About the Author

Howard Shaw was educated at Taunton School and The Queen's College, Oxford, where he read Modern History. He was commissioned in the Royal Artillery during National Service and taught at Harrow School from 1961-1997, where he was at different times a House Master, Head of History and Registrar. In 1966 he was elected a Schoolmaster Fellow of Emmanuel College, Cambridge. He has broadcast on seventeenth-century Puritanism on the old BBC Third Programme, contributed to *History Today* and written an historical study, *The Levellers*.

He turned to fiction as a form of light relief and his first detective novel, *Killing No Murder*, was published in the USA, France and the UK. He has written two further crime novels, *Death of a Don* and *Pageant of Death*, the first of which won critical acclaim in Britain and the USA, was a Mystery Guild Selection, and was later re-published in the prestigious BBC Black Dagger series as a prime example of the genre.

Also by Howard Shaw

(History)
The Levellers
(Biography)
Thomas Hardy: An Autobiography in Verse (Ed. E. Wilson)

*****

(Fiction)
Killing No Murder
"This is a real attention-grabber, worth the money and the time. The author makes an impressive debut with this book..."
News-free Press, Chattanooga, USA

Death of a Don
"Cambridge may incubate the best traitors but Oxford can pride itself on fiction's best corpses, a tradition worthily and wittily upheld here..." Christopher Wordsworth, *The Observer*

"Howard Shaw revives the peculiar pleasure one associates with collegiate murder... this traditional recipe is served up with verve and a conviction all too often absent in present day whodunits." Matthew Coady, *The Guardian*

"...a genuine, entertaining Oxford detective story."
Anthony Lejeune, *The Daily Telegraph*

Pageant of Death
"Chief Inspector Barnaby is just the right mixture of intelligence, tact and intuition..."
Huon Mallalieu, *Country Life*

BETRAYAL IN BURGUNDY

HOWARD SHAW

Matador
9 Priory Business Park
Kibworth Beauchamp
Leicestershire LE8 0RX, UK
Tel: (+44) 116 279 2299
Fax: (+44) 116 279 2277
Email: books@troubador.co.uk
Web: www.troubador.co.uk/matador

ISBN 978 1780884 882

British Library Cataloguing in Publication Data.
A catalogue record for this book is available from the British Library.

Typeset in Book Antiqua by Troubador Publishing Ltd
Printed and bound in the UK by TJ International, Padstow, Cornwall

Matador is an imprint of Troubador Publishing Ltd

For
Jamie, Gemma,
Mark and Stephen.

PROLOGUE

The wide Burgundy sky was cloudless. The sun burned down, scorching the uplands. Only in the wooded valleys was there relief from the heat. Along the River Yonne, villages and hamlets had closed their shutters. Even the birds were silent, though a pair of buzzards quartered the parched fields below Mailly-le-Château, sunlight glinting on their red-brown wings as they circled to catch the thermals.

On the Canal du Nivernais, following the valley and the river, the hotel barge Léonore, its name picked out in white letters on the bow, was the only boat moving. The skipper inched closer to the bank beneath the shade of overhanging trees. He made a final adjustment to the wheel and turned off the engine. 'Make fast!' he shouted. At the bow of the long, ungainly vessel a girl of about twenty in shorts jumped ashore with a rope and secured it to a tree. At the stern a young man hammered a steel peg into the ground by the towpath and attached his rope. The skipper, also young, no more than thirty, brown from days in the sun and wearing a naval cap at a jaunty angle, turned to his passengers gathered under the multi-coloured umbrellas shading the upper deck.

'Right, ladies and gentlemen, this is St.Pierre. We'll be stopping here till after lunch. If you want coffee or a drink, there's a bar in the village square. It's run by a Madame Breton. She speaks a bit of English and knows we're coming. There's a thirteenth-century church you can't miss. Not very well looked after. Big church, small village. There are some medieval wall paintings badly damaged by damp, if you're interested in that sort of thing. Then I know one or two of you want to see the

Commonwealth War Graves. They're in the cemetery at the far end of the village. It's no distance. Go straight past the church and stick to the main road. We'll be serving lunch on board at one o'clock, as usual. For those who look forward to the wine, we've got a nice Irancy Pinot Noir. Very local, very good. And Chef bought some more cheese in the market at Châtel-Censoir this morning. He tells me he's restocked the St.Agur you polished off last night.'

The guests, mostly elderly or middle-aged, gingerly crossed the gangplank the young man had placed between the boat and the bank and set off towards the red-roofed houses and church spire visible beyond the trees lining the canal.

Last to land were a frail-looking woman and a middle-aged man. She was slim and white-haired, wearing a wide-brimmed straw hat and flowered dress. She clutched the man's arm. He was well-built and looked fit, though his hair was flecked with grey; he wore a linen suit and a panama hat with a green and blue band that might have been the colours of a cricket club.

The woman spoke. 'Most of them will go to the bar.'

'There's no hurry. We'll take our time.' The man was solicitous.

'It's hot.'

'It'll be cooler in the trees.'

The majority of Léonore's guests were soon sitting at tables outside Madame Breton's bar. A few of the more energetic strolled towards the church, its entrance shaded by plane trees.

The couple crossed the square and walked slowly up the main street. The few shops were closed. Apart from two cars parked under the trees by the church, St.Pierre seemed deserted. They reached the edge of the village where there were farm buildings, overgrown and derelict, and a new bungalow with a trim garden.

'There it is.' The man took off his hat and wiped his face with a handkerchief.

The sun beat down on the white road leading out into the

countryside. A hundred and fifty yards beyond the bungalow, exposed and treeless, was the St.Pierre cemetery. A field of sunflowers, heads bent in the heat, climbed the hill behind it. The iron gates of the cemetery were half open as though no one had bothered to shut them; the stucco on the walls was crumbling. The whole place had an air of decay.

They went inside, the man leading the way. Around lay the usual furniture of a French cemetery: ornate family tombs, one or two new and polished, others dilapidated with age and neglect; photographs of the deceased in elaborate frames; plastic flowers, occasionally real ones. Near the gate a watering can stood by a dripping tap.

'Over here, Mother.' The woman had fallen behind. She joined the man in a corner where seven identical headstones stood next to each other. Unlike many of the other graves, they were trim and well looked after. A plaque on the wall recorded the responsibility of the Commonwealth War Graves Commission.

'He's at the end.' The woman pointed. She took off her sunglasses and put on her normal spectacles. She was dry-eyed, but frowned with concentration, holding up a hand against the sun. The man took off his hat.

The headstone, clean and white, with the RAF crest and the motto *'Per Ardua ad Astra'*, announced simply: Flying Officer James Chalmers, Royal Air Force. 1st June, 1944. Age 24.

The woman read the words aloud as though she was alone. Then: 'I'm glad we came. I've put it off for too long.'

'I'm glad we came, too. I've been living with ghosts. It closes a chapter.'

'Not really. It's only half the story.' Again the woman seemed to be communing with herself. Turning to the man, who was putting his hat back on, she said: 'Do you notice anything strange?'

'No. Just seven headstones.'

'Nothing at all?'

'Seven in a Lancaster. All killed. Not unusual. They were difficult to get out of when they'd been hit. The death toll in Bomber Command was enormous.'

'You're very detached.'

'It's a long time ago. Remember, I never knew him.'

'I can hardly forget that. It seems like yesterday to me.'

The man moved close to the woman and in spite of the heat put an arm round her shoulders. 'Is it very upsetting?'

'It brings it all back.' Her eyes were hard, but the hint of a tear trembled above the wrinkles of her right cheek. 'We were very happy – for such a short time. Just one summer. I hoped for more of a reaction from you. I wish I'd come before.'

'Why didn't you?'

The woman did not answer at once, but took out a handkerchief and touched her right eye without smudging her make-up. 'Fear,' she said.

'Fear?'

'I said it was only half the story. I didn't want to face the whole of it. Can you still not see anything peculiar?'

The man studied the seven headstones, military, precise, ordered. 'No.'

'Look at the date.'

'1st June, 1944. Just before D-Day. You told me that.'

'Look at the others.'

The man pushed up his sunglasses and studied the other headstones. 'That's odd.' Sweat stood out on his forehead. His voice had changed. Previously detached, his tone now suggested interest in an intellectual problem. 'The date's different. The rest were killed in 1943 – 19th July.' For the first time he looked directly down at her. 'They've made a mistake.'

She looked up at him in turn. For a woman in her eighties she was well preserved, the beauty of youth still apparent behind the mask of age. 'No, there's no mistake. That's the rest of the story. I've never told you the whole truth.'

'Why not?'

'Protecting myself. Trying to protect you.'

'I'm a big boy now.'

She was not smiling, but her expression had altered as though she might do so at any moment. 'You look like him.'

'And so I should.'

'You want to know the rest?'

'If you want to tell me'

'You ought to know. You have a right to know. But you won't like it and I shan't enjoy telling you.' Again her expression changed. Her eyes, still hard, matched the tone of her voice. 'Yes, it's time I told you the truth.'

She turned away from the graves and linked her arm with his. He felt the change of mood. He was not sure whether she was seeking comfort or trying to reassure him.

'Let's go and have a drink,' she said.

England 1943

1

It was still dark. Lancaster Z-Zebra lost height as it crossed the Channel and headed back to England. James Chalmers pushed the control column forward and eased himself into a more comfortable position, relaxing for the first time since taking off from Wynton Thorpe. The throb of the four Merlins was reassuring. While other pilots saw it as a matter of pride to be among the first to land, Chalmers believed in nursing his engines and had throttled back substantially. The plane dropped several thousand feet, but was still higher than the grey and white cotton-wool cloud obscuring the Channel. The crew had not spoken since leaving the French coast. After the hazards of the Ruhr the worst was over.

Chalmers's mind wandered. Discipline ingrained by training and fifteen successful missions warned him to stay alert, but his imagination could never be stopped, even at moments of high tension. At twenty-three life had barely begun. Up till now he had never really considered the reality of death. Operations from Wynton Thorpe and loss of friends had changed that. Now he was swinging in the opposite direction. The odds against survival of the full tour of thirty missions were depressingly short. His mind's eye, stirred by the sight of doomed aircraft over Germany, vividly portrayed the hundred and one ways he and his crew might die.

Enough of that. Would he get back to Oxford when it was all over? He had been up at Queen's reading Modern Languages when war broke out, but membership of the University Air Squadron and his pilot's licence had drawn him into the RAF almost immediately. He was enjoying Oxford.

Work not too strenuous, plenty of games and music – he was a first-class pianist – a good circle of friends. But it would be tame after this. How would he cope with normality when he had experienced more of the realities of life and death than most men see in a lifetime?

He eased his back again. The throb of the engines reverberated through the aircraft, pulsing into his body through the control column, filling the cockpit with sound. He looked at his flight engineer, Sergeant John Stafford, beside him. He was aware of Chalmers's sidelong glance, but did not speak. They knew each other well enough to share relief without communication.

Chalmers remembered his first operation when he had brought back a dead mid-upper gunner and counted himself fortunate to have got back at all. Since then he had become more confident and his men had developed a trust that grew with each safe return. That was a burden. Luck was as important as skill. Besides, he knew how much he depended on them. Stafford, burly, gruff, a motor engineer with Aston Martin before the war, was something of a magician with the engines; he seemed to detect trouble before it happened. His navigator, Flight Sergeant Stephen Beresford, ascetic, unworldly, was the best in the business. Tucked away in his curtained cubby-hole, he was in many ways the key member of the crew, his accuracy in plotting unerring, his dry sense of humour raising spirits at the tensest moments. He, too, was a university man, a physicist from Cambridge. Z-Zebra was the only aircraft in the squadron with such intellectual weight; it made them the butt of jokes at the White Hart where they drank on the evenings they did not fly. He relished the memory of an overheard comment from his instructor on the Lancaster conversion course. Asked how he was coping with his 'intellectual' pupils, he was terse: 'Bloody nuisance,' he said.

Down to his left was a break in the cloud. Strangely, Chalmers was always more at ease when there was a carpet of cloud; irrationally, he felt it would bear them up if anything went wrong. He recalled his first flight in a Tiger Moth and the fear engendered by the chessboard of woods and fields far below in the Chilterns. Now he looked at the blackness of the Channel through the ragged greyness.

The Channel. He had crossed it on a ferry during the last months of peace in 1939. He and an Oxford friend went to Paris, ostensibly on a cultural trip to look at the Impressionists, in fact for sexual adventure. He had read Somerset Maugham's cynical short story *The Facts of Life* and anticipated initiation into manhood with a combination of excitement and terror. In the event his nerve failed. While his friend returned to their cheap hotel off the Boulevard St.Michel with tales of derring-do under the tuition of a lush, middle-aged woman only too eager to take a young Englishman's money, he met a hungry-looking girl down by the Seine whose wan face and thin legs excited pity rather than lust. Full of self-disgust and fearful of some form of infection, he fled. To compensate he took refuge in Henry Miller, banned in England but published in Paris. His nerve failed again on the return ferry and he threw the books overboard rather than brave the customs.

France was not new to him. His mother was friendly with a French family and he had for years spent a substantial part of the long summer holiday with them near Avignon. As a child he had not understood his mother's friendship, but later realised the Frenchman was a man she might have married if their backgrounds had been different. They met very young and had obviously been attracted. But he was a Catholic and she had a strict Baptist father for whom Catholicism was anathema. Both married others, but the Frenchman maintained the link and invited his mother to send her son for holidays at his château in the Vaucluse. Sometimes his mother and father went as well, but most years he had gone on his own and as a result now spoke French like a native. It was the main reason he had chosen to read Modern Languages at Oxford.

The plane lurched in an air pocket; instinctively, he tightened his grip on the control column. His eyes pricked with tiredness. Memories of Oxford, his first flights and visits to France proceeded with a certain logic. His next thoughts were random, a kaleidoscope conjured by a wandering mind. His first pint of beer, loathsomely bitter but drunk with panache in a country pub on the way back to his school after an away match at Blundell's; his uncharacteristic flash of anger when the ground staff were clumsy getting the body of his dead gunner out of his turret after that first operation; the embarrassment when asked by an invigilating don to change his red socks for grey ones the morning he had unwittingly broken the subfusc dress code during an Oxford examination; the girl with nice legs and trim figure he had fancied at a school dance. He had not yet kissed a woman and envied those who boasted of their sexual conquests. His rear-gunner, Freddie Shorthouse, small, curiously ugly, enjoyed the favours of a harem of women who pursued him at all points of the compass.

He turned on the intercom. 'Pilot to Rear-gunner. You awake, Freddie? We haven't heard your dulcet tones recently.'

'I'm awake all right. Bloody cold back here, Skipper. How much longer?'

'Just over an hour, if the Prof's got it right. All under control, Einstein?' Chalmers respected Beresford's scientific skills without understanding their fascination. As with Stafford's unique relationship with engines, he was baffled by those whose interests were technical rather than aesthetic.

'Navigator to Pilot.' Beresford was always precise. 'You should see the Beachy Head searchlight shortly.'

There were more breaks in the cloud now and Chalmers could see the light standing upright in the sky ahead. 'Spot on, Stephen. Give me a course west of London. We don't want to be the target of some trigger-happy ack-ack man who doesn't know a Lancaster when he sees one. We'll stay out in the country.'

'Right, give me a second. I'll take us round over Reading. It'll add about fifteen minutes.'

As they crossed the coast, a white-fringed line showed where the sea met the land. Chalmers remembered the poet Arnold's lines: '*The long line of spray where the sea meets the moon-blanched land, Listen! you hear the grating roar of pebbles which the waves draw back, and fling, at their return, up the high strand.*' Evocative. And apt. He had forgotten the name of the poem, but the final lines came back: '*And we are here as on a darkling plain swept with confused alarms of struggle and flight, where ignorant armies clash by night.*' Apt indeed. A pity he couldn't share it with Beresford, but he had long ago discovered that his navigator was as insensitive to literature and the arts as he himself was to matters scientific and technical.

'Come on Chalmers,' he said silently to himself. 'Concentrate.' Aloud he said: 'We'll be coming in over the Fosse Way, chaps.' He invariably pointed out notable landmarks during cross-country training flights, sometimes to his crew's irritation. Thinking about it, he wondered if he drew attention to his intellectual capabilities to compensate for his lack of sexual experience. He suspected most of his crew had had a woman.

'What the hell's that, Skipper?' This was Leslie Ricketts, the wireless operator, a cheerful young man with bright red hair. An electrical apprentice in Leeds before joining up, he was the youngest member of the crew and immensely proud of the sergeant's stripes awarded at the end of training.

'Roman road, Les. Straight as an arrow across the centre of England. Exeter to Lincoln. Masterpiece of engineering.'

'Perhaps we could land on it, Skipper, if we run out of juice.' Stafford spoke for the first time.

'If we run out of juice, it'll be your fault, Staff.'

'They're going well tonight. They've fixed the port inner at last.' Stafford had a running feud with the ground engineer. Both were proprietorial about the aircraft and its four twelve-cylinder engines.

'Rear-gunner to Pilot. Drinks on McTavish tonight. I doubt if he hit Essen at all. All that way, acres of flak, night fighters, everybody bloody freezing and he probably dropped the lot in the Rhine.'

Flight Sergeant Hugh Robertson, the bomb-aimer, still lying prone in the nose of the aircraft, was a Scotsman, sometimes morose, not noted for putting his hand in his pocket. For no good reason he had been accorded the nickname McTavish. 'Stop complaining, Rear-gunner,' he retorted. 'We've done fifteen trips and you haven't shot down anything yet. Probably flogged your guns to that bookie in Lincoln.'

Chalmers recognised the sense of relief. The humour was there, too, on the outward journey, but it was tense and apprehensive.

'Come on, 'Tavish. You heard me open up. I nearly got that 110. Frightened him off.'

'Aye, but nothin' to do with your guns, Freddie. He saw your face. Tha' was guid enough.' Robertson's humour was simple, his accent thick.

'Well, we've got back. My lucky knickers again.' Shorthouse was impervious to insults about his appearance, believing they sprang from envy of his success with women. 'I wouldn't fly without them. Besides, they're the best thing I've found for cleaning the perspex in my turret. She's promised me another pair after this trip. She's a good girl.'

'That's the last thing she is if she has anything to do with you, Freddie. I've always been sceptical about your knickers. They didn't save her, did they?' Chalmers often kept aloof from the banter, but on the home run was happy to take part.

He pushed the column forward again and the altimeter turned as they lost more height. The cloud was breaking up fast now. The four propellers formed shining discs in the light of a rising moon. As always, the smell of oil permeated the cockpit. He found it reassuring. Unbidden, the title of Arnold's poem drifted into his mind. *Dover Beach* – yes, that was it.

'Who's on for a thrash tonight?' Stafford, at twenty-eight the oldest member of the crew and the only married man, took the initiative as he often did. He had a notable capacity for beer and an endless supply of dirty songs.

Before anyone could answer Chalmers exerted his authority. 'We'll talk about a thrash when we get down. Concentration now. Keep your eyes peeled. Particularly you, Freddie. We don't want to be bounced by some Jerry hanging around looking for an easy killing. Remember what happened to Harry Pickard.'

He could not have been more brutal. They had trained with Pickard's crew and had all been on the base when Pickard got back from Berlin and was shot down on his final approach by a German intruder waiting for a vulnerable returning bomber. They took part in a rescue operation that was no more than the picking up of bodies. He knew that would shut them up.

'Navigator to Pilot. Ten minutes to touch-down, Skipper.'

'Thanks, Stephen. Time to get out of your hole, 'Tavish. I don't want your blood and guts all over my feet if I make a mess of things.'

Chalmers was mildly irked that Robertson always had to be reminded, and irritated with his own impatience. It showed how tired he was. Again he was falling into a reverie. Freddie's mention of his lucky knickers stirred his lust. Highly sexed but wholly celibate, he had private fantasies that invaded his mind like the lines of poetry. Once, over Frankfurt, surrounded by flak, responding to Robertson's instructions during the bombing run, he was shocked to find himself holding the aircraft steady and at the same time imagining running his hand under the skirt of a girl he had seen at the White Hart.

'Flarepath any time now, Skipper.'

Chalmers peered into the darkness. 'Any sign, Staff?'

The flight engineer was looking out as intently as he was. 'There it is, Skip. Einstein's done it again.'

'Seen. Well done, Stephen. We can't do without you.'

Ricketts got clearance from the control tower and Chalmers turned towards the lights, two parallel lines of jewels in the darkness.

'Undercarriage down.'

'Undercarriage down,' echoed Stafford.

'20 degrees of flap.' Chalmers was terse now.

'Flaps down.'

'Home sweet home. Watch out, we're going in. Eyes skinned, everyone.'

The approach was good. Chalmers brought the Lancaster to a near-perfect touch-down, the sort of landing he prided himself on. As the wheels squealed on the tarmac, he was day-dreaming again. It was the same girl. His hand was moving up her thigh to the softness above her stocking and she was easing her legs apart.

2

Mary Kenyon was awake. Her auburn hair framed her face on the pillow as she turned to the still-dark window. The first returning aircraft had woken her and she counted each one as it landed. The two other girls in the sparsely furnished billet were sleeping. Clothes were scattered in lockers and on the regulation brown folding chairs by each bed.

Fifteen so far. She always knew which way they were coming in and visualised the final approach. Down over the ruined castle at Morby, across Maydon Woods, finally sweeping over the ploughed fields of Lower Braxton Farm. She could see them braking on the main runway before turning onto the perimeter track. She had woken to count them home since she had been at Wynton Thorpe. It was the least she could do.

Mary was twenty-one, a quiet girl from Shropshire. Her father, a country vicar, was protective of his only child; her mother, the backbone of the family, was resilient and, many said, hard. It was her mother who had urged her to volunteer for the WAAF; her father had been doubtful, worried about the men. In the event Mary, though naïve in many ways, had got on well. She had trained as a driver and was now as adept at driving a three-tonner or fuel bowser as a Humber staff car. She often drove aircrew out to their aircraft before an operation. Now she counted them back.

Another plane touched down. She closed her eyes. Two to come.

Some of the men she knew well, others, particularly the

replacement crews, hardly at all. Losses had been heavy recently. The previous week there had been a disastrous raid on Berlin when the squadron had lost four aircraft and twenty-eight men were posted missing. One was a pilot who had asked her for a date. She had said 'Yes' and shed tears when he didn't come back.

It was warm in the hut. She stretched her leg, searching for a cool piece of sheet. She liked the other girls, though they were very different from her. Mixing with all sorts and conditions since joining up, she realised her good fortune. Or was that the way to put it? Perhaps it was just that she saw how sheltered she was. She had been to a girls' boarding school in a remote part of Wales and never done a job; the others were from the town. Dot was a factory girl from Lancashire and Barbara came from London. Both took a light-hearted view of life and, compared with her, were experienced with men. Dot had a boy friend in the army but did not regard that a handicap to finding others on the base; and Barbara, who had been to Roedean and was socially a cut above both of them, was well-known as a flighty piece who enjoyed a good time with anyone willing to supply it. Mary felt inadequate. Listening to Barbara's polished accent, she remembered the way her parents had arranged elocution lessons when she picked up rural Shropshire nuances in the village. 'Round the rocks the ragged rascal ran,' she had repeated endlessly to satisfy the retired schoolmistress hired for the purpose.

The aerodrome had gone silent. She imagined the Group Captain standing in the control tower as he always did waiting for the returning aircraft. The base commander had a reputation for not suffering fools gladly, but no one was more concerned for the safety of the crews, no one worried more about the laggards. No longer able to fly himself, he saw it as his duty to see them safely back.

She was almost dropping off when the drone of engines emerged from the distance and another plane landed. Again the crescendo of noise as the Lancaster pulled off the runway and taxied past the billet. One to come. The recent arrival had not switched off its engines before she was aware of another aircraft making its approach. All back. She imagined the Group Captain knocking out his pipe, picking up his cane, and going back to the officers' quarters in the old manor house around which the aerodrome had been built. She was asleep before he reached the bottom of the stairs leading down from the concrete control tower.

* * *

Chalmers and his crew climbed stiffly out of Z-Zebra, carrying their parachutes. A three-tonner had drawn up by the tailplane, driven by the same WAAF corporal who had taken them out before take-off. She, too, was tired, having been up all night, but she had checked her make-up. She put on her brightest smile and went up to Chalmers, whom she knew a bit.

'Welcome home, sir. Good trip?'

For a moment the contrast between the roar of the engines, suffered for four hours, and the silence of the airfield was overwhelming and Chalmers did not respond. He took off his helmet and ran his hand through his hair. Slim, fresh-faced, brown hair tousled, he looked like a smiling sixth former. Behind him the Lancaster's engines made the characteristic cooling sounds that gave an aircraft a life of its own.

Eventually, he said, 'Yes, thanks. Everyone else back?'

'All safely gathered in. You're the last, sir.'

'The skipper gave us a tour of the Fosse Way,' volunteered Stafford. He, too, had taken off his helmet, revealing a mane of shaggy blonde hair. With deep-set eyes he looked older than his twenty-eight years.

'Better late…' said Robertson.

'Shut up, `Tavish,' said Shorthouse. 'Don't even think about it.' He winked at the WAAF corporal. 'Hello, Maggie. How's tricks?'

The girl smiled, but did not respond.

They moved slowly towards the lorry. The tailboard was down and they threw their parachutes in before climbing up themselves. Heavy flying boots and clumsy gear made it difficult and they used the rope hanging down to hoist themselves in. It had rained and the perimeter track glistened in the masked headlights of the three-tonner as it drove round the airfield to the wooden hut used as a briefing room.

'If we'd come straight back, I'd have been in bed with Brenda by now,' grumbled Shorthouse. He enjoyed his reputation and drew attention to it at every opportunity. His most recent conquest lived in the village that gave its name to the airfield. 'God, I'm frozen. Every bloody rear-gunner needs a woman to warm him up.'

Chalmers ignored him. The relief of another safe return was fading into overwhelming tiredness. Sitting by the tailboard, he listened to the swish of the tyres on the damp surface and tried to assemble his thoughts for debriefing.

The WAAF corporal changed down clumsily as she reached the end of the perimeter track and turned towards the huddle of buildings at the northern end of the airfield. The crew groaned and laughed at the grinding of the gears.

'What about that thrash, Skipper?' said Stafford.

'All right, Staff. Seven o'clock, the White Hart. Any defaulters?'

The chorus of agreement was almost unanimous. Only Stephen Beresford was doubtful. Unlike Chalmers, who had hardly looked at a book since coming down from Oxford, Beresford hoped for an academic career after the war and tried to keep up with his subject. He was actually preparing a learned paper to be delivered during his next leave.

'Come on, Einstein. We can't do without you. We shan't find our way back.'

Past experience showed that Beresford was persuadable. One of nature's loners before joining up, he had discovered the

14

pleasures of being part of a team and now found it flattering to be wanted. Likewise, he was getting used to alcohol, barely touched before. 'All right,' he said. 'As long as 'Tavish is paying.'

'Girls?' said Shorthouse. 'Brenda would like to come. How about it, Skipper?' They deferred to Chalmers on social as well as flying matters. He was an officer with a public school education. Only the mid-upper gunner, Brad Alcock, a young Canadian untouched by English class inhibitions, reacted against them.

'Aw, come on Skipper. Women all round.'

'Why not?' said Chalmers. 'Got one for me, Freddie?'

'I can rustle up enough for everyone, Skip. What's your taste, `Tavish?' Shorthouse was in his element. 'As a married man, I don't suppose you're interested, Staff ?'

Stafford had introduced his wife to the crew one week-end when she came up from London. She was a pretty woman who obviously adored him and they were all envious. 'Nothing to stop me being sociable,' said Stafford, laughing. 'We're not all like you, Freddie.'

The Bedford stopped at the briefing hut. The Intelligence Officer, a cadaverous man with a service hat too big for him, was waiting and they settled round a table vacated by an earlier crew. A map of Europe dominated the end wall, cheap curtains blacked out the windows. There were cartoons by Fougasse round the room, one warning that 'Careless talk costs lives', as if they needed reminding. Another, French in origin, showed a peasant standing outside a brothel pulling out the linings of empty pockets; the caption read, 'Avant partir en operations prenez garde que les poches sont vides!' A WAAF served hot tea and tots of rum. All except Chalmers were smoking. The air was thick with smoke from previous crews.

'You took your time, Jamie.' The Intelligence Officer liked Chalmers and it had become something of a joke that Z-Zebra was usually one of the last. 'Quick tour of the Loire châteaux?'

The reply came from Alcock, a spare, raw-boned man, who had said little since landing but now spoke in his broad transatlantic accent: 'No, sir. The skipper took us over the Fosse Way. Good for the education of an ignorant Canadian bum, I suppose, but a daft way back to Wynton. I didn't even I know the Romans came to Britain.'

'I'm surprised you've heard of them at all,' said Beresford. 'You colonials think the world started yesterday.' He got on well with Alcock and regularly pulled his leg.

Alcock, a replacement after the mid-upper gunner's death and appreciative of the way he had been welcomed, responded in kind. 'What was your university, Beresford? Wormwood Scrubs? Or was it Dartmoor? I haven't got the hang of the English education system.'

The Intelligence Officer was sensitive to the badinage of returning crews. He felt guilty his life was not on the line and thought his questioning must seem impertinent after what they had been through. They were not to know of his medical problems or that his younger brother had been killed over Hamburg six months before. 'Right,' he said, 'let's get on with it. Any problems at the start, Jamie? All straightforward joining the stream over Southwold?'

The interrogation followed its normal course. Chalmers took the lead, but the others chipped in to give information on events over the target and the skirmish with the night fighter. Eventually the Intelligence Officer, who had been taking notes, stood up and released them.

'O.K., that'll do. We've been stood down for two nights, so you can relax. It's been a pretty satisfactory night – but not for Essen. Well done.'

Chalmers went out into the fresh air. The cloud had cleared and the moon was high over Maydon Woods. Spring was on the way, but the air was cold and there was no hint of the dawn. In the fields beyond the perimeter fence a dog fox barked.

'Bed,' said Chalmers. 'I'm cutting breakfast. I could sleep

for a month.' He turned to Stafford. 'You rustle up the troops this evening, Staff. Rendezvous by the old mulberry tree. I'll lay on transport.' Still carrying his parachute, Chalmers set off to his billet behind the Officers' Mess. The others, all sergeants, turned in the opposite direction.

'You get some sleep, Skipper,' shouted Shorthouse. 'I'll fix the girls.'

3

Freddie Shorthouse had breakfast in the Sergeants' Mess and before cycling off to join Brenda in the village left a note for Dot Braithwaite with one of the WAAFs in the cookhouse. Dot was one of his few failures. She had never taken him seriously and they remained friendly. It was short and to the point.

Dot Love,

The Zebra's having a bash tonight and we want some skirts. Can you bring your lot?

Don't let me down, there's a good girl. Who knows, there might be a kiss in it! Seven sharp by the old mulberry tree.

Love,

Freddie XXX

Dot was a plump, dark-haired, girl whose charms were physical rather than intellectual. In winter she wore tight sweaters and in summer off-the-shoulder peasant blouses and gypsy skirts. Freed from the respectability of her parents' terraced cottage in Oldham, she had taken full advantage of the male company available and, if asked, would have said she was enjoying the war. She knew Freddie better than the others.

She got Freddie's note at breakfast. Back in the billet she tackled Barbara, a willowy blonde with blue eyes and enviable complexion who had never been known to turn down any sort of invitation and was unpacking some nylon stockings received in the post from an American admirer who flew from a nearby base.

'All back last night. Celebrate with Freddie's lot? How about it, Babs?'

'Why not? I'm not doing anything, are you?'

The contrast between Dot's Lancashire accent and Barbara's cut-glass Roedean tones was acute, but they got on famously and formed the central axis of the billet. Dot turned to Mary Kenyon, who was making her bed. Mary was the unknown quantity, the quiet one whose response could not be predicted.

'Mary?'

'I'll come.'

'I think that Canadian lad's the one for me,' said Dot. 'What's his name?'

'Brad. Brad Alcock. Got a farm in the wild west. Play your cards right and you might end up owning acres of prairie or a rocky mountain.' Barbara was a realist who often thought in property terms.

'What's your choice, Mary?'

'I don't know them very well. Freddie shot me a line once, but he's not my type.'

'Nor mine,' said Dot.

'I haven't met the others. Their navigator looks nice,' said Mary. 'What's his name?'

'Stephen,' said Barbara. 'Stephen Beresford. Freddie says he's the best navigator on the station. Bit of an intellectual, like their skipper. Cambridge and all that. He might do for you, Mary. You said you were good at maths. Too clever by half for me.'

'And me,' said Dot

'He's a bit dry,' said Barbara. 'I want someone with blood in his veins.'

'Blue blood?' asked Dot, raising an eyebrow. Jokes about their different backgrounds were part of the chemistry between them.

'I don't care what the colour is as long as there's enough of it.'

'And as long as it goes to the right bits.' Dot enjoyed trying to shock.

'Freddie will get some others,' said Barbara. 'And Brenda will be there. She wouldn't trust him on his own. Right, we'll all go – and I shall wear these,' she said, holding up the nylons. 'Nothing like a piece of lease-lend. Robert won't mind – Robert won't know.'

They all laughed, but Mary felt detached. She liked them both and envied their confidence. Her sheltered background made her nervous in male company. Going out with them, she felt like a younger sister and always waited for them to make the running. But she wanted to go, she knew that. Away from the claustrophobic Shropshire vicarage, relishing the warmth of new and unlikely friendships, she was daily becoming more independent. Like Barbara, laying out the nylons on her bed, she was planning what to wear.

* * *

The White Hart at Wynton Parva was a simple country pub. But it was old and its history, recorded in copperplate by a local historian, hung in the lounge bar. Under the Tudors one of its owners was fined for overcharging, put in the village stocks and so battered by outraged villagers that he went insane; during the Civil War Oliver Cromwell spent a couple of nights there before the battle of Winceby and his troopers slept in the stable. There were low black beams and inglenook fireplaces to provide comfort in winter. Before the war it had served local farmers, their labourers, and the occasional commercial traveller on his way to or from Lincoln.

War had brought changes. Incendiary bombs, jettisoned by a Heinkel after a raid on Birmingham, destroyed the old stables and damaged adjacent cottages. The following year large numbers of Irish navvies descended on the village to build the runways and billets for the bomber base, startling the locals with their language and alcoholic capacity. Then, as the Lancasters arrived and Bomber Command began its campaign against Germany, RAF crews and ground staff turned to the White Hart for normality and relaxation in an abnormal world.

The licensee was one Herbert Kitchen, a rotund man with mutton-chop whiskers whose extensive waistline was held in by a wide leather belt. His deep voice, joviality and heavyweight presence suggested a latterday Falstaff. His wife, an improbably small woman with fair hair and a certain elegance, seemed ill-matched to her husband's air of bonhomie, but together they created an atmosphere of genial hospitality. They had welcomed the cement-dusted labourers during the building of the base and now showed understanding and tolerance of the young fliers. With no children of their own and no other means of helping the war effort, they felt warmth and responsibility for the boys – they thought and spoke of them as boys – who risked their lives night after night.

' 'Evening, Bert,' said Chalmers, heading his crew.

'Good evening, sir,' boomed Kitchen. He always called the officers 'Sir', reflecting his experience of the trenches in the First World War. 'And what's your pleasure this evening?'

'Pints all round, Bert. And whatever the ladies would like. We'll have a couple of jugs as well. No one got the chop last night. We shan't be the only ones.'

Kitchen, more sensitive than he looked, winced at the casual "No one got the chop", but understood the jargon and its evasion of brutal realities. 'Right, sir. Seven pints coming up while the ladies make up their minds. That'll take a while.' He laughed, a rumbling sound rooted in his vast girth.

The ladies were shepherded by Shorthouse. He had secured a full house by asking three other WAAFs and bringing Brenda. He held an elbow here and a waist there as he collected the orders. Brenda, a big blonde with good legs, seemed unfazed by the way he touched them all and was laughing. As long as she was on hand she believed she had him under control. Dot made a bee-line for Alcock, and Barbara, after an initial word with Chalmers, was soon laughing with Stafford.

Mary gave her order last. She never knew what to drink, but had heard her aunt ordering 'Gin and It' at a hotel in Ludlow and subsequently discovered it was palatable. 'Gin and It, please, Freddie.'

The drinks arrived and Mary found herself standing next to Chalmers. As usual, and mentally kicking herself, she took refuge in a trite remark: 'Good to be back?'

Chalmers had seen Mary several times, including the occasion she had driven his crew out to their aircraft before a raid on Frankfurt, but they had never exchanged more than conventional pleasantries. He had been attracted, but thought he detected a certain untouchability. He looked at her auburn hair, grey-green eyes, and the gentle but veiled expression with its hint of sexuality.

He smiled engagingly, the lines of his face relaxing. 'You don't know how good. Did someone say you were Welsh?'

'They may have said it, but I'm not. I come from Shropshire. I went to a boarding school in Wales, but I'm English – like you, I suppose. Or are you Scottish, with a name like Chalmers?'

'I'm English. There was a Scotsman somewhere a long time ago.' Chalmers looked down at the fullness of her body, modestly revealed in the blue dress with its pleated skirt. He wondered why he had not spoken to her properly before. She crossed her legs. She had good legs, too. 'One of my Oxford tutors lives in Shropshire. We went up there for a reading party before the war. He made us walk along Offa's Dyke in the rain, then we had musical evenings with a string quartet.'

'Do you play?'

'I'm a pianist of sorts, but several friends are string players. My tutor plays the cello.'

'I love music, but I'm very ignorant. I can play the piano, clumsily. I once had to play for the hymns in my father's church when the organ broke down.'

'Your father's a vicar?'

'Yes.'

'That's frightening.'

'You're joking.'

'Of course. It doesn't do to be too serious these days.'

As Mary relaxed, her conversation became more natural. 'I've thought about how difficult it must be for you. One moment you're drinking here in the White Hart – log fires, beer, girls. The next you're over Germany in a world I can't begin to imagine. I always count the planes back.'

'We were last in this morning. We often are. It's become a sort of joke. Freddie gets fed up because he wants a cuddle with Brenda.' Chalmers waved his glass towards the pair, their arms now round each other.

'I've never been up.'

'It's fun over England. I was learning to fly at Oxford before the war. Started in a Tiger Moth.'

'Have you ever baled out?'

'Good God, no! I'd be terrified. Seriously, I'd only do it if I had to. But when the chips are down you don't have a choice. None of my lot has baled out, but they would if I told them to. What made you join the WAAFs?'

Mary looked at his unruly hair, the enquiring eyes, soft and sharp at the same time, and the fullness of the lips above his chin. She suddenly realised how physically attractive he was. And she liked the way he threw the conversational ball back. She even detected a nervousness not unlike her own and unexpected in a man with a pilot's wings on his tunic. 'I just wanted to do my bit. I wasn't going to university and I hadn't got a job. I think I wanted to get away from home, too. Tell me about Oxford. I'm envious of that.'

'I was enjoying it. Queen's is a nice college. Sociable but not snobbish. A lot of men from the North – all easy to get on with.'

'Modern Languages, someone said.'

'French and German. But I wondered if it ought to be

Music. All my friends were musical. The chap next door on my staircase was always complaining.'

'Favourite composer?'

'That's unfair.' He laughed.

'Why?'

'Too revealing. Too difficult.'

'You're not trying to hide?' Mary realised with a frisson of excitement that she was flirting.

'All right, Schubert. He couldn't write a dud tune if he tried. Do you know the String Quintet?'

'No. I've heard some of his songs. And I like the Unfinished Symphony. I told you I was ignorant.'

'I'd like you to hear the Quintet. It's pompous to say it, but it's the piece of music that convinced me of the existence of the soul. I've got the records in my room. Will you come and listen some time?' Chalmers, too, was relaxing. He could not talk to any of his crew about music, even Stephen Beresford, who was tone deaf. 'I've got the Unfinished as well – Thomas Beecham.'

'That would be nice.'

'This evening?'

'Why not?'

'We must stick around for a bit and down a few more drinks, but Staff will start singing later and we can slip away.'

Chalmers was aware he sounded almost conspiratorial. He did not want to let his crew down, but for the first time in his life he had found an attractive girl with interests similar to his own who seemed as inexperienced as he was. Life, he had decided on a risky raid on Hamburg, was for living.

'Are you sure? Don't they need their skipper?'

'I wouldn't leave them if it was just a stag do. But it was Freddie who wanted girls and they all agreed. They'll probably end up at the hop in Wynton Magna and several will peel off before the evening's out. No harm in us going first. Your glass is empty. Same again?'

The evening progressed much as Chalmers predicted.

24

Other crews came in, some joking that Z-Zebra was usually last back but always first to the White Hart. Shorthouse went to the piano and Stafford started to sing, initially a modest song about a milkmaid from Yorkshire. Barbara, who had since discovered he had a wife, still stood at his elbow. Dot, in one of her tightest sweaters, was laughing at one of Brad Alcock's jokes which she did not really understand. Robertson, more at ease with women than with men, had his arm round a ginger-haired Scots girl who, like him, supported Glasgow Rangers.

Chalmers went across to Beresford, who stood slightly apart sipping a pint of beer. 'I'm off, Stephen. I'm taking Mary to listen to some Schubert. Ring Corporal Willets at the base if anyone wants to go to the hop in Wynton Magna.' He nodded towards Shorthouse, who was playing the piano with Brenda's arms round his neck. 'Make sure Freddie behaves himself.'

Chalmers guided Mary towards the door with a tentative hand on her upper arm and they went out into the village street. The blackout was strictly observed and the contrast between the light in the pub and the darkness outside was at first overwhelming. But it was a cloudless night and as their eyes adjusted they realised they were standing under a canopy of stars.

'I had a word with Kitchen. One of his mates will take us back to the base. He runs a taxi service – strictly unofficial. Gets petrol from his brother who's a farmer.'

They waited about five minutes before the man arrived in a battered Hillman Minx. Chalmers opened the rear door for Mary before getting in by the driver. He did not want to seem too forward by getting in beside her. She, in turn, was relieved he was not taking liberties.

Back at the base they went to Chalmers's room, where he made cocoa and wound up the gramophone.

'You ought not to be here, you know. "Other ranks" in an officer's room. Bad form.' He spoke the last two words with exaggeration and laughed. Without realising it, he too was flirting.

'Very bad form,' she mimicked. 'I won't make a noise when I go.'

'I don't care if you do. A night over the Ruhr puts petty rules in perspective.'

Schubert's Quintet opened, its beauty still clear through the medium of the shellac records. They listened in silence at first, then as the first movement drew to a close Chalmers said: 'He wrote it the year he died, during the summer. Do you know, it wasn't played in public until more than twenty years later?'

'He wasn't very old, was he?'

'Just over thirty. It's staggering what he managed to write. Now listen to this.' He turned the record and put on the second movement. The opening bars of the Adagio, magical and serene, filled the room.

'See what I mean? It's got an ethereal quality I've never heard anywhere else.'

Mary was struck by its beauty, but felt out of her depth. 'I hadn't even heard of it.'

'He knew he was dying. You can hear that.' Chalmers's enthusiasm began to get the better of him. 'You know he scored it for two cellos? Quite unlike Mozart and Beethoven. They always went for two violas.'

'You're running ahead of me. Let's just enjoy it.'

'Sorry.'

They sat in easy chairs side by side but did not touch. Later, when the Quintet finished, Mary looked across at him. His eyes had closed during the last movement and he was now fast asleep. The feelings she sensed within herself were warm and protective. She watched his chest rising and falling, then got up and took off the record. He did not stir.

It was eleven o'clock. She had not the heart to wake him, so left a note on his desk.

Thanks for a lovely evening. You're the first person who's talked to me about music. I'm an ignorant but willing pupil. She paused and looked across at him. His vulnerability gave her strength.

26

I'm slipping out very quietly. No one will know I've been here. I should like to hear the Schubert again. Mary.

As she left the room she almost brushed his shoulder with her fingers. Almost, but not quite.

4

Over the next two weeks the weather was poor, with wind, rain and low scudding clouds. Visits to the White Hart were frequent and Mary and Chalmers got to know each other better. They listened to music again and one wet, squally afternoon went for a walk in the lanes round the aerodrome, ending up in a teashop in Wynton Magna. There were dark-oak wheelback chairs, chintz curtains and an open fire. They hung their dripping coats and hats on the stand by the door and sat down at a table by the fire.

'You look like a drowned rat.' Chalmers was laughing, the creases by his eyes wrinkling up in a way Mary found attractive.

'Thanks – I thought it was going to clear up.'

'You're an optimist.'

'Isn't that a good thing?' Mary rummaged in her bag and eventually produced a handkerchief to wipe the rain off her face, then handed it to him. Though their conversation had become more natural since that first night, they still fenced formally round each other. She looked down at her sensible walking shoes covered in mud and the damp hem of her plaid skirt. She was amazed at how relaxed she was.

A waitress in a black dress, white cap and apron came to the table. She looked no more than sixteen, the sort of girl filling in as older women went into factories or joined the forces. 'Tea?' she enquired.

'Yes, please,' said Chalmers. 'And some toast, perhaps?' The note of query reflected the doubt affecting orders in wartime eating places as supplies became scarce.

'Oh yes, sir, or we've got home-made scones. Ma's been baking this afternoon. And there's home-made raspberry jam, too. I helped pick 'em. There's even real butter, though we can't let you have much.'

Chalmers looked at Mary before ordering scones. 'Nice girl,' he said when she had gone. He was conscious of the waitress's developing figure and the sway of her hips as she retreated.

'Do you mean "Pretty girl"?' asked Mary, smiling.

'Perhaps I do. Do you mind?'

'I saw you looking at her.' She became bold. 'I think I was jealous.'

Chalmers blushed. It was his greatest handicap and had been with him since prep school. 'Sorry,' he said

'You're blushing.'

'Can't help it. Always do when I've been caught out. Difficult for a chap who likes to make out he's a bit of a dashing blade.'

'Not very flattering for a girl to be taken out and have her escort admiring a young waitress. A girl likes to feel she's the centre of attention.'

She turned her chair sideways to the table and stretched out her legs in front of the fire. Ostensibly she was drying her shoes and the hem of her skirt. In fact, she was showing off her legs. They both knew it. And both knew something else: they were more at ease than they had ever been with any member of the opposite sex.

Chalmers recovered swiftly. 'I'm flattered you're jealous. But I'll tell you something about men. They like pretty women and they'll look at all of them. That's the nature of the beast. But appreciation of the general leads to admiration of the particular. Now I'm looking at you.'

Mary laughed out loud. 'Fraud,' she said.

The waitress reappeared bearing tea and scones. She put them on the table with an obvious sense of pride. 'There we are. The scones are good, though I say it meself. Ma's a dab 'and at scones and cakes. She does lots o' weddings.'

When she had gone to serve another couple who had just come in, Chalmers stretched forward and touched Mary's hand. It was a fleeting motion, swift, unrehearsed, nervous. 'I fly over Germany, I drop bombs that kill people, I try to keep my crew safe – but I've never had a girl friend and I'm likely to make a fool of myself.'

'It was fun this afternoon. Getting wet. Not exactly a spring day.'

'We'll fly when it clears up.'

'I'd rather you didn't have to fly again.'

'Talking about the spring reminds me of a bit of Chaucer I can quote. Did you do the Canterbury Tales at school?'

'It wasn't a very academic school. We spent a lot of time on deportment and how to reply to invitations. I'm very good at walking a straight line with a book balanced on my head and I know how to answer a bishop's invitation to dinner. Tell me about Chaucer.'

Chalmers pointed through the window at the rain falling outside. 'All right,' he said, 'I'll show off:

Whanne that Aprille with his shoures sote
The droghte of Marche hath perced to the rote,
And bathed every veyne in swich licour . . . That's how it begins, and that's about as far as I can go. Except for the line *'Than longen folk to go on pilgrimages.'*

'Very impressive, if I knew what it meant.'

'It's about April showers and nature awakening in the spring. Sorry I dried up. I used to know most of *The Prologue.'*

'Are you sure it's decent?'

'Not much wrong with *The Prologue. The Miller's Tale*'s a different matter. We looked up the dirty bits in the library. Did you really have to walk with a book on your head?'

'Of course. It was part of the routine. Like changing your knickers every day and your vest on Sundays.'

'It's given you a nice straight back.'

'I don't like the spring. It sets off emotions I don't understand. I prefer autumn – falling leaves, bare trees and bonfires. These scones are good.'

'I wish her mother cooked for us in the Mess. What your food like?'

'It could be worse. The grease needs to be seen to be believed and some of the cookhouse girls need a good scrub. But I eat more here than I do at home. Do you prefer the spring or autumn, Jamie?'

She had only called him by his name a few times. The step from 'Sir' to 'Jamie' had been difficult.

'I prefer autumn, too. Decay rather than green shoots. Perhaps we're both a bit melancholy. Are you drying off?'

A light steam was rising from Mary's skirt. She lowered her legs and tucked them under her chair. 'The fire's hotter than it looks. I'll soon be cooked on one side.'

She was aware she was taking the initiative, drawing him out in a way she didn't think she was capable of. Chalmers was flattered. At boarding school since the age of seven, he had learned to keep his emotions under control. Both his prep and public school had been for boys only, as had his Oxford college. He had no idea whether he was attractive to girls or not.

Mary busied herself with the teapot and cups. 'I expect you like the tea in first, the posh way.'

'No, I like the milk first. It doesn't mix properly the other way round.'

'Any brothers or sisters?' Mary asked.

'Only child. What about you?'

'Same here.'

'Did you ever want any?'

'I did when I was little. The other children at the village school seemed to have them and I was the odd one out. As I grew older, I saw there were advantages in being an 'only'.'

'I saw the advantages straight away.' He was smiling again.

'Christmas and presents always centred on me. My mother once asked if I'd like a brother or sister. I was very clear that I didn't. I suspect she was relieved. She had me late and I don't think she and my father would – how shall I put it? – would have been excited by the prospect of creating an extra.'

'Where do they live?'

'Father's dead. Sudden heart attack mowing the lawn. A very suburban death. Mother still lives in Wimbledon.'

'You don't sound very concerned.'

'To be honest, I wasn't. I was only about nine. My father vanished early every morning to the City and was never back by my bedtime. I just knew him as a man with a bit of a temper who happened to sleep with my mother. Mother's always been more important, but even she became remote once I went away to school. Are you close to your parents?'

'I suppose I am. Daddy's a pet, if that doesn't sound too silly – a father-daughter closeness. My mother loves me too, but she's tougher and holds the whole thing together. Daddy's terribly conscientious and the parish likes him, but Mummy makes sure nothing goes wrong.'

'Boy friends?'

This time it was Mary's turn to blush. 'We never saw boys at school and Mummy and Daddy didn't want me to meet boys from the village.'

The door opened again and three elderly ladies, all wearing hats, came in and fussed with raincoats and umbrellas. They were well known to the waitress, who helped them settle at what was obviously their usual table. One of them, white-haired, florid, with a hat dominated by a large pheasant feather, continued the conversation they had been having outside. 'I wouldn't mind,' she said, 'if they could get back a couple of hours later. They wake me up the moment I've managed to get to sleep. Sleep's precious when you reach our age.'

'And they make so much noise with their engines when they've landed. I think they do it on purpose,' said the smallest woman, sharp-featured and wearing steel-framed spectacles. 'They always wake up Bertie. He gets very upset.'

'You'll have to tell him there's a war on.'

'It's difficult to explain to a dog. He already wonders why he gets so much horse meat.'

'I'm sure they don't do it on purpose, dear,' said the third woman, a comfortable body with a kindly face. 'I expect they're very tired too, when they've been up all night. It's a long way to Germany, you know. And very dangerous, I'm sure.'

So taken up were they with their own conversation, they did not notice the young officer with his back towards them. The pheasant feather waved and the strident voice beneath it set off on a new tack. 'My nephew in the navy says we ought to spend more money on ships. He says Hitler would have invaded in 1940 if we hadn't controlled the Channel. He says we shall lose the empire if we don't concentrate on the fleet.'

'The RAF had something to do with stopping Hitler, dear,' offered the emollient woman. 'Remember what Mr Churchill said. And I think it's high time we got our own back. I'm glad when I hear on the news we've bombed Hamburg or Berlin. Don't forget who started it. I can put up with a few engines in the early morning if we give them a dose of their own medicine. My cousin Gladys was killed in Coventry, remember.'

Their voices were loud. Chalmers looked at Mary and squeezed her hand. The humour of the situation was not lost on either of them. Quietly he said, 'Sorry about Bertie.'

'Poor Bertie. You'll have to fly more quietly, Jamie. I'm ashamed of you, waking up the whole neighbourhood.' The diminutive Christian name came more easily each time.

'I'll get the Germans to stop our engines before we get back. I expect we could glide the last hundred miles if we tried hard enough. Can't have the old biddies losing their sleep.'

'Or Bertie.'

'Certainly not Bertie.' They burst out laughing.

The waitress came and put two logs on the fire. 'We're burnin' wood most of the time,' she said. 'We chopped down a tree in the orchard last week. Apple wood smells nice, don't it?'

Chalmers was watching the waitress, particularly the way her skirt tightened over her thighs as she bent down. Mary for the first time in her life felt a genuine pang of jealousy. She determined to keep the initiative.

'Still assessing 'the general' in order to appreciate 'the particular'?'

'What?'

'I saw you watching her bend down.'

Chalmers did not blush this time. 'Come on. Let's get back to the base.'

He paid the bill and collected their raincoats from the stand by the door. Three faces topped by three hats watched as he helped Mary on with her coat. Chalmers smiled at them. 'Sorry about the engine noise, ladies. I'll try to keep it quieter next time.'

Outside, he took hold of Mary's hand firmly and they set off back to the aerodrome in the rain.

5

The weather changed. The isobars on the charts of northern Europe at Bomber Command's High Wycombe headquarters opened out at last. The old oak-framed barometer Chalmers had brought from home and hung next to his reproduction of Cézanne's *Mont Sainte-Victoire* swung from Change to Fair. Walking to breakfast in the Officers' Mess, Chalmers sniffed the air like an animal, noted the high cloud and the stillness of the daffodils beginning to fade in the grass by the front door.

'We'll be on tonight,' he said to another pilot as he collected a kipper from the sideboard. To a white-coated mess waiter he said: 'Coffee, please,' before the latter could enquire whether he preferred that or tea.

'Two to one the Ruhr,' said the other, a pilot well into his second tour. 'They know we're coming and we can't keep out of those bloody red areas. They've got us stitched up.'

Chalmers sat down and prodded his kipper. The man was a purveyor of gloom and he usually avoided his company. 'What about Berlin? Good for propaganda.'

'Worse than the Ruhr. So much fuel you can hardly get off the ground. Last time we went Johnny Carpenter and Digger Johnson got the chop. We lost more than fifty. That's over three hundred and fifty men in one night. I'm not happy doing that just for propaganda. You're a Varsity man, aren't you? What do you think?'

'It's always easier to defend than attack. How else can we get back at them? Besides, the Russians expect us to do something.' As he spoke, the sun lit up the dining room, revealing smears on the windows. 'There you are. First time we've seen it in a fortnight. We can't leave Berlin out of it. Did you go down to the East End during the Blitz?'

The other man grunted and ate the remainder of the meal in morose silence. He was a notorious grouser whose crew put up with him because he always brought them back.

By eleven o'clock Chalmers's earlier prediction had been fulfilled. The target was unknown, but the squadron had been alerted for a night operation and Z-Zebra was one of the crews to fly. Chalmers took his crew out to the aircraft for routine tests. The Lancasters were ranged round the airfield, each on its own oil-stained tarmac pan. Z-Zebra was at one of the furthest points from the main buildings, partly shielded from the wind by an outcrop of Maydon Woods, ancient woodland covering this part of Lincolnshire since the days of the Danelaw. The ground staff had built themselves a ramshackle wooden hut under the trees where they brewed up and sheltered from the weather. A petrol bowser was parked under one wing. Bombing up had started on the far side of the airfield and WAAF drivers were bringing bomb trains from the dump. Here and there engines were running.

'All under control, Uncle?' Chalmers spoke to the ground engineer, a grey-haired man who loved the aircraft he serviced and scolded the pilots who flew them if they brought them back damaged. Known universally as 'Uncle', he had cycled across from B-Baker, just landed after a flight test.

'No problems, sir. Daily inspection A.1. The engines sounded sweet this morning. The port inner's using a bit of oil. Well within limits. Any gen where you're going?'

'Not yet. Fuel load will give us an idea.'

'Still waiting. Rumour says Berlin, but you know what rumour is.'

Rumour was wrong. By the time Chalmers and his crew had completed their checks it was known the target was Stuttgart. Chalmers was only mildly interested; as far as he was concerned, one target was much like another. Beresford would get them there, he trusted his men to do their jobs efficiently, and his own confidence grew with every safe return. He would not have admitted it to anybody, but he was more concerned about Mary.

He knew he was, as parlance had it, 'slow'. He had held Mary's hand and on one occasion, guiding her through a door, had daringly put a hand on her waist. But he had not kissed her. He had not yet told her he was entranced by the way she stood, ankles close together in her court shoes, the way she walked, her skirt moving in the provocative way he recognised but could not describe. Going back to his billet for an attempted sleep, he took a decision. He would kiss her before taking off.

His batman had made his bed and tidied his room. A window was open and there was the faint smell of polish. The three books on his bedside table, Evelyn Waugh's *Decline and Fall*, a paperback edition of Burke's *Reflections on the Revolution in France*, and a collection of poems by Keats, were stacked in a neat pile. On top lay the letter received from his mother that morning. It was full of the homilies he associated with her. He was adjured 'to write to the Jenkinsons', who had entertained him on his last leave, 'to be sure you pay your mess bill on time', and 'not to drink too much'. Chalmers slipped the letter into a drawer. He thought of the friends he had seen dying in blazing aircraft: it was difficult to believe his mother could not recognise his independence or manhood. He wished he could love her. All he could see was the grimace of disapproval when she found his school reports less than perfect.

He opened the door and shouted for his batman: 'Jones!' He wasn't optimistic, but the batmen had a kitchen down the corridor where they congregated for tea.

'Sir!' He was in luck. Jones, an idle but willing fellow enjoying a quiet cigarette with a couple of mates, came running. A small, wiry Welshman, he had a reputation as a fixer.

'We're on tonight, Jones. Pre-briefing 4 pm. Wake me at 3.30 with a cup of tea, will you? And, Jones …'

'Yes, sir?'

'You know some of the WAAF drivers, don't you?' They had talked about them in the past and he knew he was on firm ground. 'Have a word with the girl who does the rota and see if you can get Mary Kenyon to take out Z-Zebra tonight.'

Jones grinned. 'Aye, aye, sir. I'll do my best. If I can't fiddle the rota, I can probably get one of the girls to do a swap.' The Welsh lilt in his voice was strangely warming.

'Keep it under your hat.'

Jones put his hand to his forehead in mock salute. 'Mum's the word, sir.' He had done one or two things for Chalmers beyond the call of duty and enjoyed the footing of apparent equality.

Chalmers took off his tie and trousers, got onto the bed and pulled the bedspread over him. Before shutting his eyes, he opened a school atlas he kept in the bedside cupboard to check the exact position of Stuttgart. He hadn't been there before and geography had never been his strong point.

It seemed he had barely closed his eyes when there was a knock at the door and Jones reappeared, carrying a tray with a cup of tea on it.

' 'alf past three, sir. Tea as ordered. And…' – he dropped his voice – 'Mary Kenyon'll take out Z-Zebra and B-Baker. They don't know the times yet.'

Chalmers swung his legs off the bed. 'Good man, Jones. I knew you could do it. Thanks for the tea. I'd better get weaving if I'm going to make it.' He was already getting out of his underpants and climbing into the woollen combinations he wore for operational flying. Jones withdrew. As a good working-class boy he was always shocked by the readiness of public-school officers to strip off in public.

At pre-briefing Chalmers, Beresford and Robertson sat together while the Squadron Commander and Navigation Leader went through the route details. Inevitably, the course went close to some of the Ruhr flak areas marked red on the map.

'How many going, sir?' asked the pilot of S-Sugar, a young Flight Sergeant on his first mission.

'About three hundred – Lancasters, Halifaxes and Stirlings. A major effort.'

Chalmers saw the relief on the man's face. He remembered his own first operation and the illusion of safety created by weight of numbers. After all, they couldn't shoot everyone down. He made his own notes, but knew Beresford's appreciation of problems was better than his. Navigation had never been Chalmers's forte. He recalled the time in training he lost his way completely and only got back to Booker in his Tiger Moth by following the Princes Risborough railway line through the Chilterns. He thanked God for sending him the best navigator in the squadron.

Back in the fresh air the three men stood for a moment outside the briefing hut and looked over the airfield. The cloud was high and a freshening wind lifted the windsock by the control tower. The Lancasters stood silently like carved stone birds. Bombing up was complete, here and there fuel bowsers were still at work. Above them, flying high and leaving a con trail, a single American B-17 headed south.

'Wonder where he's going,' said Robertson.

'No idea,' responded Beresford, 'but I'm glad the Yanks do the daytime shift. At least we can creep about in the dark.'

Chalmers turned back to his billet. 'See you at the main briefing. Get Freddie there on time. The adjutant blew his top when he was late for the Mannheim trip.'

Now Chalmers was free to daydream about Mary. His physical nature drove him on – he fantasized about kissing her, holding her to him – but there was more to it than that. Why did he tell her that Schubert's String Quintet convinced him that Man has a soul? As a boy he followed traditional Anglican worship in the school chapel because it was compulsory and he was confirmed when his mother expected it; at Oxford he attended the college chapel because two friends from his old school did. Somehow Mary had drawn him out and he had spoken about the soul as though it was a concept he had considered from every intellectual angle. But in the short term he was going to kiss her before he flew to Stuttgart.

He went back to his room, took out a writing pad, sat down at his desk and began to write.

Dear Mary,

I don't suppose you will ever read this, but just in case things go wrong tonight I should like to leave you a little memento. The truth is that I am falling in love with you. I am ashamed I have not said anything, though I suspect we both recognize what is happening. You say I am complicated, but really I'm very simple. I've never been close to a girl before – can I say we're close? – but for the first time I feel something I have not known before and it centres on you. I love the way you walk, the way you smile, the way you ask about music – and I long to kiss you. I have just made a vow to kiss you tonight before we take off. If I get back safely, you will never know what I am writing. If I don't, someone will give this to you. Look after yourself, Mary. You have made life good, so I have every intention of coming back. If I don't make it, play the Schubert for both of us.

Love,

Jamie.

He put the letter in an envelope on which he wrote *Miss Mary Kenyon*, and left it on top of Waugh's *Decline and Fall*. It would not be missed by anyone clearing his room.

***

Chalmers went to the Mess for his operational supper of bacon and eggs. Both items were in short supply and only given to those actually going on a mission.

'Flying tonight, sir?' checked the waitress before putting the plate down in front of him.

'Oh yes, I'm on tonight.' He winked, 'but I'd rather be at home in bed.'

The girl, a pretty brunette new to the Mess, blushed. She was only slowly getting used to the humour of men whose lives were on the line; she had no idea Chalmers was thinking of someone else entirely and screwing his courage to the sticking place for a first kiss.

After the meal he went to the main briefing, sitting with the rest of his crew in the smoke-filled room. A red ribbon on the wall map behind the briefing officer indicated the route. Flak danger areas and German night fighter bases were also indicated in red. The officer himself, cheerful, optimistic, indicated salient points with a billiard cue. As he did so, Chalmers watched the reactions of his crew. When he first arrived at Wynton Thorpe, an old hand, a skipper well into his second tour, told him he studied the faces of other crews and tried to predict from the strains he saw who would not survive the raid. Sadly, he claimed he was often right.

So Chalmers looked at his own men. Beresford had already made a sheaf of calculations, his thin face wholly absorbed. Hugh Robertson looked bored, but Chalmers had been his skipper long enough to know this was misleading; he was concentrating. Freddie Shorthouse was only paying attention to those items which might concern him directly; he was smiling and Chalmers found himself thinking of John Wilkes, the eighteenth-century rake whose ugliness did not preclude a rampant sexual life. Brad Alcock was smiling, too, looking round as if surprised to be in England rather than Canada; his ruddy complexion always made him look ineffably healthy, as though he lived permanently out of doors. Leslie Ricketts, red hair standing up like a brush, absurdly young, took in every word; for him it was an adventure in which he intended to make no mistake. The only man looking strained was John Stafford; he admitted sleeping badly and a mark near his lip showed he had cut himself shaving; but his blonde hair was brushed with care and he still exuded the confidence of a man who has cracked most of life's problems. Chalmers relaxed; the old hand's advice did not worry him. He suspected his crew shared the fears he had long ago admitted to himself, but they were not showing it.

The briefing came to an end. 'Good luck, gentlemen,' said the squadron commander, who was leading the raid himself. 'See you over Stuttgart.'

Chairs and tables were pushed back, the door opened and the crews went out into the dark to change, draw flying rations and collect parachutes.

***

Outside the Nissen hut the lorries waited to take them to their aircraft. Mary had parked her Bedford nearest to the door. A byzantine web of manipulation organised by the batman Jones had led to a transfer of aircraft between herself and another driver. She spent longer in front of the mirror when she realised the switch had been made.

The crews came out of the hut. The drivers shouted: 'A-Able and S-Sugar'; 'Charlie, Dog'; 'F-Fox and M-Mother'. 'B-Baker and Z-Zebra,' shouted Mary, less stridently than some of her colleagues.

The skipper of B-Baker, one Flight Sergeant Croft, was first to Mary's Bedford. He made to get into the cab with her, while his crew clambered into the back. He had opened the door, but before he could hoist himself aboard a firm hand closed on his shoulder.

'Sorry, Crofty, I'm pulling rank.' Chalmers smiled, but his grip on Croft brooked no contradiction. 'This driver needs to be shown the way and I've arranged a course of instruction.'

Croft, a pilot with whom Chalmers had drunk at the White Hart, did not demur. The mutual respect of the two men crossed the divide between officer and NCO and they treated each other as equals. 'Of course, sir. Important to get the navigation right, particularly before take off. I'll climb in the back and make sure none of mine go AWOL. After that Essen trip one or two might bale out before we get to dispersal.'

'My lot are all aboard. Except Shorthouse, of course. Give a shout when he's in.'

Chalmers got in beside Mary, who was watching with a deadpan face. The smell of oil was strong in the cab.

'You fiddled this,' she said.

A shout from the rear and a thump on the back of the cab indicated that Shorthouse was aboard. A wag in the back, one of Croft's crew, called out: 'Piccadilly Circus, please driver – and step on it.'

'Go to B-Baker first,' said Chalmers.

'That's an order?'

'That's an order.'

Mary raised an eyebrow as she set off round the perimeter track, the hooded lights only showing the rear of the lorry immediately ahead with its white-faced cargo. Her lips were moist and slightly parted, her eyes bright in the shadowy light reflected from the Bedford in front. She had no idea why she usually said something trite at a moment of emotional crisis, but she always did. She said: 'I hope it's a good flight.' She didn't mean that at all. What she wanted to say was: 'I want you to put your arms round me, I want you to be safe.'

'I hope so, too.' Chalmers, overfilling the seat in his heavy flying gear, touched her left arm. 'I'm going to give you some instructions. Be a good girl and follow them precisely.'

'Very well, sir,' she replied obediently, reverting to the flippant flirting characteristic of so much of their relationship. 'My lord's wish is . . .'

The lorry ahead turned off to towards D-Dog, just visible in its masked lights. Mary accelerated and they drove to the further reaches where the Maydon Woods pressed against the perimeter fence. They passed Z-Zebra and reached B-Baker.

Chalmers wound down his window. He shouted: 'B-Baker, gentlemen. All change.'

The tailboard dropped with a bang and seven crewmen clutching parachutes climbed out. Flight Sergeant Croft came round to the front. 'Good luck, sir.' He grinned. 'In all senses.'

'*Bon voyage*, Crofty. See you at the White Hart.'

Mary reversed before turning back for Z-Zebra. Chalmers said: 'Drive right up to the tail. I want my lot to be able to get straight in. I don't want any of them coming up the front here.'

'Why not?'

'You'll see.'

She drove round the port wing of Z-Zebra and drew up with the cab beyond the tailplane; the rear of the Bedford was next to the short ladder leading into the aircraft. Several ground staff were waiting.

Chalmers twisted in his seat and leaned towards Mary. 'I wanted us this way round because I'm going to kiss you and I don't want to provide a cabaret for that lot.' It was dark in the cab, the only light coming from the glow of dashboard instruments. Chalmers's left arm stretched across her and pulled her forward; his other arm went round her shoulders and held her firmly as their heads drew close. Their noses touched clumsily.

'I told you I was inexperienced,' said Chalmers.

Mary giggled. 'Come here,' she said. She put her hands each side of his face and drew his lips down to hers. Her lips were soft and yielding and Chalmers was aware she had somehow taken charge. The kiss was long and warm. Mary, clutching him through the bulk of his flying gear, detected a masculine smell of which she was previously ignorant. Eventually Chalmers, conscious that most of his men were now aboard the aircraft, eased himself away.

'More,' Mary said.

'Greedy girl. Not now, darling. Tomorrow, when we're back.'

44

'Take care of yourself, Jamie.' Her voice was soft.

'I will. I've got something to look forward to.'

'So have I. Keep safe. God bless you.'

'If anything goes wrong, there's a letter in my room.'

'I'll be waiting. I don't want a letter.'

Chalmers picked up his parachute and was last up the ladder. Only Shorthouse, just ahead of him, noticed the delay in his exit from the lorry. 'Come on, Skipper. I thought you must be after that WAAF driver. She's a bit of a looker, but I'm told the goods aren't for touching.' Then Shorthouse remembered Chalmers and Mary had left together that night at the White Hart and saw he might have been tactless. 'Sorry, Skip.'

Chalmers ignored the remark. 'I'm glad you managed to get here, Freddie. We were ready to send out a search party. Getting another pair of knickers? Come on, we've got an appointment over Stuttgart.'

Mary watched Chalmers vanish into the Lancaster, then drove back to the vehicle park. Inside, the sudden happiness equally suddenly died. She turned off the engine and the lights. All round the airfield the Merlins were starting up.

6

From the squadron's point of view the raid was a success. Two aircraft had minor flak damage, but there were no injuries and initial reports suggested accurate bombing. Z-Zebra had an uneventful flight and, for once, was not the last to land. The only problem occurred over the target when Alcock announced he needed the Elsan. He spent the bombing run sitting on that undignified throne in the rear of the plane, trousers round his ankles, nether regions freezing. Les Ricketts took over his gunnery duties amidships and was disappointed there was nothing to shoot at.

'I could do this all the time,' said Ricketts, when Alcock returned. 'It's more fun looking out than it is in my dark hole.'

'You wouldn't know a Messerschmitt from a Halifax,' the Canadian drawled. 'Give me back my guns. I shall feel safer – and so will everyone else.'

'That's not what you said a few minutes ago,' said Ricketts. 'You seemed in a hurry. I thought you were baling out.'

'If it was like that every time,' said Chalmers as they climbed into the Bedford, 'I wouldn't mind going more often.'

'Speak for yourself, Skip,' said Shorthouse. 'I've better things to do.'

Mary was driving back from dispersal, Chalmers beside her. 'I'm off duty this afternoon,' she said.

'We'll know by then if we're on tonight. If there's no flap, we'll go out. Meet you by the bus stop in time to catch the three o'clock. We'll have a walk – tea where the old biddies were and perhaps you'd like to go on to the flicks in Lincoln?'

'Sounds nice. I'm glad you're back. I didn't want that letter.'

'I'll get rid of it now. I've got time to tell you the gist of it.'

At 2.30 p.m. the squadron was stood down. Fog was predicted and Bomber Command would not risk returning aircraft finding their bases fogbound. Chalmers and Mary caught the bus at three and by twenty past were strolling down a country lane in the direction of Wynton Magna. The sky was clear and they walked in pale spring sunshine with a hint of the mist destined to turn into the forecast fog. There were primroses on the verges and a haze of green on hedgerows.

'Why did you kiss me last night?' asked Mary.

'Because I wanted to. Ask a silly question, get a silly answer.' He paused, looking straight at her. She tilted her head at an angle, a smile on her face he was beginning to recognise. 'You're looking smug,' he said.

'I wanted you to kiss me. Does that sound wanton?'

'Pretty shameless from a vicar's daughter.'

A horse, curious, friendly, came over to a gate in the hedge. Mary stroked its muzzle. 'You're a nice old chap. I haven't got any sugar.'

'I like their eyes. Do you think we'll live long enough to be put out to grass?' Chalmers put his hand over hers.

'I've got an apple. Would you like that?' She felt in her pocket and held out an apple bought earlier at the NAAFI. The horse took it, crunching with enthusiasm. 'Not too fast. You'll get indigestion.' The horse rolled its eyes and looked to see if anything else was on offer. Then it started to cough.

'You've done it now,' said Chalmers. 'Are you sure they eat apples? You've probably killed it.'

'They do in Shropshire. Perhaps this chap's a townee like you.'

The horse lost interest when it realised nothing else was forthcoming. It coughed again and snorted as it turned away. Another cough.

'He's got a sore throat,' said Mary. 'Did you think of me over Stuttgart?' Even as she spoke, she regretted the self-centred question. Barbara would never have been so obvious.

47

'You don't think I was going to forget my first real kiss.'

'It was mine too.'

'I once had an exploratory peck at a school dance. But it wasn't a real kiss. She was just the one everyone had a go with. I didn't want to be left out. You know what boys are.'

'I don't think I do.'

Chalmers studied Mary's trim figure. She was in civvies, wearing a fawn spring overcoat, open at the front, revealing a high-necked beige sweater and heather-coloured skirt. He had certainly thought of her over Stuttgart. How much he could say about that was a different matter. 'I planned that kiss like a military operation,' he said.

'I'll bet Freddie guessed what we were up to.'

'I expect he did. You've heard about his lucky knickers?'

'Everyone has – certainly all the girls.'

'You'd never guess how many of us have lucky charms. We're an odd lot.'

'What have you got?'

'Nothing. But I always make sure I put my left flying boot on first. Hangover from school. I scored my first fifty after putting my left cricket boot on first and after that I always did it with cricket and rugger boots. As I said, we're an odd lot. Les Ricketts has got a teddy bear his mother gave him. He wouldn't fly without it. The only one who isn't superstitious is Stephen. He says we're living in the Middle Ages. He's probably right.'

'I'd like another kiss.'

Chalmers slipped his arm inside the open coat and pulled her to him. 'You smell nice.'

'My faith in Guerlain is restored. A Christmas present from Daddy. Pre-war stock from a shop in Ludlow. He wasn't sure it was a good idea. He thought the wolves would gather.'

'This one has.'

Their kiss was long and unhurried. His hand slid down to the small of her back and would have gone further, but he heard a lorry approaching and pulled away. It was collecting milk churns from local farms and made a noisy, clanking progress.

'I don't mind being seen,' she said.

'It's all very well for you. You just hide your face in my chest. Come here.' He pulled her to him again and kissed her roughly. The hint of ruthlessness was strangely exciting.

'Mmm. I like that. Again?'

'Tea,' he said. 'We'll have to get cracking if we're going to the flicks as well. We had a plan.'

'You always stick to plans?'

'I'm a creature of habit. I'm not very good with the unexpected. I suspect you're more spontaneous.'

'I probably need organising.'

They both laughed. For the first time in her life Mary felt a mature woman. Looking at his uniform with the wings over the left breast pocket, she realised she was becoming proprietorial. For his part, Chalmers was managing to forget Z-Zebra and the dangers of the night sky. He looked at Mary and saw his world transformed. He knew he had fallen in love, just as he had said in his letter.

In the teashop they were served by the same ingenuous girl. 'Nice to see you again,' she said, putting them once more at the table by the fire. 'Better than last time, isn't it? Almost like spring. Would you like Ma's scones and the raspberry jam?' She had on the same figure-hugging dress.

Mary looked at her sympathetically, aware of the girl's anxiety to please, confident she posed no threat. She took the lead: 'Yes, please. We'll have just the same.'

Chalmers sat back, happy for Mary to order. He said: 'The coven hasn't arrived.'

'Bertie might be ill.'

They laughed again. The shared humour was part of their bond.

'Do you like opera?' he asked unexpectedly.

'I've never been. There's nothing like that up in the Welsh Marches.'

'It's a strange art form, but I went several times before war broke out. The first I saw was Puccini's *Il Trittico*, up at Oxford. That's three one-act operas, not often done. I particularly liked the first – *Il Tabarro*. It's gloomy, set on a barge on the Seine in Paris.'

'*Il Tabarro* ? What does it mean?'

'The Cloak. All about a jealous husband who murders his wife's lover and wraps the body in a cloak.'

'Would I like it?'

'You'd like the music. Tremendously evocative – there's a theme right at the beginning representing the flowing of the river and it's there all the way through. It's meant to be socially realistic – ordinary working people, not kings and nobles. Probably influenced by Zola. Read any Zola?'

'No. You see how ignorant I am. Are you sure you still want to go out with me?'

'Don't be silly. When the war's over I'll take you to the opera. *Il Tabarro*'s too dark. We'll go to something cheerful. Mozart's *Figaro*, perhaps. That's a marvellous start.'

'I'd like that. I love you telling me things. I wish I'd had a proper education.'

The waitress returned and busied herself with cups, saucers and scones. Mary watched Chalmers eyeing the high heels and tight skirt. Gently her shoe touched his leg under the table. 'Forget the general and concentrate on the particular.'

'You do watch me, don't you?'

'A pretty lame excuse when you first made the distinction, but I like the idea as long as the particular comes first. You see how gullible I am.'

'I want to kiss you again.' He looked round the teashop. A middle-aged couple were talking quietly in a corner; two women with full shopping baskets were discussing a piece of local gossip, their voices rising as they expressed disapproval, falling as they shared another titbit.

'That's a nice idea.'

Chalmers leaned across the table, put a hand on her cheek and kissed her. Then he sat back suddenly. 'Sorry,' he said. 'Short rations. My back hurt. It gets stiff flying a Lancaster.'

'Excuses.'

'If we get to the flicks, I promise you a proper cuddle. I've always envied the chaps in the back row.'

They finished their tea, Chalmers paid the bill and they set off to find the bus to Lincoln.

* * *

As a cinema the Rex had seen better days, but the war brought big audiences if not rejuvenation of past splendour. When Chalmers and Mary arrived, there was still a queue for the one-and-nine seats. Chalmers bought tickets for the two-and-threes in the circle and they didn't have to wait. Upstairs an usherette tore their tickets in half and guided them up the sloping floor to the rear. Her torch probed the darkness, revealing the worn carpet and faded red plush seats.

They apologised as they stumbled past various sets of knees before settling down against the wall at the end of a row. Chalmers had no intention of having to get up for latecomers. The trailer of a modest but patriotic war film was showing, followed by the equally patriotic Pathe News, with its crowing cockerel and cheerful commentary. It praised Allied successes in Russia and North Africa and laughing women making shells in a Midlands factory. By the time the censor's certificate for *Gone with the Wind* appeared Chalmers and Mary were huddled together, arms round each other in comforting warmth.

Above them the projection beam cut across the darkness. The drama of the American Civil War unfolded: Atlanta burned, Scarlett O'Hara struggled, suffered and survived, Rhett Butler showed his contempt. Blue cigarette smoke drifted upwards through the light, creating constantly changing curlicues, fantastic, insubstantial.

Mary's head was on Chalmers's shoulder, his arm round her. She said: 'I think I love you, Jamie.'

There was no response. She repeated, 'I love you, Jamie.'

She was aware of the depth of his breathing. He was again sleeping the sleep of exhaustion. Mary sensed new emotions: maternal protectiveness and guilt that she was responsible for getting him away from the base where he could have been asleep in his bed. They only confirmed what she had said. She loved him.

7

L ooking back at that summer of 1943 much later, Mary's memory was selective. Cloud and rain vanished and all she saw were warm days of flowers, birds and butterflies. Likewise, she forgot the nights of waiting as Chalmers and Z-Zebra worked through their tour; she remembered only the joyous reunions, rowdy evenings in the White Hart, idyllic walks and picnics.

One afternoon in May they had a picnic in a field fringed by Maydon Woods, just beyond the aerodrome. The squadron had been out the night before and had been stood down. The airfield was silent, the only sounds the cooing of pigeons and buzzing of insects in the early summer warmth. 'That was good.' Chalmers brushed crumbs off his open uniform jacket and lay back against the oak in whose shade they were sitting. 'I could sleep for a century.'

Mary tidied plates and glasses into a basket and moved from her side of the rug to sit by him. She nestled into the crook of his arm, the skirt of her pale-yellow cotton dress spreading round her.

'Being in love's a big responsibility,' said Chalmers. 'It's bad enough looking after my Zebra zoo, but the thought of not getting back and you waiting for me . . . I never want to let you down.'

'Difficult last night?' Mary sensed his mood.

'Wickenby lost one. We saw him go down. That tall chap who captained their cricket team against us last Saturday. I liked him.'

'You'll come back. I sit on your shoulder. I shan't let anything happen.'

Chalmers slipped a little lower down the tree and pulled her closer. 'I want to ask you a question.' Like so many of his decisions he was about to say something he had considered, rejected, and then resurrected on the spur of the moment. 'Don't say anything until I've finished.'

'All right.'

'I want you to marry me, so this is really a proposal. But I'm not a good bet for marriage at the moment. I don't want to give you a husband who may not be with you long.'

'Jamie, don't speak like that. Don't even think it.'

'I told you not to interrupt.'

'I don't always do as I'm told.'

'Hush, darling. We both know the truth. You've seen them go. Johnny Smithies, Sandy Protheroe, Peter Mitchell, 'Figgy' Jones – that's the last three months. I shall need to be very lucky to get through this. I know the odds. I've been lucky so far – that's why Freddie and the others trust me. So I want to marry you, darling, but not now, not yet. I want to offer you a future, something secure.'

'I like it when you call me "darling". It's possessive. I'll marry you, Jamie, you know that. Just tell me when you want me.'

'I still haven't finished.' The mock irritation of his tone reflected the style of so much of their conversation. 'You'll have to be more obedient when we're married.'

'Don't you believe it.'

He looked down at her bare knee and put a hand over it. 'One day we'll be married, Mary. But in the meanwhile,' – he paused – 'if I could get some leave, would you come to London for the week-end? Forget the war for a couple of days. A concert perhaps, or a theatre, and dancing afterwards. I'd like to show you off at the Savoy.'

'It sounds terribly extravagant. Of course I'll come. I'm sure I can get leave. I gave up my last lot to Dot when her father was ill and she took some compassionate. I'm owed some.'

'It'll have to be short notice – and we might have to postpone at the last moment. But we both know that.'

'How shall we go?'

'Train. We can get a lift to Grantham and it's straight through to King's Cross. As a matter of fact I did think about going by car, but it's too far just for the week-end – and it would mean black market petrol.'

'You haven't got a car.'

'Not yet. But Arthur Palmer's put his MG up for sale and I thought of buying it. What do you think?'

'That little red one outside the Mess? The one with a pointed tail?'

'That's it. M-Type, 1932. They raced at Brooklands.'

'It would be fun in weather like this. Why does he want to sell it?'

'He's got some debts. Nothing wrong with it as far as I know. He says it leaks a bit if you have to put the hood up. Anyway, it would take too long to get to London. We'll go by train. So you said "Yes" to my proposal?'

'Which one?'

'Both of them.'

Mary smiled at the way he had wandered away from a marriage proposal to talk about the car. He was, she thought, just like a little boy. 'Yes,' she said, 'to both.'

'I suppose I'll have to get a ring one day. I'm not sure I can afford a car as well.'

'Well, it's a question of priorities,' she responded. 'I can see the problem.' She put an arm under his jacket. 'Mind you, a ring would be nice. And I'll have to show you off to Daddy.'

'What sort of ring would you like? Have you got a favourite stone?'

She didn't answer immediately. Then she sat up, pulling away from him. 'I think we can do without a ring until we know we're really going to be married. I've had a nasty thought.'

'What's wrong?'

'A poem. You remember quoting Chaucer and I said I'd been badly educated? Maybe it wasn't as bad as all that. There was a poem we read – I expect you know it – it's called *Bredon Hill*. I can't remember who wrote it.' She looked at him enquiringly. 'You do know it, don't you? I expect you know what I'm going to say.'

'I know the poem. But I don't know what you're going to say. A.E.Houseman. Comes from a collection called *A Shropshire Lad*. Doom and gloom in the Welsh Marches. Young men marching off to death in war or about to be hanged in Shrewsbury gaol.'

'I expect that's why we were given it to read. A lot of the girls came from Shropshire and Herefordshire.'

'What were you going to say?'

'Well, you know what it's about. It's very sad. A young couple out in the countryside – lying on Bredon Hill looking at the view, making plans for their wedding. It's summertime, like it is now. Then what happens?'

'Winter comes and the girl dies. She goes to the church alone – to be buried.'

'It's best not to make too many plans. Let's enjoy the present. Forget the ring. I'm happy just to be with you.'

'I like Housman. Very melancholy. I first met *A Shropshire Lad* through Butterworth.'

'Butterworth?'

'English composer. Friend of Vaughan-Williams. He set several of the poems and wrote an exquisite piece called *A Shropshire Lad*. Killed in the Great War. He won an MC.'

Mary gave him an affectionate nudge. 'I might have guessed you'd know more about it than I do.'

'You didn't tell me what your favourite stone is – for the ring.'

'A sapphire? I like blue – my favourite colour.'

'We can have fun looking at rings, even if we don't get one yet. Perhaps in London?'

'Perhaps,' said Mary. 'Now do I qualify for another kiss as I said "Yes"?'

***

Chalmers and his crew did two more short operations, then high pressure brought a heat-wave to Western Europe. Clear skies and bright moonlight effectively stopped night bombing. The squadron was stood down. Chalmers put in for week-end leave and got it immediately as neither he nor his crew had taken any since the start of their tour. Mary was able to get a forty-eight hour pass as well.

She had said little to her room-mates about her relationship with Chalmers, but snippets of information had made them curious. She concealed her feelings under a façade of flippancy, but they knew about the country walks and visit to the cinema. Like the older sisters they often seemed, they offered gratuitous advice for the visit to London.

'Sounds promising,' said Dot one evening. 'I fancy an officer, but I'm not daft enough to think one of them would fancy me. My Lancashire accent can't compete with your King's English.' She stated it as a fact, without envy. 'He took you in the two-and-threes, didn't he? I've only ever been in the one-and-nines.'

'How are you going?' asked Barbara. She had washed her hair and was getting ready for an evening with her American.

'Train – from Grantham.'

'What are you going to do?' asked Dot. The dark eyes in her pale, Madonna-like face showed genuine interest. Like Mary she had never been to London.

'He talked about a concert and dancing.'

'Two nights, eh?' said Dot. 'Time for progress, duckie. Where does he live? Nice country estate somewhere?'

Mary took no umbrage at the inquisition. She knew it was kindly meant. 'Wimbledon,' she said. 'He's got a mother who still treats him like a child.'

'I should watch her,' said Barbara. 'She won't want anyone nabbing her little boy. I had one of those. Thought I was after her precious son.'

'I expect you were,' said Dot. Her friendship with Barbara was based on scrupulous honesty.

'Perhaps.' Barbara held up a blue dress in front of herself. 'What do you think?' She included them both in the question, but was looking at Dot.

'The pink does more for you. Tighter in the places that matter. Depends how far you want to go. Is Robert coming up to scratch.?'

'He's all right.' She did not sound enthusiastic. 'Nice smile – and generous. Brave, too, but naïve, like most Yanks. Prefers a glass of milk to a glass of beer. Right, the pink it is.'

Barbara turned back to Mary. 'You'd better find out where he's taking you dancing. You'll need something smart. Have you got a nice evening dress?'

'That green one I wore at the Christmas party.'

Barbara looked doubtful. 'It's pretty, but a bit young and covered up. You ought to have something more sophisticated.'

'He mentioned the Savoy. I've heard of it.'

'That settles it. We've got to get you dressed up.' Barbara's concern for Mary had overtaken her interest in her evening with Robert. 'I've got a lovely dress at home that would do the job and I reckon it would fit you a treat – probably better than me. You've got a better bust. Ice-blue silk and black lace, little straps on bare shoulders. Would you like to borrow it? Daddy could get it here.'

Mary's initial feeling that she was being patronised was swept away by the warmth of the offer. 'I'd love it – if it's no trouble.'

Barbara put an arm round her. 'Of course it's no trouble. We're going to get you kitted out. Proper military operation. We'll get the dress. If you don't like it, we'll find something else. Ciggie?' She held out a packet of Capstan, screwing up the silver paper and tossing it into a wastepaper basket.

'Thanks.' Mary had not smoked before joining up, but

sometimes did now to be sociable. The others smoked as a matter of course. She did not inhale and they laughed at her.

'Time I got going,' said Barbara. 'They've got a hop this evening and we're having dinner first. He's used to my time-keeping, but he'll be disappointed if I'm too late. He's not trained yet.'

Mary and Dot were having a domestic evening, getting the billet ready for the weekly inspection. Barbara had already made her contribution by scrubbing the floor so that she could go out with a clear conscience. When she had gone, the others cleaned the windows and tidied the kit layouts in the cupboards over their beds. Mary polished the final window, then said: 'I'm going out for a bit. It's a lovely evening.' She enjoyed their friendship, but as an only child sometimes found the constant company claustrophobic.

Outside, the warmth of the day hung over the aerodrome. A blackbird was singing in an elm by the WAAF billets and the sky glowed red and yellow as the sun went down. In the nearest hangar a mechanic was working on an engine and there came the irregular clink of metal on metal; from the airfield came shouts from an impromptu game of cricket played by the ground staff; in the village a dog barked, as though it needed to make its mark before night fell.

Mary didn't want to meet anyone, so she walked behind the main hangars before setting off through the grass inside the perimeter fence. The sun was still strong enough to cast her shadow before her, and the grey concrete of the control tower was softened by the evening light. The silent Lancasters, camouflaged, with black undersides, had lost something of their menace.

"Evening, Miss.' An RAF Regiment guard patrolling the perimeter fence with an Alsatian broke into her reverie. 'You all right?' The dog sniffed at her shoes.

She was standing by the tailplane of M-Mother, looking out at the dark shape of Morby castle catching the last of the sun. 'Enjoying the peace and quiet. How long are you on for?'

'Only just started. Night guard duty all this week.' He eased the rifle slung over his shoulder.

'Hard luck.'

'Better than going up in one of these things. I take my hat off to 'em. I was drafted into the RAF, but I've kept my feet on the ground. Safer – much safer.' He was a young man with a rough, pugilist's face. The Alsatian sat down, realising its routine had temporarily come to a halt.

'Isn't it quiet?' she said. The dog in the village had stopped barking, the cricketers had gone in. Then, almost imperceptibly, the drone of an approaching aircraft emerged from the silence. Sunlight glinting on its wings, a Lancaster flew into view, losing height, lowering its wheels. It made a circuit before landing and taxiing to the main hangars. 'I knew it couldn't last,' she said. The engines coughed into silence. Various ground staff surrounded it.

'Replacement for the one lost on Monday,' said the sentry. 'They're expectin' it. Probably a woman delivery pilot. Amazin' what they get up to these days – savin' your presence, Miss.'

'Rather her than me. I don't think a flying helmet does much for a woman. Though, come to think of it, Amy Johnson had plenty of admirers.'

The guard followed a line of thought of his own. 'It'll finish one day. And I s'pose the bombin's helpin'. But we're losin' one 'ell of a lot of good men. I must get off. Sar'nt Smith'll 'ave my guts for garters. Time to check into the guard room. G'night, Miss.' The Alsatian stood up obediently and the pair continued their tour of the perimeter fence.

Mary, too, started back. The sun had gone now, leaving an orange and purple glow; the airfield lay in twilight. The guard had brought back reality. Happiness was a commodity in short supply. She felt the elation of her love, but the reality of Bredon Hill was not far off. There was no point in looking beyond the week-end.

8

L ike most trains during the war, the London express was crowded and late. It was already behind schedule when it arrived at Grantham and thereafter its progress was only spasmodic. Chalmers travelled first class when in uniform and managed to get two seats, Mary sitting beside him next to the window. She had spent a long time considering her wardrobe and was wearing a simple flowered cotton dress with high-heeled sandals. Not having been to London before, she had put on stockings in spite of the heat. The prospect of Barbara's fashionable décolleté dress at the Savoy was thrilling, as was the thought of the Royal Charles Hotel, where Chalmers had booked them in. She had never stayed at a grand hotel, let alone in London.

There were four others in the compartment: a middle-aged businessman in a pinstripe suit reading The Times; a major in the Gunners with the sort of moustache that suggested he had been a regular before the war; a bespectacled, dry-looking man who might have been an academic; and an elderly woman in a lilac suit, grey-haired, having the air of one for whom a first-class carriage was a natural habitat and wearing a smart black hat with a feather. Chalmers put their suitcases in the luggage rack over their heads. No one spoke.

Past Peterborough, the train picked up speed, its white smoke hanging above the fields. Surreptitiously, Chalmers took Mary's hand. He said: 'Do you like trains?'

She looked at him and saw it was a serious enquiry. 'I suppose so.'

'I think they're romantic. I had a model layout in the attic when I was a boy. I'd like to go on the Orient Express. Perhaps we shall after the war – if we haven't bombed it to smithereens. Did you know there was a bad accident at Grantham?'

'No.'

'You don't mind talking about it while we're actually on a train?'

It hadn't occurred to her. 'Tell me.'

'At the beginning of the century. The Night Mail from King's Cross was meant to stop at Grantham, but it went straight through the station at sixty miles an hour and crashed disastrously when it hit the branch line to Nottingham on the other side. They never found out why the driver didn't stop. He'd done the journey for years, so should have known where he was. And he had a fireman who might have done something. No explanation – a lot killed, including the driver and fireman.'

'Strange the fireman didn't do anything.'

'Difficult. An engine driver's a bit of an aristocrat. Firemen are usually young – it takes courage to question a driver's decisions. The chap on our engine now is only a youngster, the driver's a middle-aged man.'

'You noticed?'

'Oh, I always look at the driver– and the engine. We've got an A3 Pacific.'

Mary smiled. Only the day before he had been talking about butterflies and now he was on trains. She imagined tidy compartments in his brain: Lancasters, history, music, butterflies, poetry, trains. She felt her own mind was a clutter of trivia not worth dragging into the light of day. Chalmers was thinking quite differently: he was frightened of boring her. The back of his hand was against her thigh and he could feel her suspender through the thin cotton dress. It was exciting.

The train slowed to walking pace and then stopped. Flat countryside stretched on both sides; trees in full summer foliage stood in hedgerows surrounding fields of corn. In the distance a church tower indicated a village. The window was open; everything seemed to have come to a standstill in the heat. Someone coughed in an adjacent carriage, the engine exhaled steam.

'Adlestrop,' said Chalmers *sotto voce*, leaning towards Mary.

'What?'

'Adlestrop. A station in the Cotswolds. There's a poem about it – Edward Thomas. It was a day like this and his train stopped there. He managed to capture the heat, the silence, the world holding its breath – like now. It's one of those short poems you can't improve. I've got it back at Wynton.'

'You're showing off. You want me to feel ignorant.'

'Men have to show off. You know that.'

Their conversation was carried on in an undertone, but Chalmers spoke this last more loudly, catching the eye of the woman in the lilac suit. Sensing the invitation, the woman, her face creasing in sympathetic lines, said, 'That's certainly my experience.' She saw the twinkle in Chalmers's eye and spoke across him to Mary. 'We women don't need to, do we, my dear?' She put her book down in her lap.

'Does Adlestrop mean anything to you?' asked Mary.

'Nothing at all. And I don't know anything about trains. Except that ours is going to be at least an hour late.'

Chalmers looked at his watch. 'You're right.' Then, smiling: 'I thought the monstrous regiment would gang up against me.'

'On leave?' asked the woman. She was impressed by his pilot's wings.

'Forty-eight hours.'

'Fighters?'

'Bombers.'

'Of course, you got on at Grantham – bomber country. My son's in the navy. Destroyer, somewhere in the Far East. We haven't heard from him for two months.'

Both had left openings, both knew they would respect the unspoken conventions of wartime conversation. They would not ask questions which might lead to 'careless talk'. 'What about you, my dear?' With the poise and confidence of an experienced hostess, the woman brought in Mary. She saw she was not wearing a wedding ring.

'I'm just a camp follower. In the WAAFs – a driver.' It was almost the first time she had held social converse when so obviously attached to Chalmers. She did not want to let him down.

'I was a nurse in the Great War. I met my husband on the Western Front when he was brought in from the trenches. He was lucky. We thought that was the end of war. How wrong we were!'

'Too many mistakes at Versailles,' said Chalmers.

'We didn't think so at the time,' she responded, a shade curtly. 'You're right, of course. We can see it now.' She was calm and unruffled. 'Nice plans for the week-end?'

The train jerked into motion. Gouts of smoke funnelled upwards from the engine and the driving wheels slipped on the rails, struggling with the heavy load.

'We're going to the Albert Hall this evening – assuming we ever get there. Myra Hess playing Beethoven's Fourth Concerto, Boult conducting. Schubert's Ninth in the second half. We're staying at the Royal Charles for a bit of luxury.'

'He's trying to educate me,' said Mary. 'A difficult job. He's introducing me to Schubert.'

'I like music,' said the woman, 'but I've never been to the Albert Hall. You won't go wrong at the Royal Charles. Mind you, they're short-staffed. A friend took me for a cocktail about a month ago. I felt guilty when I thought about young men like you risking your lives. It must be difficult to see civilians living normally.'

'It's more difficult trying to adjust to ordinary life after a night over Germany. Mary keeps me sane.' He took her hand again and put it back between them. He liked the feel of the suspender. 'But at least we sleep in decent sheets in our own beds. I wouldn't swap it for the army. You never know where you're going to sleep there.'

The major, apparently asleep, took mention of the army as an invitation to join the conversation. A sandy eyebrow, curiously contrasted to his dark hair, rose quizzically. 'I'm not too worried where I sleep. I wouldn't go up with one of you lot for all the tea in China. Lancasters? Stirlings?'

'Lancasters, thank God!' replied Chalmers. 'You can't get the height with Stirlings. Are you Field or Ack-Ack?'

'Field. 25-Pounders. I've got a week's leave and I'm going down to Somerset to see my wife and children. Only the second time this year.'

The train picked up speed. The countryside flashed past, a series of cameos barely perceived before vanishing: a field of sheep, a canal with a barge going into a lock, a gaggle of geese waddling up a lane leading nowhere, allotments and elderly men with bent backs, tumbledown sheds. They managed to catch up ten minutes of lost time in the last part of the journey. Conversation stopped as they made their way through the dingy, smoke-blackened houses in the approach to King's Cross.

King's Cross was crowded. A shaft of sunlight cut down through the smoke, lighting up the platform as the train disgorged its load. Chalmers got down the lilac woman's case and went to look for a porter for her. The woman leaned towards Mary. 'Look after him, my dear. He wants to give you a lovely week-end, but he's very tired. He's a good man. I'm envious! Be nice to him.'

Mary blushed. 'I'll do my best. I love him.'

'I know.' She gently touched Mary's hand as she stepped down from the carriage. She repeated, 'Look after him.'

Chalmers reappeared with a porter. 'Thank you so much,' said the woman. She touched his hand, too. 'Take care of yourself over Germany – and I hope you have a really good week-end.' She smiled, her face falling into its sympathetic lines.

'We'll take our time,' said Chalmers. 'There's no need to rush.'

'It was nice of you to get a porter for her. I'm just happy to be alone again. She was a pleasant woman, but I don't like sharing you.'

Outside the station they joined a queue for taxis. Opposite was a bomb-site where an office block had been destroyed in the Blitz. Grass, weeds and the occasional buddleia grew unchecked in the rubble; the adjacent warehouse had kept its roof but the windows were shattered. Further down an exposed staircase and a fireplace half way up a wall covered in dark-green wallpaper showed where a private house had stood. Chalmers had seen them before, Mary had not.

'I'd no idea,' she said.

'Worse in the East End. I told you I had an old Nanny who lived in dockland, didn't I? The whole street was flattened. She was lucky. She was in Kent staying with a farming cousin that night. Most of them had nowhere else to go. Her husband and one of her sons were killed.'

'It makes bombing Germany easier.'

'They started it, we'll finish it. I just hope there aren't too many nannies. Anyway, it's the only way we can get back at them.'

Mary was still looking at the bombed house. 'It's like a doll's house. All its privacy stripped away. You wonder what happened to the family.'

He took her hand. 'You're a good girl. I've been hardened. That's what war does. I suppose that's why I prefer to talk about music or poetry.'

Taxis were scarce, but they eventually reached the front of the queue. 'The Royal Charles,' said Chalmers. 'Can you take us down Regent Street and through Piccadilly Circus?' He wanted to give Mary a tour.

'Right, Guvnor,' said the elderly driver, impressed by the uniform and the destination. 'One problem after the Circus.

They've found an unexploded Jerry bomb at Hyde Park Corner, so they've blocked off the Knightsbridge end of Piccadilly. 'ow about going through Trafalgar Square and up the Mall? That suit you?'

'Sounds fine.'

Mary looked out at London. They left the seediness of King's Cross and moved into the West End. Every now and then there was more bomb damage, but Mary enjoyed looking at streets whose names she had heard of. 'It's exciting,' she said.

'Better before the war,' said Chalmers. 'Drab now. Look – a barrage balloon.' He pointed south over the river where a silver balloon showed up between the buildings.

He looked at his watch. 'Half-past four. The concert's at half-past seven. Bags of time to get changed and have a drink before we go out. I've booked a table at Verreys later.'

'Verreys?'

'Restaurant. We passed it just now in Regent Street.'

The taxi arrived in Ebury Street and drew up in front of the Royal Charles. A grey-haired, liveried doorman took their cases and showed them in. 'I retired once, sir, but got hauled back to the colours when everyone else was called up.'

Chalmers eyed the medals on his chest. 'You did your stuff in the last one. We want to forget the war for a couple of days.'

'It's quiet at the moment, sir. We're not full.' He led them into an extravagant foyer dominated by an Art Deco chandelier. A sort of proscenium arch decorated in cream and gold gave onto a lounge with a fountain shaped like a wedding cake. At the reception desk a trim woman in black greeted them. 'Flying Officer and Mrs Chalmers? Ah, yes. You wanted a really peaceful room. We've kept the Yellow Room for you on the first floor. It overlooks the garden, so there'll be no noise – unless Mr. Hitler decides on another visit. You'll find all the air raid instructions in your room, but please don't hesitate to ask if there's anything you'd like clarified. We still have full room service – though one or two of our girls are young and inexperienced, I'm afraid. Ring if you need anything.' She summoned a porter standing by the lift with an imperious wave. 'John, take Flying Officer and Mrs Chalmers up to the Yellow Room, please.' She gave him the key.

Throughout this exchange Mary stood to James's right. As it progressed and the full horror of the situation dawned on her, she retreated slightly behind his shoulder. She knew she was blushing, but there was nothing she could do about that. On the first floor they went down a wide, thickly-carpeted corridor before being ushered into a comfortable room with walls decorated in the palest primrose. Heavy yellow brocade curtains hung at the two eighteenth-century sash windows; a large double bed with an elaborate yellow counterpane dominated the room. The porter had a slight limp, Mary noticed, in spite of her agitation.

'The Yellow Room, sir,' he announced, as if unveiling one of the Wonders of the World. He turned to Mary. 'I hope you'll be comfortable, Madam. We're trying to keep up standards in spite of the conflict.'

Chalmers, unaware of Mary's confusion, was enjoying himself. He had never stayed anywhere so grand before. 'Thanks very much. We'll be fine.' He slipped the man half a crown.

'Thank *you*, sir.'

The door closed and James turned to Mary. 'Like it, darling? I hope . . .'

'Jamie . . . Jamie . . . I don't know what to say. It's all my fault . . . I didn't know . . .'

'Darling, what's wrong? It's strange for us both, but . . .'

'I had no idea you had this in mind. I'm so sorry.' Her eyes were wide, searching his face. 'It never occurred to me you were booking a double room. We'd never talked about it and I assumed . . .'

'What did you assume?' He held her gently.

'To be honest, I didn't think about it at all. I never thought we'd . . . we'd sleep together till we were married. When you asked me to come away for the week-end . . .'

Chalmers was horrified. 'Darling . . . I'm so sorry. I've never done anything like this before and I suppose I was too embarrassed to talk about it. I just assumed when you said you'd come away . . . I had no right . . . I'm so sorry.'

Mary clutched him, hiding her face in his shoulder. 'We both assumed . . . different things.'

'I shouldn't have jumped to conclusions. I'm an insensitive fool.'

'Don't be silly, darling. I'm sorry, too. You must think I'm really stupid.'

James recovered his equilibrium first. 'Come on, love. Let's see the funny side. We've both been a bit daft. But it's not going to spoil our week-end. We'll get round it like we get round everything else. You have this room. I'll see what else they've got. The porter said they're not full.'

'Oh, Jamie. It's our lovely week-end.'

'Our week-end's not going to be touched. I'll get this room sorted out, then we're off out. Come on, give me a kiss.' They kissed and rubbed noses in a way they had done on special occasions.

'Am I being selfish and old-fashioned?' asked Mary. 'I know the war's changed a lot of the rules.'

'Look, darling, I love you too much to do anything you don't want. I was always taught that if you want something badly enough, you'll wait for it. Mary, my Mary, I shall wait for you. Now, come on. Get unpacked and get your glad rags on. I'll go and see if they've got a garret for me.'

Apart from the embarrassment, there was no problem. Chalmers got a single room on the floor above and was soon in the bath. He lay back and closed his eyes. The war was miles away. He could think of nothing but his folly. Why hadn't he checked they were on the same wavelength? It was ridiculous to have thought Mary would jump into bed the moment he asked her. A vicar's daughter from the country who had never been to London: he must have been mad! Partly, it was his own unfulfilled sexual drive; he had fantasized about sex for so long and at last it seemed within reach. Then there was the atmosphere in the Mess. Other officers made no secret of their success with women, often one-night stands with no pretence of love. Life was cheap and they had every intention of living it to the full. How pathetic to die in a flaming coffin over Germany without having had a woman. Perhaps he should have stayed with that sad girl down by the Seine.

Mary was also in the bath and consumed with self-loathing. What a fool she was! Why in heavens name had she behaved so stupidly? If she was honest, the answer was fear. Fear of pregnancy. At the end of their final term at St.Chadd's, leavers were given a talk about sex and marriage by the doctor and the chaplain. The former emphasized technicalities and possible diseases; the latter stressed morality, values and the penalties of backsliding: together they painted a fearsome picture for inexperienced girls. They might joke and laugh afterwards, but it was nervous laughter and they did not forget the warnings. Mary knew the shame of an illegitimate child would crucify her – and her parents. She would never be forgiven.

So she lay back, looking at her slim waist and flat stomach, regretting that Chalmers was in a room somewhere above her, even wondering if she could change her mind. 'Look after him,' the woman in the train had said. She was worldly-wise, had seen their love and assumed they would be sleeping together. But she was not looking after him. She was not comforting him for those nights over Germany. She had seen his dream of a perfect week-end crumble like broken glass. He had played it down, joked in the way he always did, but the disappointment was in his eyes. Barbara and Dot would have been different.

Enough of that. Self-pity was not admirable. She got out of the bath and started to dress. She was pulling on one of her stockings when the phone rang. She took a moment to find it.

'Hello?'

'Is that my beautiful date for this evening?'

'Jamie, I'm so glad you've rung.'

'How long will you be?'

'Ten minutes. I'm nearly decent.'

'I'll be down in five.'

Mary felt the depression lifting. She was not as elated as she had been earlier, but Jamie's humour was infectious. 'Come as soon as you like. Come quickly.'

9

Despite its unpromising beginning, the week-end was a success. The concert, like so much else, was a novel experience for Mary. Sitting in the red and gold amphitheatre, she took in the formality, the ritual, the sense of occasion. Relaxed though she was, she followed every beat of Boult's baton and revelled in Myra Hess's meticulous performance of the Fourth Concerto and the energy of Schubert's last symphony. Her obvious pleasure so delighted Chalmers that he felt they were back on an even keel.

Dinner at Verreys confirmed the warmth between them. Mary was keeping Barbara's dress for the Savoy. Tonight she wore a white silk blouse, a full black taffeta skirt edged with small pink and mauve flowers, and high-heeled, silver sandals; for the first time she had put on a pearl necklace given her by her grandmother and intended, she presumed, for this sort of occasion. The idea of a smart London restaurant made her nervous, but Chalmers's uniform gained respect and she felt some of it rubbing off on her. For his part, James was also nervous, though he worked hard not to show it. He wanted to give the impression he dined out regularly when, in truth, he had never taken a girl out in the West End before. The crisp white tablecloth concealed feet and legs and they touched beneath it, eyes meeting in mischievous understanding.

'Sorry,' said Mary. 'For being so stupid.'

'I'm the stupid one. I ought to be keel-hauled for being so crass. You should sack me straight away.'

'I might not get any more concerts. I'm loving this evening. That was a really nice woman in the train today.'

'I liked her hat. That black feather was smart.'

'Everything was out of the top drawer. Did you notice her shoes?'

'They made her legs look good.'

'You're shocking, Jamie. She could have been your mother. Do you always look at a woman's legs?'

'Of course.'

'I know – it's the 'general' and 'the particular' again. Weren't you going to tell me something about 'the particular'?'

Chalmers made sure his foot was touching hers. He took a sip of Beaujolais, then said, 'You've got the best legs at Wynton Thorpe. Even Freddie says so. And I'll tell you something else.' The alcohol was working. 'When we sat in the train today, I could feel your stocking suspender through your dress. One day I want to see more of your legs.'

'I expect you will.' Mary enjoyed the sexual innuendo. 'I hope you'll come and say goodnight tonight.'

A cough indicated the lurking presence of the wine waiter. In the moment of silence while he poured, the line of conversation was broken. Momentarily he was transported from the comfort of the restaurant with its plush seats and shiny brass fittings to the sky over Germany. Fragments of flak struck the aircraft. Over the intercom he heard the scream of his mid-upper gunner and the noises he made as he died. He'd lived with it for months now. No wonder he lost his temper when they were getting the body out later.

'Jamie, are you all right?' Mary fingered the pearl necklace.

'Darling, I'm sorry.' The waiter had gone. 'What did you say?'

'What's wrong? You weren't with me.'

'One of those moments I'm trying to forget. Sorry – sorry, darling.' He smiled reassuringly. 'What did you say?'

'I said I hoped you'd come and say goodnight.'

'Try to keep me away. Like the wine?'

'I'd love anything tonight. I've hardly ever had wine before, and I've never been to a place like this. We hardly drink anything at home. Daddy keeps a decanter of sherry for guests, but that's about it. I only know about Gin and It because of an aunt. Are you sure you're all right?'

The rest of the evening passed in warm flirtation and their arms were round each other as they approached the foyer of The Royal Charles. They separated coyly as they passed the reception desk, but Chalmers pulled Mary close the moment the lift door closed. They went down the deserted corridor to Mary's room. She dropped her handbag on the bed and opened her arms. Chalmers sat down on the sofa opposite the bed and pulled her onto his knee.

***

An hour later Chalmers left for his own room. In that time they shared more intimacy than before. Mary's blouse was unbuttoned and her skirt up her thighs. When he finally said goodnight, she asked him to stay. 'It would be nice,' she said.

Chalmers held her firmly by the shoulders. 'It would be nice. But it's not what you really want and I'm not going to take advantage now. We're not going to spoil things just because I've been an idiot.'

She didn't argue. The fear was there and she loved the way he was sticking to their original decision.

'Breakfast?' he said. 'What time? Tell you what. Whoever wakes up first rings the other and we'll decide on the spur of the moment. Not too much planning. There's enough of that at Wynton.'

Chalmers undressed quickly and was soon in bed. He had drawn the curtains to avoid being woken by the early summer light, but had left a small gap and could see the moon. He thought back to the girl by the Seine and a subsequent occasion in London early in the war. He and another pilot had gone to London on a thirty-six hour pass for a show. Afterwards they dined in Soho and drank a good deal. Dinner over, he told his companion a tall story about visiting a friend and saw him off in a taxi. In fact, stirred by the girls offering themselves in doorways, he intended sexual adventure. The Blitz had only recently moderated and it was dark in the black-out. The girls had torches which they shone on their legs and high heels.

'Hello, darling.' A girl with a faint Irish accent spoke from a doorway in Wardour Street. Her face was in shadow, but there was warmth in her voice. The torch revealed good legs.

'Hello,' he said. As fearful as he had been in Paris, he had no intention of going all the way. 'I don't want to go to bed,' he said. 'Will you give me a kiss?'

'I don't kiss.' The voice was firm, but still somehow welcoming. 'Anything else?'

The darkness and anonymity emboldened him. 'Could I cuddle you – feel you?'

'Come down here.' The girl took his hand and led him into a narrow alley behind her.

'How much?' he asked.

'How long?'

'Five – ten minutes?' He could not mask his nervousness.

'A pound.' The voice was blunt, uncompromising, but the sympathetic tone remained.

He fumbled in his pocket. The girl helped with her torch. The light fell on her face. She was young, barely twenty, with curly brown hair. She was illumined only briefly, but long enough to show a face still marked by innocence.

'Come on, then.'

He moved closer, his shoes inadvertently touching hers. 'Sorry,' he said. 'Tell me if I do anything you don't like. I'll stop the moment you say.'

'You're a gent.'

It was a spring evening and he had a raincoat over his uniform. She wore a thin cotton dress and looked cold. He put his arms round her, smelling cheap perfume. He felt she came closer for warmth. His hands slid down her back, touching the belt of her dress, then going beyond it. He was trembling. Intuitively, he knew she understood. He was glad he had chosen her.

'You can do more than that,' she said. 'No one can see.' Her thigh moved against him.

He held her with his left arm and let his lips brush over her cheek. Then he moved so that he could run his hand over one of her breasts. It was full and firm. Her hair was over his face smelling clean and washed. Her arms were under his raincoat and pulling him closer. 'Sure you don't want to come upstairs?'

'This is enough.' His hand was at the hem of her dress. He pulled it up, feeling the top of her stocking and the softness of skin above it. 'All right?' he asked. She made no reply. If anything she moved closer. For five minutes he held her, his hands exploratory, tentative.

Eventually he pulled away. 'Thanks,' he said. 'That was . . .' He searched for an apposite word and failed.

She flashed the torch. 'You're a pilot.'

'Yes.'

'And a gent. You'll find a nice girl. Look after yourself.'

She touched his face with her hand, and then she had gone.

Now, lying in his single bed, he knew he had found the girl. There remained a residue of gratitude to the unknown who had taken his money and shown understanding. He moved his head to see the moon. He was back in the night sky over Europe. Whenever Mary asked about raids he made light of them and changed the subject. Perhaps tomorrow he would say things he had not said before.

Mary, too, looked at the moon. She was standing at the window in her nightdress, happier than she had ever been. Below, the classical lines of the garden stood out, the moon etching the flowerbeds and hedges with white light and shadow. Part of her was sorry not to have been more persuasive in trying to get James to stay. His hands on her body, hesitant and inexperienced, had been comforting as well as strangely exciting. The other part of her, the greater part, knew he had done what she really wanted. But their closeness had made her aware of strains in him which had nothing to do with their relationship.

She drew the curtains and got into bed. The billet at Wynton seemed a million miles away.

***

Saturday dawned warm and clear again, the sort of day that makes an optimist feel better, a pessimist worse. They did not go down for breakfast until nearly ten. Most other guests had left the dining room by the time they arrived. Waiters hovered, napkins were unfolded, choices made. The smell of freshly made coffee and toast pervaded the room.

'Decadence,' said Chalmers. 'To quote Oscar Wilde, we are living entirely for pleasure.'

'Tell me what we're doing today.'

'Well . . . we're concentrating on this evening, so I thought I might show you a bit of London. It's going to be warm again. How about a picnic? We could stroll round some of the sights. Tower of London? You can't go in these days, but you could see it from the outside. Tower Bridge? St.Paul's? Houses of Parliament? We can't do everything, but you could see quite a lot. Then back here to get ready for the Savoy.'

'Can we see all those things?'

'We could try. They're a bit scattered, but we can take a taxi or two. The hotel will make up a picnic .'

'Isn't that extravagant? Couldn't we get something from Joe Lyons?'

'This is a treat. We're living for the present.'

They finished breakfast and spent the day in the leisurely way Chalmers had suggested. First, they went to the Tower of London. Standing on the site of the scaffold on Tower Hill,

Chalmers gave an impromptu history lesson on some of the unfortunates executed there.

'Lady Jane Grey?' Mary asked.

'No, she was beheaded on the Green inside the Tower. Her husband Guildford was executed here. She watched from her window up there and saw his body taken back on a handcart before she was killed herself.'

'Gruesome. Did she love him?'

'No. It was a political marriage – her parents forced her into it. They were pawns of ambitious people. She could have saved herself if she had been prepared to become a Catholic.'

'I would have done.'

'So would I. But we live in a different age. Jane believed it would be betraying the True Church. She stuck to her guns.'

'I'd have been too frightened to go through that rigmarole in the Tower. I'm not very brave.'

'You're brave enough to take me on.'

They took a taxi past St.Paul's and down to the embankment for a drink at The Royal Oak. They ate their picnic on a bench under the trees, watching the boats and, further down river, the silver barrage balloons over the docks. Afterwards they looked at bomb damage at the Palace of Westminster and the sandbags piled round the ministries in Whitehall. Here and there officials scurried about in bowler hats, carrying gas-mask satchels and rolled umbrellas. From the Cenotaph they took another taxi to Piccadilly and had tea in a Lyons teashop. Mary loved it, catching up on a world she had only heard about. Chalmers was conscious of the drabness, the uniforms, boarded windows where bomb blast was not yet repaired, the repetitive propaganda posters.

'That was marvellous, Jamie,' said Mary, back at the hotel. 'But my feet are killing me.'

'I'm not surprised. Those shoes weren't made for walking.'

'Beast! All that talk about showing off legs and now you criticise my high heels.'

'That's men for you, darling. Thoroughly unreasonable. Come here.'

They were alone in the corridor outside Mary's room. He pulled her to him roughly and kissed her. She gave way to his strength; her lip felt bruised. His eyes were open and she saw a touch of cruelty in the left one; oddly, she found it exciting.

Chalmers looked at his watch. 'Darling, we must get organised. Bath? The table's booked for eight. I want to see you in this dress of Barbara's – and I've got to struggle into my dinner jacket. Hope I can do the tie. My scout helped me at Oxford. He had a low opinion of the way I did it.'

'You've been spoilt.'

'Probably. Now listen. I'll get changed and I'll come down to collect you. Perhaps there's a zip or something I can do up. Give me a ring when you're ready.'

The anticipation of the dinner dance buoyed them both. When Chalmers came down, Mary fulfilled his greatest expectations. The full-length ice-blue dress with its thin black shoulder straps and delicate black lace decoration over the bust was classically simple and obviously expensive, the perfect foil for her pale skin and auburn hair. As Barbara had predicted, it showed off the fullness of her breasts and hips and the silk moved with all the style of an exclusive creation.

'Darling, you're breathtaking. How's my tie?'

She straightened it marginally 'You'll do for me.'

The doorman hailed a taxi. Inside they sat close together on the worn leather. 'Difficult to believe this,' she said.

'For me, too.' He put his hand on her thigh. They barely spoke again before they reached the Savoy.

Once settled at their table overlooking the Thames, Chalmers ordered champagne. He had spent hardly anything since being commissioned and was determined to spare no expense. The sommelier, a tall man with a long nose and aloof manner, hovered while he tasted it. Chalmers wished he was still wearing uniform. Subconsciously he felt he wasn't getting the respect of the previous evening; the waiters must wonder how a young man was apparently avoiding military service. 'Very good,' he said, hoping he sounded confident.

When the waiter had gone, Chalmers raised his glass. 'Here's to us.'

'To us.' Mary took a sip. 'I've never had champagne before.'

'I had it a few times at Oxford, but I don't know anything about it. There's a confession for you.'

'It's nice.'

'So it should be for what it cost.' Chalmers looked round the room. 'I wonder who all these people are,' he said. The men were mostly middle-aged, the women younger.

'Some may be like you – out of uniform for the evening. Probably a general or two.' Mary sensed the resentment behind his question. 'Come on. We're enjoying ourselves. I don't suppose you'll bring me here very often when we're married.'

'Probably not. We'll just be a comfortable couple. The local pub will have to do. Or I may not take you out at all.'

'I'll settle for that. I just want you safely back on the ground.'

'I tell you what. After the war, when we're married, we'll come here every year on the anniversary of this week-end. How's that?'

'Lovely. I'll hold you to that, darling.'

They were finishing their pudding, a chocolate confection which in view of rationing it was surprising to find on the menu, when Chalmers sat forward and took her hand. 'Mary, I want to tell you something.'

She detected a change of mood. 'Go on,' she said.

'You know I don't say much about flying.'

'Tell me.'

'Simple really. I'm frightened.'

'I think you all are. Les Ricketts says he's terrified – but he'd hate to think I'd told you. Says he wouldn't go if he didn't have you as skipper.'

'They think I'll get them home.'

'And you do.'

'So far. But that's luck. The odds against getting back are shortening. Look at the losses this year. We've only got to be picked up by an efficient Jerry and we're dead ducks. The fact Les and the others trust me makes it worse. One day it will be our turn.'

'You're a good pilot, Jamie. They all say so.'

'I know what I'm doing, but that's got nothing to do with it. It's luck in the end. If you're the one they go for, there's precious little you can do. Once they see your exhausts you're as good as finished.'

A young man with exquisitely coiffed hair who had been playing the piano during dinner finished a Chopin Nocturne, closed the piano lid and retired. A seven-piece dance band in white dinner jackets arranged themselves by the dance floor.

'I wonder what his war work is,' said Mary, indicating the pianist.

Chalmers wasn't listening. 'I've watched them go down. Sometimes it's over quickly. A massive explosion, no chance for anyone. Sometimes it's slow. A burning engine, a skipper wondering if he can put it out, weighing the chances of getting home, giving his crew a chance to bale out. I imagine it all. The frantic grabbing of 'chutes, the panic. And I hear the screams of wounded men who know they won't get out. My first trip I lost Geoff Spearman. I've never told you that. I shan't forget his screams. He was dead when we got home. Couldn't do a thing.'

Mary listened. For the first time she saw behind the façade of humour. She was pleased the barriers were crumbling.

He went on: 'So I'm frightened – we're all frightened. But we don't admit it. We laugh and joke. I can see them doing what I'm doing. Jokes about Freddie's women, Freddie's knickers, jokes about 'Tavish and Scotsmen, jokes about anything. It's all there as we take off. It wears thin by the time we cross the enemy coast. But do you know the worst thing?'

She shook her head.

'When we're in the middle of the flak and see planes going down, I thank God it's them and not me. I saw a Halifax over Cologne. Its port outer caught fire, but it flew on as though nothing had happened. At one point I thought the fire was out and there was just smoke. Then the flames broke out again, fiercer than before. I could imagine the pilot struggling with the controls, wondering whether to tell them to get out. And then, suddenly, for no apparent reason, it heeled over on its back it and it was too late. One moment the plane was there, the next it was a flaming torch falling out of the sky. Stafford was next to me and Tavish was down in the nose. We all saw it. No one said anything – not till we got back. But I know what I was thinking. I was thinking about the charred and twisted bodies they'd find in the morning and I was glad I wouldn't be one of them. Not very heroic.'

Mary took hold of his hand across the table. 'But totally natural. I'll bet the others felt the same.'

The band was playing a jaunty American tune and two couples were dancing.

'They didn't say so.'

'What did they say?'

'Said he should have dived to put out the fire. All criticism, technical – right, up to a point. Not my reaction.'

'You didn't ask about their feelings?'

'Their feelings didn't matter. I was too ashamed of my own. I wanted them to die to save me.' His nails bit into her hand.

'Jamie . . .Jamie.' Momentarily words deserted her. Then she said: 'I'm glad you told me.'

'Why?'

'I don't want a hero I can't compete with. I want to feel there isn't anything you can't tell me. You've just done that.'

Their eyes met. Chalmers saw the love he had been slow to recognise. Mary saw love, too, but strain and tiredness as well.

She determined to get him to bed earlier than he planned. 'Come on,' she said. 'Am I going to get a dance?'

The rest of the evening fulfilled both their expectations. Mary, stimulated by alcohol, feeling more sophisticated in Barbara's dress than anything she had ever worn before, grew in confidence. But the Cinderella feeling persisted. The Savoy and its denizens were part of a dream she could not normally aspire to. She envied the woman at the next table. Clearly bored by her elderly escort, she watched smoke curl upwards from her cigarette in its ebony holder like a louche character from a Noel Coward play. Mary felt provincial and gauche. Chalmers, freed of the burden of confession, revelled in the possession of the most attractive woman in the room. Perhaps for the first time in his life he was completely happy.

***

Back at the Royal Charles Mary led him into her room. The yellow curtains had been drawn, the bed turned down, her nightdress laid out.

'A perfect evening,' she said. 'Thank you, Jamie.'

Chalmers's hands ran over the silk of her dress as they had all the evening. 'I like this dress.'

'I want you to stay.'

He kissed her, pulling her close. He knew she would do anything. If he wanted her now, he could have her. And he did want her. 'I'll stay.'

A shiver ran through her. It could have been desire or fear.

'I'll stay because I want to love you and cuddle you. I'll stay, but I'll sleep on the bed, not in it. We'll be as close as we can be before we're married.'

'A woman could change her mind.'

'She could – and she might on the spur of the moment. Come on, don't tempt me. Eve has much to answer for.'

Chalmers went up to his room, got ready for bed, put on

his dressing-gown, then came back. Mary was at the window, looking out at the moonlit garden. He stood behind her, put his arms round her waist and kissed her neck.

'I'm sorry I'm not allowed to change my mind,' she said.

'Someone must stay in control.'

She turned and looked up at him. 'Why you?'

'Because I'm an officer. I outrank you. You'll do as you're told.'

Mary laughed. 'What a nerve!'

She got into the big double bed. Chalmers lay down beside her. For half an hour they kissed, stroked, caressed and explored, the thin sheet between them. Then Mary realised his breathing was deeper; his hands, soft, gentle, increasingly confident, were no longer moving over her. He was asleep. She eased herself into a comfortable position, her head on his shoulder, her naked breasts against his chest. Within minutes she, too, was asleep.

And so in strange unfulfilment were confirmed a love and trust granted to few.

10

The journey back to Wynton on Sunday was an anti-climax. Chalmers and Mary watched the miles pass, conscious of each other, barely aware of fellow passengers. They said little.

'Hatfield,' said Chalmers, as the train passed through a station. He didn't want to speak, but felt anything was better than letting the approaching separation pull them apart. 'Elizabeth was at Hatfield House when her sister Mary died and she became Queen. She'd had a tough time – some of it in the Tower.'

'Bloody Mary – Calais on her heart?'

'Yes – it was under her Lady Jane Grey got the chop. Elizabeth might have followed if she hadn't been careful.'

'One of my heroines at school. I never understood why she didn't marry. She could have had anybody she liked.'

'She'd seen her sister's disastrous marriage to a foreigner. And it would have been asking for trouble to marry one of her own subjects. Too much power to one man and it would have upset the other nobility. Anyway, look at her mother – Anne Boleyn.'

'She got the chop, too.'

'Hardly a model for a happy marriage. Besides, Elizabeth didn't like taking decisions. Always changing her mind. Typical woman.'

A train passing at speed in the opposite direction forced Mary to delay her reply. Smoke came in through the open window. 'That's unkind,' she said.

'Nonsense. Men are just as odd, believe you me. Do you know, I'm beginning to feel very possessive about you. Do you mind?'

'I'm the same. I could be very jealous.'

Both were laconic; Wynton was taking over. He wondered how his crew had spent the week-end and how long it would be before the next operation. Mary, too, was back with realities. Her gratitude to Barbara for the loan of the dress was balanced by the thought that she and Dot would want a blow by blow account of her time away. What should she say? They would certainly think her strange – stranger than they thought already.

The train made good time through the flat Huntingdonshire countryside, the evening sun warming stone cottages, throwing shadows from trees. Chalmers watched a water tower recede into the distance. How ironic that the train taking them back to the uncertainties of Wynton had none of the hindrances that had made the journey to London so slow.

They reached Grantham only a few minutes late. Chalmers knew there would be others going back to the base, so they waited for the platform to clear. He had no wish to advertise their relationship. For the same reason he had arranged for a discreet fellow pilot, one Peter Anderson, to meet them with his car.

Doors slammed, the guard blew his whistle and waved his flag. The train pulled out, leaving its smell of coal, smoke and oil. Chalmers went off to reconnoitre the station yard, leaving Mary on the platform. She stood unobtrusively to one side of a trolley piled high with mailbags, next to a fire point with its bucket of water and stirrup pump. Behind her a rusting metal advertisement recommended *Mazawattee Tea*. Alongside two posters extolled the virtues of Virol. *Growing boys need it*, urged one; *Anaemic girls need it*, said the other. Mary recalled being given it by her school matron, who spooned it out compulsorily to a queue of girls before breakfast. Apart from Virol's supposed advantages, the close contact gave that fearsome woman the opportunity to inspect the efficiency of their ablutions. Mary could still feel the pain of having her ear tweaked when she failed the inspection and was sent back to wash again.

'Not here yet,' said Chalmers. 'Let's go into the waiting room. Out of the way of prying eyes.'

'You're ashamed of me.'

'Frightened of rivals, darling. I don't want them to know I've got the girl with the best legs on the base.'

The waiting room was warm and stuffy. There were dead flies on the window ledge. On the cream walls L.N.E.R. posters featuring the *Flying Scotsman* promised speed and sybaritic delights; alongside was a pre-war photograph of Scarborough with donkeys, children and women in hats pulling up their skirts to paddle. The last time Chalmers had been to Scarborough there was barbed wire on the beach and skull and crossbone notices warning of mines. He remembered a poem by Hardy about flyblown photographs in a railway waiting-room, but said nothing.

'You know when I shall think about last night?' said Chalmers.

'When?'

'The next op – during the bombing run. That's the worst bit. You'll help me.'

Mary knew she shouldn't say it, but she did. 'You could have had more to think about.'

Chalmers took her by the shoulders and looked straight at her. 'That's enough of that. I shall think about the whole week-end. You looked a million dollars. See if you can persuade Barabara to give up that dress.'

'I can't ask her.'

'I can. Ah, there's Peter.' Anderson was looking up and down the platform.

'We'll say goodbye now,' said Chalmers. They had one last gentle kiss before emerging. The evening sun etched the decorated fringe of the station canopy on the platform. Chalmers touched Anderson on the shoulder from behind. 'Hello, Peter. Thanks for coming.'

'Sorry I'm late. No excuse. Except to let you have a bit more time together.' His smile was affable, his face even more youthful than Chalmers's.

'Any flaps?'

'The weather's changing. We've been warned for ops. How was the Savoy?'

'Sheer luxury. I've never been anywhere like it.' Mary only knew Anderson slightly, but warmed to his quiet personality.

'Don't worry, I haven't been there either,' said Anderson, smiling. 'Too pricey for me. Jamie's always been a social climber.' The two men had trained on Lancasters together and had the sort of bond that created. He turned to Chalmers. 'Are you buying Palmer's M.G.?'

'I might as well have it for the rest of the summer. Then we shan't have to depend on an unreliable fellow like you. Come on, let's get going.'

Anderson's Rover stood in a corner of the station yard next to a 3-tonner picking up soldiers returning from leave to a nearby camp. They were joking and swearing in equal measure. A corporal checking off names as they climbed into the back saluted Chalmers and Anderson punctiliously, yet managed to eye Mary's legs as she got into the car.

The drive back to Wynton was completed in relative silence. Anderson spoke once or twice, but sensed their mood. They reached a previously agreed spot on a lane at the back of the airfield and Mary got out.

' 'Bye, darling,' she said, leaning into the car.

They touched hands briefly and then she had gone. Anderson drove straight back to the Mess.

'Thanks, Peter,' said Chalmers. 'Just tell me when you want a good turn.'

'I'll take you up on that. Sadly, I can't compete in the female stakes. You're a lucky bastard. But I'll borrow the M.G. if you buy it. You never know what talent I might find with a little job like that. Anyway, I'm concentrating on survival. Two more ops and I'm home and dry.'

'Lucky bugger. I'll join you when I've unpacked. Line up a couple of gins and stick 'em down to me.'

Back in the Mess Chalmers was relieved to find his billet deserted. He didn't want to talk to anybody. As he opened the door of his room, a Lancaster flew low overhead before turning into the wind to make its approach across the Maydon Woods. The week-end was over.

***

Mary was less fortunate. Both room-mates were there. Barbara had washed her hair and was now doing her nails, her open dressing-gown revealing stockings and not much else. Dot had been on duty and still wore her uniform; she had taken off her tie and put on glasses to carry out sewing repairs to some colourful underwear. Their heads turned as Mary opened the door.

'Hello,' she said. 'I'm back.' She put her case on the bed. 'Anything gone on here?'

'Tell all,' said Barbara. She always took the lead, often without sensitivity.

'What about?'

'You know what I mean.'

'You mean the Savoy?'

'She means *all*, ducky,' said Dot. 'Come on, love, you know how curious we are.'

Mary hung her gas mask satchel next to the other two behind the door and started to unpack. 'We had a really nice time,' she said. 'James loved the dress.'

Dot put down her needle and turned in her chair. '*All*,' she said. 'Don't dare leave anything out.'

Mary looked at them. She was smiling, the quiet smile they had never penetrated. Inside, she wanted to share the intimacies they were waiting for, but shied away from telling them. She loved the camaraderie of the billet – so different from her school – but could not unbutton in the way they could.

'Well,' she began, 'the train got in late. We spent a good deal of time looking round London. James knows his way about and a lot of the history. The hotel was very grand. There were telephones and wirelesses in the bedrooms, and a porter carried our cases. The first evening we went to the concert and had dinner at a restaurant called Verreys. We went everywhere by taxi. I haven't done that before. I saw the Tower, the Houses of Parliament and Buckingham Palace – and a lot of bomb damage. I hadn't realised how bad the Blitz was. Seeing the remains of the insides of houses, the wallpaper, the broken staircases – it brought it all home. It makes sense of what we're doing to them now.'

'We're waiting,' said Barbara. 'I didn't lend you a dress for a history lesson.'

'I felt really good in it. He was really impressed – he said other men were looking at me.' She looked at Barbara. 'I'm terribly grateful. I bought you both a little present.' She searched in her case and took out two boxes of expensive soap bought in Piccadilly. 'Thanks, Barbara. I shan't forget. James wanted me to persuade you to sell me the dress. I said I couldn't ask you.' She immediately regretted what she had said. 'Sorry, I didn't mean to say that.' Mary did not resent the questioning – she had expected it – but she realised she was talking for the sake of it and tears were not far away.

'You goose! Of course you can have it. On one condition.'

'Yes?'

'You tell all. Dot and I have been good girls and we've been envious of you living it up. Now, come on, don't be a spoilsport. Spill the beans.'

'We did lots of kissing and cuddling. Jamie's good at it.'

'Ah, *Jamie*, is it? That's promising.'

'He booked a double room?' This was Barbara.

'Yes.'

'So you slept together?'

Mary was taking things out of her case, putting them methodically on the bed. 'Yes and no.'

'Yes and no?' Dot picked up her needle again.

'It means I was a fool. To be honest, I'm ashamed of myself.'

Barbara and Dot were aware of a change in her tone. She sounded tearful. Dot put down her needle and put an arm round her. 'Don't worry, lovey. We're only being nosey because we're jealous. You've got a nice man there.'

The sudden kindness brought tears nearer. 'He's a good man – and I love him. I just wish I'd behaved differently.' She sat on the bed. 'He loves me, too. I don't want him to fly again.'

'Don't tell us any more,' said Dot.

'I was such a fool. I made him go to another room.'

Barbara unwound the towel on her head and bent forward, drying her hair. Her dressing gown fell open revealing her nakedness underneath. She looked at Mary with new warmth. 'I can understand.'

'Can you? I wanted to change my mind, but Jamie thought I didn't. He stayed with me the second night, but we only kissed and cuddled with a sheet between us. He wouldn't do anything he wasn't sure I wanted.'

'You're a lucky girl.'

'We met a woman on the train. She told me to look after him. I let him down.' She looked up at Dot, whose arm was still round her shoulders. 'You would have loved him.'

Dot looked doubtful. 'I might not have done. I talk a lot, but I've only slept with two men. I'm not an easy touch. You were right to do what you wanted to do. He'll probably respect you more.'

'I want him to want me, I want him to take me. He could be flying again tomorrow.'

The words were the boldest she had ever spoken. Jamie had never had a woman. Jamie could be killed any day. She had put petty social conventions first. She was frightened and selfish And he had understood. She wished he hadn't. She remembered the cruel eye, the rough kisses. That was what he wanted, and so did she.

'The dress is yours,' said Barbara. 'I knew it would suit you better than me.'

'I can't take it. I shouldn't have said anything. The truth is I'm upset it's all over. He wants to marry me.'

'Of course he does,' said Dot. 'He'd be mad not to.' She gave Mary a hug and went back to her sewing. 'I'd like to find one like him.'

'And I don't want him to fly.'

'Bloody war,' said Dot.

Barbara was more practical. 'Come on, you two. You wouldn't have met him if it hadn't been for the war. He'd be up at Oxford reading Voltaire and Goethe and you'd be mouldering in the Welsh Marches making cucumber sandwiches for the church fête. And don't you dare give me that dress back.'

Mary finished unpacking and went across to Barbara, now doing something to her toenails. 'You're a brick, Barbara, and I'm lucky to be here with you and Dot.' She couldn't put an arm round her, but touched her on the shoulder. Then she turned to Dot, who was cursing gently, having pricked her finger. 'Thanks, Dot. Sorry to be so daft. I wish you'd been there to keep me on the straight and narrow.'

Barbara and Dot looked at each other. Dot said: 'The truth is, Mary, we're envious. We've both got boys running after us, but you've got something better than that.'

The feelings Mary had been suppressing flooded over her. She remembered how she had once cried at a Christmas nativity play in her father's church, the gentle eyes of the pony pressed into service as a donkey stirring emotions she couldn't explain. She sat on her bed and burst into tears.

11

The warm spell was coming to an end. The barometer next to *Mont Sainte-Victoire* moved towards Change. When Jones woke Chalmers with his morning tea on the Tuesday after his London week-end there was more cloud than blue sky.

'Mornin', sir. 'alf-past seven. Red sky in the mornin', shepherd's warnin'. Reckon you'll be flyin' soon.' Jones had never been up in an aircraft, but enjoyed being the bearer of news, however gloomy. By lunch it was known the squadron was going to Augsburg, a first visit and a long trip. 'Nothing like novelty,' said Chalmers as they went through routine checks in Z-Zebra.

'What goes on there?' asked Stafford.

'Probably children's toys.' Chalmers had become disenchanted with recent target explanations.

'A bloody long way. I hope Einstein knows how to get there. I've had enough of that red patch round the Ruhr.'

'We'll go further south,' said Beresford who had come forward. 'Probably across Belgium and back across France. How's your French, Skipper?'

'Not bad. I'm not planning to use it till this lot's over. You do your stuff, Einstein, and I'll make sure she gets us back.' He patted the control column. 'No problems, Uncle?' he shouted through the open cockpit window to the ground engineer. The engineer raised his thumb. Round the perimeter, a train of bombs hauled by a tractor approached.

In the afternoon Chalmers tried to sleep as usual. It was difficult because he had not seen Mary since the previous day.

She had gone to Peterborough to pick up a new lorry and hoped she would be back in time to take him and his crew out to Z-Zebra. Before briefing Chalmers wrote another letter. He didn't want to, but any omission was tempting fate. Assembling his thoughts, he looked out of the window at an impromptu game of cricket played by a handful of ground staff. They had taken off their jackets and looked incongruous in braces. A large man batted, a large man bowled, smaller men fielded. It reminded him of junior games at school. He could imagine the batsman stalking off with bat, ball and stumps if he was out.

He wrote quickly:

My own darling,

Here is another letter I hope you won't read. I'm sure I'll be back, but I don't ever want you to feel I was not thinking of you. Mary, my Mary, you must know by now that you have transformed my life. I should like to think I have done something for you, though I don't want to be so arrogant as to claim it. I feel we are as close as it is possible for two people to be.

If you do read this, don't forget there are lots of possibilities, so don't jump to the worst conclusion. You have given me every reason to stay alive. But if it is the worst, keep a little bit of yourself for me and remember the good times this summer. If I am not there, I want you to look after yourself and then, if you meet a good man you can love – I have tears in my eyes as I write this – let him look after you in the way I hope I would have done. Above all I want you to be happy.

Goodbye, my darling. If I have gone, it will be a lonely path because you are not with me. Listen to the Schubert.

I love you.

Jamie.

As an afterthought, he jotted down some words that had been going round in his head when lying on his bed in the afternoon:

The passing show knows nothing of our love
What we endure,

The pain and pleasure
Of a golden chain
Is ours alone.
I love you. XX.

Not Shakespeare, he mused, but it says something about us. He left the envelope on his bedside table.

Briefing confirmed Beresford's route prediction. Assembly would be over Dungeness, followed by a dog-leg course across Belgium to the Rhine. They would attack Augsburg from the north, before swinging west to return across France.

'Not too bad,' said Beresford.

'Could be worse,' said Chalmers.

'Not much,' said Robertson.

They were packing up their notes when Arthur Palmer, a tall man with prominent ears and a moustache, stopped at their table. He was the skipper of G-George. 'Hell of long trip,' he said. 'Anyone would think we wanted a Cook's tour. I wonder they didn't include Munich as well while they were at it. Want to fix the car, Jamie, before we go?'

'They think we enjoy it. Happy with a cheque?'

A beatific smile lit up Palmer's face. 'Of course. And if you get the chop, I'll be down to the bank so fast they won't realise you didn't make it – or I could just take the car back and no one would know.'

'Callous sod.'

'Realistic, old man. After all, if I get the chop the cheque won't be cashed.'

'And if we both get the chop,' said Chalmers, 'some other bugger will pinch the car.' The two were friends and the banter was characteristic. 'I'll bring the cheque to supper.'

'It's got a full tank. My generosity knows no bounds.'

'Courtesy of one of His Majesty's bowsers, I know. How about a guarantee?'

'On a '32 car? I wasn't born yesterday, old boy. Anyway, the cash will have gone. Maureen's expensive.'

'Maureen?'

'Red Cross driver in Lincoln. Nice blonde job, and buxom – plenty of fore and aft. But she thinks a man's money is for spending. High maintenance job.' Palmer touched him on the shoulder. 'See you later.'

After the bacon and egg supper the crews assembled for the main briefing where there was emphasis on Augsburg's contribution to German marine diesel engines, as well as damage to morale from a deep penetration attack. The meteorological officer predicted cloud cover for the outward flight and broken cloud over the target.

'Sounds O.K.,' said Palmer, changing into his flying gear next to Chalmers.

'It always does. How often do they get it right?'

'You've become a cynic, like me.'

'I'm a realist. They have to make it sound straightforward.' Chalmers zipped up his fur-lined flying boots, making sure the left one went on first.

'She's a good looking girl,' said Palmer.

'Maureen?'

'Your little WAAF piece.'

Chalmers knew one or two officers were aware of Mary, but had no idea how far gossip had spread. 'She's a nice girl.' Reticence made him shift attention away from her. 'You've got Maureen.'

'Maureen's splendidly pneumatic, but you've got a real looker. Brains too, if she can cope with you. What's her name?'

'Mary. She's a country girl from Shropshire – father's a vicar. Now come on, Palmer, we've got an appointment over Augsburg. That's enough gossip for one evening.' The use of the surname was a reversion to the sort of schooldays both had experienced.

Mary was back in time and her new Bedford was nearest the Nissen hut when Chalmers came out. He squeezed in beside her and they touched hands affectionately. 'I spent most of the day hanging about,' she said. 'It should have been ready

when I arrived, but of course it wasn't. I had to kill two hours.'
She looked at him. 'Augsburg's a long way.'

'Better than the Ruhr or Berlin.'

'I wish you weren't going. Or that I could come with you.'

'You couldn't put up with Freddie's jokes or Tavish's depression.'

The familiar shout came from the rear: 'All aboard, Skipper.' Mary set off towards the blue lights of the perimeter track. The tailboard rattled as no one had bothered to pull it up.

Chalmers put his hand on her thigh. 'I've written another letter.'

'I don't want a letter. I'll be waiting. No excuses accepted.'

Chalmers appreciated her lightening the moment. He responded in kind. 'I'll be there. You can't get rid of me that easily.'

They dropped the B-Baker crew, then came back to Z-Zebra. The Bedford's lights illuminated the black underside of the aircraft, casting shadows across the dispersal pan. At night the plane had an air of menace. Without being told, Mary drove round the port wing to the rear, leaving the back of the lorry towards the aircraft.

She turned towards Chalmers. 'Come back safely, darling. I love you.'

They had a quick kiss. 'Think of me at one o'clock.'

'One o'clock?'

'Approximate time on target.'

'I'll say a prayer.'

And then he had gone, clutching his parachute, joining his crew round the plane.

Mary drove back to the vehicle park. She felt cold, though it had nothing to do with the temperature. She got out, straightened her skirt and hat and went to join the group of ground staff waiting by the control tower to see the planes off.

Standing under Z-Zebra, Beresford gave one of the wheels a kick. 'It's a long way, Skip. I hope they've got the weather right.'

'So do I. We go near their night fighter base at Echterdingen.' He changed the subject. 'You went back to Cambridge at the week-end?'

'I had a drink with my old tutor at the Hat and Feathers. I've asked him to read the paper I'm working on. He's a fine physicist but unreliable on the political front. Bit of a Leftie. Supported the Nazi-Soviet Pact then changed his tune when Hitler invaded Russia. We get on all right if we stick to academic things.'

'Criticism of area bombing?'

'Quite the opposite. We can blast everyone to hell as long as we help the Red Army. Can't understand why we don't launch a Second Front now. Strange man. That's something I've learned from our lot. If I ever get back to the university world, it's a lesson to remember. Too many academics think they can lay down the law because they're clever.'

'I'd like to finish my degree. But I don't know what I want to do later.' He looked towards B-Baker where aircrew and ground staff were also waiting. The flare path had been turned on. It was like a theatre before the curtain rises. 'Odd conversation to have. If we get the chop tonight, the future won't be a problem for any of us. I can only say that to you.'

There was a small report from the area of the control tower and a green Very light climbed into the sky.

'Right,' said Chalmers. 'Let's get the show on the road.' The others were already stubbing out cigarettes and climbing aboard.

Chalmers settled into his seat and adjusted his helmet. He switched on the intercom. 'Everyone O.K? No problems?' He slid back the cockpit window to communicate with the ground staff and within seconds all four Merlins were alive, joining the cacophony of noise breaking out all over the aerodrome.

Stafford checked his dials. 'Looking good, Skip. Pity. I hoped we could have a night off.'

'No such luck. Anyway, Einstein's done his homework. He'd be browned off to waste it. Isn't that right, Stephen?'

'Don't you believe it. Who wants to travel all the way to Germany with a load of lunatics? I ought to be paid extra, considering the company I have to keep.'

There was a double report and two green Very lights climbed upwards.

'Right,' said Chalmers. 'Any complaints, gentlemen?' Then, before anyone could reply, 'Glad to hear it. Silence, please, I'm busy.'

Through the window he gave a thumbs up, waved the chocks away, and released the brakes. Slowly, cumbrously, the heavily laden aircraft moved forward. Concentrating on keeping a safe distance behind B-Baker ahead of him, Chalmers remembered Palmer's remark. Mary had brains, too. He had not thought about it. Palmer was right, of course. He was lucky to have found her. Then, looking at the blue lights edging the perimeter track, he recalled a production of Mozart's *Magic Flute* he had seen at Covent Garden. The Queen of the Night, surrounded by stars, had moved across the stage between similar lights. What strange, unpredictable tricks the mind played.

Mary stood watching the take-off. She usually liked to be quiet, thinking her own thoughts, but for some reason she turned to the young woman next to her, a nurse in the Medical Officer's surgery. They had not spoken before. She was thin, wearing a cheap summer dress and shapeless cardigan, her blonde hair covered in a headscarf. 'You've got someone going?'

'Sort of. You?'

Mary nodded. 'Z-Zebra.'

'M-Mother. Rear gunner. Name's Tom. He gets so cold in that turret. I knitted extra-thick socks, but he's still cold.'

Mary looked at her pale face. 'Serious?'

'I am. I think he is. He's kind and generous. Comes from Liverpool. I'm a London girl. You serious?'

'Yes.'

'Tom tells me not to get too serious. Says there's big risks. He doesn't talk much about it. Your chap?'

'Says the same. He's skipper of Z-Zebra.' Mary was glad she had spoken, but felt guilty for saying her man was a skipper. It sounded boastful.

The first Lancaster, Q-Queenie, began its take-off. Engines roaring, it moved forward, slowly at first but with increasing momentum. Its tail wheel was off the ground by the time it passed the knot of spectators and they followed its lights into the sky as it lifted into the darkness. The next aircraft was in position before the first was airborne.

Chalmers eased Z-Zebra forward in the queue until it was their turn. 'Stand by,' he ordered. He shared the tension they all felt. Apart from the bombing run, the take-off of the heavily loaded aircraft was the most stressful part of the operation. He slid the cockpit window closed.

'Green,' said Stafford, as the control tower flashed its lamp towards them.

Chalmers opened the throttle, the noise level rose and every part of the aircraft vibrated. He released the brakes and Z-Zebra surged forward, wings rocking, throbbing with sound and energy. 'Full power,' he ordered, and Stafford, leaning forward close to him pushed the throttles to their fullest extent. The flare-path flashed by on each side and the accelerating lights took him back to the Queen of the Night. He couldn't remember the name of the singer. Had she been German? The tail wheel lifted, he pulled back the control column and they were airborne.

'Undercarriage up,' said Chalmers. 'All right, you can relax.'

'Thank Christ for that,' said Shorthouse, notoriously nervous on take-off. 'Now I've only got to worry about freezing.'

'Just make sure you're on the ball when we get into the stream, Freddie. We don't want to hear from you before then.'

Chalmers knew the others liked Freddie, but could find his humour wearing. Minutes later he said: 'We're over the sea. Test your guns.'

Short bursts of tracer cut into the night sky. Z-Zebra climbed into cloud and the cabin went dark. Then they were into clear air. Stars pricked the black velvet of the sky and white snowdrifts tumbled beneath them. Chalmers throttled back, but they were still climbing as they approached Dungeness where the bomber stream was forming.

In spite of the black-out it was possible to see towns edging the sea. Beresford, working at his table behind the pilot, identified them when Chalmers asked. Beneath them the seamless chain of sound created by the bombers drifted down to sleeping households. At Dungeness a searchlight pointed upwards, indicating the assembly point. Chalmers said: 'We're on time – 16000 feet. Keep awake.' His tone reflected his own tension,

'Rear-gunner to Pilot. Lancaster behind and a thousand feet down.'

'Just make certain it's a Lancaster, Freddie,' said Chalmers. 'Don't forget the Mosquito that turned out to be an M.E 110. Aircraft recognition not your strong suit. You use your energies elsewhere.'

'It's all right, Freddie, we're just jealous,' said Stafford.

Shorthouse had a thick skin. 'I hope you're all as wide awake as I am,' he said.

'Navigator to Pilot,' said Beresford. 'Ten minutes to the Belgian coast.'

'Right, we're on the way in. Eyes skinned.' Chalmers was crisp and firm.

The Lancaster had climbed to 18000 feet and was on course for the coast just south of Ostend.

* * *

Mary and the nurse waited by the control tower. The drone of the last aircraft faded and silence descended. The other watchers drifted away and they were on their own.

'Eerie, isn't it?' said Mary. 'What's your name?'

'Edna.'

'I'm Mary. I'll be waiting when they get back. I collect B-Baker and Z-Zebra. Will you be getting up?'

'I always do. I wait for Tom.'

'I'll look out for you.'

'Thanks.'

They walked back together. Mary touched Edna on the shoulder as they separated to their billets. 'I'll be thinking of Tom as well as Jamie,' she said.

'Thanks.' Edna looked like a wounded animal. 'Thanks,' she repeated.

Mary walked behind the hangars back to her billet. She was cold again, very cold.

12

Along the coast of Holland, Belgium and France the German radar aerials swept the sky. Plotting crews speculated about possible RAF targets.

Beresford turned on the intercom. 'Navigator to pilot. Enemy coast ahead.'

'Two Lancasters to starboard, Skipper,' Alcock reported. 'We're not on our own.'

Chalmers held the aircraft steady as it flew across Belgium at just over 200 miles an hour. He searched the sky with renewed intensity. Some miles to port searchlights appeared and desultory flak came up, falling well short of Z-Zebra's height. 'Florennes,' he said. 'Night-fighter base.' He was more relaxed than usual. Was it increasing confidence born of over twenty safe returns? Or was it Mary, the woman he loved and who loved him? He took one hand off the control column and waggled his fingers in the glove. Beneath him his parachute felt hard and he moved to ease his muscles. To his right Stafford studied his gauges.

Beresford completed a calculation and came up again. 'Navigator to pilot. Thionville turning point seven minutes. Important to get it right, Skipper,' said Beresford. 'Too far south and we hit the flak at Metz.'

'It's all right, Stephen, I don't want to go there any more than you do.'

Chalmers was concentrating hard now. Just ahead through broken cloud a string of yellow flares lit up the sky. 'Turning-point markers,' he said. 'New course, Stephen.'

'New course 110 degrees.'

'Roger. New course 110 degrees.' Chalmers put the Lancaster into a shallow bank to port, now heading for the Rhine and the flak gap between Karlsruhe and Mannheim. He touched the rudder bar gently as the plane returned to level flight.

They were just above the cloud and from time to time they dipped into it. When they did so, Chalmers felt more secure; however good its radar, no night fighter looking for his tell-tale exhausts would see them from underneath. But there was a hint of silver on the four propellors as the moon rose and that brought new dangers.

'Crossing the Rhine, Skip,' said Beresford. 'North of Karlsruhe. Flak?'

'Not near us. Something going on up north. Searchlights, flak, flares.'

His sense of well-being would not go away. With Mary behind him he was a man in his own right and could cope with anything. She was, as she put it, 'sitting on his shoulder'. Shorthouse and his women, Stafford and his pretty wife, the other girl friends temporary and permanent, fell into perspective. It was not just that he was the skipper: he was a man like them. Childish though it sounded, he wanted to shout out, 'I'm in love with a woman and she loves me.' He remembered his last words as he climbed out of the Bedford. 'Think of me at one o'clock.' He knew she would. Time and distance seemed to pass more quickly and the familiar sounds of the aircraft were more comforting than usual. He was taken by surprise when Beresford announced the second turning-point: he banked steeply to head south.

'Time on target ten minutes,' said Beresford.

'More cloud,' said Chalmers. 'We're not going to see much.'

But he was wrong. As they approached Augsburg, the cloud broke up and they could see the city under bombardment. Coloured flares, red and green, hung in the sky. Searchlights fanned upwards, some hitting the base of the cloud, others probing the upper atmosphere. Flak exploded in tight black balls, each with a flashing centre. On the ground, the city was burning. Smoke, black and grey, together with the dark red of fire, showed up in the light of the flares. Looking at the colours, some sharp, some faded, Chalmers was reminded of a medieval tapestry. Then, shocked by the death and destruction the maelstrom of light, colour and smoke represented, he imagined a new circle of hell.

Over to starboard, a good mile away, a searchlight caught a Lancaster. It tried to side-slip away from the beam, but before it could escape two other lights had swung onto it. Chalmers watched, hoping cloud would cut off the lights. He had once been caught in searchlights and imagined the blinding brightness in the cabin, the pilot struggling to twist out of danger. Already flak was flowering dangerously close. The Lancaster was diving now, but the searchlights followed every move. 'Get rid of the bombs,' said Chalmers to himself. 'Give yourself a chance. Get rid of the bloody bombs.' His feet were cold, but he could feel sweat down his back. Another searchlight swung across to the beleaguered aircraft. It looked doomed.

He was right. The plane was surrounded by flak when its motion suddenly changed. It seemed to lift in the air as a burst of flak appeared immediately beneath it and there was a flash of flame from an engine before the whole aircraft disappeared in an explosion of blood-red fire and smoke. Briefly a burning wing and shattered tailplane reappeared as recognisable parts of an aircraft before the rest disappeared as a cascade of flaming fragments falling out of the sky.

'Christ!' said Stafford.

'Concentrate,' ordered Chalmers. He looked at the pattern of green, red and yellow markers ahead. 'Target coming up. Bomb-aimer, stand by.' A detached part of himself worked automatically while another part responded to the horror just seen. Steadying the aircraft for the bombing run, he imagined the helpless crew blown into the night, the latest victims of Dante's inferno.

'No parachutes,' said Stafford.

Beneath them, through ragged cloud, the flashes of exploding bombs appeared in the darkness close to the patches of fire. Outlined against the fire, much lower, another four-engined aircraft crawled across the city. The searchlights swung nearer, looking for a new victim. The flak crept closer, too.

***

Mary was woken by a strange noise. At first she couldn't think what it was, then she remembered. She had set her travelling alarm clock to go off at 12.45 a.m. and put it under her pillow. It was loud enough to wake her without disturbing the others. She slid a hand under the pillow and turned it off before checking the time by its luminous hands. 12.55 a.m. It was late: it always was. Through the window opposite she could see stars and a crescent moon. By its light she saw the familiar objects of the billet: clothes on folding chairs, metal wardrobes, gas masks on pegs behind the door, the black stove with its chimney, distorted and sinister at night. Her companions were asleep, shapeless humps beneath the bedclothes.

The hand of the clock had moved infinitesimally. 'Think of me at one o'clock.' He was over Augsburg. 'Please God, keep him safe.' She had a vision of her father's church in Shropshire, the grey tower next to the manor house, the yew shading the lych-gate. As a child, sitting in the dark oak pews, she had stared up at the Gothic arches searching for the green man whose effigy was up in the roof of the nave. Later, she had prayed for a longed-for friendship before a Christmas term at boarding school. 'Please God, may I be in Margaret's dormitory. Please God . . .'

It was different now. She tried to imagine the flak over Germany. She couldn't manage it. James had described it, but the picture wouldn't come. She was aware instead of the fair hairs on his arms caught in the sun during a picnic, the gentle smile when he set off to find another room at the Royal Charles, her own protectiveness when he fell asleep, as he so often did. 'Please, please God, keep him safe. Please bring him back to me.' No sound came, but she articulated the words, her lips moving against the sheet. Then, thinking that sounded selfish, she added, 'Please keep them all safe. Please God bring them all back.'

She was only partially awake. Half-formed pictures of their week-end came and went. The woman in the train, so sympathetic; the blitzed house at King's Cross, with its violated privacy; the feeling of sophistication as she dressed for the Savoy. She was warm and Jamie was probably cold. When they spent the night together, he had told her how cold his feet got at twenty thousand feet. She had hugged him and promised to keep him warm. He snuggled up and, as he often did, quoted poetry. He talked about 'the poppied warmth of sleep', a phrase she had managed to remember. Keats, he said. She had promised to read the whole poem, but had not yet done so. She felt guilty. She would be punished: he wouldn't come back. She opened her eyes and shivered in spite of the warmth. Augsburg was a long way. He wouldn't be back for hours.

***

The flak was thicker. Chalmers could see the exhausts of another Lancaster slightly higher and just ahead of them. The searchlights to starboard had not yet found another prey.

'Pilot to Bomb-aimer. She's yours, Tavish'

Robertson lay in the nose trying to get the red and yellow markers into his bomb-sight. 'Bomb doors open. Left – left – steady, steady. Right – steady. Left – left – steady, steady.'

Chalmers touched the rudder bar gently. It was one of the most dangerous moments of the whole flight, but his euphoria remained. The imagination he could not control had Mary on his knee, his hand under her skirt. Strangely, he noticed that Robertson's Glaswegian accent was less marked when giving his orders. Around them the flak intensified; over to port ground fire came up like a string of scarlet beads.

'Steady – steady. Nearly there – hold her, Skip. Steady – steady. Bombs gone. Steady for the photo. Bomb doors closed.' Robertson intoned the ritual words.

'Well done, Tavish, well done. Let's get out of here.' Chalmers's response was equally ritualistic.

Five tons of bombs fell away and Z-Zebra, relieved of her load, lifted upwards. Beneath them the flashes of anti-aircraft guns formed a counterpoint to exploding bombs. A bank of cloud drifted towards them and Chalmers buried the aircraft in it.

'Navigator to pilot. New course 275 degrees.'

'Roger – 275 degrees. Thanks, Stephen. Homeward bound, men. Well done, everybody.'

Two flak explosions under the port wing, closer than anything before, maintained the tension just when it might have evaporated. Fragments of shrapnel sounded against the fuselage. Chalmers put the aircraft into a shallow dive, banking to starboard to pick up the new course. In his mind's eye he saw again the exploding Lancaster, the death of seven men. Aloud he said: 'Keep your concentration. We're not home yet.'

Searchlights, flak and fire fell behind as they turned away. Darkness out of light. For a while they continued in cloud then emerged into clear air. Above stars speckled the sky, a mystical universe, remote, detached, yet somehow beneficent; beneath, patches of grey-white cloud hid the Black Forest in the darkness below. Chalmers toyed with the idea of a flippant remark about German history, but thought better of it. His own daydream was drifting back to Mary. She was wearing the ice-blue dress and they were dancing at the Savoy. He held her tightly, feeling the warmth of her thighs through the thin silk.

Freddie Shorthouse suddenly came on the intercom, his voice urgent: 'Fighter – fighter. Corkscrew – corkscrew port. Go . . . Go now.' There was a touch of hysteria. 'Go now,' he shouted.

Chalmers reacted instantly, pulled the column over, throwing the Lancaster onto its port wingtip, letting it slide downwards in the often practised manoeuvre designed to throw off a fighter attack. Behind, he heard the rattle of Brownings as Shorthouse opened fire. The whole aircraft strained with complaint. Beresford swore uncharacteristically as items on his plotting table slid away from him, destroying the meticulous order he maintained there.

'J.U.88,' said Alcock. He, too, opened fire, his guns spraying the night air as the Lancaster side-slipped away. The smell of cordite drifted down the fuselage.

Chalmers pulled back to level flight. Ahead there was bank of cloud shaped like a human head. He made for it, pushing the stick forward to increase speed.

'Still there,' reported Alcock. 'Coming in fast.'

Again, the crackle of gunfire; again, Chalmers threw the aircraft into the corkscrew motion. This time German tracer curved over the starboard wing as the Lancaster fell away to port.

They reached the haven of cloud and Chalmers levelled out. The cabin went dark. 'Praise be,' he breathed. Aloud he said: 'Skipper to gunners. Well done. With luck we'll have cover for a bit.'

'Wasn't sure when I first saw him, Skipper,' said Shorthouse. 'Thought he was a Lancaster. Then the moon showed him up – out of range, waiting his chance. Sheered off when I opened fire.'

'Couldn't get at him, Skipper,' said Alcock. 'You dived before I saw him properly. He came in at a different angle the second time. Too fast to get in my sights.'

'Sounds like a beginner. He'd have done better biding his time. We'll lose him in this cloud.'

'Navigator to Pilot. Crossing the Rhine.' Beresford's academic tone had a calming effect. 'Try to cut out the aerobatics, Skipper. You've messed up my table.'

For a time they flew steadily westwards, then, once more, the cloud thinned, drifting over the cabin in grey wisps, before breaking up completely. Z-Zebra emerged into clear sky, the moon glinting on wings and propellors.

'Sharpen up, everyone,' ordered Chalmers. He peered out at the darkness. They would be on a radar screen somewhere and the return leg took them close to two fighter bases. Twice he tightened his grip on the control column when he thought he saw another aircraft; each was a false alarm, a trick of the light and a tense imagination. To his relief, there was another bank of cumulus cloud ahead.

The intercom crackled. It was Shorthouse again. 'Another one, Skipper. Closing fast. Corkscrew port. Go port now.' His voice was more controlled, as though correcting the panic conveyed earlier. The urgency was still there.

Once more Chalmers threw the aircraft to port, sideslipping, falling away into the darkness.

As he levelled off, Shorthouse came back: 'Still with us. M.E.110. Followed us down. Coming in again. He's firing . . . He's . . .'

Shorthouse's voice dissolved in a scream of pain and the noise of exploding cannon shells. The aircraft shuddered. The sound was magnified in the enclosed space, giving the impression of massive damage. The controls shook and Chalmers felt a series of impacts immediately behind him. Absurdly, even as he imagined total disintegration, he blessed the designer who had fitted a bullet-proof back to the pilot's seat. Tracer appeared from behind, and he knew the port wing had been hit. The cloud was closer. Stafford's eyes were on him, waiting for him to produce deliverance. Again he went into the corkscrew manoeuvre, the controls stiff, response sluggish. 'Pilot to Rear-gunner. Are you all right, Freddie?'

The aircraft reached the cloud and darkness enveloped them. 'Pilot to crew. Report back. Freddie, are you O.K.?' Silence. 'Stephen, are you O.K.? Les? Brad?' There was no reply.

He turned to Stafford. 'Get down there, Staff. It may just be the intercom.' He was not optimistic.

The smell of cordite was now joined by that of smoke. 'Get up here, Tavish,' Chalmers said. 'We've got problems.' Robertson climbed out of the nose. 'Stay here till Staff gets back.' It was a crisis and he had to be calm. He could not show his feelings of near panic.

Stafford plugged into the intercom at the rear of the plane: 'Bloody mess back here, Skip. Les and Brad are goners. Stephen's hurt – unconscious. Something's burning, but I can't see what. Can't tell about Freddie either. His turret's been hit. He's making a noise. He's alive.'

'Concentrate on the fire. Tavish, go and help. I can manage here.'

The aircraft was pulling roughly to port, the control column twice the normal effort. They were still in cloud. Chalmers knew they had swung off course and if Stephen was out of action he had to get home without him. Panic returned. He could do it, but Stephen would do it better. Les and Brad were dead. He'd got to know them well, the salt of the earth in their different ways. His responsibility. He thought of the first dead man he had taken home and recognised the feeling of guilt. He had met Les's mother, a comfortable woman whose husband had died down the pit and who took in washing to make ends meet. She was enormously proud of her son's three stripes and Chalmers had promised to look after him. What a fool to promise anything! He saw again the immolation of the Lancaster coned by searchlights.

Stafford came on: 'The oxygen's buggered up, Skip. We've got to lose height.'

Chalmers pushed the stick forward. He hoped the cloud base was low. Anything to keep the cloud. The chances were the fighter had lost them, but he could not be sure. He watched the altimeter as they dropped below ten thousand feet.

Stafford reappeared. 'Fire's out. It was Les's wireless stuff. Totally u/s. Les has had it. No pulse, blood all over his head. Brad's a terrible mess . . . terrible. Tavish is giving Stephen morphine. He's covered in blood and oil. Stomach, I think. He's bad. Freddie's alive – he's making a whimpering noise – but everything's jammed. I can't get at him. There's hydraulic oil everywhere and a fucking great hole in the floor.' Trying to forget the horror that was Brad Alcock's body, he spoke in a monotone. 'Can we make it?'

'He hit the port wing.'

'Smoke,' Stafford said.

No flames were visible, but smoke streamed away from the port outer engine.

'Extinguisher,' said Chalmers, pushing the extinguisher button. There was no obvious effect.

'Could be bad,' said Stafford. 'Feather it, Skipper.'

'Right, close it down.' Chalmers always deferred to Stafford's knowledge of engines. The propellor windmilled to a stop. There was still smoke.

Chalmers felt the effect on the controls as the port wing dropped. He was struggling back to level flight when he saw the gyro compass.

'Now we've lost the bloody compass.' The expletive fell oddly from his lips; he had never been taken over by the culture of service swearing as readily as others. Stafford would be aware he was under strain. 'If I can work out where we are, we can still make it. Depends how serious the fire is.' He indicated the smoke. As he did so, the cloud thinned before breaking up; they were in moonlight again. 'That's all we need.'

He looked sideways at Stafford. 'Help Tavish with Stephen and Freddie. Get back here as fast as you can. I can cope for the moment.'

He wondered if he was speaking the truth. There was damage to the controls and with an engine out it was hard to stay level. He felt cold and there was sweat down his back again. He looked again at the useless compass, then up at the stars. A moment's calculation was enough. They were flying south-west instead of north-west. They had probably been doing so for some time. He looked out at the smoking engine. The odds were stacking up against them.

13

The three engines were going well. Chalmers had managed to turn north-west. He looked to the north where, miles away, searchlights fingered the sky. If he was not too far off course, it could be Strasbourg. He looked up through the canopy at the North Star. It was approximately where he expected it, but he remembered the scathing comment of the burly warrant officer who had initiated him into the mysteries of navigation: 'Mr Chalmers, sir, you couldn't find your own home if your mother wasn't holding your hand.'

How far south-west had he gone? If it wasn't Strasbourg, what was it? He was nursing the engines, but he needed Stafford back. There were no clouds to hide in now. The nearest, a Himalayan range miles to starboard, seemed to be mocking him. It was going to be a long run home.

Stafford reappeared. 'I don't think Stephen's going to make it. You'll have to do without him, Skip.'

'Freddie?'

'Can't get at him. He's bad. Tavish is having another go.'

'We're miles to the south and mighty vulnerable – a lame duck wandering about, flying low. Just the job for an ambitious Jerry.'

He looked out at the night. The stars had changed. Beautiful, ethereal, even beneficent before, they were now cold observers; Thomas Hardy's view of a malignant fate destroying mankind's endeavours seemed apt. He was aware of another town, but had no idea what it was. There were no searchlights or flak. Eastern France, it must be. Dijon? Or were they further south? His forearms ached with the pressure on the control column.

The intercom clicked. It was Robertson. 'Freddie caught it in the back. I've given him morphine. He'll have to stay where he is.'

'Make him as comfortable as you can, then get back to Stephen.'

The normal vibration of the plane had been joined by noises indicating damage. Chalmers knew the idiosyncracies of Z-Zebra like any car owner and recognised alien sounds. He had dropped to five thousand feet and was on a heading north-west, but it was all he could do to hold it. Nevertheless, he felt some normality had been restored. Tired though he was, unbidden thoughts continued. The last half hour had been like a Kafka novel: moments of rationality followed by bizarre twists over which he had no control.

Stafford looked at the feathered engine. 'Smoke's thinning,' he said. 'We're going to make it.'

Chalmers approved the optimism. That was why he had chosen Stafford when the crew was made up. He could never have worked with the only alternative, a gloomy Celt from Cornwall who saw nothing but disaster. At the same time he faced another fact. If anything else went wrong, baling out would only be an option for Stafford and Robertson. Shorthouse was stuck in his turret and Beresford was unconscious. He would have no alternative but to try to put the plane down.

The thought had barely formed when a flicker of light appeared on the port outer, vanished, then reappeared more strongly. Chalmers and Stafford saw it at the same time, a blue and yellow flame licking the engine and streaming behind the wing together with renewed smoke.

'So much for the extinguisher,' said Chalmers. 'Grab your chute, Staff. You and Tavish are getting out. I'm going to put her down. Tell Tavish.'

Stafford looked at him then went to the rear, climbing clumsily over the main spar. Seconds later, or so it seemed, they were both at his shoulder. 'We're staying,' said Stafford.

Chalmers felt a flash of anger. Every ounce of effort was going on the controls and his crew were disobeying him. He looked out at the wing where the fire glowed fiercely. 'It's an order,' he said. 'Bale out.'

'If you're staying, Skipper,' said Robertson, his Scottish accent thick, 'so are we. You'll need help.'

'And I've never trusted my 'chute,' said Stafford. 'I know the girl who packed it.' He eyed the burning engine. 'Besides, it's bloody cold out there.'

Chalmers's anger died as rapidly as it was born. 'Last chance,' he said. 'You're disobeying an order, but I understand why. I'm not going to argue. I'm going to put her down on anything remotely flat.' Z-Zebra dropped lower and out of the darkness the first landscape features appeared.

The moon lit up a countryside of woods and hills. Chalmers had cursed the moon earlier, now it was essential. His inner voice made a silent plea to God and, as if in answer, he saw the river. Ahead and over to port, glinting white and silver, a ribbon of water twisted away from them. The Seine? The Loire? He tried to remember the rivers they might cross. It was running roughly north.

Stafford and Robertson had seen it, too. 'Down there?' hazarded Stafford. 'Wooded on the right bank, open on the left. The fire's worse.'

'We can't mess about,' said Chalmers. 'I'll risk one circuit to look at it, but we haven't any choice. There are trees, but that open patch looks possible. Now you will obey orders. Tavish, get back to Stephen. Put him behind the main spar. Crash-landing drill. Staff, strap in and help me here.'

Discipline and self-preservation took over. 'Good luck, Skipper,' said Robertson. 'I'll be praying.'

'So shall I. Hope He's listening.'

116

Both Chalmers and Stafford had their hands on the control column. Chalmers allowed the port wing to dip. The aircraft banked in a wide circle, losing height and bringing the ground into focus. They crossed the river and, still banking gently, looked across at the possible landing place. They were low enough to see the contour of the higher hills and the woodland dominating the countryside. Here and there a solitary farm or cottage appeared.

'Ground mist,' said Chalmers. All down the valley a veil of mist clung to the surface of the river and spilt into adjacent fields. 'Help and hindrance. Shows where it's flat, but it'll make it difficult. I'm going down on the left where it spreads over from the river. That's as flat as we're going to get. Right, let's get lined up.'

Action took over. Imagination, so unreliable, so uncontrollable when he had time to think, was neutralised. Lives depended on his skill. Momentarily, looking at the flaming engine and the river, he thought of the trials of Earth, Air, Fire and Water in *The Magic Flute*, but even as the idea formed it dissolved. He was aware of the void in the stomach all frightened men know.

Once more the great aircraft swung round over the river. There was heavy vibration and he could only keep the control column in position by forcing his leg against it. The fire had spread to the wing and sparks had joined the smoke. An explosion was possible, but there was nothing he could do about it. Beneath the wing as they levelled out he saw a church tower and a village clustered on a hill. Beyond, parallel with the river and barely visible through the mist, were a canal and railway. Directly ahead, between the river and the woods, were what looked like water meadows. There were trees, but he thought he could see a passage through.

He was lined up at last. He felt the sweat again. They were dropping fast, but every inch of space was vital, there was no question of overshooting or going round again. He had swung closer to the river than he intended, but the fields were more level than he had thought.

They were into the mist, its insubstantial whiteness drifting past, breaking up as propellers and wings cut into it. 'Stand by,' said Chalmers. The port wing was dropping, the flames were worse. He pulled the throttles back, and let the aircraft sink. The cockpit was dark again. 'Please God, no fire,' he prayed.

The last seconds seemed endless; Chalmers even wondered if the mist had made him misjudge height totally. Then Z-Zebra hit the ground belly first. The noise was indescribable, even to ears deadened by hours of engine roar and vibration. Eyes closed, crouching forward, no longer with any semblance of control, Chalmers thought the aircraft was disintegrating. Thrown forward by the sudden deceleration, he lost all sense of individual sounds in the vortex of noise. Z-Zebra swung to starboard, heading towards the river and the trees and there was nothing he could do about it. An excruciating pain surged up through his leg. To his right, something struck the aircraft and Stafford was thrown across him. He opened his eyes long enough to see the engine flaming to his left and trees straight ahead. Pointlessly he clutched the control column. He tried to protect his head. His arms no longer responded. There was fire. There was water. Then, mercifully, all was darkness.

***

Dawn came up slowly at Wynton Thorpe. First light revealed streaks of grey cloud in a pale aquamarine sky. There was no wind and the orange windsock hung limply by the control tower. Birdsong greeted the first aircraft to land. B-Baker was among them and Mary collected its crew.

'Reasonable trip?' she hazarded to Croft, who had joined her in the cab.

'A ruddy long way. I could sleep for a thousand years. Jamie not back yet?' They were passing Z-Zebra's empty pan.

'You know him, Crofty. Always last.'

'Probably looking at a French cathedral.'

'Flak?'

'Not as bad as the Ruhr.'

'Fighters?'

'No one came near us. One of the most uneventful trips we've done.'

They were edging round each other. She was looking for reassurance and he knew it. As she dropped him at the interrogation hut, another plane made its approach. She went straight back to Z-Zebra's pan. She was not going to miss Jamie.

Twelve, thirteen, fourteen. Two to go. S-Sugar, the most recent arrival, taxied to the far side of the airfield. Above, the strips of cloud were now edged with pink and it was lighter. Mary wound down the window of her door, letting in the early morning coolness. She wanted to get rid of the Bedford smell of oil she told herself; more realistically, she wanted to hear the distant sound of an aircraft.

"Morning, Miss.' It was the duty sentry, the same man she had met before her London week-end. His turn-out was immaculate; his Alsatian sensed a pause in operations and sat down.

'Peaceful night?'

'I miss my kip. You never catch up during the day.'

'No excitement?'

'Nothing stirring – a few badgers over by the woods.' He looked across to Morby Castle and the surrounding woodland. 'Mind you, the night before I caught a young'un from the village trying to 'alf-inch a push-bike be'ind the Sergeants' Mess. Right little tearaway, 'e was. Reminded me of meself when I was 'is age. I give 'im a clip round the ear'ole an' told 'im not to be daft. No point in getting' 'im in real trouble. An' I'd have to write out a report. Writin's not my strong point, you might say.'

Mary was not listening. His shiny boots, she noticed, had dew on them.

He sensed her inattention. 'Most of 'em back, then?'

'Two to come.'

'You keeps a count?'

'Don't you?'

'Can't say as I do. I don't know none of 'em, y'see. You got someone flying?'

'Yes.'

'An' 'e's not back yet?'

'No.'

The sentry was not one of nature's most sensitive men, but knew he was on tricky ground. ''E'll be on 'is way, Miss – you mark my words.' He pulled on the dog's lead, tightening his grip on the webbing of his rifle. 'Yes,' he said reassuringly, 'you mark my words.' And then he had gone.

As the crunch of his boots faded, Mary was aware of another plane in the distance. She focused on the squat shape of the castle and a Lancaster appeared, flying low. One engine was stopped and it made straight for the runway without doing a circuit.

Mary closed her eyes. 'Please, please God, make it Jamie. Please God, make it Jamie.'

She kept her eyes tightly closed as the aircraft landed. When it was approximately level with her, she opened them. It was O-Orange. The disappointment was palpable, a depth of feeling never experienced before. Her eyes were dry, but tears were not far away. She remembered her headmistress's words on the occasion her parents had failed to turn up at school for a long-anticipated week-end visit. 'We don't cry, do we, Mary? We all have to get used to disappointment.' Subconsciously she pulled back her shoulders.

O-Orange pulled off the runway and taxied to the eastern side of the aerodrome. Its engines died away. Again there was silence, apart from a lark climbing into the sky beyond the perimeter fence. The first rays of sunshine touched the top of Morby's ruined keep.

Another twenty minutes passed, each one adding to Mary's despair. A tentative tap on the door broke her concentration. She looked down and saw the nurse, Edna, standing with a bicycle. She looked tired, but had done her make-up and her blonde hair was brushed with care. Mary saw she was really rather pretty. Her concern was for Mary. 'I heard Z-Zebra's not back,' she said.

Mary managed a smile. Last night she had felt patronising. Now she felt nothing but warmth. 'Tom safe?'

'One of the first.'

'I'm glad for you.'

'He may have landed somewhere else, you know. They do that if they're in trouble.'

'I know.'

'Tom didn't see anyone go down.'

Mary put a hand out of the window and Edna took it. Mary saw the sympathy in her eyes. 'It's difficult,' she said.

'Jamie, isn't it?'

'We're going to be married one day – when this is all over.' She spoke with a certainty she did not feel. The shadow of the headmistress loomed. We don't cry, do we?

'Tom's asked me, too. We're waiting till the end of his tour.'

'Known him long?'

'Since he came to Wynton. I didn't take him seriously to begin with. But he's a good man – and generous. He wants to be a painter and decorator when this lot's over. He makes me laugh. And he wants children.'

Mary gave her hand a squeeze. 'You're a lucky girl.' She could not stop herself adding, 'I thought I was,' and knew how self-centred it sounded. 'Sorry.'

Edna gave a squeeze in return. 'Come and have some breakfast. We'll see if there's any news.'

'All right. Put your bike in the back.'

They drove back to the vehicle park, then walked to the cookhouse. Inside, Mary's emotions were tied in a small hard knot, dry, tight and private. She saw the care Edna had taken with her appearance. She was wearing nylons and expensive-looking court shoes. She thought of the time she had taken over her own make-up. Only a handful of people who had been on night duty were in the cookhouse. Mary toyed with a mug of strong tea while Edna, warm-hearted Edna, produced optimistic, anxious possibilities. 'Even if they were shot down, I expect they baled out. He may be free in France, not even a prisoner of war.'

Mary was impatient, but desperate not to be rude, unfeeling. She took Edna's hand and said, 'I must get some sleep.' She had underestimated the girl and was honest enough to admit it. 'Thanks for looking after me. You're right – I mustn't look on the black side.'

But she did. As she made her way back to the billet via the path behind the hangars, she was coming to terms with the truth. She would never see Jamie again.

Burgundy 1943-1944

14

Something was pricking him. Chalmers felt it in the ear first, then on his neck. It was dark, totally dark. He tried to move and a stab of pain thrust itself up his right leg. He moved an arm and felt in the area he believed his head to be. It was soft and somehow bigger than usual. He was faint and dizzy. His hand, too, as he moved it upwards was pricked. He opened his eyes, but it remained dark. Some sort of bandage was covering his head and one of his eyes. There was a rural smell. *He was alive.*

A voice, a female voice, said in French: 'He's moving.'

A man responded. He could not catch the words.

There was a hand on his shoulder, a gentle hand. He wanted to speak, but nothing came. The exploration of the pricking of his ear and neck produced an explanation: he was lying in hay or straw. He moved his head and the dizziness increased.

The touch on his shoulder was repeated. The female voice spoke again, this time in English, with an accent: ' 'ello.'

He moved again, trying to pull himself into a sitting position. The pain in his leg bit into him. He lay back, more faint than before. Disconnected ideas floated through his mind. The plane was sinking into the mist. He could see flames. He could feel water. *The Magic Flute* chords echoed and re-echoed. Air, Earth, Fire and Water. A snatch of Shelley learned at school merged with Mozart. '*I am the daughter of Earth and Water, and the nurseling of the Sky . . .*' His mind was working after a fashion.

'Lie still.' The voice was soft. 'You're safe.'

He was drifting off. There were stars above, mountains and valleys of cloud below. A voice was saying, 'Keep your belly in the cloud. If they see your exhausts, you're a goner.' A prep school cricket coach said, 'Left elbow up, right up. Get to the pitch of the ball. If you don't, you're a goner.' Pain was there, too, coursing through his leg. He was in the mist, there were trees ahead. The picture faded.

Somewhere beneath him an animal shifted its feet. An animal? There were swirling layers of mist, props and wings cutting into it. Animals. Would there be animals beneath the mist? Space was running out. He gripped the control column, willing the plane down. It was swinging towards the trees. There were flames, and water . . .

Water. Someone was trying to get water between his lips. The soft hand was on his shoulder again. He opened his eyes. A dark-haired young woman was looking down at him. Curiously she seemed to be at the end of a tunnel. She was smiling and holding a lantern. Its flame flickered.

' 'ello,' she said.

He wanted to reply, but only a dry sound came out. He felt the water slip down his throat. He tried again. This time he managed it. 'Hello,' he said.

'You're safe,' she said. 'You must drink.' More water went between his lips. Even more ran down the side of his face.

'Where are they?' The words were there, just.

'They?'

'The others . . . Tavish, Staff . . .' His hand moved over his head. Speaking made every part of it throb. 'Freddie? Einstein? My friends. Was there fire? There was water, wasn't there? There were bound to be fire and water.' He was not making sense.

'Do not talk. We talk later.' The voice was comforting, struggling with an unfamiliar language.

He felt the hand again. He was conscious of another presence. A male voice muttered something he did not hear.

The girl spoke. 'You sleep now.' He felt a sharp prick in his arm, sharper and deeper than the straw. The face at the end of the tunnel faded. He was unconscious within seconds.

When he awoke it was light. He lifted the edge of the bandage and blinked at the sunlight streaming through a crack in the wall. He moved his head and looked around. There were rough beams, cobwebs, and the tiles of a roof no more than six feet above him. Every part of his body protested when he moved, but he shifted enough to see that he was lying on hay in what appeared to be the loft of a barn. His right leg was strapped to a piece of wood. He turned his head to the left where the top of a ladder was sticking up through the hay. The rural smell was still there. Somewhere a blackbird was singing. Faintness came back when he moved his head.

He lifted a hand and examined it, then the other. Both were bruised, but there was no sign of burning. He felt the side of his face. It was swollen, rather as it had been when he'd had toothache as a boy. He moved his left leg. It responded. The right leg was a different matter. Any movement sent slivers of pain through the rest of his body. He turned towards the ladder. 'Hello,' he said.

There was no reply. He lifted his head and spoke more loudly: 'Hello.'

Above him, over the opening in the wall, a butterfly fluttered in a spider's web. Momentarily it distracted him. The Lancaster was in the searchlights. 'Corkscrew port,' he said aloud. His lips were dry. Then, for the first time since regaining consciousness, he thought of Mary. It was warm in the loft, but a shiver ran through him. He had let her down. She would be waiting. She would think the worst, she was bound to. They had joked that if he didn't get back it would be his fault. 'I'll always be here,' she had said. 'You're the one wandering off.' 'I'll never let you down,' he had said. But he knew the realities; he was not sure she did. She would get his letter. 'I don't want your letter,' she had said. The butterfly, a Small Tortoiseshell, its wing torn, made a supreme effort, broke free and vanished into the morning air.

How long had he been there? Fact and fantasy merged as he drifted on the edge of consciousness. There had been voices, French voices. He remembered being carried. Where were the others? He opened his eyes and moved his head to make sure he was on his own. There was no one else. Just piles of hay and the ladder poking through. Somewhere beneath him the animal was making noises. A horse?

There were voices again. They were outside and speaking French. Fluent himself, he caught the odd word. They were talking about a doctor. Then they were beneath him, a man and a woman. He heard feet on the ladder. He turned his head and a woman's face appeared, pale, not made up, the face at the end of the tunnel.

"'ello, you awake?' she said. The smile was warm. She was young and pretty, somewhere in the mid twenties, with full lips and high cheekbones. Dark-brown hair fell naturally round her face. She wore a simple cotton dress with small white flowers.

Chalmers responded in French. 'Where am I?'

'You speak French, Monsieur?' The girl could not hide her surprise.

'Where am I?' he repeated.

'You're safe. In a farm near Châtel-Censoir.' She relaxed into her own language.

'Châtel-Censoir? Where's that?' He remembered trying to work out where he was before coming down. He saw the ribbon of river, the mist, a church and houses on a hill.

'Burgundy – northern Burgundy. The valley of the Yonne.'

'The Yonne?'

'A river. Your aeroplane's in it. The Germans are looking at it.'

'The plane's in the river? Where are the others?'

She knelt beside him, modestly adjusting her dress. She put a hand on his shoulder, just as she had before. 'You were the only one we could save.'

128

'There were four others. They were alive when we came down. Where are they?' He knew he sounded hysterical. 'Where are they?'

'The others are dead.'

'They can't be. Staff was next to me. He helped me land. They can't be dead.' An inner voice told him he was trying to avoid guilt.

'Tell me your name.' The woman was leaning over him.

'James. James Chalmers – Flying Officer. We'd lost an engine, the compass was useless. They can't all be dead.'

'You're safe. We got you away before the Germans arrived.'

'They were in the plane.'

She took his hand; she knew the effect her words would have. 'The man at the back was drowned. The tail broke off and was under water. There were four bodies in the middle of the plane. They were under water, too, but we couldn't see how they died. You were still in the cockpit. The man next to you was covered in blood – something had hit his head. We couldn't do anything. We had to get you out.'

Chalmers looked away. He had failed them all. He closed his eyes, summoning dignity to face this calm girl. He wanted to cry. In his mind he was going through it again. He felt the swing towards the river, saw the trees ahead.

'You were lucky we were there,' she said.

'Lucky?'

'We saw everything. We got you out.'

Part of his brain told him he should be asking who 'we' were and why they were in a remote French field in the small hours of the morning. Emotionally, he could only think of the men who had trusted him. The deaths of Ricketts and Alcock he had somehow absorbed before the crash, rather as he had adjusted to the loss of the engine. Devastating, terrible, yet comprehensible. But the others had been alive, depending on him. Poor, infuriating, boastful Freddie; Stephen the Prof, intellectually a cut above them all; 'Tavish, morose, taciturn, the butt of every joke within the magic circle, always defended outside it; and Stafford, whose maturity made the rest of them feel like schoolboys. He had let them down and he had survived. And now a pretty French girl was holding his hand, comforting his tears of self-pity.

'Could you manage to eat something?'

He shook his head. 'No thanks. My throat's dry.' He let his head drop back onto the hay and looked up at her.

'More water? Milk?'

'Milk would be nice.'

'I'll get you some. Your leg's broken. The doctor's coming back. He gave you an injection.'

'Why were you there?'

'Where?'

'In the field where we came down.'

She got up, putting a finger to her lips. 'Too many questions.' She brushed bits of hay off her dress and, stooping beneath one of the roof beams, went back to the ladder. His eyes followed her. 'I shan't be long,' she said. Her head disappeared.

Beneath him a horse – definitely a horse – snorted. And Chalmers, who could not recall shedding tears since his first day at prep school, was crying. He wanted Mary. He wanted her to tell him it wasn't his fault. She gave him confidence, made him feel he could cope with anything. What would she say if she were there? He tried to visualise her sitting where the French girl had been. 'Think positively,' she would say. 'You're alive.'

He looked down the length of his body. His boots had been removed, but he was wearing the rest of his flying kit; there was blood down the front and the left arm of his jacket had been cut away; the strapping on his right leg was some sort of leather. The watch on his wrist had been smashed. He wiped the tears with the back of his hand; the hand was shaking.

The young woman reappeared with a glass of milk. She knelt beside him. 'Can you hold it?'

'I'll try.' He managed to lift himself onto an elbow and took the glass. Her eyes were brown, with dark lashes. The milk was thick and creamy. He sipped it through bruised lips. 'That's nice.'

'This morning's milking. One of my jobs.'

'You keep cows?'

'A small herd.'

'They can't all be dead.'

'We had to concentrate on you before the Germans got there.'

'We?'

'My father – some others. We heard you were in trouble before we saw you. We saw the flames. We guessed you'd try to get down.'

'Are they your fields?'

'No. We've brought you to our farm, ten kilometres away. The Germans are looking for you. They know the pilot isn't there. They may come here.'

Chalmers's thought processes were confused, but the presence of a rescue party puzzled him. 'Why were you there? Did I ask that before?'

'You did. I didn't answer.' She was smiling again, an engaging smile involving a minimum of facial movement but warmth in the brown eyes. 'It's better you shouldn't know for the time being. We can't guarantee they won't find you. You're not well enough to move.'

'How did you get a doctor?'

'He was in the field. He bandaged you up. He realised your leg was broken. There may be other things. He wasn't able to look at you properly. You were lucky.'

'Lucky?' He turned his head away.

'Sorry.' She held his hand. 'How do you feel now?'

He tried to smile. 'Bruised,' he said. 'Bruised all over. The leg's painful. How long have I been here?'

'Two days. We've only managed to give you water.'

'What's your name?'

'Chantal.'

'Milkmaid?'

'Farmer's daughter. There have been Lejeunes at La Rippe for generations.'

He drank some milk. The dizziness had returned: he was on the edge of consciousness.

'We?' he said again. He put the glass down carefully and lay back in the hay. Above him the terra cotta tiles, roughly fitted together, spoke of a simple farm. 'We?' he repeated. The pain of his leg would not go away. Why should farmers and a doctor be in the fields in the small hours?

'The doctor says you'll be here for some time.'

'He lives in the village?'

'Mailly-le-Château. Village above the river. He's coming when he's finished morning surgery. He's got a good excuse. Grandfather's not well.'

'Excuse?'

'The Germans watch doctors if they think there are injured English flyers around.'

He was wandering again. 'Did the plane catch fire?'

'The fire spread from the engine when you touched down. We thought there would be an explosion. The river put the flames out. Smoke and steam everywhere. We were surprised to find you alive.'

'There's a horse down there.'

'Two of them. They work the farm.'

'What will you do if the Germans come?'

'Hope they don't find you. We'll take the ladder away and close the trapdoor. It can't be seen if we pile hay underneath. They can't tell there's a loft here – it's not obvious from the outside.'

'You've done it before?'

There was a slight pause. 'Yes. Now I've work to do. Is there anything else I can get you?'

'I'm fine.' Then, realising he was saying it for the first time, he said: 'Thanks for everything, Chantal. I must be losing my manners.'

'I'm sorry about your friends. There was nothing we could do.' She touched his hand and stood up. 'Now I must go. Someone will be back soon.'

He was alone with his gloom. Aloud he said: 'Please God, forgive me.' There was a rushing noise in his ears, a biting pain in his leg near the ankle. In imagination he was kneeling in one of the uncomfortable pews in the chapel at Queen's. 'Please God, look after Mary.' Then he passed out again.

He had no idea how long he had been unconscious when he felt someone touching him. 'Chantal?' he said, eyes still closed.

'No.' The voice was male.

He opened his eyes. A middle-aged man, sallow, black-haired, with a small moustache and humorous eyes, was bending over him, feeling the bandage on his head. 'Doctor?'

The stranger smiled. 'You speak French. That makes a change.'

'I was studying it at Oxford when the war started. Better on set books than idiom. I know my Corneille and Racine. I've stayed in France a lot . . . my mother brought me.'

'No one's even tried *oui* or *non* before. It will be a pleasure to treat you.'

'Doctor ...?'

'Gambert, Jean Gambert.'

'Why were you there when we came down, Doctor? Did you look at the others?'

'We had our reasons. There was nothing we could do for them. You were fortunate.'

'That's what Chantal said.'

'We'll talk about it later. Now I want to examine you properly. I had to be quick when we picked you up. Hold still. Tell me if anything hurts.'

'What's wrong with my head?'

'Not much. You've got a gash across the scalp. That's why I put the bandage on. It's only temporary. I'll dress it again and get the bandage off your eyes. Something gave you a crack on the side of the face, too. You've got a black eye coming up nicely. Headache?'

'Terrible. Was there fire?' Chalmers was soothed by the sensitivity of Gambert's hands.

'You're concussed – nothing worse, I think. There was fire, but not in the cockpit.'

'My leg's gone, hasn't it?'

'I've seen worse. We'll get a plaster on when we've cleaned you up. Chantal's bringing everything we need.'

The dizziness and sickness came on again and before Chalmers could reply he relapsed into unconsciousness.

When he came to he felt different. He was still lying in the hay but was wearing a pair of clean pyjamas. His leg was in plaster up to the knee, the pyjamas cut to accommodate it. Gambert and Chantal were there, washing their hands in a bucket.

'Ah, you're awake,' said Gambert. 'Bad bruising everywhere, but I can't find anything else. The leg's a clean break. You must stay quiet to get over the concussion.'

'Thank you, Doctor. Thank you, both.' He tried to smile at Chantal, who was drying her hands.

'Chantal's got the blood off you. No shaving. You must let the bruising on your face recover. Not hungry?' Gambert's bedside manner was brisk.

'No, I feel sick.'

'We'll get something into you this evening. That's all we can do for the moment. Now you must sleep.' Gambert took Chalmers's clothes and dropped them through the trap-door before following down the ladder. Chantal picked up the bucket.

'Did you wash me all over?'

She laughed, an attractive sound. 'All over. Do you mind?'

He found himself blushing. 'Did *you* mind?'

'You're not the first. We've had RAF men before.' She took the bucket to the ladder and handed it down to Gambert. 'Now go to sleep. I'll bring you soup later. And you have to eat it. Doctor's orders.'

The day passed. Chalmers knew nothing of individual hours, but sensed the heat of mid-day when birdsong was muted and the farm lay silent. Later, he was aware of renewed activity: cows in the yard, a dog, a van driving in and later leaving, men talking. In the distance he heard an occasional train. The light began to fade. The thought of food no longer brought on faintness and sickness. His leg throbbed, but the pain was more bearable. Not far away someone was playing a simple tune on a piano; the occasional false note grated. So he wasn't the first RAF man they had looked after. His mind was getting into gear at last. He had heard of families helping aircrew shot down over France and had actually met a pilot who had escaped through Spain to rejoin his squadron. He had fallen on his feet. He looked down at the fresh plaster and realised the absurdity of the thought. It was dark when he heard voices approaching again.

He raised himself on an elbow. First to appear was a lean man with a weather-beaten face, suspicious eyes and a drooping moustache. He wore rough farming clothes, a beret, and carried a lantern. Chantal followed, with a bowl, a jug, and something wrapped in a napkin. 'My father, Jacques,' said Chantal, when she had struggled through the hole. 'He helped get you out.'

Chalmers looked straight at him. 'Thank you, Monsieur,' he said.

'You must eat. Chantal has brought soup. Asparagus – we had it ourselves. And freshly-made bread.'

'Thank you for getting me out.' He looked at Jacques Lejeune's worn features, estimating his age. Fifty? Sixty? He tried to imagine him climbing into the cockpit of the Lancaster. Difficult. He tasted the soup. The bread was still warm. 'It's good,' he said appreciatively.

'You've been asking questions.' The voice was sharp.

'I'm very grateful for all you did. I wondered what you were doing in the field at that time in the morning.'

Lejeune had put the lantern down and squatted in the hay where Chalmers could see him. He lit a Gauloise. 'You know there is resistance in France?'

'You're in the Resistance?'

The eyes in the unshaven face gave nothing away. 'There is resistance. We're on the edge of the Morvan. Difficult country for the Boches. Hills, forest – remote, not easy to get at. There were several of us there when you crashed. Mere chance we were there.'

'Chantal said you've had RAF men before.'

'You know nothing about that. The doctor says you'll be with us for a while. You'll stay up here. Later we'll make you more comfortable.'

'What will happen to my crew?'

'The Germans got them out. They'll treat them correctly. A Lancaster came down at Pontaubert in June. They buried them at Avallon. Proper military ceremony from the Luftwaffe. They treat dead Englishmen better than live French. We've got to concentrate on you. They'll give up if they don't get you in the first week.' He inhaled the cigarette. His tone mellowed. 'It's a change to have someone who speaks French.' He stood up. 'Gambert will come again tomorrow. Get some sleep now. If you need anything, tell Chantal.' The brusqueness returned. 'Goodnight, Monsieur.' He retreated down the ladder.

Chantal got up, too, picking up the lantern. 'Nothing you want?'

'No thanks. I'm feeling better.'

'We're going to take the ladder away and pile hay underneath. Search parties have been in St.Pierre today. We're

136

taking no chances. I'm leaving bread and cheese in case it's difficult for us to get back in the morning. Don't try to contact us. Wait for us to come to you. If you hear any sort of search, stay completely silent. Remember what would happen to us if you were found.' Chantal, previously the epitome of gentleness, was suddenly tough. Then she smiled. 'Be a good boy and you'll be all right. Goodnight. I'm leaving this bucket for you . . .'

He watched her walk to the ladder, skirt tightening over her hips as she held her dress to negotiate the narrow opening. For some reason he remembered the pathetic prostitute by the Seine. As a thought it made no sense at all. That girl had been thin and hungry, Chantal was rounded and well-fed. He must be light-headed again.

The ladder was taken, the trapdoor closed and for the next twenty minutes Chalmers heard activity beneath him. He was asleep before the barn fell silent.

It seemed he had barely shut his eyes when he was awoken by a cockerel heralding a new day. Distant cockerels responded. Clearer-headed now, he was conscious of the rhythm of the farm. A female voice – not Chantal, he would have recognised her – spoke to hens in the yard below and someone rattled a bucket; a dog barked in response to rivals across the valley; someone pumped water with a hand-pump; cows came in for milking; there were snatches of indecipherable female conversation and the clattering of crockery. The train was there again, distant but clear; a small local train, he hazarded. At one point he thought someone was coming to see him and was disappointed when he realised it was the horses being led out. Once more he drifted into sleep.

His dreams were troubled. He saw again the useless compass and the flaming engine. In some bizarre transposition he found himself in Freddie's rear turret, wounded, unable to get out, trusting the pilot – himself – to make a successful landing. Then he was with Beresford and Robertson, huddled behind the main spar, helplessly awaiting the impact. He had known they would get the chop one day, but had always played it down. As Skipper that was his job: to keep them going back for more. He had done it too well. Now he had been found out. They were dead and he was alive. He was back in the cockpit, mist drifting past, the plane swinging towards the trees.

He awoke, the depression of the dream hanging over him. He looked for his watch, then remembered it was broken and that Chantal had taken it. He felt hungry and wondered whether to start on the bread and cheese.

He was stretching for the cloth in which it was wrapped when he became aware of noises alien to a farmyard. Initially it was the sound of a lorry drawing up. Then a man's voice shouted in German and feet, feet booted and military, landed on the stone of the yard and scattered purposefully. Chalmers's German was not as good as his French, but he picked up the key words repeated by whoever was in charge. 'Schnell! Schnell! Kick it open if you have to.' There were other voices, too, speaking a language he did not recognise.

He lay back and looked up at the tiles. Another moment of truth. He would be found, Chantal and her family would be shot. His failure was total and there was nothing he could do. He closed his eyes and prayed. 'Help me, dear God. Help me.' That was selfish, a schoolboy's prayer. 'Sweet Jesus, keep us all safe.'

15

He lay completely still. He could hear his heart and felt that even the twitch of a muscle would draw attention to his presence.

Outside, sounds of the search drifted upwards. Someone was hitting something, perhaps a door, perhaps with the butt of a rifle. Someone else had kicked a door open. He heard it give way and swing on its hinges. *'Schnell! Schnell!'* repeated the guttural voice. Listening to the feet, he reckoned there were at least six men. A dog was barking.

A voice he recognised as Lejeune's spoke calmly: 'Nothing needs kicking, everything's open here. Stop fussing, woman.' This last shouted to someone indoors. An unknown female voice shouted at the dog: *'Tais-toi!'*

Lejeune moved away, but Chalmers could still hear him talking. The man he was speaking to, presumably the German in charge, responded in bad French. Lejeune was asking what they wanted and inviting a total inspection of his farm. His tone was at once conciliatory and brusque. 'Look where you like,' he said, 'but don't frighten the old man. He's in bed. He's an old bastard' – Chalmers heard him spit – 'but I don't want him dead yet. The doctor says he needs complete rest.' Lejeune, he realised, was something of an actor.

The voices faded, the search continued, feet moving in different directions, doors opening and shutting. Initially, they concentrated on the far side of the yard. Pigs squealed; the dog barked again and this time Lejeune shouted at it; someone knocked over a bucket. Then silence when they moved out of the yard.

Tentatively, Chalmers stretched for the bread and cheese. Hunger overcame the caution keeping him motionless. The bread was fresh, the cheese something unknown to him. Whatever it was, it was good. He was still eating when the sounds of search arrived beneath him. Boots, voices, stable doors opening and shutting.

'Full of hay,' said Lejeune. 'Right to the roof.'

'Put your bayonets on and stick them in,' said a German voice. 'He'll come out fast enough.'

Lejeune was encouraging. 'Go on, stick them in. Give it a good poking. The only person you'll find is Dupont's wife without her knickers. I found her here last week with the postman. The old fool married a woman half his age. *Imbécile.* Everyone told him. He only did it to get her two fields at St.Pierre.'

There was crude laughter from one of the Germans who understood French, then, after five minutes of noisy activity, they had gone. Eventually the searchers returned to their lorry which revved its engine in apparent frustration before leaving the yard.

When it had gone there was silence, broken only by the hens outside. He made an effort to sit up and it was easier than he had thought. His head was spinning again, but it was only momentary. The pain in the leg remained and the weight of the plaster drew attention to it. Easing himself forward on his bottom, he moved to the opening in the wall where the spider's web shimmered in the light. It was no more than a crack and he could see why it did not reveal the presence of a loft.

Pulling himself closer to the wall, he peered out. It was much as he had imagined. The farmyard was immediately below; to his right was the house, a substantial building of rough stone covered in creeper, its sun-bleached shutters closed against the heat; opposite was another barn, similar to the one he was in, with a rope and pulley tackle for lifting items from the yard and exterior steps to the top floor; to the left a rough track led out to an orchard. Chickens pecked below and one of the horses, tethered to a post on the far side, was drinking from a trough; a haycart stood beyond it, the shafts on the ground. In one corner an old plough and other rusty implements lay in a heap, weeds and nettles growing through them. Shadows from the house stretched across the yard. Butterflies flitted in the grass of the orchard.

The door of the house opened and an elderly woman in a black dress and dun-coloured apron came out carrying two buckets. Her hair was grey and drawn back in a bun; her face, also grey, was wrinkled and worn. She walked with measured tread to a water-pump a few yards from the door. Putting one bucket down, she adjusted the other beneath the spout. She took the handle and pumped until the bucket was full, then moved it and replaced it with the other. The action gave the impression of such weary repetition that she might have been doing it since the beginning of time. She picked up the buckets and went indoors. A black and white cat crept along the wall of the barn opposite. Chalmers could hear pigeons and thought he could see a *pigeonnier* above the trees of the orchard. He was feeling thirsty and wondered how long he would be left on his own. He leaned against the wall and closed his eyes.

He awoke some time later. Shadows had lengthened and it was cooler. Twilight was not far off. The door of the house opened and Chantal emerged carrying a basket in one hand and a jug in the other. He admired her straight back and the way her dark-blue peasant skirt swung as she walked. She vanished beneath him and he heard her shifting hay with a fork. Eventually the trapdoor opened, the ladder reappeared and her head emerged. She had put on lipstick and looked younger.

'I thought you'd forgotten me,' he said.

'They've gone.'

'You've been a long time.'

'We had to be sure. They're searching farms the other side of Mailly.'

'They sounded thorough.'

'They're always thorough. They went everywhere – except up here. The Cossacks tipped everything over in the old man's bedroom. I thought they were going to kill him when he swore at them.'

'Cossacks?'

'Russians. They joined the Germans and are used against the Resistance. They've got a camp near Saint-Florentin. One of them wanted to burn down all the farms within ten kilometres of Châtel-Censoir. The German NCO shut him up. You must stay here for the time being. Later we'll get you into the house. Easier for us. We shan't have to bring everything up here.'

'How did you get me here?'

'It was difficult.' She laughed at the memory. 'You were strapped onto a stretcher, Doctor Gambert tied that piece of wood to your broken leg and we hoped you wouldn't wake up while we were throwing you about. Fortunately you were unconscious. One of the men from St.Pierre thought you were dead. Said it would be easier to drop you in the river. I've got some food. You must be hungry.'

Chantal opened the basket and laid out on a white napkin what to Chalmers looked like a delicious picnic. There was fresh bread, butter, ham, more cheese, a jug of milk and a bottle of red wine. 'Farmers eat better than people in the towns. There's a big black market. We sell things like eggs on it. The Boches and Vichy take so much. You like wine?' she asked.

'I don't know much about it, but I like it.'

'It's a *vin ordinaire* from Lebrun over the river, but we all drink it. Probably the only vigneron in Burgundy who doesn't sell to the Germans.' Chantal was sitting in the hay with her arms round her knees. 'Do you know, the Hospices de Beaune gave one of their best vineyards to Marshal Pétain last year? It's been renamed Clos du Maréchal and had a fancy wall built round it. A lot of people are loyal to Pétain.'

'They'll look silly when the war's over.' He was eating hungrily.

'They thought Pétain did the right thing in 1940 – a lot of us did. Everyone let France down – the politicians, the army, the British. He was the old hero. What else could he do?'

'Strange to hear you say that. I thought the Resistance hated Vichy and all it stands for.'

'Things have changed. Vichy's collaborationist now, but Maman won't hear a word against the old man. She had two brothers at Verdun. They trust Pétain before De Gaulle. Laval's a different matter. And the *Milice* are appalling, even Maman agrees about that.'

'*Milice?*'

'Vichy police. The shame of France – traitors, scum. Dangerous to us, too, because they know more about France than the Germans. More likely to know when we're lying. There'll be a reckoning one day.'

'Isn't it difficult to have your mother's family sympathetic to Pétain?'

'Poor Maman's pulled in so many directions. She doesn't trust anyone. I had a brother, Robert. He was killed near Sedan when the Germans invaded. Her only son. She loathes the Germans. She's even prepared to think the English may help. She doesn't like the English much. Papa persuaded her we have to work with you. She said she would help the Resistance when she discovered Dr.Gambert was part of it. His son's a prisoner of war.'

'And you?'

'I admire the English for holding out when everybody else collapsed. I support De Gaulle, though I can see Pétain didn't have much choice. I loved Robert. He was a year older than me. When he was killed, I knew I'd do anything to get the Boches out. We're very complicated.' She smiled the ambiguous smile he had come to recognise in the short time he had known her.

'You spoke English to begin with. Where did you learn it?'

'Convent school in Auxerre. One of the nuns was English and gave lessons to anyone who wanted to learn.'

'You speak well.'

'Not as well as you speak French. We'll stick to that.'

He poured some wine, but felt awkward that she was not drinking. 'Didn't you bring two glasses?'

'No.'

'Share mine. I don't like drinking on my own. Tell me about your family.'

'She took the proffered glass and had a sip. 'There you are. You have most of it. There's my sister, Marguerite – she's younger than me. Robert would have inherited La Rippe. She showed no obvious emotion, but the muscles in her face tightened. 'You joined the RAF straight away?'

'I was up at Oxford. Most of my year volunteered when we saw what was happening. I was already learning to fly.'

'I would have liked to go to university. Not many women do in France. My English nun wanted me to try – she saw I liked reading and music and said I had a brain. But I was expected to help on the farm, even more so when Robert was called up for the army. Like most farming families, the land's everything.'

'Who's the old lady in black pumping water?'

'It's a long story.'

'I'm not going anywhere.' He smiled, picked up his plastered leg and moved it to a more comfortable position.

'You're able to laugh at yourself.'

'Tell me about the old woman.'

'My grandfather married late. He had two children – my father, Jacques, and his brother, Maurice. Maurice is a bachelor, he lives here – and is a bit simple. My grandmother died when Maurice was born, so my grandfather needed help with the children, particularly when it was clear Maurice was backward. He hired a woman from the village to live in, look after them and clean the house. She was just a servant.'

Chalmers noted the apparent contempt of 'just a servant' and recalled how badly his mother's friends treated their servants at the château near Avignon. He liked Chantal and felt a pang of disappointment. Something must have shown on his face, because she stopped. 'Go on,' he said.

'I thought you were going to say something.'

'No, I was beginning to be interested.'

'Well, Célestine – that's her name – Célestine was a woman in trouble. She'd had an illegitimate child who died after only a few weeks. Her chances of marriage in a respectable village were thin. So she came here, cleaned the house and looked after the children. But she was a good-looking woman and grandfather was lonely. After a while she became something more than a housekeeper, if you see what I mean. She would have liked him to marry her, but he'd had enough of marriage with my grandmother – she had a fiendish temper – and he wasn't going to be hooked again. They did a sort of deal. Bed – his bed – the two boys, housekeeping. No marriage, no dowry, but a house for life. She was a poor woman with no prospects and it must have seemed reasonable. They stuck to the bargain. He's not well now, but she nurses him and works about the house. The boys grew up and they have a sort of affection for her because she looked after them. But she was always a servant, never one of the family. Papa married Maman young – an arranged marriage really. Célestine stayed on and worked for everyone, helping my mother when we were born. Grandfather's treated her worse since he's been ill and more dependent on her. Maurice is closest to her as she's always done so much for him. The rest of us take her for granted. She and Maman don't always get on. She resented Maman taking things over. All very natural.'

'Very French.'

'Probably. But things happen in England, too. I've read about them.'

'Not in Wimbledon.' He looked at her puzzled face. 'That's a joke, an English joke. Tell me about Marguerite.'

'Marguerite works in the dairy with Maman when she's not helping at a shop in Mailly. Butter, cheese, cream. I do most of it. I ought to be there now. You've lured me away.' She stood up, brushing off hay in a way he was coming to recognise as characteristic. Her features seemed to have softened since he first saw them.

He pulled a face and grimaced as pain cut through the bruising. 'I shall be lonely.'

'Enough to eat?'

'Marvellous. I haven't thanked you properly. The wine's like nectar. Bring another glass next time.'

Chantal closed the trapdoor over her head and negotiated the ladder carefully. For the first time she saw that Chalmers was different from the others. Up to now he had been a problem, an unexpected problem to be dealt with kindly and expediently, but a distinctly temporary problem. Now she wondered. The fact that he spoke French fluently was entirely new and – she had to admit it – she was attracted physically. She had had men friends, but this man was different.

Chalmers was sorry to see her go. He wondered whether this was disloyal to Mary. He longed for Mary. He lay down, shut his eyes, and went back to the night at the Royal Charles when they had slept together and explored each other's bodies. He wanted to be with her, to laugh with her, to show he could be the sort of man she wanted. He detected she found it hard to believe she had fallen for someone really reliable. What innocents they had been. *Were*. He must get the tense right.

He stretched to where Chantal had put a small pile of belongings from his pockets. Aircrew flew with few personal items and he never took his main wallet, but he had an old one and in it there was a photo of Mary that never left him. He pulled it out. It was a simple shot taken one sunny evening after a picnic near East Kirkby. She sat under a tree, her skirt spread round her. Auburn hair framed her face – partially in shade because he was not a good photographer – a face radiant with happiness. Her features, regular, yes, but intensely individual, had relaxed into a smile of warmth and love he wanted to preserve for ever. What was she doing? She would jump to the worst conclusion. Positive she might be, but she was also realistic: she had seen too many men not come back to have illusions. He saw the chalk writing on the squadron operation board: *Z-Zebra: F/O Chalmers – Missing*.

He finished the ham, had another drink of wine and lay back. For the first time his mind was working normally. Part of him was back at Wynton Thorpe, holding Mary, loving Mary, asking mundane questions, wondering what Palmer had done with the cheque. But none of that was real. Reality was here in France. He had a broken leg, he was lying in a bed of hay dependent on strangers taking enormous risks on his behalf. Reality was a sick headache, pain running up through his body if he moved too quickly. He was drifting off again. *The Magic Flute* was never far away. Earth, air, fire and water. He had promised to take Mary to an opera. That's what it would be. She would enjoy the drama, and she'd love the Queen of the Night. He could tell her about the strange way it had crept up on him. Then he thought of Stafford and the others, particularly young Les Ricketts. 'Don't worry Mrs Ricketts, I'll make sure he comes home in one piece. He's a good lad.' They'd trusted him and he had failed. He saw the butterfly in the web. 'Corkscrew port.' A Lancaster coned by searchlights disintegrated in a monstrous explosion. Twisted bodies, burnt bodies, lay in depressions made by their fall from a great height. The disconnected alleyways of his mind were full of pictures.

He was woken by a car driving into the yard. It was dark. Its lights flashed briefly on the tiles above his head before being turned out. Its doors shut quietly. Chalmers felt more alert than at any time since the crash. When its engine stopped there was silence, followed by voices. A door opened and shut. He sat up and manoeuvred himself to the crack in the wall. There was light in two of the downstairs windows of the house, but the curtains were drawn. The sky was cloudless and he looked up at the stars. The last time he'd looked at them he was struggling to plot a course north-west. He recalled twisting his head, the vibration of the control column, the silver river snaking away from him, the mist in the valley, the burning engine, and the relief when he saw the patch of flat land. Why should a car arrive in the middle of the night?

He was dozing off when one of the horses beneath him whinnied. He jerked awake in time to see the door of the house open, light spilling into the yard. Three men came out, one of whom he recognised as Gambert. Lejeune stood in the doorway in his shirtsleeves, a candle on the table behind him. He raised a hand in farewell before closing the door. The three got into the car, turned on the lights and pulled quietly out of the yard. The whole effect was of conspiracy, secrecy.

Curiosity was growing in step with physical recovery. The depression brought on by the death of his crew was still there – it would never lift – but he knew he was at the centre of something he did not understand. Why had they been in the fields? What was going on? His talk with Chantal had made him aware he had only a simplistic, one-dimensional view of events in France. Now the search was over he was going to ask questions. He worked his way back to his flattened patch of hay and lay down. In the roof roosting birds settled down after the disturbance in the yard.

He had no idea of time, but pictures formed and reformed in his head, the exhausting form of waking dream experienced earlier. Mary was with him, but he could not see her face. He was meeting her father, a grey man looking like Lejeune, wearing a dog collar. When he said he wanted to marry Mary, he looked doubtful. Someone was reading *Bredon Hill* aloud:

'They tolled the one bell only,
Groom was there none to see,
The mourners followed after,

And so to church went she,
And would not wait for me.'

Yet he was in a church and Mary was there somewhere. Freddie Shorthouse, poor ugly Freddie, was in a front pew with an arm round a big blonde. The rest of his crew were there, but he could not see them. In a pew at the back were the women from the café, one wearing the hat with the pheasant's feather. Through a window he saw Arthur Palmer arriving in the M.G. He was waving a cheque. The landlord of the White Hart, stomach held in place by his belt, was in the pulpit. 'And what is your pleasure this evening, gentlemen?' Somehow he transmogrified into Dr Gambert, washing his hands in a bucket. Chantal was there, too. Sleeves rolled up, scrubbing a table, back straight, skirt swinging. Then he saw Mary. She was giving an apple to a horse. It coughed. Beneath him one of the horses snorted and shifted its feet.

He opened his eyes: the moonlight had moved. Eventually, he fell asleep.

16

Chantal Lejeune undressed quickly and slipped into bed. Around the room heavy oak furniture reflected moonlight. It had been a tiring day and there was sensuous pleasure in stretching out in the cool sheets. But her mind was not as relaxed as her body and ideas chased each other as she adjusted to a comfortable sleeping position. The search had been tense, but it had happened before and she was reasonably confident the loft was safe. In any case there was no reason for the Germans to suspect them: they had merely been sweeping the area, covering every farm. Her father's caution had been extreme from the start; there was nothing to link them to other groups.

She looked out at the moon and the outline of the distant woods. Tired, yes, and tense, but that was not the thought at the forefront of her mind. It was something to do with the Englishman. The fact that he spoke French was interesting and certainly different from the others. It was, she decided, as her mind drifted on the edge of sleep, his helplessness, his dependence. She thought of the pale limbs she had washed, the vivid bruises on his shoulders and face, and the leg she had helped to plaster. But it was more than that. It was the way he had drawn her out in conversation and the way she had responded. She had not discussed her mother's sympathy for Pétain or her own education at the convent with the others. She had fed them, too, but none of them had wanted her to share his meal. 'Didn't you bring two glasses?' Chalmers had asked. And his name. She had eventually discovered the names of the others, but she had asked James almost immediately.

She opened her eyes and glimpsed cloud edging over the moon. Then she realised what had pulled them close. The fate of his crew. Their first exchange when he was barely conscious, almost before he knew where he was, had forced her to reveal the truth. He had asked because it was his prime concern; she had been honest because that was her nature. She could have prevaricated, waited until he had recovered. Instead she had told the truth, a truth bringing tears to his eyes. Her sympathy for this helpless man as he faced the implication of what had happened had removed barriers. When she saw him next it was natural to fall into personal conversation. She shifted her head on the pillow and fell asleep.

Her sleep was dreamless. She woke once. Something roused the dog in the yard – a fox perhaps – and he barked briefly and loud enough to wake her. She did not open her eyes, but for a few moments her mind was in gear and in those seconds she thought again of Chalmers. It was not that he was particularly handsome – he was just like many men, firmly moulded, masculine, normal. She sensed the strength of a leader of men, but he was in her care and he was happy to depend on her. She stretched and within seconds was asleep again. The storm that broke later did not disturb her at all.

***

Jacques Lejeune, too, had a good night's sleep, before being woken by the rain and thunder. He never thought the search would unearth anything and they had no reason to suspect La Rippe. He had cultivated contacts with Germans in both Auxerre and Clamecy and knew he was not on any list. But whatever the precautions, chance was the ultimate arbiter. It would only have needed a sharp-eyed searcher to notice the crack in the wall. His father was useful: bad-tempered with illness he had acted as a lightning conductor, swearing at the intruders, drawing attention to the house rather than the barns.

More concerning was the news brought by Gambert, Georges and Henri. They had all been there the night of the crash and it was a badly timed visit so soon after the search. But they had known nothing of it and needed to speak to Lejeune urgently. Georges ran a bar by the river and rumour had reached him about arrests in Clamecy and Quarré-les-Tombes. Links with these groups were minimal and he was not concerned that suspicion would endanger them, but they were part of the chain dealing with Allied airmen and if they had been discovered there would be nowhere to send his latest arrival. Once his leg had healed they wanted to send him on his way like the others. Lejeune and Gambert had plans for the development of their group which would be handicapped by the long-term presence of an English pilot. Georges had good news, too. The Germans had lifted their roadblocks and assumed their quarry had drowned in the Yonne.

Lejeune had gone to bed some time after his wife Marie and she was up before him. When he woke she was sitting in front of her dressing-table in her blue dressing-gown. Dark-haired, with mature, still-attractive features, she was doing things to her face. 'You were late last night,' she said.

'Gambert came – and Georges and Henri. Something's happened at Clamecy. Georges picked it up from a bargee. The abbey, too, if the rumour's right.'

'Storm last night,' said his wife. 'Dying away now.' Outside a distant rumble of thunder confirmed her words.

'Chantal can find out. She must go to Clamecy.'

'They don't know anything about us, do they?' said Marie, starting to brush her hair. 'You've always said…'

'Nothing at all. Stop fussing.'

'I was worried about the old man. I thought the Cossacks would kill him.'

Lejeune sat up, scratching himself and feeling the stubble on his chin. 'The Boche N.C.O. had them under control. The old man helped, though he didn't know it.'

'Célestine was worried.'

'She loves him. You've never allowed for that.' Lejeune sat on the edge of the bed and tightened the cord on his pyjama trousers before standing up and scratching again.

'She takes advantage. She's a servant.'

'She won't forget.' Lejeune lit a cigarette and inhaled deeply before expelling a cloud of smoke. His mind was elsewhere. 'We must get him into the house. Whatever's happened at Clamecy we can't get rid of him with a broken leg and we can't keep moving the hay. He can have Robert's room. The Boches won't come back.' He started to dress, pulling on a rough shirt and working trousers.

'When do you want Chantal to go?'

'This afternoon. She's too busy this morning – and the pilot's got to be fed. We can't trust Maurice to do that and Marguerite's needed at the shop. Maurice will do the animals, I'll get the milk to the station and you can do the cheese and cream for Châtel-Censoir. Everything normal.'

'Célestine can help me.' Marie, stood up. 'And she can get Robert's room ready. You're sure it's safe?'

He grimaced. 'Important none of the locals know – at least for the time being. Keep him away from windows. Gambert'll get him fit and we'll get rid of him. We'll pass him on unless the chain's gone. Gambert has the excuse to come to see to the old man.' Lejeune went across to his wife and put a rough hand on her shoulder. 'Trust me.'

'I do.' She took his hand and held it against her cheek. It was a solid marriage and they had grown close over the years. He kept details of Resistance away from her to protect her. She in turn did not ask awkward questions. 'Safe for Chantal?' she asked.

'She's a sensible girl. Takes after her mother.'

'She was as upset about Robert as we were. They were close. Closer than Marguerite.'

'She's younger. A good girl – takes after her mother, too.

She'll help with anything, but I'm going to keep her clear of this other business. I don't want her involved. Not yet.'

'We're all involved. One false move and they'll shoot us all. How soon can we get rid of this man?'

'Chantal will find out.'

'And if the line's gone?'

'There are other lines. I'll find something.' Lejeune had moved close to his wife again. 'Don't worry. I'm looking after you . . . after all of us. Come on. Chantal doesn't know she's going to Clamecy. Célestine doesn't know she's working in the dairy. And we've got to feed the Englishman – he doesn't know anything.'

'Interesting he speaks French.'

'Chantal likes him.'

'Did she say anything about Jean-Claude? She never says much about her men friends.'

'You want to marry her off. We need her on the farm.'

'If she married the right man, he could work on the farm too.'

'Jean-Claude wouldn't be any use. *Pouf!* Doesn't know a cow from a sheep. Besides, you've always talked about marrying money. You thought that man Picard from Paris might interest her. She didn't like him.'

'She only saw him once. Anyway, the war's altered everything.' Marie returned her husband's touch on the arm. 'I miss Robert.'

Jacques did not respond at once. His craggy face fell into the lines of despair Marie remembered when the news came. 'I miss Robert, too. I think of him more than I talk about him. You do the same.'

'Never let us down. Or himself.' She felt for his hand as they shared the bond of unhappiness. 'That was a terrible day.' She looked out of the window. 'Do you know what Madam Morelle said last week? She's an insensitive woman.'

'What?'

'She said Chantal's a good match now' – she paused – 'now she hasn't got a brother.'

'She's an old witch. And full of envy. The Morelles have been envious of our land for years. They've always wanted our field by the canal. The old man made sure they didn't get it. He wouldn't give up an inch of land – and nor would I. One reason you married me.'

'She's married off four daughters.'

Outside a cockerel was crowing and there came the sound of the pump as Célestine collected the first water of the day. Lejeune tightened a thick belt round his waist and made for the door. 'I'm going to see the Englishman.'

The farm normally had a pace of its own, established round the rhythm of the seasons, the demands of the animals and the local markets. Today Marie sensed an unusual urgency and wondered what the presence of a visitor in the house would mean. She dressed quickly and went down to the kitchen where Célestine had already prepared *le petit déjeuner*.

17

Chalmers was woken by the sound of rain and thunder. The horses below stirred uneasily. Eventually the storm died away and he lay on his back, looking at the tiles above, listening to the final drops of rain. He moved gingerly, testing the points of pain. A door opened and he followed someone's progress from the house into the stable. He thought it was Chantal and was disappointed when Lejeune's head appeared.

'Good morning, Monsieur. You slept?'

Chalmers pulled himself into a sitting position. 'Yes, thank you.' He could not stop himself saying: 'I heard a car.'

'Ah.' Lejeune remained with his head through the trapdoor. His eyes, sharply appraising, flicked over Chalmers. 'Ah, yes.' There was a distant rumble of thunder. 'I have good news. No road-blocks. They think you drowned.'

'How do you know?'

'Girl with a Wehrmacht boy friend in Coulanges. Keeps us informed.'

'Us?'

'There's bad news, too. I'll tell you in the house. Gambert says we can move you. More convenient for us – and for you. I've brought these.' He threw over a pair of battered slippers.

Their eyes met. Chalmers detected a degree of warmth for the first time. 'I hope it won't be too difficult,' he said.

'Gambert's coming back, my brother will help – and so will Chantal. That's enough.'

Lejeune had still not shaved. It made Chalmers conscious of his own growth of beard. He was meticulous about shaving.

The prospect of hot water and a proper wash was attractive. Thinking about meeting other members of the household, he looked down at his leg and the pyjamas torn to accommodate the plaster. 'Have you any clothes?' he asked.

'My son's clothes – Chantal told you about Robert – some will fit. You'll have his room.' The brusqueness was there again. 'I'll be back later.' His head vanished.

It was encouraging that the doctor considered him well enough to move, even more so that the Germans had given up their search. But bad news, too. He lay back, feeling his bruises. The spider, its web damaged by the escaping butterfly, was carrying out repairs. It was raining again.

The morning passed. The rain stopped and the sun came out. Again the sounds of the farm: a cockerel crowed, cows were milked, chickens fed, horses led out. He heard Chantal's voice and others he did not recognise. He wondered if the farm employed anyone apart from the family. He could see it was more substantial than a simple peasant farm. Some way off, a church bell tolled. What was that? Then he remembered. The Angelus. He had played cricket against Downside, the Catholic public school in Somerset. At noon the Angelus sounded from the abbey and the Downside team stopped whatever they were doing and doffed their caps. For a batsman it was disconcerting to find a bowler halting half-way through his run-up. Now it was strangely reassuring to have a point of reference in a foreign land. The Millet painting, *The Angélus*, came to mind: a farm worker and peasant woman standing in a field reverently recognising the moment as the noontide bell tolls across a bleak landscape. Sentimental? Certainly, but memorable, too. Why else remember it now? And another picture. Millet again, *The Water Carrier*: a peasant woman in clogs carrying buckets of water exactly like Célestine in the yard. He felt transported back to nineteenth-century rural France.

Shortly afterwards a car came into the yard and he heard Gambert. He thought this might lead to an immediate visit, but the doctor went into the house and he had to wait a further ten minutes before voices came in his direction. Lejeune appeared first, followed by another grey-haired, unshaven man in a beret. He was a heavier version of Lejeune, with a more prominent nose, thicker lips and watchful, childlike eyes. He carried a rope but did not speak.

'My brother, Maurice,' said Lejeune. 'We're going to get you down.'

Chalmers found himself speaking as though in an English drawing room. 'I hope I'm not being too much trouble.'

Gambert, who had remained at the top of the ladder, took charge. 'Get yourself over here. We'll put a rope round you and lower you through the hole.' His head disappeared and the ladder was taken away.

Sitting in the hay, Chalmers looked up at the Lejeune brothers. They were wearing identical boots, black, stained and weathered, the comfortable boots of countrymen. Without speaking, Maurice Lejeune took the rope, put it round his chest twice, under his arms, and secured a knot behind him. His brother checked it. Feeling the tightening knot, Chalmers imagined a hangman's noose. He looked up at them, toyed with the idea of a joke then thought better of it.

He looked down. Gambert and Chantal were immediately beneath, staring upwards. 'Put your feet into the hole . . . gently, gently,' said the doctor. 'Make sure the plastered leg's well clear of everything. Now don't worry. You've got two strong men there.'

Chalmers eased his legs into the hole and sat on the edge. It reminded him of simulated parachute jumps. The Lejeunes took the strain and he let himself go, dropping slowly through a tunnel of hay towards Gambert and Chantal. When he reached them, the doctor took his weight, pulling him backwards, while Chantal held the injured leg as he sank into the hay. 'I'd rather bale out than do that again,' he said.

Chantal was dressed for going out, wearing a fresh white blouse and flowered skirt. She lowered his leg gently while

Gambert undid the rope and reached across to one of the stalls to pick up a pair of wooden crutches. Worn leather, polished by previous patients, covered the supports under the arms.

'I got them back from Monsieur Pouget yesterday – the baker in St.Pierre. Broke his leg falling off his delivery cart out at Sery. His horse bolted, frightened by a low-flying Luftwaffe aircraft. James, isn't it?'

'Yes.'

'I'm Jean. Better than too much formality. You're going to be here some time.'

'Right – Jean.' Chalmers found it difficult to call a doctor by his Christian name, particularly one to whom he owed his life.

Gambert and the Lejeunes watched as Chalmers took his first tentative steps.

'I'll soon get the hang of this,' he said, then nearly toppled over and had to hang on to the open door. 'Blast!' he exclaimed.

'*Merde* is better,' laughed Gambert, who had some English.

Chalmers readjusted the crutches and tried again. This time he made it through the door into the yard. The air was lighter after the storm; here and there damp stonework steamed in the heat of the sun. He looked upwards at the barn and could hardly see the crack where the light went in and the spider laboured for its prey. No wonder the Germans had missed it.

'Well done, Monsieur.' Lejeune was encouraging.

Chantal put a hand on his shoulder in a spontaneous gesture. 'You must be hungry. I've done something special.'

'I'm hungry all right. I thought you'd forgotten me. What have you done?'

'*Coq au vin*. You'll only get it at a farm these days. Let's find some clothes.'

'Not *le coq* I heard this morning?' he said.

'No, he's safe for the time being.' She held the door and Chalmers hobbled into the kitchen, which opened immediately onto the yard. The room was warm and dark. One wall was filled by a heavy oak dresser with ornate china plates and an ancient pair of scales. Opposite, a kettle steaming on it, was a black, wood-burning stove. A smoothing iron stood on its iron-rest. The table in the centre of the room, damp from a scrubbing, was covered with cooking pots. In a corner onions hung from a wooden beam. An open pantry door revealed slate shelves and a pair of rabbits hanging from a hook. Oil lamps and candles confirmed what he suspected: the farm had no electricity. There was a strong smell of cooking.

Chantal saw him glance at the onions. 'There was ham there, too. We hide it now. The Germans would take it.'

He paused to enjoy the aroma and to lean on the table. Crutches were more difficult than he had imagined. As he did so, Célestine came in from an inner room. She was just as he had seen her before, wearing the faded black dress with its skirt only inches off the ground. She must be, he thought, in her late seventies. He was reminded of Millet's peasant faces, tired, grey, devoid of hope. For a moment he thought Chantal was going to ignore her. To his relief she introduced him.

'Célestine – Flying Officer Chalmers – James. He's going into Robert's room.'

Chalmers propped himself on a single crutch and held out his hand. '*Madame – enchanté.*'

Célestine did not speak, but held out her hand and inclined her head.

'I've put some of Robert's clothes on the bed I think will fit,' said Chantal. 'Bring them down and he can get dressed.' It was apparent that Célestine had not been included in discussions and was surprised to see Chalmers in the house. 'We'll be in the sitting room. He can change there.'

Célestine's only comment was 'I'll lay another place.'

Gambert stuck his head round the door. 'I'm going. I'll look in tomorrow.'

Chantal turned to Chalmers. 'We're eating in the front room. Normally we have meals in the orchard when it's hot, but we can't take risks. Come through.'

They went into the dining room. The windows looking onto the orchard were open, but it was a claustrophobic room with more nineteenth-century furniture. There were heavy maroon curtains and walls covered with family photographs. A cross, black with an ivory figure, occupied a central position between two of the larger photographs. The table was laid for lunch. Chantal opened another door, ushering him into a dark room where the shutters were closed.

Célestine reappeared carrying clothes. 'Robert was near your size. Don't know about the shoes.'

'We'll leave you,' said Chantal. She was aware of Célestine's coldness and felt protective. 'Shout if you want help. Marguerite and Maman will be here in a minute. Maman's in the dairy, Marguerite's been at the shop in Mailly. I'll look at *le coq*.'

Chalmers put the crutches to one side and sat down. Automatically he picked up the socks and put them on. He remembered the M.O. at Wynton saying he could always tell a public school man because he put his socks on first and took them off last. Chalmers had replied, 'Absolutely essential. Nothing but bare boards or cold lino in any dormitory I've known.' He worked his way upwards. The underclothes were big and shapeless, but shirt and trousers fitted pretty well. To his relief, the shoes were a near perfect fit. He left the jacket as it was so hot.

There was a mirror over the fireplace and he staggered across to look at himself. His right eye was surrounded by red, black and yellow bruising that ran down the side of his swollen, unshaven face. His eyes were bloodshot as though he had had a night on the town. Perhaps for the first time he realised how lucky he had been.

'May I come in?' Chantal knocked on the door.

'I'm decent,' he replied. 'Though I can't see that it matters after you've nursed me. I'm not coy.'

'I don't want you to think French girls are forward. I've read books. Some say Englishmen came to France before the war to meet girls.'

'Don't believe everything you read.' He felt a twinge of guilt. 'You're all dressed up.'

'I'm going to Clamecy. Half an hour on the train from St.Pierre.'

'Is that the train I heard ?'

'Yes. It goes through Châtel-Censoir. I may see your plane.'

'I hope you don't.'

'Why?'

'It reminds me of the others. If I'd managed it better, they'd still be alive – all of them. They were my friends. Why are you going to Clamecy?'

'Papa wants me to go.' She looked away, ashamed she had touched a sensitive nerve.

'To buy something? Sorry – nothing to do with me.'

'As a matter of fact it is. I've a school friend there who'll know more than we do about what's going on. Marguerite and Maman will be here in a minute. Marguerite thought you wouldn't live. I told her you would.'

'How did you know?'

Chantal shrugged. An observer would have said she was flirting. Her eyes were wide, the hint of a smile played about her lips. Chalmers fiddled with the belt round his trousers, trying to tighten it. As he did so, he heard voices in the kitchen.

'They're here,' said Chantal. She shouted: 'We're in the parlour. James is down.'

They came in and Chantal introduced them. Marie Lejeune, short, Mediterranean-looking, wore a blue blouse, matching blue cotton skirt and sensible shoes. Marguerite was also dark, with bright, dancing eyes. She wore the plain green dress she kept for working in the shop. Prettier than Chantal was Chalmers's first impression and probably less responsible. She looked about twenty. Her hair had been blown out behind her on her bike ride from Mailly.

'Worse than we thought,' said Lejeune, who followed them in.

'Leave it till food's on the table,' said his wife, leading the way back to the dining-room.

Maurice Lejeune, who had been waiting by the door, sat down clumsily, his guarded eyes suggesting events were moving too fast for him. He had the habit of licking his lips and from time to time chuckling as though appreciating a private joke. The others paid no attention. Célestine put a steaming pot in front of Marie Lejeune. It was apparent that in domestic matters Marie was the key figure. Chalmers could see why she and Célestine did not always hit it off. Célestine waited now while Marie filled a plate for the old man upstairs. When it was ready, she took it up, eventually returning and taking her place at the bottom of the table next to Maurice.

By the time she was back Marie had served everyone. She nodded approvingly at Chantal. 'It smells good,' she said. 'You should cook more often.' She wiped her hands on a napkin and looked at her husband. 'Now, what's the news?'

'Bad. Georges picked up rumours from the bargees at *Les Pêcheurs* – and Gambert's heard things too. Arrests at Clamecy and Quarré-les-Tombes. And they've searched the abbey. The line's been broken.'

'The Englishmen?'

'What Englishmen?' asked Chalmers, involuntarily.

Lejeune did not respond at immediately, carefully cutting meat on his plate before consigning it to his mouth. The light caught the stubble on his chin, showing flecks of grey. He looked at his wife. 'We don't know.' To Chalmers he said: 'We weren't going to tell you. Safer that way. What you don't know, you can't tell.'

'Of course. Totally understood. Very sensible.' Chalmers sensed the rebuke.

Lejeune's mood was dark. 'But if you're going to be here any length of time, there are things I'll have to tell you. We don't know who's been arrested because we don't know names. Simple security. They don't know ours either. Chantal's going to Clamecy.'

'Isn't that dangerous?'

'Less dangerous than anyone else going. Nothing suspicious about a visit to a school friend. And it's easier for women to move about. A lot of couriers are women.'

Maurice spoke for the first time. 'I want to go to Clamecy.'

'Not today, Maurice.' Marie was firm.

'I want to go on the train.' His voice was on a monotone, like a deaf man.

'You've got to plough the upper field. Remember? You said you'd do it this afternoon.'

'I like the train.'

'Another time,' said his brother, as though to a child. 'There'll be another time.'

Maurice grunted and looked disappointed. Célestine touched his hand. Marguerite gave him a sympathetic smile. Chalmers was picking up the nuances of family life, realising how backward Maurice was. Unaccountably he was laughing again. 'I like the train,' he said.

Lejeune ignored him. 'I told you there is Resistance here,' he said. 'It's always difficult for the government in the Yonne – right through history. The Boches know they've got a problem. Too many hills, too much forest, too few roads. Some villages haven't seen a German since the invasion. We had an escape line for British and American fliers. It may have gone. You could be stuck here now even if you hadn't broken your leg.' He took a piece of bread and mopped up juice from his plate. He looked at Célestine. 'How's the old man?'

'Better than yesterday. He had a good night. He tired himself shouting at the Cossacks. He was waiting for lunch – thought it was supper.'

Lejeune looked again at his wife. 'Any news?'

'Anna Masson had her baby last night – another girl. That's

her fifth. Claude's upset and blames the curé. He more or less promised a boy after the fourth. Anna persuaded Claude to give money to the church on the strength of it.'

'More fool him. I wouldn't give a penny to a priest.'

'You're prejudiced. You always have been when it comes to priests. I'm surprised you came to church to marry me.'

'We all make mistakes, Marie.' Lejeune smiled at his wife with a warmth giving a good indication of the strength of their marriage.

Marguerite was laughing. 'I'm not going to get married. I don't want any babies.'

'No one will have you,' said her father.

'There won't be any young men if the Boches take them all to Germany for forced labour. You won't have a choice.' This was her mother.

'So much for your precious Pétain,' said Lejeune.

Marie shrugged. 'What else could he have done?'

'He's living with the consequences – and that means collaboration. He's a foolish old man, if not a wicked one. Vichy's lined up with the Boches.'

Chalmers looked round the table. Chantal caught his eye. This argument had been going on a long time and she knew each step. Marguerite, who had sparked it off, was not listening. Célestine was silent in a world of her own.

Maurice spoke: 'I want to go on the train.'

Chantal welcomed the interruption. 'Next time, Uncle. I promise.'

'I got proper coffee from Madame Lousteau. First time this month,' said Marie.

'What are we giving her?'

'Eggs. Next week.'

'Bartering,' said Lejeune, looking at Chalmers. 'We're in a stronger position than most.'

The meal continued with similar disjointed conversation. Chalmers wondered how far his presence was inhibiting them or whether it was normal. Chantal looked at her watch. 'I must go,' she said, 'if I'm going to catch the 2.30.' She got up. 'Wish me luck.'

She left the room with her father. When he came back, he signalled to Chalmers to go into the parlour. His wife and Marguerite were discussing a hat in a magazine. Célestine was clearing the table, putting the chicken bones into a bowl to make soup.

'I'll plough the upper field,' said Maurice. He spoke normally and stood up, brushing away crumbs.

Lejeune joined Chalmers in the parlour and indicated the largest chair. 'That's the most comfortable.'

Chalmers positioned himself clumsily, put the crutches to one side and lowered himself into the chair. Chalmers saw for the first time that Lejeune's eyes were more than watchful and suspicious. They were intelligent. He wondered what he was going to say.

For his part Lejeune had also been carrying out character assessment. And he had taken a decision.

18

The heat was building up again. Chalmers wiped a handkerchief over his forehead, but did not take his eyes off Lejeune. He was beginning to feel trusted. He knew he was a problem, but guessed the fact that he spoke French gave him an advantage not shared by his predecessors.

'We only had the others a couple of nights. You could be here some time.'

'Not just my leg?'

'Not just your leg.'

'If it's not safe for you, I'll go.'

'You could be useful.' Lejeune changed tack. 'You understand about my brother?'

'It must be difficult.'

'We look after him – and we can't let him know much.'

'What does he understand?'

'He knows Robert was killed and he doesn't like the Germans. He knows we have secrets. He's never said a word about the RAF men we've had here. He can't be involved in anything. He wasn't in the field when we picked you up. He's good with the animals. He ploughs the straightest furrow on the farm.'

'Tell me about the escape line?'

'We think it's broken. We've had three men. The next link was at Clamecy. We'll know when Chantal gets back. We're stuck with you.' There was the hint of a farmer's smile.

It was a relief to know humour was part of his make-up. Chalmers said: 'There are other groups?'

'The communists are strong in Laroche-Migennes – a

167

junction on the main line south from Paris. Trains change engines there. They made the first trouble in the Yonne. The Gestapo moved in – plenty of arrests, innocent and guilty. Locals weren't pleased they'd stirred things up. There's been more trouble in the Morvan since the forced labour decree. Men have gone into the forest. We help feed some of them.'

'Why were you in the fields when we came down?'

'That's where you could be helpful.'

'How?'

'It depends what happened at Clamecy. There are two Englishmen. They're in touch with London. London wants to send supplies – arms, explosives. They want a dropping place for a *parachutage*. Gambert thought those fields might do. What do you think?'

'From a flying point of view, they'd do well. The river's clear from the air and it's easy to approach down the valley. Would it be safe on the ground? What about the Germans?'

'We can trust the local owners and some will help. There are woods to hide things, separate tracks out, and the road's the other side of the river. Difficult for the Germans to get at even if they realised something was going on. There aren't many nearer than Auxerre. A few are billeted in St.Bris and Coulanges, but there's nothing to take them out into the country. And the girls who go with them have enough sense to keep their mouths shut. There are patrols, but they're predictable. Until your plane came down they hadn't been to Châtel-Censoir for two months.'

'Anti-aircraft batteries?'

'By the railway station in Auxerre. More at Migennes. Nothing nearer. They were in action last month when there was a raid on the junction. Didn't hit anything.'

'Have you got a map?'

'I'll get it.' Lejeune left the room.

Chalmers put his hand up to the bruising on his face. The mere thought that he might be valuable was encouraging. He detected the change in Lejeune and was warming to the man. Up to now he had been cold, detached, coping with an unexpected problem. Since coming into the house, Chalmers almost felt welcomed.

Lejeune returned, bringing a well-used map of the Yonne. His finger, coarsely grained with physical work, pointed. 'That's where you came down – near Châtel-Censoir. We're here at La Rippe. Follow the river and the railway' – the finger plotted a course – 'and you come to Auxerre. Over here is Migennes where the Reds are.'

'That's miles away. A plane could approach from the south without going anywhere near it. Nothing down here?'

'Nothing. No Germans, hardly any French. Hills and forest for miles. One of the Englishmen said we'd need lights. Cars, torches – or fires. And he wanted measurements. That's what we were doing when you appeared. Could a plane get in there?'

'You couldn't get a Lancaster down. Not with me flying it, anyway.' Their eyes met again, Lejeune conscious of the bitterness behind his remark. 'A Lysander, perhaps.'

'What's that?'

'Small high-wing monoplane. Short landing and take-off. Special services use them for bringing people to France and taking them out. How did the Englishmen get here?'

'Parachute. Dropped near Lormes. There are other Maquis groups there.'

'Is there often mist?'

'Sometimes in summer.'

'Are the fields really flat? I'd need to see them. Is the ground firm or wet? What about the grass? Could you get any trees down?'

Lejeune almost broke into a smile; Chalmers recognised the expression he had seen in Chantal's face at the end of the tunnel before he was fully conscious. 'You'll see for yourself. Then we'll try to get hold of the Englishmen if they've survived.'

'They may not have done?'

'Can't tell. They were in Clamecy. It depends where they were when the Germans moved in.'

Lejeune was thawing, but his suspicion of outsiders was palpable. His eyes might occasionally reflect friendliness, but they also flickered with distrust. Chalmers detected the instincts of a peasant family which had prospered.

'When will Chantal be back?'

'Can't say. There's a train that gets into St.Pierre at 7.15. She usually comes on that. If she sees young Pierre, she may be later.'

'Pierre?'

'Young man in Clamecy – helps in his father's shop. He'll inherit it one day. She's been out with him a few times. Marie thinks he's all right.' For the first time Chalmers felt he was sharing a family confidence.

'Nothing to do with the Resistance?'

'No. His parents are Pétainist.' Lejeune eyed him. 'Will you help?'

Chalmers looked down at his leg, picked it up with his right hand and moved it to a more comfortable position. He was trying to conceal his feelings. From being an incubus, an unwanted guest, he might be valuable. His spirits lifted in a way they had not done since learning of the death of his crew. He looked at Lejeune. On each occasion their eyes met for longer. 'I'll do anything you want – anything at all.'

'We'll wait for Chantal. Then we'll know the worst. Now we've got to deal with you. We've moved you, but you won't be able to go out – not yet anyway. Too many people we can't trust. Now listen.' He leaned forward and Chalmers saw the depth of the lines running away from his mouth and eyes and the grey in his hair. Lejeune was older than he had thought. 'No one's likely to see you, but if anyone comes you're a cousin from Provence. You used to go there before the war. You know Vaison?'

'Vaison-la-Romaine? Yes. The family I visited showed me the Roman remains.'

'Our cousin used to live there. Your French is good enough – but not with a Provençale accent. A Lejeune married a girl from Vaison during the Great War. We haven't heard from them for years – don't even know if they're still alive – but you can be their son. You came here to help on the farm, had an accident and your leg was plastered by Gambert. We stick to the truth as far as possible.'

'What sort of accident?'

'You were helping with the hay and fell down from the loft. Gambert was here looking after the old man. The problem is papers. You haven't got any.' He fingered the stubble on his chin. 'We can probably get some. It's only a problem if the Boches come. It's more important to get the accent right for the locals. There aren't many strangers in rural Burgundy. There's a distinctive Provençale tang. I'll coach you.'

'I hope I won't let you down.'

'So do I. I'll tell you about the family later. You stay inside till it's dark.'

Chalmers looked at the unshaven face, the dishevelled, collarless shirt, none too clean. For a moment he was conscious of the paradox of the situation. Here was he, Captain of Cricket and Rugger at school and college, Flying Officer and skipper of a Lancaster bomber, taking orders from a scruffy French farmer. But he was in Lejeune's hands and he recognised a leader when he saw one. Speculating about the Gambert-Lejeune relationship, he guessed Gambert's professional and intellectual skills deferred to Lejeune's personality.

Lejeune stood up. 'I'm going to see Maurice. Stay away from the windows. If anyone comes you lie low until I say otherwise. Don't trust the postman. He may be all right, but we're not sure about his sons.'

'But you know about him. I heard you telling the Germans about his frolic with Madame Dupont.'

Lejeune's face broke into a genuine smile. 'They had a shock when I found them. Minouche Dupont has a reputation.'

'How does Chantal get back from St.Pierre?'

'Bicycle – fifteen minutes. Been doing it for years.'

Lejeune pointed across the valley through the open window. 'Those fields are ours, as far as the vineyard. That belongs to Blanchard. He sells wine to the Germans, but he's all right. The Blanchards have been here as long as the Lejeunes. We keep the cows in the bottom field, down by the river.'

'Where did we come down?' He still thought collectively in spite of the deaths of his crew.

'Over there, between Châtel-Censoir and St.Pierre.'

'Is that the Yonne?'

'It goes through those woods. There's a canal too, and the railway.'

'I saw them through the mist. It's amazing how clearly I remember the last moments. Where does the river go? I've never heard of it.'

'It joins the Seine at Montereau. In the old days they used to float logs from the Morvan forests all the way to Paris.'

A heat haze hung across the valley. A buzzard circled the trees by the river, its mewing cry the only sound. Butterflies fluttered in the grass and wild flowers bordering the lane.

'It's quiet.'

'Nothing to make a noise. German aircraft sometimes. Few cars – no petrol. The doctor gets some. We've got some for emergencies. I must see Maurice. Come up to your room.'

He abruptly opened the door and left Chalmers to follow. Chalmers got to his feet, picked up the crutches and moved as fast as he could. Lejeune had not even left the door open and one of the crutches got caught on the handle. Oddly, he appreciated Lejeune's apparent indifference; it gave him an independence he felt he had lost. Lejeune stood at the top of the stairs watching his progress with interest rather than concern.

'You're improving,' said the Frenchman. The landing was dark, but Lejeune opened a bedroom door and the sun lit up striped wallpaper and brown curtains. There was a carved oak wardrobe behind him. Everything seemed to have been made in the nineteenth century when, Chalmers guessed, the family had first touched prosperity. 'This is your room.' Lejeune stood aside to let him pass.

It was the brightest room he had seen, the first to escape the shade of trees or shutters closed against the heat. The windows were open and the sun streamed in. Military photographs confirmed Robert's previous presence. A large china bowl decorated with flowers stood on the washstand together with a matching water jug; a clean towel hung over a wooden clothes-horse. Opposite the window was a simple iron bed. It had been made up and more clothes laid out, presumably by Célestine.

Lejeune stood at the window overlooking the yard. The farm lay in a hollow surrounded by woods and open fields. 'We make cider,' he said, indicating the orchard. 'The press is in the barn. Célestine does that. The arable's over there – up to the trees. There's Maurice.' At the edge of the woods a pair of horses and a man were ploughing.

'Very isolated.'

'We don't want visitors. There's another farm down the lane. Beyond that there's a hamlet – Magny. More Blanchards, no Germans. I must go.' The curtness returned. Lejeune realised it was the first time anyone had slept in Robert's room since his death and he remembered watching Robert dressing there for his first day at school.

The leg was hurting now. Chalmers said: 'I'll stay here for a bit.'

Lejeune grunted and left. Moments later Chalmers saw him making his way towards the top field.

***

Chantal arrived at about half-past seven. The last bit of lane to La Rippe was uphill and she was flushed and breathless when she got off her bicycle.

Making sure he was concealed from the lane by the heavy maroon curtain, Chalmers sat at the window of the parlour waiting for her. His future, indeed the future of them all, might depend on the news from Clamecy. And he had missed her. The afternoon had been difficult. Lejeune had retreated into his natural brusqueness, Marie Lejeune's distrust of Englishmen had become apparent, and Célestine was uncommunicative; Maurice's limitations were obvious and although Marguerite was flirtatious enough to get his attention, her immaturity was off-putting. He went to meet Chantal in the yard.

'Hello,' he said, squinting into the sun.

Her brown arms were bare and she looked younger than she had in the darkness of the loft. Her breasts pushed tightly at her blouse, making her waist look more slender than it was. 'Hello,' she replied, smiling. She was pleased to find Chalmers waiting for her. 'Feeling better?'

He nodded. 'Less bruised – and I'm getting the hang of these things. News?'

'Worse than we thought. I've been all over Clamecy. I'm tired.'

'Tell me.'

'They got everyone, including André. They knew the houses to go to, and they've searched the abbey. They're still going through the villages on the Morvan side.'

'André?'

'Headed the Clamecy group. Code name.'

'The Englishmen?'

'One caught with André, the other got away.'

'What about this end? What about – your family?' He nearly said, 'What about you?'

'We'll soon see. Papa says they don't know names and can't

give us away even if they're tortured. I hope he's right.' She touched his leg. 'Still painful?'

'Better. I've never broken anything before.'

'Where's Papa?'

'Up with your grandfather. Your mother's there as well.'

'I must see him. He'll want to know.'

Later that night in bed, watching the moon climb over the woods, he remembered Chantal's arrival. He had been waiting for her, he told himself, because her news was urgent. But there was more to it than that. He could see her slowing the bicycle, letting it fall to the right, her foot touching the ground. As she did so, she slipped off the saddle, automatically holding the fullness of her skirt with one hand to keep it clear of the rear wheel. It was a practical action born of years of repetition, graceful and sensual, the skirt moulding to the contour of her body. For the first time he admitted the thought lurking at the back of his mind: he hoped she hadn't stayed to see Pierre. There was something about her that caught his attention every time she moved, an attraction any man would recognise. It was disloyal to Mary, he knew that. She would joke about recognition of the general and the particular. She trusted him and that made it worse. He wanted Mary, but she didn't even know he was alive.

The air cooled. Towards the woods an owl was hunting. He had put out his candle and its smell lingered. He was covered by a sheet, nothing more. He had discarded Robert's pyjamas, which were scratchy and thick. His weight sank into the depths of the feather-bed, reminding him of the time he had as a child once slept with his grandmother in a feather-bed that seemed enormous.

Chantal was at the forefront of his mind, but he applied himself to his impressions of the family. Jacques Lejeune, he decided, loved his wife, deferred to her opinions, but took his own decisions. He had eaten early and cycled off to discuss Chantal's news with Gambert. Marie Lejeune controlled the domestic household and expected her daughters to fit the pattern she dictated. In both cases he detected disappointment: Chantal's independence was not easily directed, while Marguerite's flippancy was a source of irritation. Maurice's problems were no longer an embarrassment to any of them. He had talked about trains again at supper and having been promised a treat at the end of the week fell asleep before the meal was finished. Célestine's silence seemed disapproving of everyone. She worked in the kitchen and on the farm, but spent any spare time with the old man. The servant status was obvious, but the relationship upstairs gave it a dimension the others could not question.

The sky was clear, the moonlit countryside stark and white. No wonder Bomber Command tried to avoid the moon. He remembered the relief when he buried the aircraft in cloud. They should have stressed that more in training. The emphasis had been on sticking in the stream, checking wind speeds, getting the right height, watching the turning points. Survival had nothing to do with that.

The woods on the skyline were etched in outline with a million stars above. He marvelled at their beauty, pondering Man's insignificance in a universe he did not begin to comprehend. The stars were beneficent once more, not the cold observers of the death throes of Z-Zebra. He closed his eyes, his head aching. Half waking, half sleeping, he was back in the oak-panelled form-room at school where 'Beaky' Brewster, his inspirational English master, dishevelled and chalky, was holding forth on *Paradise Lost*. He was at the point where Satan and his fellow angels, cast out from heaven, rouse themselves from the pit of Hell before plotting revenge against the Almighty. 'Look at the sense of struggle,' Brewster said, sweeping his hand over his hair as he did at moments of excitement. 'Look at the defiance. Milton the Puritan turns Satan into a hero. *What though the field be lost? All is not lost; the unconquerable will, and study of revenge, immortal hate, and courage never to submit or yield: and what is else not to be overcome?'*

The words floated in memory and he realised his gratitude for being made to learn so much poetry by heart. Chaucer, Shakespeare, Milton, Keats, Shelley – acres of it were at his disposal. He could quote almost as freely as Brewster. Quite unbidden, Milton's description of Satan's discovery of God's newly created world drifted back. He spoke the words aloud:

'Far off the empyreal Heaven extended wide
In circuit, undetermined square or round,
With opal towers and battlements adorned
Of living sapphire, once his native seat,
And, fast by, hanging in a golden chain,
This pendant world, in bigness as a star
Of smallest magnitude, close by the moon.'

Then he saw it. He knew why the words had come back. *The golden chain.* Plagiarism. The impromptu little poem he had left for Mary was an unconscious echo of Milton. *The passing show knows nothing of our love. What we endure, the pain and pleasure of a golden chain, is ours alone.* He might have known he was not being original.

The Fall of Man. Satan had reached his goal and set about his mission of revenge. In the dreamland of his mind the words took on a new significance. He loved Mary: that was certain. And she was waiting for him, going through agonies of uncertainty. She would have his letter, she would see his love. It would be no consolation.

And now there was Chantal. She was not Mary, he did not love her, but she was *there*. She was attractive and he sensed something between them. The Fall of Man. Could he even begin to compare himself with the wretched Fallen Angel and the temptations of the Garden of Eden? He was twenty-three, had touched the doors of death and never had a woman. Was it wrong to consider the possibility she might give the fulfilment he longed for? She had a lovely smile, she was warm and conscious of her attraction for men. The way she walked, back straight, skirt swinging, eyes hinting at something

177

indefinable: she knew the effect she had. Or was he being foolish, looking at a desirable woman who had not even noticed he was male?

He lay back. The moon had climbed higher. Robert's pictures were clear on the wall: Robert drinking with friends in Lille; Robert with fellow soldiers on the Maginot Line; Robert shooting wild boar in the Ardennes. Had Robert had a woman? The photographs showed a man with the Lejeune nose, pale but confident. Chalmers judged he and Robert were roughly the same age. And Robert was dead. Nothing hinted at a girl friend, nothing suggested he had become a man in the truest sense.

He closed his eyes, no longer reining back his imagination. Chantal was bending over him. She was kissing him, her tongue running between his lips. Her fingers, soft and light, ran over his chest. His arm was round her waist, pulling her down. He felt the fullness of her breasts against him. He was thinking of Mary, wanting it to be Mary, guiltily aware it was not. The waking dream faded as he fell asleep.

19

The next days passed slowly. A series of thunderstorms reduced the temperature and Chalmers spent a good deal of time in his room trying not to get in the way of farm routine. He went downstairs for meals eaten on the scrubbed table in the kitchen and observed the family. The first surprise was the influence of the old man. Though Jacques appeared to take most decisions, the figure upstairs retained an authority on farm matters no one dared flout. Jacques accepted this reluctantly and Chalmers suspected his Resistance role was a form of escape. Likewise, Marie deferred to him and this increased the tension between her and Célestine. Chantal took responsibility for Chalmers as she had in the barn. She dressed his head wound several times, eventually removing the bandages and allowing him to shave. More than once she came upstairs to talk before he went to bed. Marguerite, initially frivolous, had, he discovered, a serious side and, with Célestine, helped look after Maurice, whose main contribution was heavy labour in the fields. Bizarrely Chalmers saw parallels with Orwell's Boxer.

He was not bored. Life on a remote Burgundy farm was vastly different from the Mess at Wynton. But there were few books and he was thrown back on his own devices. He borrowed a map from Lejeune and brought it to life by relating it to pictures in a faded guide to local churches and châteaux he found. He wondered if he would see any of them: the thirteenth-century cathedral at Auxerre rising like a great ship above the trees fringing the Yonne, the exquisite Château de Ratilly in the Puisaye, the Château de Chastellux in the depths of the Morvan. After dark he concentrated on getting some exercise outside and improving his technique with the crutches. And all the time he watched Lejeune, monitoring his comings and goings. He did not ask questions, waiting for Lejeune to confide when he wanted to.

The initiative came one day after supper when it was getting dark. Lejeune took him aside and led him into the yard. He carried a bottle and two glasses. 'It's safe out here. You need fresh air. We'll have a drink.' It was a warm summer evening, the sun setting beyond the orchard, swallows still hunting. He led the way to a wooden seat and table on the edge of the orchard, Chalmers hobbling after him. They faced away from the farm towards the woods. Chalmers dropped the crutches on the ground beside him. 'I'll be glad to be rid of these. Has Gambert said how long I've got to keep the plaster?'

Lejeune ignored the question. 'They buried your friends three days ago,' he said. He poured some red wine.

'Where?'

'St.Pierre. The cemetery on the road to Mailly. All done properly. Luftwaffe guard of honour.'

Chalmers was silent. He had tried not to think about his crew. But the guilt was there. He was conscious of Lejeune watching him. 'How do you know?'

'The curé at Mailly told Gambert.'

'They were good men. Brave men doing a job. They trusted me.'

It was Lejeune's turn to be silent. He looked towards the woods, now losing their clarity in the fading light. He took out a cigarette, lit it and exhaled into the still air. 'You did your best. Events take over. Like Robert, like the arrests.'

'I wish I'd known.'

'We'll take you there. Have you wondered where I've been recently?' He seemed almost to be hinting at friendship. 'You're very discreet. Gambert likes you. We're working on the next move.'

'The fields?'

'And other things. You're the first problem. With the chain it was simple. You stayed a couple of nights and we passed you on. You're not fit to move anyway. We've come to a conclusion, but you have to agree.'

'Go on.'

'He smiled a warm smile. 'We want you to join us – to stay here. Your French is good, our group is small enough to keep the secret and you can be useful.'

Chalmers drank some wine. He felt equal measures of pleasure and nervousness. 'Your group – how small?' he asked. The question concealed his emotions.

'Three others – together with me and Gambert. They helped get you out.'

'What about the family?'

Lejeune hesitated. 'The old man doesn't approve. Marie knows a good deal and doesn't approve either. But she won't let us down.' He eyed Chalmers. 'Chantal's committed. She'll never forgive the Germans for Robert.'

'I'm flattered. And I like it here.'

'I must tell you something first – about the Clamecy group. One of the Englishmen is dead. The Germans said he was shot trying to escape, but that's not what we heard. The Frenchmen have been taken to Paris and they'll be shot too when the Gestapo's finished with them. If you join us, you lose any protection as a prisoner of war. You'll wear civilian clothes. If you're caught you'll be shot just as we shall.'

'You've saved my life.' Chalmers had already considered the possibility of being thought a spy the moment he put on Robert's clothes. 'I'll join. On condition you tell me everything – I'm a fully paid up member.'

'Agreed.' Lejeune's terseness returned. He held out his hand and Chalmers took it. Both grips were firm.

'There's a bat,' said Chalmers. It was a degree darker now and the first stars had appeared. A bat from the barn flew in a circular route from the yard to the orchard and back to the yard again. It distracted them from an emotional moment.

'You'll be more use when you can walk. We're based on Mailly-le-Château. I'm the nominal leader because I started it with Gambert after Robert's death. The others have their own reasons. You'll meet them soon. We've passed on fliers, we give food to the men in the forest, and we're in touch with the Reds at Migennes. We help distribute their newspaper – *Le Travailleur de l'Yonne*. We don't agree on a lot of things, but . . .' He shrugged. 'We were going to get a link with London through the Englishmen. That's where you come in.'

'Go on.'

'The Englishman who was killed was going to organise groups here. The one who got away was a wireless operator. He's in the Morvan and safe. London will support us if we can organise a dropping zone. But we've got to show we know what we're doing. The arrests in Clamecy have damaged us. You can convince them we're still in business. Tell them about the fields. You can vouch for us. We need weapons, ammunition, explosives.'

'They haven't sent anything yet?'

'London only heard about us recently. They need to be convinced we're worth it – and that we're genuine. The Morvan's difficult for the Germans. We know the forests and they don't, but our organisation's new. There's another group down at St.Léger, the Vauban Maquis. They picked up arms and ammunition dumped in the forest by French troops retreating in 1940. They derailed a German military train near Nevers in the spring. The other side of Quarré-les-Tombes there's the Maquis Camille They had the first *parachutage* in Burgundy. Apart from the fliers we've done nothing.'

Chalmers sipped his wine. Selfish thoughts were uppermost. If contact was made with London, they would know he was alive. Mary would be told. Conversely, of course, if he stayed at La Rippe he would not see her until the war was over and God knew when that would be. He said: 'So we get hold of the wireless man. How do we do that?'

'He's in the Morvan. We can get him here. But we need to be sure about the fields. We'll take you to see them. They'll listen to you. There's a curfew, but it's safe now the roadblocks have gone.'

'Your security's better than Clamecy?'

'If we'd been careless, we'd have been picked up by now.'

'You want to take me while I'm on these?' Chalmers indicated the crutches.

'We can't wait. The wireless operator's our only hope. There's no point leaving him in the forest. We've made contact and he'll come the moment there's something to send. With the collapse of Clamecy, he can join us. You'll prove we're genuine. He's suspicious, but he's got to trust somebody.' Lejeune leaned forward, his face relaxing into the comfortable lines normally reserved for private moments with Marie.

It was dark now, and the moon was rising. It was still warm and the smell of Lejeune's cigarette hung in the air. From the house came the sound of a piano. Chalmers had first heard it lying in the barn. In his delirium he had not been sure whether it was real or not. Now someone was playing the opening bars of the Moonlight Sonata. 'Who's playing?' he asked.

'Marguerite. She had lessons from a woman in St.Pierre. She doesn't practise enough.'

'The piano needs tuning. Where is it?'

'My mother played. It's in her old bedroom, next to the old man. It's only been tuned once since she died.'

'Can I play sometime?' He had played regularly on the Mess piano at Wynton. Apart from Mary, it was the thing he missed most.

'You play well?'

Chalmers's understatement came to the fore. 'Not badly. But I haven't practised much recently – like Marguerite.' The piano came to a halt amidst a flurry of mistakes and Marguerite went back to the easy opening.

'We can't afford to let it give you away. The sound comes out in this direction and it's difficult to hear in the lane. You can play as long as we see who's around.' Lejeune had taken off his beret and his grey hair was almost blond in the moonlight. The wrinkles round his eyes had relaxed. He stretched a hand across and touched Chalmers, a gesture not made before. 'That sounds smug, James. My apologies.' The defences were coming down. 'We'll look at the fields tomorrow evening.'

The next day Lejeune cycled off after milking and reappeared in time for lunch. Chalmers, who tried not to get in the way at lunchtime, was in his room watching Chantal collect eggs from the hen-house in the orchard. Lejeune knocked and came in. 'This evening you'll meet them all. They're pleased you want to join us.'

Later, after an early supper, a battered black Citroën drew into the yard. Lejeune nodded at Chalmers and they went out to the back door. '*Bonne chance,*' said Chantal, carrying dirty dishes to the sink. She smiled over her shoulder.

Chalmers caught her eye. 'Thanks.'

'In the back,' said Lejeune. Chalmers put the crutches together and arranged them on the worn leather seat. Lejeune got in beside the driver, a young man with narrow shoulders, a thin, pointed face and unruly black hair. His inscrutable eyes reminded Chalmers of a sullen boy at school who sat in the back row and made trouble for masters.

'This is René,' said Lejeune. 'Works at his father's smithy and garage in St.Pierre. We can't do without him. René – this is our pilot, James.'

The young man ignored the introduction and did not look round. 'Safe,' he said. 'No roadblocks.'

'René's brother was killed in 1940, like Robert,' said Lejeune. 'He'll do anything.'

René put the car in gear, backed out of the yard, and turned into the lane. He drove on sidelights in the light of the moon. 'We'll see your plane,' he said.

'Will they move it?' Chalmers asked.

'They left the Lancaster at Pontaubert a long time. That was in a wood. Yours will be a problem for barges on the river. They'll have to do something about it.'

Chalmers looked out of the window. Having studied the map, he had a good idea where they were. 'How long?'

'Ten minutes,' said Lejeune. 'We drive slowly. Nothing to draw attention. It's still before curfew.'

'Curfew?'

'Applies more in towns and villages than out here. If the Boches get excited about something it's brought forward. It was 9 p.m.in Migennes when the Reds started trouble.'

When the lane was under trees, Chalmers felt secure, but as in Z-Zebra, he felt the whole world was watching when they emerged into moonlight. At length after a stretch of woodland running parallel to the railway and the river René pulled off the road and eased to a standstill under the last two trees. 'There it is,' he said.

Chalmers couldn't see it at first. Then, as his eyes acclimatised, he saw the unmistakable outline of the front half of his Lancaster in the river near the opposite bank. There was no sign of the tailplane, but one wing and two engines were clear of the water. The fuselage was in shadow and largely submerged; the exposed wing with its RAF roundel glinted in the moonlight, as did the whirls and eddies of the river flowing past it.

Had he been asked to write down his feelings at that moment, he could not have done so. He saw again the flames, the mist, and relived the eternity before impact. In the background were the trials of Fire and Water and a gallery of spectral Banquos, indistinct, tortured with fear and reproach. The aircraft and the darkly-flowing river mirrored and magnified his depression. He recalled the Paul Nash painting, *Totes Meer*, a sea of aircraft wreckage, seen on a visit to London. And Mary was there too, trusting Mary, whom he adored, who believed – and made him believe – he could do anything. What folly! He could not even stop himself lusting after a French girl he had only just met.

He said: 'Aren't there any guards?'

'No,' replied René. 'Unless they were brought back this evening. There were guards until the bodies were recovered. Now the local gendarmes watch it during the day, but they go when it gets dark. Dussault keeps us informed. He owns the fields.'

'I've seen enough,' said Chalmers.

They drove on for another mile, then turned right, crossed the river and came back the other side, this time down a farm track. 'You see what I mean,' said Lejeune. 'There are several tracks like this we can use for getting stuff away. With donkeys or horses we could use rougher paths. And there are hiding places in the woods. We could keep everything this side of the river secret – as long as the Germans don't pinpoint the landing area. It's ideal for us. Depends how it is for the RAF.'

'Monsieur Dussault?'

'Sympathetic. His wife won't let him join us, but they won't give us away. He lost his father at Verdun.'

They were soon in the woods again, then, quite suddenly, René turned into an open area of grassland. 'What about it?' asked Lejeune. 'You came down through that gap in the trees.'

They left the car in shadow and walked into the moonlight. The field stretched extensively to left and right, fringed by trees. Chalmers looked in the direction of his own final approach. 'Châtel-Censoir up there?'

'Seven kilometres.'

'It's flat enough.' He bent to look at the grass. 'If Dussault can keep animals cropping it as short as this, a plane might get in. Getting off again would be different. It's wide enough – I could see that coming down. We need to check the length – and the trees. Come on.'

Chalmers's call to action did something to lift his depression. He hobbled in the direction of the place where he had come down, Jacques and René on either side. Briefly, he was in charge. 'We'll get to the end,' he said, 'then you two can stride out a measurement to the edge of the wood. I'll enjoy watching you.'

Lejeune pointed again: 'You hit the ground about there.'

'I overshot in the mist. But no excuses. I ought to have made it. Without mist a plane could get down more quickly than I did. There'd have to be lights, but you could do that – torches or car headlights. Is it dry right across to the river?'

'Water meadows over there, but the river bank here's high – no flooding. Dussault confirmed it. Said he'd once lost a cow over the edge that couldn't get back. There are bushes here and there – you destroyed some of them – and there are rough patches. It's not flat all over.'

'Good as a dropping zone. Better than getting a plane in or out.'

'A *parachutage* is the most important.'

'Now the length. I'll meet you back at the car.'

Lejeune and René set off towards the far end, counting their paces. Chalmers, shadowed by depression, hobbled towards the river looking for signs of his crash. At first he could see nothing, then one of his crutches slipped and he realised he was standing on the track of the Lancaster's progress towards the river. The earth was furiously churned and four ridges and furrows showed the gouged-out progress of the engines, the line of the port outer scorched black. Here and there bits of metal littered the ground. He went a few steps forward, but stopped when the track veered towards the river. He had seen enough. He turned away and went back to the car. He reached the shadows and was aware of the smell of a cigarette.

'Hello, Englishman.' A voice spoke in English from the darkness.

In spite of the warning smell, Chalmers jumped.

'Over here, by the car.'

Chalmers dug in the crutches and went further into the trees. At first he couldn't see anyone, simply bright bits of the car shining in the light filtering through the leaves; then he saw the glow of a cigarette and two figures. One was tall, one was short, both were holding bicycles, both were smoking.

'Friends of Monsieur Lejeune?' he hazarded in French. Taken off guard, he was recovering.

The taller of the two propped his bicycle against a tree and came forward. He was thin, hatless, with dark hair and a lean, bony face. 'We helped get you out. I am Henri, this is Georges. Georges did more than I did, he's stronger. He got into the cockpit and undid your harness. Welcome to *La Bourgogne*.' He held out his hand.

Chalmers took the proffered hand. 'Thank you for everything. You saved my life.'

'Gambert said you had a good accent. He was right.' Henri's voice had a hoarse quality, as though his throat was dry or he had been shouting.

Georges had come forward and also taken his hand. He had square shoulders and a firm grip. In the dim light Chalmers could see his features were rough-hewn, his hair short. He looked like a boxer, the type seen in booths at fairgrounds. He was not loquacious. 'You were covered with blood. I didn't think you'd live. Gambert thought you might.'

'Where are Jacques and René?' asked Henri.

'Measuring the fields.'

'We were standing here,' said Georges, 'that night.'

'We heard you a long way off,' said Henri. 'Jacques thought you were a German. Gambert knows more about engines and guessed you were a Lancaster. Then we saw the flames. Gambert said you were trying to get down. When you went round in a circle, we knew you'd try here. There's nowhere else.'

'You were lucky,' said Georges.

'It doesn't seem like that to me.'

'The mist was thick. We thought you'd crash. You did well.'

'Not well enough. My crew died.'

'You could have hit the trees.'

'I could see the gap. The problem was height. I couldn't see the ground. How long did it take the Germans to get here?'

'Three hours. There's no garrison here. No patrols. They had to come from Auxerre – and someone had to tell them about it. It took about ten minutes to get you out. We were well away before they arrived.'

'Ah, you've met.' Jacques and René appeared in the moonlit opening. 'Bigger than I thought,' said Lejeune. 'Nine hundred metres or thereabouts, about four hundred wide.'

'I'd guess that's pretty good. The river makes it easy to find. Landing's a different matter. I've never flown a Lysander. You say there are places to hide things. Where will you eventually take them?'

'It depends what we get. Some will come to La Rippe, some can stay in the forest.'

'When's the wireless operator coming?'

'We're going to him. I don't want him at La Rippe. The Germans can pinpoint a signal. We'll move him about.'

'When?' asked René.

'The sooner the better. Tomorrow?'

René shrugged in a way Chalmers recognised as characteristic. 'Why not? Same time?'

'You'll lose Geneviève,' said Henri. 'She won't put up with you being out every night.' The older man, taller than all of them, ruffled René's hair. 'Different for me. Alphonsine can't wait to get me out of the house.'

'Geneviève will get used to it.'

'Don't bank on it,' said Lejeune. 'Women are difficult.'

'You've got a good one in Marie,' said Henri. 'Alphonsine's been difficult from the first. To start with she thought I was out with someone else. Now she wishes I was.'

Chalmers enjoyed the badinage. He noticed Georges had not joined in. He turned to him. 'What do you do, Georges?'

For a moment it looked as though Georges was going to ignore him. Then he removed the cigarette from his mouth. 'Bar,' he said. 'I run a bar in Mailly. Down by the river.' He replaced the cigarette.

'That's why we got him to join us,' joked Henri. 'Free cognac.'

'Good for gossip,' said Lejeune. 'We know what's going on.'

'You serve Germans?' asked Chalmers. It was a naïve question, but he wanted to see how Georges would react.

Henri replied for him: 'He would if he had to. No point in making trouble. It hasn't arisen yet. No Germans in Mailly. I run the grocer's shop and I serve anybody. There are some Frenchmen I don't like, but you can't be choosy in business. Every franc counts.'

Georges spoke again, this time not removing the cigarette. 'No one wants trouble.'

Lejeune took charge. 'We'll contact London now you've approved the fields. You'll drive tomorrow, René, and you must come, James.' He turned to Henri and Georges. 'You two stay at home. All right?'

Chalmers was impressed by Lejeune's authority and clear thinking which the others obviously respected. René might be taciturn, but he was committed. Henri and Georges, the one so tall, thin and voluble, the other so bulky and monosyllabic, reminded him of a theatrical comedy team. Only slowly was he coming to terms with the fact that these men had saved his life.

'We wanted to meet you,' said Henri, as Chalmers got back into the car. His tone was serious. 'We were lucky when Clamecy collapsed.'

'We kept our distance,' said Lejeune. Henri and Georges stood back as he got in beside René and slammed the door. 'I'll be in touch,' he said through the window.

René drove onto the track leading back to Mailly, leaving the other two to pick up their cycles. Out of the trees they turned onto the lane, equally deserted. They crossed the Yonne and climbed the hill into the little town. Lights behind shutters hinted at life, but there was no street lighting. The curfew appeared firmly in place. Lejeune pointed out of the window. 'That's Henri's shop. And Georges's bar – *Les Pêcheurs* – is down that hill in Mailly-en-Bas. We'll go when you're fit.'

'Interesting church,' said Chalmers, looking at the turrets on the church dominating the square.

'Concentrate on what's important,' said Lejeune. It was the first time he had given any sort of rebuke and Chalmers concluded he was under more strain than he had thought.

René re-crossed the Yonne and stopped at La Rippe. 'Tomorrow,' he said. 'Eight. I'll be here.' There was no further conversation. Chalmers watched the tail-lights retreat down the lane.

20

The next day Chalmers saw how effectively Lejeune concealed his double life. To all intents and purposes he followed a normal farming routine. In the morning after doing the milking with Chantal and taking the churns by horse and cart to the station at St.Pierre he cleaned out the pigs with Maurice. In the afternoon he helped Célestine and Chantal with the cheese and the day-old chicks for the Châtel-Censoir market. Only when he came in for the evening meal did he pay any attention to Chalmers.

'René will be on time,' he said, washing his hands in the kitchen sink. 'Never lets us down.' The lines on his face, deeply moulded, were emphasised by the sun coming through the window over the sink. He had shaved, the first time for about a week.

Apart from helping Célestine with the water pump and hens in the morning, Chalmers spent most of the day indoors. It had been considered safe for him to play the piano in the afternoon and he now sat at one end of the kitchen table watching Marie and Célestine prepare supper. Lejeune sat by the open door, smoking.

'You play well,' said Lejeune. He knew nothing about classical music, but had enjoyed listening.

'The piano's better than I thought. Playing's relaxing – I used to play after a raid.'

'You could give Marguerite lessons,' said Marie. She had been baking and her plump forearms were dusted with flour.

The door opened and Chantal came in from the yard, a pile of washing in her arms. 'Give Marguerite lessons in what?'

'Piano,' said Chalmers.

'I loved what you were playing this afternoon,' said Chantal. 'What was it? I'd never heard it before.'

'Schubert – his last sonata. Marvellous – written just before he died. Goes to the depths and stirs you up if you're a romantic like me.'

'It was beautiful. I had lessons once.'

'Schubert,' said Lejeune. 'A German.'

'Austrian – Viennese. Not Prussian. Big difference,' responded Chalmers. Momentarily he thought of Mary and the evening they had listened to the Schubert Quintet.

'Chantal didn't practise more than Marguerite,' said her mother. 'More money wasted.'

'Madame Maugin was a tyrant. I would have practised for James.' She put the washing down. 'I'll do the ironing later.'

'James is coming with me this evening,' said her father. No one asked where they were going.

After supper Lejeune and Chalmers went to the orchard to wait for René. It was still light and they sat on the wooden bench. Inevitably Lejeune was smoking. He said: 'I'm having second thoughts about you playing. I could hear you in the lane.'

'Really a risk?'

'People can't keep their mouths shut. Too many informers – too many links with the Boches. Nothing's simple.'

'It looks different from England.'

'It's easy for de Gaulle and the Free French in London. It's survival here. That comes first. Blanchard's got five children. He needs money, so he sells his wine to the highest bidder – the Germans. We're friends, but I wouldn't tell him anything. There's a woman in Auxerre whose husband is a prisoner of war in Germany. She's got a blind father and several children. A good-looking woman. She works in a brothel for German soldiers.'

'But you all want them out.'

'Some more than others. There's an industrialist in Dijon who builds lorries for the German army. He didn't agree at first, but they threatened to take over his factory without compensation. That changed his mind. Now he gets production bonuses, there are rations for his workers and he goes hunting with the *Feldkommandant*. Now he's worried that the RAF will bomb his factory. We have to compromise.'

'You compromise?'

'Who doesn't?' He shrugged. 'Vichy requisitions animals and corn and fixes prices. We make up our losses selling on the black market. And if we want to help the RAF or the men in the forest, we create camouflage. I sell cheaply to a butcher in Auxerre who's a well-known collaborator. He supplies a Wehrmacht Officers' Mess with meat and gets champagne and Chablis at favourable rates. He's bound to have told the Germans where he gets his supplies. They'll be less suspicious if we're supplying their food.'

Chalmers felt naïve. He knew there was collaboration, but imagined most condemned it. He was learning the ambiguities of occupation.

René's Citroën broke his thought processes. Again its approach was secretive, the engine barely audible; again it was on side-lights only. René saw them waiting and stopped at the entrance.

'How long?' asked Chalmers.

'Half an hour. We're meeting at Pontaubert – near Avallon. An old mill in the woods.'

Chalmers settled into the back seat. 'Where the other Lancaster came down?'

Lejeune slammed his door a second time to ensure it was shut. 'Six months ago. The crew all died.' He was matter of fact.

René was as taciturn as on the previous occasion. He had yet to make any friendly gesture towards the Englishman. Once more the car moved quietly through wooded countryside. Chalmers sat forward, looking at signposts in the gloaming. At length they passed the gates of a substantial château and drove into a village.

'Pontaubert,' said Lejeune.

On both sides of the street grey stone cottages spoke of a simple farming community. René turned on the headlights, lighting up a faded advertisement for Pernod and a closed charcuterie. The rough surface of the road rattled the car. 'No repairs since the start of the war,' said René. Beyond a substantial church with a spire, they drove down a hill, crossed a stone bridge, and turned right into a narrow lane. The woods closed in and René drove off the lane and drew up by a low building on the edge of a river.

'Pontaubert mill,' said René. He stopped near the river, switching off the engine and lights. 'I hope they're here.'

It was dark now. A figure detached itself from the building and came towards them.

'Jeanne d'Arc.' The voice was female.

'Orléans,' Lejeune responded.

'Le Renard?'

Chalmers smiled at the cloak-and-dagger exchange, then remembered he owed his life to these people. The irony of passwords recalling a French victory over the English did not escape him, but he judged it best not to comment. It was the first time he had heard the name, Le Renard. They got out of the car and he saw a comfortable, middle-aged woman wearing peasant clothes and a kitchen apron. 'They're waiting,' she said.

The mill was little more than a long, low cottage. It had a red-tiled roof in need of repair and there was a car in a lean-to shed. At the end by the river there was an extra floor and the outline of the mill wheel. Tethered near the main door was a white goat. Inside, the room was bigger than he had expected. Three men sat at a bare wooden table, the remains of a meal in front of them. On the wall were two faded photographs: one pictured a religious procession with a statue of the Virgin and villagers in Sunday dress; the other a harvest scene with a horse-drawn cart piled high with hay and labourers with scythes. A pair of oil lamps on the table shed light. Brown curtains, heavy and thick, hanging from wooden rails, were tightly drawn. The air was blue with cigarette smoke.

The largest of the men, his ruddy face dominated by heavy eyebrows, greeted Lejeune as a friend and nodded to René. The other two were watchful. The woman fetched extra glasses and filled them with red wine.

'Our English pilot,' said Lejeune. 'He's joining us at Mailly.'

'Bernard,' said the large Frenchman, holding out his hand. 'Code-name,' he added. 'Best keep it simple.'

The smallest of the men, black-haired, with a swarthy complexion and suspicious eyes, looked at Chalmers, but spoke to Lejeune. 'You saw him come down?' He spoke in French, but Chalmers detected an accent.

'Oh, yes, we saw him come down. His men drowned in the Yonne.'

The third man, fair and freckled, about thirty, wearing labourer's clothes, held out his hand. 'Peter Johnson,' he said. His cautious expression vanished, replaced by a broad grin. 'I need another Englishman.'

Chalmers adjusted the crutch under his right arm and shook his hand. 'Good to meet you,' he said, aware the formality sounded out of place. 'The wireless man?'

The other nodded. 'Arrived with Emil three weeks ago. Trained by SOE. Heard of it? I went straight into the forest when Clamecy went wrong. Only just made it. Emil didn't. This is Miguel – Spanish communist, given his life to the cause. Escaped to France when the fascists won the civil war. He's looked after me. If it hadn't been for him, I'd have been picked up with Emil. Loathes the Germans. Blames them for Franco. Wants to shoot someone, but hasn't got a gun.'

'James,' said Chalmers holding out his hand again. The Spaniard shook it, but his watchful air remained. The accent was explained. He turned to Johnson. 'Your French is good. Lived here?'

'Channel Islander. Dad married into a Jersey family and we lived there. French all the time – with the local patois. We were on the last boat out before the Germans moved in.'

Lejeune was keen to get on. To Johnson he said: 'You're in touch with London?'

'Not for four days. They know the chain's collapsed and that I'm O.K.. No point in risking unnecessary contact. They pinpoint a radio quickly if it keeps transmitting.'

'We've got the place for a drop,' said Lejeune.

'They won't drop anything until they're convinced you're in business again. They're worried about the Clamecy fiasco. They know you were part of the chain, but nothing more. Emil was going to pull the Yonne valley together.'

'James will do it.' Lejeune looked towards Chalmers.

Johnson looked doubtful. 'You're taking a risk. I've been trained for this sort of thing.'

'Tell him,' said Lejeune.

'I've agreed to stay. They know what they're doing. They'd have been picked up by now if they'd made mistakes. My French is as good as yours. They've asked for help – I'm prepared to give it. In any case I can't move far with this.' He indicated his leg. 'Besides' – he looked directly at Johnson – 'you're going to need someone now you've lost Emil.'

Chalmers was trying to rationalise ideas going round in his head for days. He liked Johnson's style and detected a sense of humour. He was merging into the French background, yet remained essentially British and untroubled by the shambles he had been dropped into. The wine had given his fresh face a blotchy look as though he was unused to it. Chalmers drank more wine himself. It was rough and he thought of Mary and the wine at the Savoy. And, he could not help it, he thought of Chantal. He was aware that whenever he thought of Mary, Chantal also came into view.

'London will need convincing. They'll help if we're properly organised and sure we're safe.'

'We can do more than save a few Allied airmen,' said Lejeune. 'If the Second Front ever comes, we could make trouble in the whole of the Yonne.'

'It'll come.'

'Not fast enough for the Reds. They complain every time I see them.'

'They're impatient,' responded Johnson. 'They want to help the Russian front. London won't come till they're ready.'

'What can we get from London?'

'They'll send the same things they would have sent Emil. Arms, ammunition, explosives – clothes, if you need them.'

'I've got a man who can use explosives,' said Lejeune. 'Henri was a mining engineer in the Congo. How soon can we get a drop?'

'Convincing them you haven't been penetrated is the important thing. James will help. Then it'll depend on the aircraft available and the moon. For the moment I'll tell them there are two separate groups – you in the Yonne valley, Bernard in the Morvan. Bernard's found his own dropping zone in the hills. Miguel's as impatient as you are.'

'When's your next contact?' asked Chalmers.

'Tomorrow – an agreed transmission time. I'll want details of your fields – grid references and so on. How are we going to communicate?' He looked from Bernard to Lejeune.

'We avoid the telephone,' said Lejeune. 'Couriers on bicycles mostly.'

'We can't rush anything.' This was Bernard. 'We've put up with the Boches for three years. A month isn't going to make any difference. I've got a vineyard to look after.' He pointed at Lejeune. 'He's got the farm. We've both got the harvest.'

René, at the end of the table eating an apple, spoke for the first time: 'The British got out fast enough at Dunkirk.' His thin face topped by its untidy black hair suggested contempt.

Chalmers was going to speak, but Lejeune got in before him. 'Unfair, René. They didn't want to be harnessed to a dying animal. There are more British being killed now than Frenchmen. Look at James's crew, and the men who died here in Pontaubert. Anyway, you're biased.' He looked at Chalmers. 'René had two older brothers. One was killed during the German invasion – I told you that. What I didn't tell you was that he lost his other brother a few months later. He was in the navy and killed at Mers-el-Kébir by the British.'

Chalmers looked at the unforgiving face. 'I'm sorry,' he said. 'I had no idea.' He remembered the attack on the French fleet in 1940 when it looked as though the Germans might get hold of it. It seemed justified, but this was not the time to say so. 'I'm sorry,' he repeated.

René shrugged, looked at Chalmers, then at his half-eaten apple. Once more Chalmers was reminded of an immature, sullen boy.

Bernard interposed. 'Business, I think. Peter will contact London, but we must be clear about the information to send. A mistake to come to the mill again – for the time being anyway.'

'Agreed,' said Lejeune. 'I'll get someone to you the day after tomorrow. The café in Vézelay – usual time. Probably Henri.' He turned to Johnson. 'Here's the map. James will show you the place for the drop.'

Twenty minutes later they were on the road to La Rippe. Sitting behind René, Chalmers looked at the outline of the head in front of him. 'I understand about your brother,' he said.

The head nodded and for a moment it did not look as though there would be a response. Then René replied: 'War. You didn't start it. But it was wrong. I loved him.'

It was a more mature comment than Chalmers had expected. Perhaps the ice was breaking. Now he thought about Chantal. He recalled her flirting about piano lessons and he saw again the taut blouse over her breasts and the fall of her skirt. Nor did he forget the softness of her hands when she dressed his head wound. He wondered if she would still be up when they got back.

***

Three days later Chantal cycled to Mailly to get news from Henri. He had been to Vézelay and reported back on Johnson's contact with London. Two facts stood out. London accepted that the Bernard and Lejeune groups were secure and had agreed the dropping zones. There was also a personal message for Chalmers. For security purposes he would remain posted as 'Missing' and no one would be told of his survival. Meanwhile it was understood he was helping the Lejeune group. He had been given a code name, 'Louis'.

Chantal, her father and Chalmers sat in the orchard after supper. The two men had glasses of wine, Chantal a glass of water. It had been a hot day and the evening sun still had warmth in it. Chantal was going through Henri's report, making sure she had covered everything. 'If we get explosives,' she said, 'London will say what they want us to do. They'll give targets.'

'I knew that.' The sinking sun threw Lejeune's shadow across the grass in front of him. 'They'll rely on James and the wireless man to keep us in order. But we only do things we want to. Remember, we face the consequences.'

'The Spaniard – Miguel – won't like it,' said Chalmers. 'He wants to take on the whole German army once he's got a gun and a round up the spout.'

'Peter's transmitting again in three days,' said Chantal. 'They want a group in the Yonne and prefer us to the Reds in Migennes. The fact James is here is important.' She adjusted her skirt with care and looked across at Chalmers. 'He makes us respectable.'

'Not too respectable, I hope. The RAF has a reputation to keep up. They're supporting Bernard as well?'

'Oh, yes. They may send someone to help him. Johnson got the impression they expect you to keep us under control. They've wasted supplies on groups rounded up when drops started. '

'The forest men need food and clothes before arms,' said Lejeune. 'You'll go to Vézelay next time, Chantal. I don't want Henri going too often. It looks odd when he's got a shop to look after. You can always be seeing young Jean-Claude at the café.' He glanced at Chalmers. 'One of her admirers. She could have hooked him years ago.'

Chantal wrinkled her nose in the way Chalmers found delightful. 'I could have had him, but I didn't want him. Spends all his time looking at the café accounts.'

'Don't mock accounts,' said Lejeune.

Chantal was looking at Chalmers, not her father. 'There are more important things than accounts. I realised that when Robert died. Jean-Claude's a good man, but dull. We only have one life. I'm not throwing mine away.'

'Resistance – the Germans?' said Chalmers.

'There's no choice.'

'Nor me.' He held up his leg. 'Dumped in the middle of France, dud leg, no one to get me home.'

'You could give yourself up. I'm told prison camps are comfortable.'

'I wouldn't have to help Célestine lug water about or muck out the cowshed. And there might be someone sensitive to look after me.' As his wounds healed he had jokingly complained about Chantal's brisk treatment of the dressings.

'Men! Robert was like you. Always complaining if there was the smallest thing wrong with him.' The humour in her voice did not cloud the affection for her brother.

Chalmers watched her. She could not claim classical beauty, but her mobile brown eyes had an attraction any man would find hard to ignore. He wondered how Pierre of Clamecy viewed them – and Jean-Claude of Vézelay. He turned to

Lejeune, now lighting a clay pipe. 'You meant it about the piano?'

'I knew there was a risk, but hadn't realised how the sound carried till this afternoon. I could hear you down by the river. You play too well. Different from Chantal or Marguerite messing about.'

Chalmers understood. 'Right,' he said. 'You're the boss.'

Chantal was leaning forward. 'You could teach me. I'd love to play properly – and I'd promise to practise.'

'You've promised to practise before,' said her father. He registered the flirtatious tone and was not sure what he felt about it.

'That was different. I've heard James play. He'd be a good teacher – I might even be a good pupil.' She had turned to face him.

He sensed her subtly playing on their intimacies – the washing, the wound dressing, the shared jokes. For his part, he looked at her eyes and her other attractions. How could he even play with ideas of wanting her? He loved Mary, and she loved him. Posted 'Missing'. She would have no idea of the truth. Love? Lust? Guilt bit into his conscience. It did not stop his next words: 'You might be a good pupil.'

'I would practise. Promise. You could be brutal and beat me if I didn't.'

'If anyone's going to be brutal, it will be me,' said Lejeune. 'Stop teasing the man.'

'I'll teach you if you want me to. That wouldn't cause problems, would it?' Chalmers looked at Lejeune. 'The sound of the piano, I mean.'

'Chantal hasn't much time.'

'Enough,' she said. 'You can't keep me working every minute. Can we start tomorrow?'

'You've got the market in the morning. Célestine can't go on her own.'

'I'll be back in the afternoon. Marguerite will be there then.'

The next day Chalmers helped Célestine and Chantal off to market, fed the hens and pigs, then pumped water for the animals. Later, he went back to the barn and helped Maurice, who was cleaning the stable and restacking hay. Chantal cycled back from Châtel-Censoir and after lunch the two of them went up to the piano in the room adjacent to the old man. For the best part of an hour Chantal showed Chalmers what she remembered of previous lessons and he commented on her performance. At one point she detected what she took to be a spasm of irritation crossing his face. She stopped playing. 'I'm no good, am I?'

He realised he was blushing. He had, in fact, been thinking of something else entirely. 'Nonsense, I'm just distracted.'

'Distracted?'

They were sitting close together, her thigh only inches from his. He detected a perfume for the first time. 'You disturb me.'

'Disturb you?'

'You've been very kind to me.'

'You're a good patient, James.'

'Did you want me to stay?'

She looked at her hands on the piano, played a few inconsequential notes. 'Yes,' she said.

'Why?'

'Looking for compliments. Typical man again! I thought an Englishman might be different. Have you been in love?'

'Have you?'

'Yes, I've been in love. I thought I was happy. I shan't make the same mistake again.'

'To fall in love?'

She shook her head. 'I was let down. I'll tell you one day. And you?'

'There's a girl in England. We're in love. We're going to be married when this is all over.'

'What's her name?'

'Mary.'

You miss her?'

'She doesn't know I'm alive.'

'Not my question.'

'Of course I miss her.'

'But you look at me. I know when a man looks at me.'

'I'm not a monk.'

'I'm not a nun.'

'I'm not a monk, but I am a man. I recognise a desirable woman when I see one. You've been good to me. I'm grateful, very grateful – and it's more than that. It's a funny thing, but I told Mary that men can appreciate more than one woman.'

'Faithfulness?'

'I'm not unfaithful.' His tone was angry. 'Go back to Chopin. The easy bit at the beginning.'

'Coward. You don't like facing your conscience.'

'Are you tempting me?'

She smiled and played a few notes. 'I wanted to know if there was anyone else.'

'And now you know?'

'It's your problem rather than mine.' She had been looking at her fingers on the keyboard, now she turned to face him. The movement of her legs pushed her knee against his. 'Isn't it?'

'You're very pretty.' Their eyes met, then they both looked away.

'And so is Mary, I expect.'

'She is. And I love her.' He was determined to be truthful. 'But she's miles away.' He put up an arm and touched her affectionately on the shoulder. 'You've made me like you.'

'Like?'

'I don't know what words to use. I'm being honest. We can be friends. I think we are friends.'

Chantal turned back to the piano. 'You're right. Let's concentrate on Chopin.'

'Very well.' His voice had become distant: he was aware of it. 'You *could* play well, if you did as you were told. That's honest, too.'

21

Chalmers slowly acclimatised himself to his new situation. He stayed under cover, but did various jobs about the farm. He proved adept at turning the mangle when Célestine was washing and he chopped wood for the winter in the yard. He was not yet allowed into the fields where Lejeune and Maurice had been joined by a labourer who cycled daily from Coulanges to help with the arable work. The man was ignorant of Resistance activities and unaware of his presence.

'Not trustworthy?' asked Chalmers one evening at supper.

'No one knows who doesn't have to.'

Marie was serving rabbit from a casserole. Maurice chuckled at another of his private jokes. Chantal caught Chalmers's eye, then looked away, both aware of a shared intimacy. She had changed into a yellow dress after the day's work. Célestine was upstairs, taking the old man his supper. Two brass oil lamps flickered on the table.

'How did the lesson go?' Marie put the lid on the casserole and sat down.

'James says I'm no good.' Chantal's eyes smiled again. 'I've promised to practise. I've told him he can beat me if I don't.'

'Never did any good in the past,' said her father. 'Always been wilful.' He was proud of both his daughters, but had always been closer to Chantal and was aware of her attraction to the Englishman.

'You used to tell me to follow her example,' said Marguerite. 'Perhaps James will teach me instead if she's no good.'

Célestine came in carrying a tray. She, too, had changed, as she always did on Sundays. Servant she might be, but this was one way she could remind them of her status with the head of the family. This evening she wore an old-fashioned, dark-purple dress, full length, very faded, with a black band round her throat and a cameo brooch he had given her one birthday many years ago. 'He enjoyed that,' she said. She sat down in her usual place at the end of the table, the place from which she cleared and served everyone else. Maurice was laughing again. No one paid any attention.

Chalmers was getting used to Maurice. 'This is good,' he said, putting butter on a piece of bread. 'I love the smell of new bread. We didn't get it like this in the Mess.' He launched into something he knew was mildly provocative. 'Was that a Red Kite I saw this morning, over the woods down by the river?' He had been struck by their total indifference to wild life. At one point he commented on the abundance and beauty of Swallowtail butterflies, which he had never seen in England. They did not understand what he was talking about.

'What?' This was Lejeune.

'Kite. Thought I recognised the forked tail.'

'There are more birds now,' said Lejeune, wiping his moustache with the back of his hand.

'Guns had to be handed in when the Boches came. Some were. Penalties are severe.'

'Did you?'

'Where do you think this rabbit came from?'

'You shot it?'

'The top field yesterday.'

'A risk?'

'The gun's well hidden. It's the last thing we'd give up. Blanchard kept his. I'd tell him if I knew the Boches were coming and he'd tell me. That *sanglier* the other day came from Blanchard – the woods near Courson. I let him have a couple of rabbits yesterday.'

'How did it start – your group?' Chalmers asked the question he had previously avoided.

Lejeune looked at Chalmers with narrowed eyes, then remembered the promise about the Englishman knowing as much as everyone else. 'Gambert was here looking at my father. He'd been in touch with his brother, also a doctor, in Villeneuve-sur-Yonne. Small town the other side of Auxerre. His brother helped a Spitfire pilot shot down near Sens. He'd baled out and was wounded. He'd lost a lot of blood and was ready to give himself up. He had no French at all, but quite by chance knocked on the door of the *boucher* in Villeneuve to beg some food. It so happened that the *boucher* had married an English nurse at the end of the Great War. They took him in and Gambert's brother patched up his wound. Then they were stuck. I'd heard rumours about an escape line in Clamecy – no more than that. Chantal has friends there and poked about to see if she could find out anything. She managed it, the pilot came here and we became a link in the chain. The others followed.'

'So no real planning?'

'No – completely local. We've no idea how long the Clamecy chain was there. From our point of view it was all spontaneous. Migennes tried to get us into something more organised, but they're Reds. No planning about the men in the woods either. Farmers feed them to stop them causing trouble. Most concentrate on keeping body and soul together. I've known Bernard for years. It was pure chance we found we were both helping the forest men – then he told me about his own group and the Maquis Camille in the Morvan. Rumour says there's more organisation in the South, and there must be links with the Free French in London, but we don't know anything about that. The messages, of course.'

'At Pontaubert you were called *Le Renard*.'

'Nickname at school. It's stuck – code-name for me and the group.'

'You rather than Gambert?'

'Most Resistance started in towns – journalists, doctors, schoolmasters. It's only recently spread into the countryside. Farmers and peasants are cautious. Most supported Pétain – like the Church. They still do. Gambert's a reliable man, but not a leader. Henri and Georges respect him because he's a doctor – and so do I. They respect me because I'm a successful farmer. Country people are suspicious of the towns. They'll follow one of their own.'

'How long have you been here – your family?'

'At La Rippe – in this house?'

'Yes.'

'Since the 1850s, before the first Boche invasion.'

'The Franco-Prussian War – Napoleon III?'

'If that's what you call it. The Lejeunes were peasant farmers for years, very small, like most peasants. Our cottage is still there at Crain. Then one of them struck gold – my grandfather. He married into the Paumiers. They'd got hold of church land at the Revolution and owned this farm. You can see their tombs in the cemetery – very impressive. But no good at producing sons. His wife inherited this house when her brother died and the land came with it. My father was their only son. The Paumiers resented the Lejeunes. Didn't think we were good enough. We were though. That's why my mother got the piano. They're all dead now,' he said with satisfaction.

Lejeune confirmed what Chalmers suspected. He'd detected the peasant attitude from the beginning: suspicion, self-reliance, hostility to anything not understood, the grasping attitude to land. But bourgeois aspiration was there, too: ambition for his children, the decoration and furniture. He recalled his own first term at Oxford, keeping quiet about his suburban background, trying to fade into a milieu where style of hacking jacket and width of trousers were more important than academic prowess.

'That's why I was sent to the nuns in Auxerre,' said Chantal.

'I wouldn't go,' said Marguerite. 'So I can't speak English.'

Chalmers looked at the sisters. The affection between them was obvious. Conscious of their differences, they were nevertheless close. At the same time he felt Chantal pulling him towards her. He sensed a warmth including him in everything she said. Marguerite flirted openly, but probably did that with any man. Chantal's eyes were on him and he trusted her in a way he felt was reciprocated.

Lejeune said: 'I want you to hear something later. The others have heard it, you haven't.'

'The messages?' asked Marie.

'Yes.'

'I'll come, too.' This was Chantal.

Lejeune looked towards Maurice and said: 'Not all of us. The messages aren't for us . . . yet.'

After supper Lejeune picked up an oil-lamp and he and Chantal led Chalmers upstairs. They went to the end of the first landing and up a small staircase leading to the second floor. Chalmers had not been up here before and was immediately struck by the quality of furnishing. The carpet was threadbare, the wallpaper faded.

'Maurice's room,' said Lejeune, as they passed a door. 'Next to Célestine. He had it when he was a baby. He got used to it and wouldn't move. He likes things to stay the same.'

He opened the next door and they went into a room with closed shutters. 'Célestine's room. She moved back when father became ill.' There were dark-brown curtains, a single bed with a blue counterpane, and beside it a small upright chair with a rush seat that reminded Chalmers of the painting by Van Gogh. Next to the window stood a washstand with a china bowl and jug, and beyond that an oak wardrobe, its single door open, revealing the clothes inside. The floorboards were wide and rough, the only covering a cheap patterned rug by the bed.

Lejeune knelt by the bed and pushed the rug to one side. From his pocket he produced a chisel and eased it into a gap between the floorboards. He twisted his wrist and the board turned on its side. He put his hand into the gap beneath and brought out a small brown rectangular box with black knobs on the top.

'Wireless,' he said. 'Dropped in a *parachutage* near Dijon. They want every group to have one. Clamecy gave it to us when we passed on the last RAF man.'

He indicated the bed and Chalmers and Chantal sat down. As they did so their hands touched accidentally. Both withdrew instantly, but for a fraction of a second they shared an unstated intimacy. Lejeune turned one of the knobs and the wireless crackled into life. Eventually American dance music emerged out of the atmospherics. He sat on the chair and looked at a fob watch he'd taken out of his waistcoat pocket. 'We're early,' he said. For Chalmers, Glenn Miller's big band sound brought a reminder of the world he had lost.

Minutes later the programme changed and they were listening to a girls' choir in London singing an anti-German propaganda song. To the tune of the nursery rhyme *Meunier tu dors* the voices, innocent, full of *joie de vivre*, sang:

'*France ouvrière et France paysanne*
N'oubliez-pas que l'Nazi c'est l'ennemi . . .
. . . Que le moulin et l'usine ralentissent
Pour l'ennemi ne faites pas le moindre effort
Vous verrez qu'un jour votre sacrifice
Vous aura tous sauvé de la mort'.

'Good for morale.' Lejeune held up his hand. 'Listen.'

Eventually, the voices faded and a cultured voice speaking immaculate French said: *Ici Londres, ici Londres. Les Français parlent aux Français.* We have some messages for our friends across the Channel.' The voice was genial, confidential, almost intimate. It spoke clearly and repeated each message slowly. 'Gaston will feed his pigs tomorrow and Jean-Marc will take his bell to the churchyard on Friday. The elephant has big feet and the lion is fit and well. Pierre must provide wine for the party and Armand will sleep with Justine tonight.'

'Cryptic,' said Chalmers. He caught Chantal's eye.

'Hope he doesn't disappoint her,' she said.

The messages continued for some minutes and ended with a rousing version of the *Marseillaise*. Lejeune replaced the wireless under the floorboard. 'They all mean something to somebody. Bernard had a message before the drop at Lormes.'

'Strange to hear the voices – and the American band. It seems only yesterday I was there. Difficult to believe I'm in the middle of France. There's a lot of activity if those messages all mean something.'

'France is a big country. You can be shot if you're caught listening.' He changed the subject. 'When Gambert takes the plaster off, we'll start work. The first thing is to get you papers. Migennes have put us onto a man in Saulieu. He can do it once he's got a photograph. He'll want your measurements and a fingerprint, too. Henri's coming tomorrow with a camera. We may stick to the story about the relative from Vaison. We'll take the advice of the Saulieu man.'

'I'm nervous about going out.'

'You'll be all right.' Chantal smiled and touched him on the shoulder. 'Your French is good.'

'The next thing's a *vélo*,' went on Lejeune. 'Georges has got one. His uncle's – he died last month. Lived near Noyers. Georges'll collect it next time he goes to Auxerre to stock up his bar. You must find your way about.'

'I've studied the map. When I've got the bike, I'll make sure I know every nook and cranny. Why do you keep the wireless here?' He indicated the floorboard.

'It's dry, and if there's a search, they're less likely to be thorough here. Célestine's an old woman and if the worst came to the worst we'd put her in bed and make out she's ill. Her chamber pot'll be on the rug and the Boches would think twice about moving it. She knows what to do.'

The next day Chalmers was sitting on a kitchen chair outside the barn trying to pluck a chicken when Henri cycled into the yard carrying a tripod under one arm. On a bicycle he looked even more gaunt than usual. A Gauloise was clamped between his lips. For his part, Chalmers was glad to be interrupted. Célestine had given him plucking instructions, but he was a poor pupil. He was relieved she had not asked him to kill the bird, but the feathers made him sneeze.

'Saulieu tomorrow,' said Henri. 'He can do the papers straight away.'

Chalmers put the chicken on a dish and stood up. 'Where do you want me?'

'Put your jacket on. Come into the dairy. I only need your face.'

'By the wall – against the whitewash.' Henri bent over his tripod, fitting a small black camera to it with the precision of a man who knows what he is doing. 'A sideline before the war,' he explained. 'Babies, baptisms and first communions. Can't get the films now. This is special. Jacques got it from Migennes. Don't smile. An identity card is serious – same as a passport. Pity you've shaved. There's still bruising, but I can get rid of most of it. I was told to make you as nondescript as possible.'

Henri took three shots, then straightened up. 'That'll do. They'll be ready for Saulieu tomorrow.'

They left the dairy, walking through the long grass of the orchard. The sun was warm; insects buzzed round them. 'Where's Jacques?' asked Henri.

'In the fields with the man from Coulanges. Maurice is there, too.'

'Maurice!' Henri laughed. 'What do you make of him?' His thin face creased into an expression that managed to convey puzzlement and pity.

'A gentle giant – a simple man. He works hard. They all work hard.' He was grateful to express honest appreciation after all they had done for him.

They walked through the trees, Henri pushing his bicycle, the tripod under his arm. The apples on the trees were ripening. Chalmers suspected he would soon be picking them. Henri put one of his long legs over the bicycle and threw away the stub of his cigarette. Chalmers felt he had been accepted.

He asked Lejeune about Saulieu when he came in for lunch.

'Saulieu? Small town – about 70 kilometres. On the N6. You can't come. Gambert will drive me. He gets petrol and can move about as a doctor.'

The next day Gambert arrived after breakfast. The photographs had come out well, almost too well. The bruising had faded, but was still there.

'He doesn't look rough enough,' said Lejeune. 'Not a countryman.'

'The man may have ideas,' said Gambert. 'He's done the English before.'

Lejeune and Gambert set off for Saulieu the moment the man from Coulanges had been given his jobs for the day. Chalmers sat in the yard with another chicken to pluck.

***

The man who created false papers lived on the top floor of a crumbling house in the square opposite the twelfth-century basilica of St-Andoche. It was a sunny day, but the curtains were half drawn and the book-lined room was gloomy. Philippe, the only name they had been given, was small and dark, wearing spectacles with metallic rims; a twitch in the flaccid skin by his mouth suggested nervousness. His questions were sharp. He picked up the photographs Gambert had put on his desk. 'Reasonable,' he said. 'Story?'

'We rely on you,' replied Gambert. 'We were going to say he's a Lejeune cousin from Provence if anyone sees him on the farm. He speaks French fluently – too well for a country area like Burgundy. Educated man, could be from Paris. He's twenty-three.'

'There really *is* a cousin?'

'There *was*. Haven't heard for years.'

'Farming?'

'Vineyard. Gigondas – near Vaison-la-Romaine.'

'Does this man know Provence? Could he talk about it?'

'He used to visit a French family at a château near St.Rémy. That's why his French is good. No regional accent.'

'Does he know Paris?' Philippe was brisk.

'No. One visit.'

'We'll concentrate on what he knows. I'll put him in Provence. He can be a remote cousin, we don't want name confusion. His papers must stand up on their own. Educated, you say?'

'At Oxford when war broke out. Studying languages.'

Philippe stared at his notes. The twitch by his mouth was more pronounced. 'We'll start from scratch. Commercial traveller's best. He can move about. He's clean shaven and looks respectable. Broken a leg?'

'Plaster off next week,' said Gambert.

'What does he know about?'

'Nothing to do with farming,' replied Lejeune with conviction.

'Wine?'

'No.'

'He won't be questioned unless he gets into trouble. He just needs the papers for checks. What *does* he know about?'

Lejeune and Gambert looked at each other. Lejeune had taken off his beret. He examined his work-stained hands, subconsciously comparing them with the soft hands of the man holding the pencil behind the desk. 'Music?' he hazarded. 'He plays the piano.'

'Music? Music teacher? Difficult. Can't go too far. Would be remembered.'

'He's read a lot – literature. French as well as English. Likes De Maupassant. Tells me I should read De Maupassant – and Zola. Have you read them? We haven't got enough books for him.'

'Books.' Philippe considered the possibility. 'Books,' he repeated. 'That's better. Books – a publisher's representative. There's a firm in Marseille I can use. Not too far from St.Rémy. He could have gone there for work. I know the owner. Capitalist, of course, but on our side. He'll put his name down as an employee. He won't need to know anything.' He looked up, the desk light turning his spectacles into opaque discs. The twitch had gone. 'Go and get some lunch. Mention my name and you'll get something reasonable at the Café St-Andoche next door. Don't hurry. This takes time. It'll be ready by three. What shall we call him? Something ordinary. Michel – yes, he looks like a Michel – Michel Duval. That's ordinary enough.'

Lejeune and Gambert went out into the summer sunlight. 'Knows what he's doing,' said Lejeune. 'I trust him. Migennes said he has everything prepared. Just fills in the details.'

'Red,' said Gambert, 'but we expected that. Beggars can't be choosers.'

'We wouldn't have known about him if it hadn't been for Migennes.'

The Café St-Andoche was more or less empty. They went inside and sat at a corner table under a gilt mirror and advertisements for Dubonnet and St.Raphaël. To one side were official notices: a warning about closing-time from the local German authority and a similar warning against alcoholism and selling drink to young people from the Vichy government. Behind the bar hung a portrait of Marshal Pétain. A middle-aged woman wiping tables eyed them suspiciously as they came in. Mention of Philippe wrought a transformation and after a delay a young waiter, no more than a boy, produced a cassoulet in which pigeons were the prime ingredient. They shared a *pichet* of red wine and some ersatz coffee. Gambert's Citroën was the only French car parked by the fountain in the square. A German military Mercedes had parked beside it. Its occupants, a Wehrmacht driver and an NCO, sat at an outside table drinking beer.

The woman, flushed with her efforts, was friendly. 'Regulars,' she said, nodding at the two Germans. 'If they weren't Boches, I'd be sorry for them. Long way from home and no one wants them here. They're honest when they've had a drink. Not enough girls, friendly ones anyway. And they can see the war going badly. Frightened of being sent to the Eastern Front and worried about their families under the bombing. How do you know Philippe?'

Lejeune was non-committal. Gambert pretended not to have heard. Lejeune countered, his voice lowered: 'You serve a lot of them?'

'It's business.'

Lejeune nodded. 'Of course. They buy from my farm. We have to survive. One day it will be different.'

'Perhaps.' Her voice was toneless, indifferent to the future. 'Philippe thinks so. I'm not so sure. Look at the Maginot Line. *Ils ne passeront pas.*' She laughed, a harsh sound. 'Pétain picked up the pieces. A lot still support him. Cognac?'

'Thank you,' said Lejeune. 'Philippe wouldn't agree, I think.' He pointed at the portrait behind the bar. 'About the Marshal.'

'Oh, Philippe!' She dismissed him with a Gallic shrug. 'He's a dreamer.' She poured three substantial cognacs. 'We all know Philippe. I knew him when he was a little boy. Believes the Russians will save the day.'

'And you?'

She shrugged again. 'They'll look after themselves, like everyone else. You know about Philippe . . . ?'

'Communist?'

'Of course. Sees politics in everything. But he enjoys a meal here and forgets we're capitalists. We get on all right.'

An elderly couple who had been eating their lunch at a table to the rear of the café paid their bill and left. The woman was all in black, the man, also in black, walked with a limp and the aid of a stick. They had the resigned look of people with no interest in anything, not even each other.

The woman from the bar waited until the door closed, then said: 'Monsieur and Madame Mercier. Had two sons. Both killed at Loos in the Great War. This war doesn't exist for them.'

Lejeune drained his cognac and turned to Gambert. 'Time to go. Thank you, Madame. The cassoulet was good.' He paid the bill.

'*Au revoir, Messieurs*. My regards to Philippe.'

Outside, after passing the Germans, Lejeune turned to Gambert. 'She probably knows what our business is.'

Philippe was waiting. 'There's the *Carte d'Identité*,' he said. 'And it's dirty enough to have been in use for some time. Dated 1941 when Vichy was still unoccupied. There's a ration book and letters from the Marseille publisher. I've put in references to music and art books. It'll stand up to any cursory investigation. He needs a good story to go with it. The publisher will support it if he has to, but keep him out of it if you can.' He stood up, holding out his hand. '*Bonne chance*,' he said. '*Vive la France.*'

Lejeune and Gambert shook hands and went back to their car. The Mercedes was still there, the Germans enjoying a joke with two girls in summer dresses who had joined them.

'They've found company,' said Gambert.

'The spoils of war. More money than Frenchmen.'

They climbed into the car and set off for La Rippe by side roads. Fields and woods slipped past and before long they were beneath the walls of Avallon in the valley of the River Cousin. The houses of the town climbed the hill above them, a tumble of untidy roofs and bleached shutters. Lejeune was looking at the papers. 'Professional job,' he said. 'We mustn't let him down. It'll depend on James.'

'He's intelligent,' said Gambert. 'And his French is good. That's the key. You think we were wrong? Something's worrying you.'

'Doctor's diagnosis?'

'I know you.'

'James is all right.'

'What, then?'

'Chantal.'

'She's a sensible girl. If you'd said Marguerite . . .'

'Chantal likes him. I know my girls.'

'Likes him too much?'

'Perhaps.' Lejeune was articulating thoughts barely admitted to himself.

'She'll fall for someone one day.'

'He's giving her piano lessons. They laugh a lot.'

'Leave it to Chantal's good sense.'

In Avallon, they were held up by a German dispatch rider giving a military convoy priority through the narrow streets of the town. 'Troops moving,' said Lejeune. 'The sort of information we can send to London. I don't want Johnson at the farm, but we'll get him nearer.'

'Doesn't Bernard want him?'

'He was coming to us. André had arranged it. He only went into the forest when Clamecy collapsed. Could you find room for him?'

'Plenty of room, but difficult to keep him out of the way in the village. Patients might see him. Georges and Henri would be no good either. Better in a farm.'

'I can't have them both.'

'Poirier?'

'He's sympathetic. His sister's a problem.'

'No worse than Maurice.'

Lejeune made a noise that sounded like assent. Auguste Poirier had a smallholding on the edge of St.Pierre and a simple sister whose grasp of reality was as tenuous as his brother's. 'I'll think about it.'

Gambert was back in time for evening surgery. As he opened the door, he remembered Lejeune's concern about Chantal. He trusted Lejeune's judgement and wondered if he could be right.

Chalmers and Chantal were in the room with the piano when Lejeune got back. Chantal was playing a Schubert Impromptu, her forehead furrowed with concentration.

'Better?' she asked, looking up at Chalmers standing over her.

Chalmers looked at her concerned face. He saw how much his approval meant and was surprised he had not understood this before. Without really thinking what he was doing, he put his arm round her shoulders. 'Much better, he said. 'You've got a lovely touch – a woman's touch.' Then, his arm still round her, he said, 'We'd better see what your father's got for me.'

Chantal looked away. For once she did not respond with a flippant remark. Something inside her was producing feelings never experienced before.

22

The following week Gambert took off the plaster. Chalmers went into the yard to practise walking without crutches and his initial delight was tempered by finding the leg weak and his balance so uncertain he had to put a hand on the barn wall to keep upright.

'You'll be fine in a couple of days,' said Gambert.

'Georges is bringing the bicycle today.'

'Don't go beyond the farm until you're sure of the leg.'

'I want to prove I can survive outside.'

'All the more important to take it slowly. You know the wireless man's coming this evening? Poirier's going to take him. He's got children and he wants the Germans out before they're grown up. Putting him in his barn. He won't join us, but has agreed to hide Johnson. I'm collecting him at the mill.'

'Now I've got papers we should be in business.'

'Details at your fingertips?' Gambert had the confidence Chalmers associated with doctors, but sensed his nervousness whenever he talked about going out.

His cover story had in the end combined the distant cousin with the publisher's representative to explain his presence at the farm. As a relative he was staying at La Rippe and his leg explained why he had not moved on. His sense of humour came to the fore. 'I've got a split personality simply by being here. Now I've been given two French names.'

The thought of a split personality was not new. Lying in bed at night he had struggled with his feelings for Mary and Chantal. It was not about which one he loved. He adored Mary and longed for her. No, it was not the certainty of love: it was more subtle, more difficult. At Wynton Thorpe their closeness was constantly confirmed. If they were not actually together, they were sending notes, planning their next meeting. All that had stopped; he had heard nothing of her for more than three months. In any case she would have imagined his death. He knew too well that the chalk-scrawled 'Missing' on the squadron board meant 'Killed' to everyone. But he was alive. He was alive, miles away and there was no guarantee of seeing her again. Pages in the book had turned. A new narrative was appearing on blank paper. The old world was the past; the reality was the Lejeune family, Gambert, Georges, Henri, and René. And in that reality Chantal was desirable. She had nursed him and was risking her life for him. From the first he had been her responsibility and he detected jealousy if anyone else did anything for him.

Did he have feelings for her at all? He wanted to laugh at the idea. Mary was everything. He had let her down and was consumed by guilt. But if he shut his eyes he could not see her; he needed the photograph in his wallet to conjure her presence. And beyond the guilt, beyond the love, he was aware of Chantal. Chantal's sexuality was difficult to ignore. There was warmth, mischief and something intangible; her solid peasant tread magically transformed the movement of her body into a sexual statement any man would recognise. He remembered the mature woman who had given ballroom dancing lessons at school creating lust in her girl-starved pupils simply through the way she moved.

Georges arrived with the *vélo* shortly after lunch. He drove into the yard in a battered green *camionette*. Chickens scattered and Marie and Chantal came out of the dairy. Chalmers appeared from the stable carrying a pitchfork.

Georges held the bicycle it in front of him. 'Not bad, eh? Three-speed gear.'

'Very good,' said Chalmers. He did not forget that this was the man who had got him out of the cockpit.

'His widow wanted to sell it. *Pouf!* She's never liked me. Didn't like her husband much either.' The usual cigarette dangled from his lip. 'She owed me a favour. I once lied for her when she was too frightened to tell her husband about one of her debts. He often hit her.' He handed the bicycle to Chalmers. 'It needs oil.'

Chalmers gingerly put his leg over the crossbar and eased himself into the saddle. Momentarily he thought of a cycle ride he and Mary had taken to a pub near Wynton Thorpe shortly before his final flight. Before going back to the base they had enjoyed a cuddle under an oak tree by the lane. 'I'm looking forward to being married,' she had said. It seemed a long time ago.

'Careful,' said Chantal, watching him get onto the cycle. She had been churning butter and a curl fell over one eye.

'I don't want anything else broken.' He put pressure on the pedal and eased forward. The cobbles were rough, but he steered a steady course towards the orchard before turning and coming back past the *camionette*. The chickens eyed him warily. He completed three circuits before stopping in front of Georges. 'That's fine. I'll lower the saddle and put more air in the tyres. A good *vélo*. Thank you.'

Georges was behind the wheel of his van. 'I must get back to Mailly.' He reversed, waved cursorily and was gone.

'Put it with mine,' said Chantal, pushing back the wayward curl. 'Now you've got it I'll start showing you around.'

'The locals will be curious,' said Marie.

'James can talk about Vaison. Who's been to Provence? Georges hasn't been as far as Dijon. Henri went to Marseille on his way to the Congo, but he's never been to Paris. *Mon Dieu*, we've hardly been out of the Yonne ourselves.' Chantal turned to Chalmers. 'I've been to Paris twice.'

'I only managed it once.' Chalmers glimpsed again the waif-like figure by the Seine. 'Got the flavour and saw some of the sights. Notre Dame, Eiffel Tower, Sacré-Coeur. What did you do?'

Chantal looked at her mother. 'Maman wanted a dress for a wedding. The time before that I was a little girl. I can't remember why we went. Dr.Gambert was at the Sorbonne. He doesn't want to go back.'

'Parisians aren't liked,' said Marie. 'Clever and too much money. But that lilac dress was lovely. Rue de Rivoli. Even your father liked it, though he couldn't believe the price.'

'Where are you putting the wireless man?' asked Chalmers.

'In the barn where you were,' replied Chantal. 'It's only one night.'

'I want to talk to him.' With his leg out of plaster, Chalmers felt fit and although he deferred to Lejeune's leadership he intended to play a full part within the group. 'I'll finish cleaning the stable.'

***

Célestine was lighting the lamps and Lejeune was upstairs with his father when Gambert returned with Johnson. The doctor dropped him and drove off without waiting to speak to anyone. The trip had taken longer than expected and he knew his wife worried.

'I was late getting to the mill,' explained Johnson to Chalmers. 'Troop movements again and Bernard wasn't taking any risks.' He looked around. 'Nice berth you've found. I've been living in a hut in the woods. They haven't the first idea how to dig a latrine. I was damned lucky not to be picked up with Emil.' Johnson's hair framed the firm contours of his face. He had lost the high colour of their first evening but struggled with the larger of the two cases he had unloaded from the car.

'London?' Chalmers asked.

'They'll support us in spite of Clamecy. I was complimentary about you. And Lejeune seems to know what he's doing.' He dropped his voice. 'He was lucky not to be swept up with the others. I've got a transmission tonight.'

'He's cautious. I've hardly seen the light of day.'

Lejeune came into the yard from the kitchen. He looked at the cases. 'Put them in the barn. That the wireless?' Johnson nodded. 'Cover it up. We'll get it into the loft when you've had something to eat.'

'I'm transmitting later.' He looked at his watch. 'Just over three hours.'

Supper in the kitchen was a strange meal. Johnson was treated like a guest and conversation was stilted. Marie and Chantal enquired after his family and the Channel Islands, Marguerite flirted; Lejeune and Chalmers, who wanted to talk about more important things, were silent; Célestine's disapproval of anything intruding into routine was again manifest. Afterwards, carrying lanterns, the three men went to the barn and put the cases in the loft.

Johnson looked at his watch again. 'It's a tight schedule in London. I've asked the questions, now we get the answers.' He opened the wireless case and spent half an hour screwing a morse key into a board and fixing an aerial to beams in the roof. He put on headphones and tuned the equipment. It gave off buzzing and whistling sounds.

'Very noisy,' said Lejeune.

Johnson held up his hand. 'Let me concentrate. They don't like me asking for repetition.'

Buzzing and whistling were renewed. The clicking of the morse key indicated contact. The headphones clamped Johnson's fair hair to his head, framing the lines on his forehead. From time to time he made jottings. At length he relaxed, removed the headphones and turned to Chalmers and Lejeune sitting in the hay. 'A drop within a fortnight,' he said. 'The next moon. They're assuming "Louis" is in charge.' He smiled at Chalmers. To Lejeune he said: 'You must say what you want. You won't get it all, but there's no harm in asking. They want lights at both ends of the drop.'

Lejeune touched Chalmers on the shoulder. 'You've made

a difference. We'll make a list.'

Chalmers stood up, brushing away hay. He appreciated the generosity behind Lejeune's remark. The bond was tightening.

Johnson stayed in the loft. Poirier was collecting him next day. Lejeune and Chalmers returned to the house where Chantal and Marie were sewing in the parlour, leaning forward in the light of oil lamps. The contrast between light and shadow and the concentration of the two women reminded Chalmers of a painting by Joseph Wright he had seen at the National Gallery. Not for the first time he wondered at the way his mind conjured pictures when more important matters demanded attention.

Lejeune held pencil and paper. 'Guns,' he said. 'Whatever they'll give us. Explosives. Something Henri can handle.'

'Oil to keep the guns in condition,' said Chalmers. 'Petrol – we need more. And medical kit. Gambert's always complaining about shortages. We should stick to essentials. Johnson says the forest men need boots and clothes. We can add them as an extra later. We've got to impress London.'

'We take our time and do things properly. The Boches won't leave France without a fight. Besides,' – Lejeune lowered his voice – 'the French aren't united. Sad, isn't it? The Boches walking all over us and we put other things first. The Right blame the Republic for everything. Vichy had support to start with and most are loyal to Pétain. They want to turn the clock back. On the other side the Reds see the chance of a new revolution.'

'Where do you stand?' Chalmers had not worked this out.

'Between the two. I don't want the Church on our backs and Vichy's a disaster. But I'm a farmer. I've got land. I want the Boches out, but not to hand everything to the Reds. I'll work with Migennes and use men like Philippe – for the time being.'

'De Gaulle? The Free French?'

'Perhaps.'

Chalmers detected suspicion in the ambiguity of the word.

The peasant attitude was still there. Marie put down her sewing. 'We don't know who to trust,' she said. 'Clamecy must have been betrayed.'

'It could have been anywhere along the line.' Lejeune lit a cigarette.

Chantal leaned back, lamplight soft on her face, hair darker in the shadow. 'Papa, can I take James out now he's got the *vélo*?'

'Not to Clamecy.'

'No – round here. Magny, Mailly, St.Pierre – perhaps Châtel-Censoir.'

'Take him to *Les Pêcheurs*. Georges will be there.'

'Tomorrow?' She looked at Chalmers.

'I can't wait to escape.' Chalmers spoke confidently, but aware of nervousness born of long incarceration. 'Should we tell Georges?'

'I'll warn him,' said Lejeune. 'I don't want him surprised.'

'What about Poirier?' asked his wife.

'He's not coming till later.' He turned to Chantal. 'When you've been to *Les Pêcheurs* come home via St.Pierre. Show him Poirier's farm – and the station. Maurice can work in the dairy tomorrow. He won't mind.'

The next day dawned sunny again; the summer continued. Chalmers woke early. The thought of getting out was exciting, but a responsibility he did not take lightly. He could mess up everything. He remembered the brutality of the Cossack voices. He put on the most anonymous of the clothes he had been given: rough trousers, nondescript jacket, a pair of shoes that had seen better days. The smarter clothes would wait until he was on the road as the publisher's representative. He met Chantal on the landing as they went down to breakfast.

'Ready?' she asked.

'As I ever shall be.'

'You'll be fine.' She looked as calm as he wanted to feel. She wore a flowered blouse and the full blue skirt. A black belt with a silver buckle emphasised her waist. Somehow she always managed to look freshly laundered at the beginning of the day. Marguerite had the same knack.

'How do you manage it?' he asked.

'What?'

'To look so . . . so fresh. No one would think you work as hard as you do.'

She lowered her eyes. 'Vanity,' she said. 'And we're lucky to have Célestine. The Blanchards had a maid, but they haven't now. It makes a difference.'

He walked behind her down the stairs. As she reached the bottom step, she paused unexpectedly and he almost bumped into her. He checked himself, then, quite spontaneously touched her hair, so gently he did not think she would notice. 'That was nice,' she said. 'Could you do it again?' Her voice was soft.

He stroked the fringe of hair curling up from the nape of her neck, more firmly this time. He remembered how he had put his arm around her shoulder at the end of the piano lesson. He had made a second physical gesture and not been rebuffed.

At about half-past ten Chantal went out to the orchard where Chalmers had been cutting grass with a scythe. He was sharpening the blade with a whetstone. Her eyes were smiling. 'Ready to go?'

'Ready to stop this job. I don't want to lose a leg. Maurice showed me how to do it, but I haven't mastered the technique. He thinks I'm daft.'

They collected the bicycles and walked to the front of the farm. The lane was deserted. The branches on the trees were motionless in the still air, the only sound a chattering magpie in the field opposite. To Chalmers it seemed the countryside was full of eyes. Chantal felt the anticipation she always sensed when she had Chalmers on her own. They set off towards Mailly-le-Château, its houses tumbled together on the side of the valley.

227

The lane dipped into a shaded hollow, then swung left up an incline into sunshine. Chalmers kept his front wheel just behind Chantal's, anxious to go at whatever speed she dictated. He was entirely in her hands. 'No one around,' he said. Relief conflicted with a feeling that he wanted to be tested in some way.

'Hardly anyone uses the lane. We might meet Blanchard's cows if he's moving them.'

The lane dropped away and the sunshine faded as they free-wheeled into a tunnel of woodland. When they emerged into the sun again, Chalmers began to relax, looking at the butterflies in the hedges. They took him back to the butterfly in the loft and his relief when it escaped the spider's web. He recalled a line in one of Hardy's valedictory poems summing up his life: 'He was a man who used to notice such things.' How odd that his mind threw up literary bric-a-brac in moments of stress.

They were going downhill again, more steeply. Chantal was a confident cyclist and flew ahead, skirt and hair streaming behind her. Again Hardy appeared, this time the poems about Emma, his future wife, riding her mare wildly on the Cornish cliffs during their courtship. He was cautious on the bicycle and still conscious of his leg. His left hand fingered the brake.

'Come on,' she called over her shoulder.

He came up beside her as they reached level ground. To their right, through the trees, the glistening Yonne curled towards the bluff on which Mailly-le-Château perched. They cycled towards the bridge over the river leading to the outlying buildings of Mailly. On the bridge was a religious shrine, neglected and semi-derelict, the sort of thing Chalmers normally stopped to investigate. He was about to ask what it was when they met the first person they had seen, an old woman in a black dress clutching a baguette.

'*Bonjour, Madame Morelle*,' said Chantal loudly, as to one who is deaf.

'*Bonjour, Madame,*' parroted Chalmers.

The woman eyed them, her face thin and lined, lips narrow and pinched. She was a smaller and older edition of Célestine.

'Stone deaf,' said Chantal. 'Grandmother to half of Mailly. Claims to be eighty, must be ninety. The biggest gossip in the village.' Chantal slowed and dismounted at the end of the bridge. 'She'll find out about you. But harmless. Lives with a spinster daughter. One of her grandsons was captured during the invasion. Still a prisoner. She remembers the war in 1870. Her aunt was raped and shot. She loathes the Germans. There's *Les Pêcheurs.*' She pointed at a shabby house by the river, its title spelt out in faded green letters over the door. 'We'll walk the last bit.'

It was warm enough for the door to be open and Chantal led the way inside through simple tables and chairs. It was dark after the brightness outside and Chalmers thought the room was empty. Then his eyes adjusted to the gloom and he saw two elderly men sitting in the corner. Both wore berets and had full moustaches. They looked, he thought, like Marshals Foch and Joffre discussing a military problem. They were playing cards. Each had a glass of red wine in front of him. They fell silent as Chantal and the stranger came in.

Chantal introduced Chalmers. 'From Provence,' she said. 'Where's Georges?'

'In the kitchen.' Georges's wife, Ernestine, appeared behind the bar. She was a big woman, bulging breasts and hips emphasised by the large flowers on her brightly coloured dress. She had a florid face and kind eyes. She looked at Chalmers with interest. Georges had primed her and she knew the part to play. '*Bonjour, Monsieur?*' A rising inflection indicated the note of query.

'*Bonjour, Madame.* I expect you heard about my accident. Bad news travels fast.'

'*Certainement.* A nasty fall, Dr.Gambert told me. Georges broke his leg when he was a boy. Fell out of a tree pinching Monsieur Croiset's apples. Served him right.' She smiled at the two old men, including them in the conversation.

'We need Michel on the farm,' said Chantal. 'The old man thinks he broke it on purpose to avoid work. Tries to rule with a rod of iron from his bedroom. Georges cooking?'

'Doesn't let me near the stove when he's got a rabbit.'

'I gave it to him,' said one of the men. 'Stroke of luck.' He winked. 'Fell over in front of me when I was looking for mushrooms near Magny. Couple of them. My wife's cooking the other tonight. *Pichet's* empty.' He looked at Ernestine.

Ernestine made an impatient clicking noise and took over more wine. 'Your liver's your own business,' she said. To Chalmers she said, 'Wine, Monsieur? Cognac? No coffee.'

'Cognac, *s'il vous plaît, Madame.*' Chalmers had never drunk brandy in the morning. 'A small one. I'm scything the orchard this afternoon.' He joined Chantal at the table next to the men.

'Provence,' said one of the card players ruminatively. 'My brother's wife went there before the war. Her sister nearly married a man from Avignon. She said it was hot. Hotter than Burgundy.' He inhaled his cigarette and looked at his cards. To Ernestine he said: 'I hope Georges gets coffee soon.'

'So do I. Black market – he hasn't been let down yet. We had some in June.'

The other man looked at Chalmers. 'Do you fish?'

It was not the sort of question Chalmers had expected. He sipped his cognac. 'No, I've never fished.'

'Pity. You could have come on Sunday. The Mailly competition.' He turned to Ernestine. 'Good entry this year?'

'More than usual. They want something to eat.'

'Georges and Ernestine organise it,' explained Chantal. 'Good for trade, isn't it?'

Ernestine looked round at the empty tables. 'It needs to be.'

Chalmers also surveyed the room. The pictures on the walls were mostly photographs of Mailly-le-Château, notably the château from which the village took its name, a nineteenth-century building of no great beauty built within the walls of the original castle. A shadow appeared across the sunlight of the door and a middle-aged man in a dowdy suit came in. He looked enquiringly at Chalmers and Chantal effected the introduction. He was the local schoolmaster, a Monsieur Ronson, obviously respected by the two older men. Chalmers thought he detected suspicion in Chantal.

'I heard there was a stranger at La Rippe,' Ronson said. He was grey-haired and wore spectacles with a metal rim.

Chantal smiled at him. 'Madame Ronson is well?'

'As well as can be expected.'

Ronson picked up a glass of wine at the bar and sat down at a table on his own. He eyed Chalmers. 'Vaison-la-Romaine, did you say?'

'The old town – on the hill. Do you know it?' Chalmers sensed a quizzing by the local busybody.

'Never been there. Roman remains, I believe.'

Chalmers was prepared for this. 'Archaeologists get excited. There's a theatre and a lot of pillars and statues.' He managed to imply a lack of interest. 'Have you been the schoolmaster here long?'

'Long enough to be accepted.' He looked at Ernestine. 'Or I hope so. The curé's been here longer.' He smiled a bleak little smile that went with the steel-rimmed spectacles. 'The Germans have moved troops into the Morvan.'

The dustier of the two old men spoke, rheumy eyes looking at the schoolmaster. 'They're after the men avoiding the labour law. They caught some last week. Lucky not to be shot. They're searching houses in Auxerre too.'

'Dijon was bombed last night.' This was Ernestine, now polishing glasses. 'The railway again. I'm glad my father moved out here.'

'They kill Frenchmen as well as Germans. There'll be more killed before this is over,' said Ronson. 'I've never liked the English. They bombed Orléans last week. There's a rumour they're getting revenge by bombing places where they were beaten by Jeanne d'Arc.'

Chalmers hoped his face did not give away his feelings. The absurdity of the idea made him realise he had much to learn about the French. At the same time he felt he was accepted.

Chantal did not look at him, but spoke bluntly to Ronson. 'We'll be glad enough when the Second Front comes. There'll be plenty of English killed then. A lot being killed over Germany now. You're too close to the Reds in Migennes, Monsieur. They'll spill anyone's blood to help the Russians.'

'The Russians are winning the war. There'll be changes when it's over. You wait and see.'

'We'll have to wait a long time.' One of the old men produced a grey-looking handkerchief, wiping his eyes before blowing his nose.

Chantal and Chalmers stayed another five minutes, then Chantal announced she was taking him to St.Pierre before lunch and the desultory conversation ended. Outside, side by side on the bank of the Yonne, they looked at each other, but did not speak until they had gone round the first corner.

'Well done,' she said. 'They didn't suspect anything.'

'You don't like Ronson.'

'I don't trust him. He was Pétainist and now he's friendly with Migennes. Not the sort of person you tell anything to.'

'The two old men seemed harmless.'

'They are. Always at *Les Pêcheurs* in the morning – and they'll be back this evening. They'll talk about you, but they accepted you. Now for St.Pierre.'

'How far?'

'A couple of miles. Flat like this.'

The road crossed open farmland, the Yonne winding through woods to their right. They had just passed a farm when Chalmers slowed and stopped in the shade of an oak. 'It's warm. I'm taking my jacket off.'

Chantal joined him under the tree. He had folded his jacket over the handlebars. She stretched out an arm and touched his hand. 'I was proud of you.'

'I was terrified.'

'Nonsense.'

Her hand rested on his, soft, reassuring. He turned his own hand over, folding her fingers into his. 'I didn't want to let you down.' He squeezed her fingers, then pulled her towards him. Her face was inches away from his, her eyes wide. The sun mottled her skin with leaf shadow. He let his cycle drop and put his free hand into her hair. She opened her lips and he kissed her. It was impulsive, without conscious thought, the urgency springing from both of them. He held her tightly. 'Oh, Chantal,' he said. 'My Chantal.'

'Don't speak,' she said. 'Don't speak. I understand.'

23

Chalmers held her for a few seconds before she pushed him away. The pleasure of his unexpected kiss did not blind her to danger. 'Not here.' She picked up her bicycle. 'Sorry. Anyone could have been looking.'

'Papa wouldn't have been pleased.'

'He wouldn't approve?'

'We mustn't draw attention.'

'Sorry again. Of course, absolutely right.' Chalmers threw a leg over his bike. 'I'd wanted to do that for a long time.'

'I wanted you to.'

'I wasn't sure.'

She did not respond. The road was as empty as it had been since they left Mailly. 'We're all right,' she said. 'We must get on.' They pedalled in silence, the only sound the tyres on the tarmac. Both were aware a barrier had come down. Just once their eyes met and they smiled before looking away.

The road twisted and the spire of a church appeared over the trees. To their right, with rising ground behind it, they passed a cemetery, crosses visible over the stucco wall. They were beyond its iron gates before Chalmers realised this must be where his crew were buried. He braked suddenly. 'The St.Pierre cemetery?' he asked.

'Not now. Too many eyes.' She knew what he wanted.

Chalmers looked down at his pedals. Again he was aware of unfamiliar emotions. He looked up. 'Right, let's get on.' He focused his eyes on the spire ahead. He wondered if she understood the guilt he barely grasped himself.

A rough farm marked the edge of the village. An empty cart stood in the yard, shafts on the ground, and a tumbledown barn was full of hay. A woman was hanging out washing, hens pecking round her. Chantal waved at her, but did not stop. 'Madame Poirier,' she said. 'Where the wireless man is going. She doesn't know about you, so there's no point in making her life more difficult. Poirier may tell her. I'll show you the station.'

They reached the square, dominated by plane trees and the church. One or two locals sat at tables outside a café. Women gossiped at the door of the *boulangerie*; through a window Chalmers could see the baker kneading dough, arms and shoulders bare in the heat of the kitchen. Chantal waved a greeting at the curé, standing in his cassock on the steps of the church. 'A good man,' she muttered. 'He'll wonder who you are, but I won't introduce you now. The station's round here.' They went past the post office and the *charcuterie* down a road bordered by lime trees and several substantial houses. 'The bourgeois part of St.Pierre,' she said.

The road forked beyond the last house and crossed a single track railway by a level-crossing. The lines were silver with use, but grass grew between the sleepers. A hundred yards up the line stood the station. There were two platforms and a siding with three empty coal trucks. A coal lorry was parked in the station yard. There was no sign of life.

'No activity,' observed Chalmers.

'A train each way about once every two hours. Links local villages with Clamecy and Auxerre. There's a Paris connection at Migennes'

'Like village stations in England.'

'I use it a lot.' She pointed at a cottage. 'Vacherot's a friend. He'd help if we had a problem. A widower – do anything for anyone. His family's run the station since the railway was built. I cycled down here to watch the trains with Robert. His wife was alive then. She gave us lemonade.'

Chalmers looked at the cottage, its grey shutters faded and sun-bleached in the heat. Without thinking he said, 'Adlestrop' and instantly regretted it.

'What?'

It was an innocent remark, but even as he made it he remembered saying the same thing to Mary on their journey to London. What a fool! Adlestrop belonged to Mary. He fumbled for a reply. 'An English poem. A train stopping at a station like this.' He could see Mary in the train, felt the suspender through her skirt, saw again the woman in the lilac suit. The guilt of betrayal was redoubled.

'Odd subject for poetry.'

'It captures the heat and the silence. England's not as big as France, but there's some beautiful countryside. I may be able to show you when the war's over.' The words tumbled out, unconsidered.

'Mary might not like that.'

'No.' Now he looked at her. 'The war's not over. I'm living day to day. I could be in the cemetery with my men.'

Chantal stood with her legs each side of her bicycle, her skirt hanging in folds about her. She was not wearing stockings and her legs were brown. Her straight back pushed her breasts forward against her blouse. It was a completely natural position, devoid of artifice, showing her whole body to advantage. 'You're different,' she said.

'How?'

'The others were grateful, did what we told them. None of them could speak a word of French. You seem at home.'

'I am.'

'And Mary?'

'She's not here,' he said simply. 'You are.'

'Convenient.'

'I love Mary. But I may never see her again. Now I've met you.'

'You can chop and change like that?'

236

'You're misinterpreting, misunderstanding.'

'Women are different.' She was under the spell of their kiss and saying things she knew she might regret.

'I hope so.'

'They're more faithful.'

'Time to go home? Célestine will have lunch ready.' He was trying to ignore the guilt. It did not stop him wanting to kiss her again.

They went back through the square. There were more people outside the café. Again Chantal waved. Everyone seemed to know her. In the shade of the trees stood the horse and cart used for *boulangerie* deliveries, the horse eating from its nosebag and nodding its head.

They did not speak until they were putting the cycles away, Chantal conscious of Chalmers's silence. 'Poirier must have collected Johnson,' she said. 'The hay's been moved. If it's like this tomorrow, we could go out again. Châtel-Censoir, perhaps?'

'I want to go to the cemetery.' His crew's death overrode everything.

Chantal was looking at him, her eyes warm. 'I understand, you know.'

'That's why we get on so well. Are you sure you can get out tomorrow?'

'Papa wants you to know the whole area. You've got to get down to Vézelay and Avallon by the side roads – and across to Cravant and Vermenton. It's easier for me to show you. Papa can't spare time away from the farm. We can go when I've done the milking. I'll ask about the cemetery. The morning's best. Locals go in the afternoon.'

'Germans?'

'No reason why they should be there.'

'I don't regret this morning.'

'Nor do I.' Her voice was so soft Chalmers barely caught the words. But he heard what she said as she shut the barn door. 'We'll have to find somewhere more private.'

237

They didn't speak again until they were inside with Marie and Célestine, who were about to put lunch on the table. 'We thought we'd lost you,' said her mother. 'Your father feared the worst. Poirier came for Johnson. He's a good man – he didn't want him.'

'We saw Madame Poirier hanging out her washing,' said Chalmers. '*Les Pêcheurs* brought out my lazy streak. I could spend a day or two there with a *pichet* and those two locals.'

'Madame Morelle saw him,' said Chantal. 'Everyone in Mailly will know by now.'

Lunch fitted the established pattern of meals at La Rippe. Lejeune talked about the farm and Marie asked about gossip brought in by Marguerite's customers at the shop in Mailly. Maurice ate noisily, laughing at his private jokes, occasionally disrupting the thread of conversation by making odd comments. Célestine was silent, speaking only when spoken to; as usual she vanished for part of the meal to take up the old man's lunch. Chalmers and Chantal were less talkative than normal, aware of each other in a way they had not been before. Afterwards Chantal followed her father into the yard and asked about the cemetery. He was doubtful.

'It means a lot. We're sticking to the relation story, so he could be looking for one of those nineteenth-century Lejeunes.'

Her father looked at her. 'I rely on your good sense. Don't stay long.'

'I'll make sure he doesn't.'

'He likes you.'

'I like him. He's in love with an English girl. You needn't worry about me.'

Her father could see she wished it otherwise and changed the subject. 'The wireless man's speaking to London. He'll have an answer about a *parachutage*. James is important. They trust him.'

The next day Chantal and Chalmers cycled to the cemetery. The sun was out again and it was warm. The gate was half open, there was no one inside. 'If anyone asks questions,' said Chantal, 'you're looking for Henri Lejeune. He's over in the right-hand corner. An old grave with a rusty iron railing. His side of the family died out. Your men are over here.' She pointed beyond several graves with substantial marble headstones. 'The Germans insisted on the best part.'

They walked down an aisle between the graves and reached six fresh mounds of earth. A simple wooden cross had been placed at the head of each. 'Who put up the crosses?'

'St.Pierre carpenter. The curé told him to when the Germans had gone.'

'I like the simplicity.' Chalmers was looking at the graves, wondering who was beneath each mound. For seconds he was back in the aircraft, sinking into the mist. Tavish and Stafford were there at his shoulder; in the darkness behind, Einstein and Freddie, helpless, ignorant of the crisis; and those already dead: young Les Ricketts, so enthusiastic and naïve, the one they all looked after; and Brad, the colonial with the strange accent they had tried to persuade to stay in England after the war. The six mounds lay in the sunlight, near enough to the wall to have a shadow creeping towards them. Chalmers closed his eyes. He wanted to pray, but words would not come. All he really wanted to say was 'Sorry.'

Chantal's hand crept into his. It was tentative, reassuring.

'They trusted me,' he said.

'Only one pilot.'

He looked down at her. 'It helps if he's competent. I was Skipper. It was my fault we were hit in the first place.'

'Nonsense.'

'You know nothing about it.'

'I know enough. The Germans shoot down aircraft every night. You have miles to go, they know you're coming. Your men knew that. I'd like you to tell me about them one day.'

She was right, of course. They would have joked and pulled his leg, but not one would have moaned. It was his conscience holding him to account. She held his hand and it was comforting. 'One day I'll tell you about them.' He looked over the wall at the white road running to St.Pierre, as deserted as it had been the previous day. 'Time to go. Where next?'

'Further down the valley. To Bazarnes, then across to Cravant and Vermenton on the N6. We'll come back the other side of the river through Prégilbert and Sery.'

The rest of the morning passed quickly as they followed the route Chantal had outlined. Here and there she pointed out farms which might be friendly or hostile. Chalmers mentally filed the information and occasionally made a mark on his map.

'Don't they really want them out?' he asked, after she had pointed out another Vichy supporter.

'Of course most want them out.'

'So?'

'In 1940 it was easier to support Pétain. Now some have doubts, but don't want to take risks. Only a few collaborate, but we can't trust them. You were lucky you didn't come down on Buisson's land.' She indicated a stretch of farmland with the roof of a farm visible over trees. 'Wealthy man, more acres than most. Dines with German officers in Auxerre. Time for lunch.'

'I'd wondered about that.'

'I've got it with me. Take the next turning left.' They had come through a hamlet of two or three cottages. A rutted track twisted away towards a belt of woodland beyond open fields. Chantal led the way and the track petered out as they entered the trees. Birds flew off at their approach and a red squirrel scuttled away. 'I've got a picnic.' She got off her bicycle and walked towards a patch of grass in a sunlit clearing.

Chalmers followed. 'You're a dark horse. I thought we were going home.'

'Don't you like picnics?'

'You don't have picnics at Oxford.' The words came glibly. He did not mention Mary or their picnics near the aerodrome.

'It's very simple.' Chantal opened a bag tied to her cycle rack and took out bread wrapped in cloth. Cheese followed, with a bottle of red wine and a couple of apples from the orchard. 'I've got glasses and knives. No plates. The ground's dry over here.' She sat down, her back against the trunk of an oak tree.

Chalmers sat beside her, nervous of his emotions. Looking at the pale face topped by dark hair, he recognised the attraction he had felt the first moment he had seen her in the loft. She put the linen cloth on the ground between them. Chalmers poured wine into the simple glasses and handed her one. 'I could get used to this. We only have wine in England on special occasions.' The London week-end was with him again. He thought of Verreys and the Savoy.

'Perhaps it is a special occasion.' She took the glass and looked at him over the top of it. She cut cheese for herself and passed it over to him.

Chalmers put his glass carefully on a flat spot where he would not knock it over, then leaned back against the tree, legs stretched out in front of him. Ahead, beyond a gap in the trees, the ground fell away and the valley lay in sunshine. 'Very peaceful,' he said. It was a trite remark, but Chantal's physical closeness and their kiss had in a way created a barrier as difficult as the one broken down. 'You've been here before,' he said.

'Only with Robert and Marguerite. We came on bikes as children. Our secret place. I haven't been since Robert died. Nor has Marguerite.'

He drank a little wine, and cut more cheese. 'What did you mean – "Perhaps it is a special occasion."?'

'No one comes here. I hoped we could have another kiss.' She moved closer and felt for his hand.

Chalmers took her hand and turned to face her. 'I was always taught it was rude to deny a lady what she wanted.' The words came automatically. Part of him responded to her warmth and flirtation; part was conscious of Mary and a betrayal he had not thought possible; and part lingered with his men in the cemetery. Chantal put down her food and moved so close her knee was against his. He put his glass down and pulled her to him.

The next few minutes were the most emotionally confused of his life. Appalled at himself, his weakness as he saw it, he nevertheless revelled in the scent of her body and the abandonment she offered. Her lips were on his, her fingers were in his hair, fumbling with the buttons of his shirt, her arms pulled him down. No longer the modest girl who had nursed him, her passion transmitted itself with a vibrancy he could not match.

He looked up at her. Above her head the leaves patterned the sky. 'You smile?' she said.

'You're a lovely girl, Chantal. Frightening.'

'Frightening?'

'I'm not very experienced.'

'I want you,' she said.

'I want you, too.'

She rolled off him and lay back. 'Take me then.'

He looked into her eyes, not daring to look at her body, though his hands moved over her.

'It's lonely on the farm.' She pulled up her skirt. 'Here,' she said. She guided his hand.

For a second he responded, his hand touching the softness of her thigh. Then he pulled back, struggling onto his knees. Desire died as rapidly as it had appeared. 'No,' he said.

She held his hands, puzzlement and disappointment on her face. 'No?'

'Not now, Chantal. Not now. I can't . . .'

She sat up. 'You wanted to.'

'I wanted to. Of course I wanted to.' He pulled her to him, hiding his face in her shoulder. 'Sorry, darling . . . I'm so sorry. It's not your fault. It's me. Of course I want you. But I can't . . . I can't . . . You understand? We've only just seen my men in the

242

cimetière.' His face was still in her shoulder and she could not see the tears in his eyes. 'I can't . . .'

She could not see the tears, but felt the sadness. She held him, putting her cheek against his. 'I understand,' she said. 'I understand.'

Above their heads a breeze ruffled the leaves. Somewhere in the distance a lorry, engine revving, struggled up an incline. In the wood a blackbird was singing.

***

Later that night he lay in bed half awake, looking at the moon and the distant woods. There was pain in his foot and calf. Cramp. He curled his toes up as he had been taught at school and the pain faded. Was it the cycling? Then he remembered Chantal. He wanted her, she wanted him, and yet he had shied away. No, not true. He had not been physically capable. He had only just seen the six mounds in the cemetery. How many of them were men in the sense that mattered? What would Chantal feel? She had offered herself and been rejected. Did she really understand? She said she did and they had seemed close as they cycled home. He clung to her last words as they put their bikes away: 'Don't worry. It was my fault. I'll come to see you.'

The corner of the barn roof was touched by moonlight. He remembered the silvered garden at the Royal Charles with Mary. She had been with him all day, even when Chantal was lying in his arms. He loved Mary, so why did he want Chantal? And he did: the desire was intense. 'I'll come to see you,' she had said. He remembered the young waitress with the tight dress in the tea-room and his distinction between 'the general' and 'the particular'. He wanted Mary. But he wanted Chantal, too. Could a man love two women? He had never thought about it in simple terms like that. Was the distinction between love and lust artificial?

243

The moon had moved. He eased his head to one side so he could see it more clearly. Yes, he wanted Chantal. She was *there*. He might never see Mary again. He closed his eyes and was back in the wood. Chantal lay in the shade, skirt up her thighs. A snatch of Herrick materialised, as it had that afternoon: *'A sweet disorder in the dress kindles in clothes a wantonness . . .'*

Somewhere in the night he heard a fox. It took him back to Wynton Thorpe, to the fox barking in the chill of the morning as he made his way across the airfield after a raid. And it brought back those moments of relief after another safe return. Would he be a man before he flew again? Would Mary understand the curious imperatives of a virginal male? Would she go to London with him?

The moon had moved again. It was approaching a cloud shaped like a human head. Within seconds he was asleep, this time a dreamless sleep.

***

He woke later than usual; the sun was higher and the sounds of the farm deeper into the morning. There was a knock and Célestine appeared with shaving water as she had done every day.

'They told me to let you sleep,' she said. Her voice was neutral in tone, as though she had no opinion of the decision.

'I must get up.' He pushed back the sheet and swung his legs to the floor.

'Chantal said you would be tired. I've left breakfast on the table.'

Downstairs, he was joined by Chantal, who had finished milking. With Célestine at the sink, Chantal treated him as though they had barely met. 'Henri's collecting papers at Migennes today. I'll be distributing them later. You could come.'

'What papers?'

244

'Something from Paris. We've had it before. *Défense de la France*. Migennes doesn't like it. It's Christian rather than Communist. But they pass it on. Henri and Georges will deal with Auxerre. The rest go to Clamecy and Avallon.'

'How do we go?'

'Train to Clamecy from St.Pierre. There are too many to take on bikes. They come in cases. We could do it in one journey if you came as well.'

'I'll come. When do we go?'

'Before lunch. Henri brings them from Auxerre. We'll be in Clamecy by early afternoon. We leave them with somebody there. They'll get the rest to Avallon. We're simply messengers.'

'But Clamecy was betrayed.'

'The escape chain. My old schoolmates do the paper round. They stayed clear when the Germans searched the abbey.'

Lejeune approved Chalmers going. 'He can see how the trains run. And you can introduce him to Clamecy. They'll know him if he has to go on his own.'

Later in the morning Chalmers and Chantal cycled to St.Pierre. The sky was grey and a wind blew from the north-west; the temperature had dropped. At first they were silent, then as they passed the cemetery, Chalmers said, 'Thank you for yesterday.'

'Just the cemetery?'

'Not just the cemetery.'

'I was insensitive.'

'I'll do better next time. If there is a next time.' He looked across at her.

'There will be. I told you – I'll come to see you.'

She was wearing a brown skirt he had not seen before, a black jacket over a beige blouse and a small brown hat. They reached St.Pierre ten minutes before the train was due. A postal van was also in the yard, its driver waiting for the morning delivery from Auxerre. A middle-aged couple stood on the platform. The man wore a shabby suit and could have been a clerk; the woman with him had a cloche hat fashionable ten years earlier. Chantal did not know them, so there was no need to introduce Chalmers.

'Put the bikes here,' she said. 'They'll be safe by Vacherot's cottage. He never asks questions. Henri will get off here. We take the cases and get on. No long conversation. We'll wait on the platform.'

She led the way up a flight of steps. They moved away from the middle-aged couple and looked up the line curving through woodland towards Mailly-le-Château. On the other side of the line a lorry had stopped by the siding and two men were shovelling coal. Overhead a flight of ducks made its way towards the Yonne. Their V formation reminded Chalmers of formation training at Booker. In the distance he heard the sound of an engine, but it was a full five minutes before the train itself emerged from the woods and drew into the station. The engine, black, smelling of oil, steam spurting from leaky joints, stopped at the end of the platform. The driver, red-faced and portly, leaned out of his cab and looked back at the four carriages while his fireman fed the firebox.

The unmistakable figure of Henri alighted from the last carriage. Chantal waved and went up to the open door, followed by Chalmers. Henri, cigarette dangling, this time wearing a soft trilby hat and loose raincoat, summed up the situation at once. He muttered, 'You can take all three', pointing to the suitcases in the carriage, each bound with a leather strap.

Henri was the only passenger to get off. He said nothing more and made his way, one arm swinging, down the platform. A black Citroën had pulled into the yard and he got in. Chalmers recognised René at the wheel. The waiting couple got on the train. The guard handed a sack of post to the postman who had come up from his van. No one noticed the brief exchange with Henri.

'Always the last carriage,' said Chantal. 'Usually empty. Fewer people see, fewer to ask questions.'

'And if anyone does?'

'Sick mother moving house. Loyal son helping with belongings. Henri's a good actor. René's reliable. Henri wouldn't want to be marooned in St.Pierre.'

She sat down by the window and motioned to Chalmers to sit opposite. The cases, each a different size, stood on the floor. Outside the only sound was the heavy breathing of the engine. 'Suppose I hadn't been here?' he asked.

'Henri would have taken the third case with him and we'd have had to make another journey.' Chantal smiled and moved her eyelashes in a way Chalmers recognised. 'I knew you would be useful.' The softness of her tone emphasised the ambiguity of the remark. She blamed herself for insensitivity the previous day and wanted to make amends. Before he could respond there was a whistle and the train began to move. Gouts of black and grey smoke were flung into air and the carriages jerked forward. Outside the terracotta roofs of St.Pierre retreated. Woods and fields replaced them and the line ran for a while parallel with the Yonne and its attendant canal.

Chalmers pushed the nearest case out of the way, stretched his leg and moved it against Chantal's. He said: 'I hoped you would come last night. I would have done better.'

'I'll come.'

'I'll be waiting.' Chalmers recalled Chantal's passion and obvious expertise. 'I'm not the first.'

'No.'

'Did you love him?'

'I thought I did. I thought I was his only girl. It was Robert's friend Gaston. We were lovers for a whole summer. Then I found out about the other girls and now I don't know where he is. Prisoner of war, they say. He told me lies. You told me the truth. You love Mary. I'm a poor substitute.'

He leaned forward and held her hands. 'You're not a substitute. I told you I wanted you. I meant that. I've wanted you since I first saw your face when I was delirious.' He looked out of the window as the train pulled into Châtel-Censoir. The station yard was deserted apart from another postal van. An old man with a dog at his feet sat outside the Hôtel de la Gare drinking wine. Steam escaped noisily again.

Chalmers released her hands and sat back in case anyone came in. Chantal was looking at him with an expression he had not seen before. This time it was her turn to lean forward. 'It's war,' she said. 'I don't suppose it can last. We'll enjoy it while it does.'

'Nothing's certain. Whatever happens, I shall never forget you.' He took her hand again. 'Just remember I said that.'

24

Half an hour later, after running down the wooded valley of the Yonne and several stops, they arrived at Clamecy. The station was little busier than the others and only a handful of people got off. A small engine was shunting trucks in a siding.

'Wait,' said Chantal. 'Let the rest go.' She got down onto the platform and looked towards the exit.

Chalmers waited until she indicated all was well then joined her. A porter was unloading luggage from the first carriage and putting it on a trolley. Another postman had appeared and was carrying two sacks to his van. The red-faced driver emerged from his cab and started to oil parts of the engine. Smoke drifted up from its smokestack.

Chantal nodded. 'We'll go now.' She picked up the smallest case. 'I'm glad you're here for the others,' she said. 'They're heavy.'

Chalmers picked up the cases. 'You're right,' he muttered. 'Is it far?'

'Top of the town – the old part. Not far, but uphill. Try to make them look light. Anything to avoid attention.' Outside the station a man was unloading milk churns from a lorry and there was the usual queue of women outside a *boulangerie*.

'Always queues,' said Chantal. 'In the cities women queue for hours and sometimes get nothing. People cycle out into the countryside on Sundays to get food.'

'There are queues in England too – and I don't suppose the *marché noir* is very different.' He put the cases down and re-adjusted his grip. 'I'd like to have seen you managing these on your own.'

'I've done it before. *Combat* and *Résistance* as well as *Le Travailleur de l'Yonne* – we've taken them all. Anyway, that's why I wanted you to come.'

'I hoped there might be another reason.'

They turned into a narrow street winding uphill. On each side half-timbered seventeenth-century houses with dark woodwork and small windows gave an indication of the age of the town. At the top a church tower with three storeys, one ornamented with elaborate gargoyles, dominated the square and the town beneath. Opposite the church a restaurant, *L'Angélus*, had its door open; on the other side a terrace looked out on the jumble of houses that was Clamecy. Beyond the roofs the curve of Burgundy's woods and hills surrounded the town.

'Next to *L'Angélus*,' said Chantal. 'The green door.'

She walked straight up to it and knocked. It was opened by a bald man wearing a baize apron. His baldness was fringed with white hair and he peered over gold-rimmed spectacles. 'Ah, Chantal,' he said. 'Come in, my dear. And your friend.' They embraced affectionately.

Chalmers followed Chantal through a hallway into a parlour at the back of the house where a fair-haired young woman of approximately the same age as Chantal sat in a window-seat darning a sock. She wore a simple flowered dress and was pretty in an unsophisticated way. He put down the cases with relief and eased his shoulders.

'This is James,' Chantal said. 'Our English pilot. He's joined us, so you'll be seeing him again. We've brought the *Défense* papers.' She turned to Chalmers. 'This is Claudette. We were at school together. Her father, Alphonse' – she smiled at the man who had come in behind them – 'is the best watch repairer in Burgundy.'

Claudette and her father held out their hands. Chalmers detected genuine warmth. He responded: 'Delighted to meet you, Monsieur. *Enchanté, Mad'moiselle.*' Chantal makes me work, as you can see.'

'She makes us all work, Monsieur,' said Alphonse, adjusting his glasses. 'None of us realised what a taskmaster she would be.' The smile in his voice spoke of affection for his daughter's friend. He picked up one of the cases. 'They're heavy. We'll split them up before we take them round.' He put them in a cupboard under the stairs. 'Never leave anything around,' he explained. 'You can't tell who may come in unexpectedly.'

'Germans?' asked Chalmers.

'There were some at the Hôtel de la Poste a few days ago,' said Claudette. 'Officers. But they went on Wednesday. A lot of activity in Avallon. New men at *Le Chapeau Rouge*. That's the Gestapo headquarters,' she explained to Chalmers. 'Rumour says they're still holding two monks from the abbey.'

Claudette had a small round face with mobile eyes; her fair hair was full of natural curls. She had continued with her darning, taking advantage of the light coming through the window. 'We know more about what happened,' she said. 'It wasn't what we thought. It started miles away. In Uzès down in Languedoc. A lawyer in the Resistance became too friendly with the wife of a man in the *milice*. The militia man found out – caught them in bed the story goes – and the wretched *notaire* gave away a lot to save his own skin. The chain unravelled as far back as the abbey and Clamecy. No fliers caught, but the line's gone. At least twenty have been taken to Fresnes. They won't get out alive.'

'Still safe to take the papers?' asked Chalmers.

'No sign they know anything about us,' replied Alphonse. 'There's always a risk'– he shrugged – 'but we haven't lost anyone yet. They thought they'd cleaned up Clamecy when they got the abbey.'

'Ersatz coffee?' said Claudette, putting down her darning. 'Cognac? I reward myself when I've finished Papa's socks.'

Chalmers looked to Chantal. He would happily have sat down with a cognac, but Chantal had indicated they ought not to stay long. She took charge naturally. 'Not today – Papa worries if I'm late. And things are happening at our end. We're hoping for a *parachutage*. James has helped.' The expression on her face reflected something more than gratitude and he wondered if the others picked it up. He was immediately back in the wood and wondering when she would come to his room. He was amazed at the way his sexual drive overrode the issue of safety.

Alphonse adjusted his spectacles. 'I look forward to seeing you again, young man. It's a pleasure to find an Englishman who can speak French. Take care of Chantal.' He nodded towards her. His quizzical expression suggested he understood their relationship. The clipped precision of his speech made Chalmers think he had probably made a shrewd choice of career in watch repairing. To Chantal he said: 'No problems with Migennes?'

'Henri didn't say anything.'

'They're well-organised now, but they didn't join the Resistance until the Germans attacked Russia. They didn't say anything the first year when de Gaulle started broadcasting from London. Orders from Moscow, though they wouldn't admit it.'

Chalmers looked at Alphonse's under-nourished face and the slender watchmaker's fingers. He wondered why he had moved against the Germans.

Alphonse answered his unspoken question. 'We got involved for the same reason as the Lejeunes. I had a nephew, my sister's boy. Killed when the Boches broke through the Ardennes. And I was on the Western Front in 1918. I never want to see another German.' His eyes, previously kindly, were hard.

'I was lucky to be found by the right Frenchmen. I admire your bravery. More difficult, I think, than dropping bombs. And I'm learning that France is a complicated place. It's simpler across the Channel.'

'We have to know who to trust,' said Chantal, getting up. She embraced Claudette. 'Time you came out to La Rippe. You could get to know James. I haven't seen that dress, have I? Suits you.'

'Got it in the market last week. Not *haute couture*. Papa was kind.' She looked at him affectionately. 'I think he wants me off his hands. Wants me to catch someone – though he'll have to darn his own socks if I go.'

Chalmers and Chantal were back at the station in good time. Chantal's shoes clicked on the pavement as they turned into the entrance; the light breeze plucked at her skirt. 'Claudette's mother died just after the invasion,' she said. 'Claudette's an only child. Close to her father and does everything for him. She sometimes comes out to La Rippe for a day or two.'

'Have they got a radio?

'No. They distribute papers – nothing more.'

The station was no busier than when they arrived. The Auxerre train had only a sprinkling of passengers. The shunting engine had assembled a goods train which now stood alongside a loading bay. A farmer and his dog were shepherding Charolais cattle into one of its trucks. The cattle were noisy and uncooperative, the farmer abusive.

Chantal put her arm through Chalmers'. 'First carriage, by the engine. Fewer people.' The nervousness he had detected in her during his first day off the farm was evaporating. He helped her into the compartment when they reached the front of the train. 'Careful,' she said. 'You don't know who's watching.'

'I'm family. I can touch you.' He looked at his wrist and remembered his broken watch.

Chantal noticed his glance. 'You need a watch. Robert had an expensive one for his twenty-first birthday – he put his old one away somewhere. It'll be French. The broken one might have given you away.'

Chalmers leaned forward, taking her hands between his. 'I liked them,' he said. 'I knew I would like any friends of yours.'

253

He looked down at their touching feet. 'When are you coming to see me?'

Chantal's eyes were on the window. She moved her feet. 'Be careful. I know too many people round here. They'd want to know about you.'

'Cousin from Provence. Stick to the story.'

'That'll do for the Germans or anyone who gets too nosy. It's more complicated if it looks as though we're – as though we're involved. I don't want to start lying to friends.'

'Claudette guessed.'

'She's different. No need for deceit.'

'Your father?'

'Papa probably knows. He only sees possible complications. He's very single-minded.'

'I expect he's right.'

'Fathers have a simple view.' Chantal glanced out of the window where smoke from the engine drifted past. 'We'll make sure there isn't a problem, won't we? After all, you love Mary. I'm a passing whim.'

'That's not fair.' He was determined she should not see herself as a second-rate stopgap. However deep his love for Mary, his feelings for Chantal were genuine.

Outside the guard blew his whistle and the train began to move.

'Claudette liked you.'

'I liked her. You've been friends a long time?'

'We were new girls together at the convent. One or two of the nuns terrified us. We were both punished with a big penance in our first week. We've been close ever since.'

'Perhaps it was a big penance to cover future sins?'

'I'll come,' she said. 'I don't want to upset anybody.' She had drawn away, but now she came close. 'I like you very much. I know I'm second best' – she waved her hand when she saw he was about to interrupt. 'It's up to us how we react.' She took his hand and placed it on her thigh. 'I'll come soon.'

Chalmers was leaning forward, too. 'I want to tell you something. You can probably guess.'

'I doubt it.'

'I haven't made love to a woman before – not properly, not completely.'

'You didn't have to tell me.'

'Was your first time long ago?'

'Long enough. No one at La Rippe knew. Father would have been horrified.'

'The nuns wouldn't approve.'

'I did my penance. I haven't been to church since leaving the convent. Mother would like me to go, but Papa doesn't make me. Célestine understands. She's had her problems, but she goes to church now.'

The train gathered speed and again ran through the woods beside the Yonne. Beyond Coulanges they passed a lock on the canal with two barges locking down towards Auxerre. The lock-keeper turned the handle to close the sluices; his wife and a little girl in a red dress were talking to the bargees; smoke curled from the chimney of the lock-keeper's cottage: it was an idyllic scene, a cameo of peace and normality.

'Difficult to imagine there's a war on,' said Chalmers. He remembered his first sight of the canal as he flew in over the church at Châtel-Censoir. Even then it had looked peaceful in the light of the moon.

'We don't know whether the war touches them or not. You could see me selling chicks in the market and never guess I did anything else. For all we know the lock-keeper is part of Bernard's group. I wouldn't know – and he wouldn't know about me.'

'Is that likely?'

'No. Most settle for something less heroic. He does his job, he's got his cottage and grows food in the garden. The bargees are the same. They need goods and want to be left alone by Vichy and everyone else. Probably more worried about whether your plane blocked the river than whether you survived or not. There's a rumour the Germans are using barges to shift heavy goods near Tonnerre. They'll be paid well. Are you shocked?'

'I expect it would be the same in England. We're lucky to have the Channel.'

'It makes me ashamed. You've risked so much.'

'So have you.' He looked down and moved his feet round hers again.

The train rattled over a bridge crossing both the river and the canal and drew into St.Pierre. They got out, Chalmers taking care not to touch Chantal. Further down two middle-aged Frenchmen smoking pipes were the only other passengers to alight. The train left in clouds of smoke and steam. Vacherot collected their tickets at the exit.

Chantal introduced Chalmers casually. 'My cousin, Michel. He's working at La Rippe. We can't do without him now grandfather's in bed.'

Vacherot, a small man with kind eyes, wearing a faded railway uniform, said: 'Don't let them work you too hard, Monsieur. Blanchard told me there was a stranger at La Rippe. I've known Mademoiselle Chantal a long time – we're old friends.' He reminded Chalmers of a GWR porter he'd known at Oxford. Perhaps railwaymen were the same on both sides of the Channel.

Chalmers said, 'We have it easier in the South. The sun ripens the grapes and we have long siestas.'

Vacherot looked about him to check no one was within earshot. 'Bombing at Migennes yesterday. I hope they don't bomb this line. I wouldn't get paid if it closed.'

'They won't bother with this line,' said Chalmers. 'I'm sure it's not important enough.' Even as he spoke, he knew he was being tactless. 'I mean, it doesn't carry any Germans.'

Vacherot shrugged again. 'War,' he said. 'The small man pays. It doesn't matter who wins.'

'But you want them out?' said Chalmers involuntarily. Out of the corner of his eye he saw Chantal look at him disapprovingly.

Vacherot turned away despondently. 'I want everybody out. The Boches, Vichy, anyone who tells me what I can and can't do. I want to be left in peace to look after the trains. That's what I'm good at. Isn't that right, Chantal?'

Chantal put a hand on his arm. 'We all want to be left alone. You'll be all right here.' She turned to Chalmers. 'They'll wonder where we are.'

They picked up their cycles from the fence by Vacherot's cottage and set off back to La Rippe. Vacherot waved farewell, a gesture somehow implying acceptance of his lot in life as well as friendship.

***

That night Chantal came to Chalmers's room. It had gone eleven and he was just dropping off to sleep. A floorboard creaked on the landing, he heard the door handle move, and almost before he was aware of her presence, she was slipping under the bedclothes beside him. She wore a simple cotton night-dress and was shivering. 'Warm me up,' she said.

'I hoped you'd come.' He moved towards her, searching for her lips.

'Not too loud. I'll stay till morning.' She moved closer, moulding herself to him. She felt his hands run down the back of her night-dress. 'Pull it up.'

'Forward hussy. You like being in charge, don't you?'

'Not really.' She meant what she said. Part of his attraction was the strength she sensed in him.

'Lie still,' he said. 'My turn to give orders.' He pulled her night-dress aside roughly and caressed the fullness of her breast.

'I prefer you to give the orders.'

257

'Mary said that once,' he said, and instantly regretted it. 'Sorry.'

'Most women do.' She ignored the apology. 'I shall remember what you said today.'

'What?'

'That you'd never forget me whatever happens.'

'I meant it.' His hand crossed to her other breast. He pressed himself against her.

She snuggled close, her hand searching out his hardness. 'You're in charge. I'm your woman tonight.'

He ran his hand up the softness of her thigh and kissed her neck. As he did so sensed a change in the balance of their relationship. From the first hours in the loft he had depended on her guidance. He had done nothing without her approval. Now her vulnerability was apparent. His nervousness evaporated. He felt the surge of confidence he had experienced after his first solo flight. As a whole man there was nothing he could not do.

'Lie still,' he said. 'Yes, you're my woman.' He nuzzled her shoulder, at the same time pulling her nightdress up to her waist. 'Yes, I'm in charge now.'

The room was dark. There was no moon and cloud hid the stars. Physical desire, sheer pleasure, controlled him. But as he moved inside her there was guilt as well. He could not escape Mary, and his mind, detached and mobile, responded as it always did. The darkness mirrored the darkness of the ancient woodland of The Chase where Alec d'Urberville seduced Tess, the source of ultimate tragedy. At the same time he remembered Hardy's fatalistic comment: 'It was to be.'

25

Four days later Henri cycled into the yard with a note from Johnson. London had promised a *parachutage* in a fortnight. There were instructions for marking the dropping zone, ten containers were promised, and a message of confirmation would be broadcast by the BBC the previous night. The message would be: 'Louis will get his rations if he is a good boy.' Henri was puzzled. 'I hope it makes sense,' he said.

Chalmers detected the irony of an English sense of humour with relief. It took him nearer home than he had been for nearly two months and was strangely comforting. He had been impressed by the risks taken by the Lejeunes, but could not easily forgive the acceptance he saw all around him. A little humour and understatement put him back on an even keel.

'One more thing.' Henri looked at Chalmers. 'London insists you and Johnson organise the lights. An English pilot will trust you to get it right.'

Chalmers folded Johnson's note and pocketed it carefully. 'We must be there early and we want six strong torches. Possible?'

'We've got them' said Lejeune. 'Bernard used bonfires in the Morvan. We can't risk that. I've had torches for months. More than six if we need them.'

'Six will do.' Chalmers was thinking as he spoke. 'How are we going to get the stuff away? Don't we need more people? The containers will scatter if there's a wind.'

'No-one else. We'll use the cart. We'll bring most of it back here. Anything we can't manage we'll hide in the forest. The

Germans never go that side of the river. When your plane came down it took them hours to find it. They didn't even know where the nearest bridge was.'

Chalmers looked at Johnson's note. 'It says "as near midnight as possible." We'll be there before dark – all of us. Then we can plan the torches.' He relished the idea that he was responsible.

'I must go,' said Henri. 'I can't leave my wife in the shop all the time.' He mounted his bicycle and left the yard without a backward look.

'Maurice can take the cart,' said Lejeune.

'Maurice? Safe?'

'He'll come back here. He won't stay for the drop.'

'There'll be just enough of us,' said Chalmers, 'as long as the containers don't scatter. We won't open them there. Back here we can take as long as we like. Chantal will come?'

Lejeune looked at him quizzically. 'You couldn't keep her away. She likes you.'

'You disapprove?'

'Chantal knows her own mind. I don't want complications – emotions.'

Chalmers eyed Lejeune's greying hair and heavily-contoured face. He looked a simple farmer, but his wisdom made Chalmers feel youthful and rash. He was right to distrust emotional involvement. 'We'll be all right. Chantal's a sensible girl and I'm not daft.' He wondered if her father guessed how far their relationship had gone. 'What about Marguerite?'

'She'll want to come. All right?'

'Certainly. We've got to see where everything lands, and it's all got to be carried.'

Lejeune changed the subject. 'I'm going to the top field. Maurice is ploughing. He can't be left for long.'

The two men looked at each other. They said no more, but both recognised mutual respect and understanding.

Three days later Chalmers cycled to the drop zone. He wanted to look at the field in daylight without distractions. And he had his private feelings. The remains of Z Zebra had been removed, but he needed a few minutes on his own. He still found it hard to believe. It seemed an age ago.

It was grey day. There was no wind and the branches on the trees by the Yonne were still. He cycled down the narrow lanes, meeting no one between La Rippe and the woods giving onto the field. He propped his bicycle against a tree and looked towards Châtel-Censoir and the line of his final approach. The drop would come in the same way. The danger was the river. Any miscalculation and they could lose everything in the river or the forest further over. He would arrange the torches at an angle to the river with the car headlights at the end. He paced out the field again. Before returning to La Rippe he knew exactly where the torches would be; he even put small sticks in the ground to mark the positions. It was the first time he had done anything independently since his arrival.

Chantal came to his room again that night. 'Not too tired?' she asked.

Chalmers pulled her close. 'I've just spent a day being useful. That's a new sensation.'

'I practised the Chopin while you were out.'

'I'll hear you tomorrow – before you start on the bread.'

'I should like that.' She lodged her chin on his shoulder. 'Your father doesn't approve.'

'What father does?'

'He thinks it's dangerous. He tightened his arm round her. 'If we had a crisis – Germans, anything – I might decide to save you first. You might do the same. We can't afford emotions. Your father's right about that.'

'Kiss me.'

'I'm serious.'

'So am I. Kiss me.'

'I'm beginning to think you're still in charge. That doesn't mean your father's wrong. We must be careful.'

'Not too careful. Life's short. The war's taught me that. We take what we can.'

Chalmers ran his hand beneath her nightdress. He knew she was right. At the same time, even as he pulled her to him, he thought of Mary and heard the voice of caution he had known since childhood.

***

The two weeks passed slowly. Chalmers spent the time exploring, sometimes with Chantal, sometimes on his own. Here and there he stopped and followed tracks into the woods. He was amazed at how empty the countryside was. He encountered no Germans and no gendarmes. As confidence grew he took to dropping into village bars for a drink, either in the morning or early evening. Everywhere he was able to merge into the scenery as the bookselling Michel Duval from Provence helping out at La Rippe. Only once did he have to struggle. A woman in the bar in St.Pierre had a sister living in Vaison-la-Romaine and wanted to talk about her. She found it hard to believe 'Michel' did not know her and it was only when he explained that he came from the old town – Vaison-en-Haut – that she relented, admitting her sister ran a café in the new town lower down.

Two days before the drop Lejeune and Chalmers visited the field and Chalmers outlined exactly what he wanted done. He also explained the problems facing the pilot and left Lejeune in no doubt that they might have a fruitless vigil.

'The cart in the wood?' suggested Lejeune. 'Near those tracks.'

'Yes – it must be close. The containers will be heavy. We'll have to do something with the parachutes, too.'

'We'll get rid of them at La Rippe.'

262

They were walking towards the Yonne, Chalmers unconsciously leading to where he had come down. The furrows gouged out by the Lancaster engines were still fresh, though here and there grass was growing through. Bits of metal remained scattered along the aircraft's track. For the first time he noticed a tree on the riverbank whose trunk had been splintered, presumably by a wing as the aircraft plunged into the water. Lejeune watched but said nothing; Chalmers registered his sensitivity. His respect continued to grow and he saw why he was the natural leader of the group.

The next night Lejeune, Chalmers, Marie and Chantal went to the top room to wait for the London message. The broadcast was on time. *'Ici Londres, ici Londres.* We have some messages for our friends across the Channel.' The voice paused, then: 'The seagulls are flying tonight. I repeat: The seagulls are flying tonight.' It paused again. 'Jean-Paul's friends will need feeding tomorrow. Jean-Paul's friends will need feeding tomorrow.' The next pause seemed longer, but that was probably an illusion. 'Louis will get his rations if he is a good boy. I repeat, Louis will get his rations if he is a good boy.'

Lejeune smiled beatifically. He said, 'Louis will get his rations.'

The voice in London continued intoning messages like an incantation. 'Jules and Camille should go to Mass on Sunday. Danton and Robespierre are alive and well. I say again, Danton and Robespierre are alive and well . . .' Lejeune turned the radio off, breaking the spell.

'I doubt if they'll see eye to eye,' said Chalmers.

'Reds,' said Lejeune. He turned to his wife, putting an affectionate hand on her shoulder. 'Louis will get his rations.'

'You've done it,' she said. 'They're taking us seriously.'

'Convinced at last?'

'I've been worried.' She looked at Chalmers. 'Mothers are always more cautious than fathers. I'm sure your mother didn't want you to fly.'

'Probably not.' He was curt, almost rude, but now was not the time to explain his tangled relationship with his mother.

'You've made the difference,' said Lejeune. 'Now we must go to bed. We'll be late tomorrow.'

'You'll check the others?' asked Chalmers. He was emboldened, almost for the first time, to question Lejeune's organisation.

Lejeune smiled. 'Don't worry. They'll be there.'

That night Chalmers lay in bed alone. Chantal came to say goodnight, but when she'd gone he curled himself into a foetal ball in the all-enveloping feather-bedding. Outside a wind had got up, moving the clouds rapidly across the sky. His last conscious thought was to hope it would drop by morning.

He was woken by the sound of Célestine filling her buckets. He lay quietly for a moment, considering the irony that an abnormal day was starting so normally. He looked at the sky. There were clouds, but they were still; the wind had dropped. To his surprise routine dominated the whole day. The cows were milked, the animals fed; Marie and Marguerite made cream and bread in the dairy; Maurice and Jacques met the labourer from Coulanges and went to work in the fields up by the woods. Only Chantal deviated from normality by cycling off to check everyone would be there on time. Chalmers, too, fitted into the rhythm of the farm, feeding the chickens and geese and cleaning out the stables again.

The first change to routine was an early supper. Maurice had already been dispatched with the cart. He was told exactly where to go and he asked no questions. Chalmers, Chantal, Marguerite and Lejeune finished their meal and set off on bicycles, reaching the drop zone in fading light. Maurice was sent back to the farm. He showed no curiosity. 'Will my supper be ready?' he asked. 'Is it pork?' He laughed aloud. 'I like pork.'

Chalmers watched him go with relief. At the same time, looking at the cart and its two horses, a thought occurred. 'Will they be all right with the aircraft?'

'How low will it be?' asked Lejeune.

'I don't know. It can't be too high or the stuff could go anywhere.'

'Someone will stay with them. Shall we get Maurice back?'

'No. Who's best with the horses?'

'I'll do it,' said Marguerite, her pale face serious in the fading light. 'I'd rather look after the horses than pick up heavy parcels.'

'All right,' said Chalmers. 'Take them further into the wood. Come back the moment the plane's gone.'

As he spoke there came the sound of a car and René's Citroën stopped under the trees bringing Johnson and Gambert. The car had barely stopped when Henri and Georges appeared on bicycles. 'Good timing,' said Chalmers. 'Now the lights.'

The twilight deepened. René moved the car to one end of the field at an angle to the river and Chalmers took the others to their positions. 'Right,' he shouted. 'Lights on.' René turned on the headlights and twin beams were thrown across the field. To each side the arms of a rough U were outlined by torches. Chalmers, holding a torch himself, was encouraged. 'All right, Peter?'

'He should see them.'

'Lights off,' shouted Chalmers. Used to the strength of the flare-path at Wynton Thorpe, he wondered how long the batteries would last. The car headlights were the last to go as René had at first not heard him.

Night came on fast. In the east a line of cloud marked the horizon and the first stars appeared; to the east a pale orange glow coloured the sky. Around them the hills were no more than black outlines. Towards Châtel-Censoir a full moon was rising.

'A couple of hours,' said Chalmers. 'We need to be ready from 11.30. The moment we hear the plane we turn on. I'll shout. Keep everything on until I tell you to turn off. He must have every chance.' He turned to Johnson. 'Anything I've forgotten?'

Johnson shook his head and looked at his watch. 'Time to kill. Anything we can usefully do?'

Chalmers turned to Lejeune. 'Dussault knows?' He did not understand why he had not asked before.

'Yes. He won't tell anyone. We couldn't ignore him. It's his land.'

Henri was lighting a cigarette. 'Cognac?' He produced a flask and offered it round. Chalmers took it to be sociable but only allowed a fraction of the burning liquid between his lips. He looked across at Chantal talking quietly to Gambert. He and she had not even touched hands in the course of the evening. They might have been strangers.

Johnson came across. 'So far so good.' The big fair-haired man had happily allowed Chalmers to take charge. Although specifically trained for France, the loss of Emil and his first experiences had shaken him. He was in awe of the pilot and happy to defer to him. 'What's that?' he said suddenly. In the distance came the sound of aircraft engines.

Chalmers was startled. For a second he thought the drop was early. Then he relaxed. 'Luftwaffe,' he said. 'Junkers 88. Night fighter.' The sound grew as the plane came nearer before passing overhead heading south-west. 'Not in a hurry. Not interested in us, anyway.'

The moon climbed above the wooded uplands towards Noyers. Around the waiting group the grass silvered and ghostly shadows appeared. Henri and Georges smoked one cigarette after another. Henri produced his flask again. Chantal went back to her bicycle and offered coffee. 'Bartered in Mailly,' she explained. 'There's food as well.'

'You're a clever girl.' The others were talking and Chalmers had moved close to her. She was holding out bread on a cloth.

'Chicken? Cheese?'

'I'll have cheese.' Chalmers took it with one hand, at the

same time slipping an arm round her waist. Making sure the others weren't watching, he gave her a kiss on the neck.

'Papa will see.'

'He knows.' He moved away and looked at his watch. 'Ten minutes,' he said.

Johnson joined them and took some chicken. 'Not long now.'

Chalmers swallowed a mouthful then shouted, 'Stand by.' He touched Chantal on the arm. She muttered, '*Bonne chance, chéri,*' and moved away to the bottom of the U without looking at him.

The others took up their places, René returning to the car, where he left the door open. Somewhere in the woods an owl hooted. Chalmers had put himself at the bottom of the one leg of the U. From there he could see all the lights. Tense and feeling responsible not only for what was happening on the ground but also for the approaching aircraft, he looked up at the stars, straining for the sound of engines. For a while he held his torch at an angle, ready for action, but as minutes passed, each an eternity, he remembered his old nanny. 'A watched pot never boils,' she said. He lowered his arm, the torch hanging at his side. He had started to wonder whether the whole affair had been called off when he caught the murmur of a distant aircraft.

'Listen!' called Henri, fifty yards away.

'Quiet!' he replied, as the sound increased.

'*Quadrimoteur,*' called Henri, his enthusiasm overcoming the discipline Chalmers had tried to inculcate.

'*Silence!*' shouted Chalmers. He was trying to work out what it was. Stirling? Halifax? It was not a Lancaster. The engines grew louder, getting nearer but not heading directly towards them. 'Halifax,' he said to himself, at the same time thinking it seemed too far south. 'Lights on,' he shouted.

The car headlights sprang to life and on each side torch beams faced upwards at a shallow angle. The engines had been fading, but now the plane had turned and the sound grew.

Then Chalmers saw it, a dark shape following the river valley. 'Please God he sees us,' he prayed. The aircraft continued its course up the river as though indifferent to them.

'*Merde*,' shouted Lejeune. 'He didn't see us.'

'Wait.' This from Chalmers. 'Whatever you do, keep the lights on.'

The aircraft had changed course again. It had gone up the valley but was now coming back across the hills to the west. Chalmers's confidence rose. If he were in the pilot's place he would do the same. Initial arrival to identify the zone, then a wide circle losing height, and another approach up the valley. The engine roar grew again; the aircraft was lower and somewhere over Châtel-Censoir. Holding his torch steady towards the approaching sound, he lived again his own nightmare: the burning engine, the church on the hill, the silver river and mist-covered fields. He would never be rid of it.

It was close now and heading straight for them. Within seconds the outline of a Halifax, its four propellers glinting, materialised over the trees, following a perfect course between the torches towards the car headlights. 'Spot on,' breathed Chalmers. At the same time, as so often, his mind resurrected words from the past. The looming presence overhead conjured Wordsworth's terrifying experience as a small boy one night in the Lake District when he imagined a mountain peak moving after him. '*The grim shape towered up between me and the stars, and still, for so it seemed, with purpose of its own and measured motion like a living thing, strode after me.*' The excitement of the moment banished the lines instantly, but again he wondered at the quirks of the human brain. The roar of the engines was deafening and the aircraft so low it appeared to grow in size as it passed overhead. Then it had gone, banking and climbing to the north-west, engines fading as quickly as they had come. Behind it left silence and the flowered silhouettes of parachutes swinging gently down from five hundred feet.

'Keep the lights,' shouted Chalmers. 'Watch them, watch

them!' The unbidden Wordsworth had vanished and in its place was a great lifting of the spirit. He had done something right for the first time since his arrival. Now it was vital not to lose anything. He had already seen one cigar-shaped container drifting close to the river and others had gone towards the woods on his left.

Most chutes landed exactly on target. Henri, Georges and Lejeune ran towards them, pulling down the billowing silk, stopping the containers being dragged on the ground. Chantal trained her torch on one that had come down beyond the car. Chalmers counted each one, mentally recording where it landed. Gambert seemed mesmerised. Statuesque, he stood in the middle of the field gazing after the vanished plane waving his torch vaguely. '*Merveilleux*,' he muttered, '*merveilleux*.'

Within a short time they found eight containers and dragged them under the trees. Marguerite returned with the cart. She was full of praise for the horses. 'They didn't like it. I didn't like it either. But they weren't difficult. Do you want it here?' She brought the cart into the open.

'Stay in the wood,' said Chalmers.

For half an hour they laboured to load the containers onto the cart, using the parachutes as padding between them. They were heavy and needed at least two people to lift. Two were missing. There was disagreement about where they might be, Chalmers thinking they had overshot into the wood, René equally certain they were near or in the river. Marguerite stayed with the cart while they searched. In the event both were proved right. After nearly an hour, Georges found one hanging in trees beyond the end of the zone; René found the other, its chute hooked onto another tree, the container half in and half out of the river.

'He did well,' said Lejeune.

Chalmers accepted the compliment. 'Lucky the breeze is light. We could have lost the lot.' His sense of responsibility remained. 'Let's get on with it.' He felt vulnerable in the moonlight. 'We must get it under cover.'

René drove off in the Citroën, taking Johnson back to St.Pierre. The remainder returned to La Rippe with the cart. They arrived in the small hours and Gambert, Georges and Henri did not go home until everything had been hidden. They agreed to meet the next day to see what had been sent. Chalmers went upstairs with Chantal while Lejeune turned out the lamps. She turned to him outside his room and kissed him. 'Goodnight, James. It went well.'

He held her to him in the darkness of the landing. 'I shall expect you tomorrow night.'

'Perhaps.' Chantal was flirtatious. 'It might depend on what's in the containers.'

'Nonsense. Even if we've enough explosive to blow up every railway in France, I shall be waiting for you tomorrow.'

She pressed herself against him and then she had gone.

Lying in bed a few minutes later, he felt as happy as he had at any time since his arrival in Burgundy. The evening had been a success and he sensed an acceptance not felt before. The warmth from Chantal was growing. They had even discussed Verlaine and Baudelaire as well as Chopin and Beethoven. Sadly, he did not think she would recognise Wordsworth's *Prelude* that had come upon him as the Halifax approached. Mary seemed in another world. Guilt was there, but it was fading.

26

The next morning brought a mild late-summer day. Pale sunshine lay across the woods and hills and there was only the hint of a breeze. Lejeune and Chantal were out with the animals by the time Chalmers was down for breakfast. Marguerite was still at the table in the kitchen, but was about to cycle to the shop. Marie was making pastry and Célestine was upstairs with the old man. 'You manage to make me feel thoroughly idle,' he said, sitting down in the place left for him.

'The animals won't wait,' laughed Marie. She looked at Chalmers. 'I couldn't sleep until you were back.'

'I must go,' said Marguerite, looking at the clock over kitchen range. To Chalmers she said, 'I hope you find the right things. Papa wants to open them as soon as he's got Maurice working.' She took down her coat hanging behind the door. 'All that excitement and I can't whisper a word.'

'See if anyone heard it – the plane,' he said.

Lejeune was back by ten o'clock. He had made sure Maurice and the man from Coulanges were working by the river. Immediately afterwards René arrived with Johnson, so they all went straight to the barn, uncovered the containers, disentangled the parachutes, and prised them open. For Chalmers it was like a bran tub at Christmas.

The first was heavy, the one they had had most difficulty lifting the previous night. 'Tinned food,' said Johnson. 'No wonder it's such a weight. Bully beef mostly.'

'Food will go to Bernard,' said Lejeune. 'Georges can take it in the *camionette*. Guns and explosives stay here.'

'If they've sent any,' said René, his scepticism still strong.

'What about this?' said Johnson. He held a pistol with an ugly silencer. 'And other guns, packed in grease.' He put the pistol down and picked up a cloth-covered Sten gun. 'Stens and ammunition. Three Brens, too. We can arm the forest men as well as feed them.'

'Explosives for ourselves first,' said Lejeune. 'If we're going to get more from London, we've got to prove we're worth it.'

Johnson was opening another container when Chantal came in from the dairy. 'I didn't want to miss it. We can use this,' she said, holding up the silk of a parachute. 'Célestine can make undies.'

Chalmers said, 'Can't leave them lying around.'

'Célestine won't let us down.' Chalmers was pleased by Chantal's loyalty. She often showed more affection for the old woman than the others.

'More guns and ammunition – and grenades,' said Johnson. 'Oil for maintenance, too.'

By the time Georges arrived with Gambert and Henri they had opened most of the containers and even René was cheerful. 'Plenty of explosive,' he said to Henri. 'Now you can show us what you can do.'

Henri's lean face suffused with pleasure as he looked at what Johnson was holding. 'That's good,' he said hoarsely, the timbre of his voice seemingly affected by his enthusiasm. 'I can use that all right. We'll prove we're better than Migennes. We'll blow up their line to Dijon.' Henri resented the Migennes Resistance because they had stirred things up without considering the consequences. His elderly mother, who lived there, had been arrested by Gestapo searching for members of the group who had killed a German officer. At one point it seemed she might be shot as a hostage.

'Clothes – and boots for the men in the woods,' said Johnson.

'To Pontaubert with the food,' said Lejeune. 'We've done well – as well as the Maquis Camille. They had a drop near Quarré-les-Tombes. The first in Burgundy.'

They spent the rest of the morning hiding things. The containers they loaded into the *camionette*. Georges and Henri were going to take them to a quarry near Avallon. 'It's flooded,' said Henri. 'No one goes there. We'll go tonight. Alphonsine won't be pleased, but I can't help that.' He always looked depressed when he mentioned his wife. Her passion for cleanliness had driven a wedge between them and he attributed his patronage of *Les Pêcheurs* to her unbridled enthusiasm for brush and broom.

By the time Maurice and the man from Coulanges came back for lunch everything was under cover and all the visitors except Johnson, who remained out of sight in the barn, had gone. Maurice filled the horses' trough with water. He said: 'Is it pork again? I like pork.' He laughed, looking at Chalmers. 'Do you like pork?' He accepted Chalmers's presence, but gave no sign of understanding who he was.

After initial embarrassment Chalmers had learned how to cope with Maurice. 'I certainly do, Maurice,' he said. 'I do like pork. We'll have to ask Célestine if we've got pork again, won't we?'

Maurice and the labourer, a man with a deformed shoulder who reminded Chalmers of a character from a Zola novel, went inside for lunch. Lejeune turned to Chalmers. 'When we've eaten, go back to Poirier's with Johnson. Johnson's acknowledging the *parachutage* to London. I want to know if they've got a specific target. We'll decide if we do it.'

After lunch Chalmers and Johnson cycled to St.Pierre. It was the first time they had been alone together for any length of time. Both appreciated the opportunity to speak frankly – and in English. 'I could have been swept up at Clamecy,' said Johnson. 'Poor Emil didn't stand a chance. The Germans had the so-called safe house. Bernard discovered what was happening and got hold of me. He didn't realise I was a wireless man, but saw I was valuable. He wouldn't have let me go to anyone but Lejeune. God, this bike's uncomfortable! We can freewheel down here.'

They enjoyed a downhill stretch on the empty lane without speaking, the air fresh on their faces. 'What training did you get?' asked Chalmers, pedalling again.

'Several weeks. I was an ordinary wireless man, but volunteered for SOE when they discovered my fluent French. Did a bit of everything. Brens, Stens and I've fired one of those Welrod things – the one with the silencer I waved about. There was an explosives course. I can use most of the stuff they've sent, but Henri probably knows more. We were shown how not to break our necks when we fell out of an aeroplane.'

'I told my crew to bale out. They'd have survived if they had.'

'Some were injured.'

'I tried to get down. I had to try.' This was the first time Chalmers had felt able to talk about it with Johnson. 'Rather you than me baling out. I could screw my courage to the sticking-place if it were life or death. You did it in cold blood.'

'I was terrified. I just followed Emil when the light went green and the man shouted "Go!" I was more frightened of being taken back to England. There were a couple of girls on my course. I couldn't have faced them.'

'Your cover story?'

'SOE provided it. I was a motor mechanic before I joined up. Over here I'm an ex-employee of a garage in Auxerre. The owner knows about me and will back me up in a crisis. His son was in the French army and escaped from Dunkirk. I'm looking for work and that covers me moving around. My papers are sound, though they haven't been tested. Nor have yours, have they? Mine look dirty and used. They're clever in London.'

They crossed the railway and cycled into St.Pierre. The baker's horse and cart stood outside the *boulangerie*; in the square by the church the curé, biretta in hand, was talking to a gendarme. A farmer's cart piled high with hay made its way through the shadows of the trees and out into the sunshine of the countryside.

'We'll talk in the bar,' said Chalmers. 'In French, remember. They're used to me here. Better than Poirier's.'

They propped their bikes against one of the plane trees and went into the bar. The proprietor, Monsieur Claudel, a gloomy man with heavy jowls, looked up from his newspaper. He wore a waistcoat with its buttons undone; his sleeves were rolled up untidily. Chalmers was now accepted without much interest. 'Wine? Cognac?' Claudel asked.

Chalmers nodded. 'Wine, please – and water. When did you last have real coffee?'

'Last month? The month before?' Claudel was not interested. The Occupation had created insoluble problems; he did not bother his head with them. He filled a *pichet* and brought it over, together with water in a carafe advertising Ricard. 'Boches in St.Pierre this morning. They're after something.'

Chalmers and Johnson sat down in a corner to avoid attention. They were talking about farm matters when two men came in and ordered cognacs. One was Ronson the schoolmaster, his companion a cadaverous older man with white hair. Ronson recognised Chalmers with a motion of his arm, then continued conversing in the sort of voice that attracted attention. 'Dalon heard it, too – the aircraft,' he said.

'Dalon?'

'Dalon. At the Mairie – Châtel-Censoir. Thought another one was down in the Yonne. The last one caused trouble. But there was nothing wrong with it. Came down, then went back up again. Something going on.'

'Not German?'

'Dalon said it was English. Four engines. And I met a boy from school, young Jean Deaud. Funny lad – bright. He knows about planes – more than Dalon. He said it was English, a bomber. He told me a name, but I've forgotten it.'

'So what was it doing?' Ronson's acquaintance gave the impression of being an intelligent man picking up information but giving little away.

Ronson leaned forward confidentially. His voice had dropped, but he still spoke as though he wanted others to hear. 'It could have been something for Migennes.'

'Migennes? You know them?'

Ronson polished his glasses with a handkerchief. Chalmers and Johnson listened, wondering how Ronson had managed to ingratiate himself with the Migennes Maquis.

'Yes,' replied Ronson. 'I've a friend – another schoolmaster – he keeps in touch. We were in the cycle club when we were younger. They're getting stronger.' He sipped his cognac and looked round the room as though realising he was being indiscreet. Chalmers felt he was acting, a clever man not risking open alliance with the Resistance but rubbing out a pro-Vichy past. He wondered how many others were doing the same.

An old woman with a grey-muzzled dog under her table looked up. 'I heard it,' she said. 'Woke the whole of St.Pierre. My husband never did hold with flying machines – always said they'd cause trouble. And he died thirty years ago.' She poured the remains of a cognac into her coffee and examined it through pebble glasses. 'Might make it drinkable,' she said.

Chalmers thought of the woman with the pheasant feather in England and that brought back Mary. 'What do you think of the Lejeune girls?' he asked. 'Attractive, aren't they?'

'Chantal likes you.'

'I owe her a lot.'

'Marguerite?'

'Pretty girl. I like the whole family. But I'm biased. They saved my life. Jacques was delighted when you turned up. He wanted to contact London, but not through any of the other groups. A shrewd man. If he'd made mistakes, he'd have been swept up with Clamecy. Marie doesn't approve, but she'll go along with anything. The dead son unites them.'

'She's pretty all right.'

'Marguerite? I saw you looking at her. You can't have Chantal.'

'I didn't have a girl in England.'

'I did.' Chalmers corrected himself. 'I have. I've got a girl I'm going to marry if I get home. She doesn't know if I'm alive or dead. Bound to imagine the worst.'

'And Chantal?'

'Honest question, honest answer. Don't know. I've told her about Mary. We get on well. She's here, Mary isn't. I'm a man, she's a woman. Is that wrong?'

Their eyes met. Later, they both felt it was the moment their friendship started. Johnson said, 'Lejeune wouldn't want Englishmen for both his daughters. I ought to look elsewhere.'

'Nonsense. Try your luck. She's choosy. She doesn't do everything her father wants.' He drank some wine and checked that Ronson and his companion were concerned with their own affairs. 'To business. Targets? Contact tonight?'

'They're expecting me.'

'What was Emil planning?'

'Reports on troop movements. Then sabotage. Communications – railways, bridges, telephone lines. Not assassination. Leads to reprisals. Perhaps arming the men in the forests. They could help when the Second Front comes.'

'We must do something ourselves if we're going to be credible. They've sent a lot of stuff. We want a soft target. We're beginners and we don't want to make a mess of it. Get it right and they'll support us, get it wrong and they won't. That's the way I read it.'

'They'll be impressed by the drop – lights O.K., everything safe.'

'Say it went like clockwork. Congratulate the pilot. He was spot on.' Chalmers poured some water. He was drinking more wine than he was used to and wanted to keep a clear head. 'So we need something simple. A railway bridge, perhaps – somewhere they don't patrol, something easy. How is it at Poirier's?'

'He's given me a room in the attic. Barely furnished – bed, chair, no carpet. Well out of the way and I can get my wires up without trouble. They leave me alone. His wife's frightened – and he tries to please her. He's worried about Ann-Marie, too. She's normal much of the time, then says something totally dotty. More bats in the belfry than Maurice and that's saying something. They've told her the story – I'm looking for a job at a garage – but she keeps asking why I don't go to Auxerre. "More garages there," she says. And she's absolutely right. For the Poiriers' sake I can't stay long. Lejeune knows that, too. I'll cycle over tomorrow to tell you what happens.'

The two fell silent, drinking their wine. Ronson and his companion talked quietly, Ronson with one eye on other customers. A middle-aged man and his wife, well dressed and known to Claudel, came in, ordered wine and sat down. The man addressed no one in particular. 'Hear the aircraft last night?'

Eyes swivelled. 'English,' he said, looking round the room. 'Dropping things. My daughter works in the café at Vincelottes – heard Boche officers talking. Not good news. We don't want the Boches stirred up – and we don't want them here. Resistance is all very well if you haven't got family. It's all right for the English – they're miles away. The Boches shot more hostages at Valenciennes the other day. We'll pay the price if the English cause trouble.'

Anonymous faces eyed the speaker. Ronson and his friend also looked, but said nothing. The woman with the dog was the only one to respond. She had ordered another cognac and poured more of it into her coffee. '*Courage, Monsieur.* They won't go home on their own. If we don't do something, the only ones to get credit for sending them back to Germany will be the English and Americans. I don't know anyone in the Resistance, but I support de Gaulle.' She spoke with a slight slurring of the speech and the room fell silent.

Claudel went over to her table. 'That's enough, Thérèse,' he said. 'No politics here. I serve anyone and I don't allow politics.' He looked round the room, mentally checking his customers, some of whom he knew were Pétainist.

'I pay for my cognac. I say what I like.'

The middle-aged couple looked indignantly at her. The man said, 'I'd be brave at your age. Remember who gets shot. It won't be you.' His wife nodded. She said: 'Anything stirred up here makes life difficult. The only ones who'll gain when the Boches go will be the Reds. Do you want that? I'd rather the Boches stayed than be taken over by Bolsheviks. My cousin in Paris says all the Maquis are Reds.'

Ronson put his glass down. 'The Reds are doing more than most,' he said. 'My friend in Migennes . . .'

Claudel, who knew his customers well, waved his arms and interrupted. 'See what you've done, Thérèse.' To the couple he said, 'We've all got to survive. I serve Germans if I have to. We all compromise. I don't want the Reds either.' He looked pointedly at Ronson. 'I'm surprised at you, Jean-Paul. You approved when the Auxerre council backed Pétain in 1940. You said how wise the Marshal was and hoped a street would be named after him. Now that's enough politics. I mean it.' He threw a napkin over his shoulder in a dismissive gesture. He poured himself an Armagnac and looked round the room as though daring anyone to defy him.

After a moment of silence, conversation resumed at a low level. Chalmers and Johnson exchanged a look. 'I'm learning,' said Chalmers.

'So am I,' responded Johnson. 'Know much about French history?'

'Pretty basic.'

'I've picked up some from my mother. Still got her French accent. They can't forget their revolution – sorry, revolutions. Each one left its mark. We got our civil war over in the seventeenth century and we've forgotten all about it. They're still going on about Liberty, Equality and Fraternity – and they all mean something different. I thought everyone would want the Jerries out, but some see them as a better bet than the Bolsheviks. And now the Bolshies are taking a lead in the Resistance.'

'Lejeune told me the Maquis Vauban in the Morvan is headed by a Communist. He says even the monks will vote for him after the war. It's not just Migennes.'

'The monks?'

'The Abbey of La-Pierre-qui-Vire – where you were being taken, in the forest. The monks have hidden RAF men. Some of them were taken away when the escape line was blown. They won't hide anyone else.'

'So tonight's important. I'll press for details in a way I haven't done before. They like to close down quickly. Think it's safer for me.'

'It is.'

'But we must get this one right. We mustn't be involved in anything daft. That Spaniard at the mill gave me the creeps. He'd get us all shot. Thank God he's Bernard's problem and not ours.'

The peace of the bar was suddenly shattered by the arrival of another dog and its owner. The dog, a frisky Alsatian puppy hoping for a game, made straight for Thérèse's mongrel and received a sharp bite for his pains. The ensuing mayhem gave Chalmers and Johnson the chance to escape. They picked up their cycles and set off in opposite directions.

***

Next day Johnson arrived at La Rippe early. He could barely contain his excitement. 'We've got it,' he said, as Chalmers joined him in the yard. 'We've got to do some homework, but it looks just right.' He was breathing heavily. 'I can't understand the French enthusiasm for *le vélo*. This machine will be the death of me.'

'Go on.'

'I'll tell you inside.' Johnson wore working clothes with grease and oil patches to confirm his role of motor mechanic. 'Can't get used to the beret,' he confided, taking it off as they went into the kitchen. 'Where is everybody?' They sat down at the kitchen table.

'Jacques is out with Maurice. The girls have gone to Mailly. Marie and Célestine are upstairs somewhere. Tell me.'

'They're pleased with us. The pilot said it was easy. Congratulated us. The lights showed up better than we thought.'

'Target?'

'Interesting – and I think we can do it. Do you know about the caves?'

'Caves?'

'Famous caves on the N6 – the main road south. The Grottes D'Arcy. Pre-historic cave paintings, animals and so on.'

'So we blow up pre-historic paintings? I don't imagine Jerry guards them. Unless they were done by Aryans.'

Johnson shared the humour of the idea. Then he went off at a tangent. 'Poirier doesn't like Jews. I was warned in training not to be surprised if the French were anti-Semitic. It's the only thing Poirier agrees with Vichy about.'

'The politics are complicated. The Dreyfus Case lives on. And they don't know who to blame for the collapse when the Germans invaded. Not our problem. Targets? Caves?'

'Not the Grottes D'Arcy – further down river. Towards Auxerre. The Germans use some of them to build aircraft. There are foreign workers there – forced labour.'

'Sabotage?'

'No – easier. There's a town south of here, Le Creusot – the other side of Autun. A steel town – the Schneider works are there. A French factory makes engine parts under German supervision. They're brought up to the caves. They come in a convoy every fortnight. No escort. It's been going on for months.'

'How does London know?'

'A commie at the factory.'

'So – what do we do?'

'The road from Le Creusot goes through wooded country.

281

If we stop just one convoy, we mess up production. London suggests one, but we could hit another later. With surprise we could make the whole thing difficult for them.'

'Right.' Chalmers was assessing the possibilities. 'Blow it up? Attack it – take the bits away?'

'Up to us. One snag. There's no escort, but the drivers are French. Not collaborators, just men doing a job. London doesn't want them hurt.'

'If there's no escort, we should be able to cope with that. When's the next one coming?'

'This week – Friday. We've got two days.'

Chalmers shook his head. 'No. We plan it properly. We can *watch* this one. Then we've time to set it up for their next trip. We're not going to be rushed. It's got to be faultless – for all our sakes. Times?'

'London was precise. The lorries are loaded during the day and leave the factory at Le Creusot in the late afternoon – five or six of them. They're heavily loaded – they go slowly. Departure time – 4.30-5.00 pm – but he doesn't know when they arrive up here. He reckons they should be in Avallon by about eight. He can't be sure. And he doesn't know if they have a break on the road.'

'We'll check this end. If Lejeune agrees – and I'm sure he will – we'll monitor it this Friday. We'll have a go at the next one – when we've chosen the best place. I've cycled down to the N6 at Vermenton, but that's more or less open country. My guess is we ought to do it in the Morvan. Rougher country – more wooded. Easier to get away and fewer locals to take the rap. The Germans will put it down to one of the Morvan groups. I'll get the map.' He collected the Michelin map Lejeune had given him and spread it out on the table. 'There's Le Creusot,' he said, pointing. 'Now what's the route?'

Johnson looked at his notes. 'Due north to Autun and north again to Saulieu. At Saulieu they pick up the main road, the N6.'

Chalmers pushed the map towards Johnson. 'What do you think?'

'Not my strong point, map-reading. But if all this green' – he pointed – 'is woodland, I should think somewhere here. Hardly any villages.'

'Before Saulieu. I agree. If the Germans are anywhere, they'll be on the main road and there's no sign they think the convoy's vulnerable. It depends on Jacques. He'll know the road. They won't be going fast if they're loaded.'

They heard footsteps in the yard and after he had knocked mud off his boots Lejeune came in. He acknowledged Johnson and went to the sink to wash his hands. 'Action?' he asked. 'London?'

'I think we can do it,' responded Chalmers. 'It's up to you. We've time to do it properly if we plan straight away.'

'Where?'

'Your choice. You say what's possible.'

Lejeune dried his hands. 'Come into the dining room. Bring the map.'

***

An hour later Lejeune leaned back in his chair. He deferred naturally to his military guests, but he knew the road they suggested and confirmed it was ideal. Nothing could travel fast and there were myriads of places for an ambush. 'So what do we do?' he asked.

'We've got to be sure there's no escort,' said Chalmers. 'If that's true, we can destroy the whole convoy – and save the French drivers. We need to be on that road this Friday when it comes through.' He looked at Lejeune. 'Wherever you think best. We check the lorries – and recce the site for getting away. We need everyone to see the ground.'

'Plan?'

'All subject to your approval, but it looks simple. This

Friday we find the approximate time they get there and check everything London says. The next time they come we'll be waiting. We block the road – a tree? a car? – and hold them up. We force them off the road into the woods, get the drivers out and Henri blows up the lorries. We've got guns. I don't see a problem. The aircraft parts will be destroyed and a fortnight's production ended.'

'The drivers?' said Johnson.

'We protect them – and ourselves. They're driving for the Jerries, so we can treat them as prisoners. Tied up if need be. They won't know us and we don't know them. Once the job's done we let them go.'

'One or two might join us,' said Johnson.

'Doubt it. They probably live in or near Le Creusot – perhaps with families. We could be destroying their jobs as well as their lorries.' Chalmers was realistic. 'They could be more hostile than the Germans.'

'Don't worry,' said Lejeune. 'They've chosen to drive.'

'Easy decision, Jacques?' said Chalmers. 'Survival? You say that's the key. Families? Jobs? Difficult.'

'They're helping the Boches.'

'What about the Maquis in the Morvan?' asked Johnson. 'Aren't we invading their territory? They'll get the blame.'

Lejeune had shaved but he rubbed his chin as if feeling the usual stubble. 'There are no private areas. I'll talk to Bernard and he'll understand. I don't even know where the Vauban Maquis or Maquis Camille operate. Bernard's an old friend. And I'll see he doesn't know too much.'

'How do we get down there?' Chalmers looked at the practicalities.

'Two cars will do it – René and Georges. You and Johnson could cycle down tomorrow, if you wanted to take a chance with the weather and sleep in the woods. This fine spell looks settled.' Lejeune pointed out of the window at the changing colours of the surrounding woodland. Autumn was not far off.

'If you got there tomorrow, you could have a plan ready for us.'

'Perhaps.' Chalmers hesitated to take instant decisions. His respect for the Frenchman was based in large part on their shared caution. He looked at Johnson. 'We could recce the whole area. We're free – they've got to keep jobs going.' He laughed. 'If it belts with rain, we'll get soaked. Is there anywhere to shelter?'

Lejeune looked doubtful. 'You might find a hunter's hut. I've a groundsheet and a couple of First World War cycling capes you could take.'

Johnson smiled at Chalmers. 'That bike'll be the death of me. I don't share the Gallic enthusiasm for *le vélo*.'

'I think we should. Jacques, show us the best place – we'll go tomorrow.'

Lejeune's rough finger probed the map, pushing north from Autun. 'This is rough country. How about there?' He pointed at a bend in the road. 'Forest either side, a long way to the nearest village, and tracks east and west for getting away. I know the place. No houses – nothing. And they'll be coming uphill at that bend. They'll have to slow down.'

Chalmers's respect for the Frenchman increased. Lejeune had chosen the same spot he would have gone for if he had been working from the map alone.

Johnson got up. 'I'll go back to the Poiriers. I'll be here before nine tomorrow and ready to leave as soon as you are. No transmission before Monday.'

When he had gone, Lejeune and Chalmers sat either side of the heavy oak dining table eyeing each other. 'You've done a lot for us,' said Lejeune. 'We can do something big now.'

'You've done something big already. You've saved men.'

'This will be more satisfying. We shall see what we've done.' Lejeune's eyes showed something Chalmers had not seen before. There was a hardness of light akin to hatred. For the first time since they had met Chalmers wondered if Lejeune was as controlled as he had thought.

27

Johnson arrived while Lejeune and Chalmers were finishing breakfast the next day. 'They're glad to be rid of me,' he said. 'Poirier's wife – Liliane – is terrified. The Cossacks were rough when they went through the place after your crash. She made me pack up the wireless before I left. She's worried about Anne-Marie. She's seen the wireless wires and thinks I'm growing a vine in the attic. Liliane's worried she may say something daft in the village.'

'Poirier's a good man to take you in,' said Chalmers. 'Give me ten minutes.'

'I've looked at the map,' said Johnson. 'There are hills. My bum's sore just looking at them. Poirier says it'll rain. Wind in the west and the Morvan hills look blue. Infallible, he says. Got the capes?'

'There's a hut,' said Lejeune.

'Safe?' This was Chalmers.

'The Boches don't go into the woods unless something attracts their attention,' said Lejeune. 'A few hunt with the local Vichy men near Saulieu. But not in the Morvan. They're as nervous of the Morvan as French governments. Célestine done your food?'

'We shan't starve.' Chalmers looked at the watch Chantal had given him. 'Right, we'll see you up that track at about three tomorrow. We'll be off the road, about a quarter of a mile. Bring a towel in case we're soaked.'

'And make sure Georges brings his bloody *camionette*. I'll get there, but I'm not riding back,' said Johnson.

'I'll do my best,' responded Lejeune. 'Georges can be difficult. He runs what he calls 'private business' with another bar owner in Crain – *marché noir*. It depends if the friend wants the *camionette* – and on petrol.'

When Chalmers and Johnson left, Chantal made sure she was there. She made no particular gesture, just a wave of the hand as they set off towards Châtel-Censoir. But Chalmers saw the expression on her face and he gave a look he hoped transmitted something special.

Initially there was little indication that Poirier's prophecy of rain would be fulfilled and they rode through empty lanes in fitful sunshine, but clouds gathered as they neared Avallon. The Morvan hills were ominously dark as they dropped down beneath the medieval ramparts and by the time they reached Saulieu it was raining steadily. They stopped at a café to put on the capes. It stood on its own, small and unprepossessing, a faded sign announcing the *Café du Centre*. Inside three or four workmen standing at the bar looked them up and down. Strangers were infrequent..

They made signs of greeting and sat down. They knew they would be the subject of curiosity, but had decided not to volunteer an explanation unless pressed. The workmen, exchanging gloomy comments about prices and the shortage of cigarettes, lost interest in them. Chalmers picked up a paper lying on the table and glanced through it. A photograph of Pétain surrounded by laughing children dominated the front page. Chalmers tossed it across the table. 'You wouldn't know there's a war on,' he said.

'They'd be closed down if they said the wrong thing. And the Marshal's popular.' Johnson nodded towards a portrait of Pétain behind the bar.

'Only a handful of people like Lejeune are prepared to take risks. They're a minority. The rest get on with things and Vichy says it's an opportunity for national revival, to scrap the mistakes made before the war. Most people at home don't realise what's going on. I certainly didn't. Look at that.' He pointed at the smiling faces in the paper. 'And René can't forgive us because we blew up their fleet at Mers-el-Kébir. I'm sorry about his brother, but it was the obvious thing to do.'

Johnson drank some wine, nodding towards the workmen. 'They're more concerned about work – and you can't blame them. The one with the moustache hasn't had a job since the invasion. I've been listening.'

The men had more or less forgotten the strangers. The woman behind the bar, a young blonde, heavily made up, served a cognac and lit a cigarette. She said: 'Another raid on Calais last night. A lot killed – mostly French.'

The man with the moustache shook his head as though the ways of the world were beyond his comprehension. 'Bound to be French. My brother-in-law lives in Boulogne. Says the raids are getting worse. A lot of talk about invasion.'

The woman shrugged with indifference and adjusted a shoulder strap. 'The Boches pay well at Madame Goulet's.'

The men laughed. 'Trade must have looked up,' said the youngest, a short fellow with slicked-back hair and prominent ears. 'The last time I went I didn't stay. Nathalie's the only one worth looking at and she was busy.'

'New girls since the Boches came. The money's good.'

'You should try your luck, Danièle,' said the man with the moustache. Ribald humour at her expense was not new.

'I'd make more than I do from you lot,' the woman responded. 'And the bed would be comfortable.'

Chalmers and Johnson smiled. Their appreciation of the humour knitted them into the group at the bar. 'Going far?' asked one of the men.

'Autun,' volunteered Chalmers reluctantly.

'You'll get wet. It's set in.'

'No petrol. *Vélos* the only way. Difficult to do business these days.' He picked up the critical tone of the conversation they had overheard. Chalmers looked round. 'Germans here?'

'A few. They're moving troops again. Main road south busy. Business?'

'Books. We're meant to be a cultured nation. God knows when I'll get petrol again.'

The man with prominent ears said: 'If you haven't got a job, you can't buy books – or anything else. They say there are jobs in Normandy and Brittany. Building Boches defences.'

'Would you go?'

'He's never been out of Burgundy,' said one of the others. 'The Boches would have to pay a lot. Perhaps they do.'

'No Nathalie in Normandy,' said Danièle, exhaling smoke.

'Calvados, though,' said one. 'It might be worth it.'

'To work for the Boches?' said Danièle.

'Work's work. You serve them, don't you?'

'We had that little corporal who'd lost his way. I was sorry for him. He was going to get into trouble. I helped him.'

'And what happens if they lose the war? What about *collaborateurs*? There'll be trouble, mark my words.' The moustached man, older than his companions, nodded to himself.

Chalmers caught Johnson's eye and they stood up together. 'Back on the road,' said Chalmers, waving a farewell.

'You won't make it before dark,' said one of the men. '*Bon voyage.*'

It was still raining. 'Bloody *vélo*,' said Johnson, remounting after wiping the seat. Within minutes they were out of the town, passing small farms in wooded countryside. In three quarters of an hour they saw two cyclists going in the opposite direction, three horse-drawn farm carts and no more than half a dozen cars.

'Lejeune was right,' said Chalmers. 'This is the road. I'm surprised they come this way.'

'They've no reason to think there's danger. The Maquis haven't done anything this side of the Morvan.' Johnson looked west as they freewheeled down a hill. 'It's stopping. Look, the sun's out.' The cloud had broken and sunlight shone through the gathering dusk.

'Not far now,' said Chalmers. 'It looks like a lane on the map – it could be just a track.'

They were in thick woodland, beech and oak on both sides; the rain had stopped but the overhead branches dripped steadily. 'I hope the hut's still there,' said Johnson. 'If it rains again, we're going to get a soaking.'

'Here it is,' said Chalmers. 'A proper lane – to begin with anyway.' It was a lane of sorts, but covered with a carpet of sodden leaves. In the distance the remains of a sunset appeared through ragged storm-clouds. It was already twilight. 'The hut should be over there.'

They set off through ferns, spraying themselves with water as they pushed through. 'I can see it,' said Johnson. 'Good God, I don't call that a hut.' He pointed to four crumbling stone walls ahead. Ivy covered the outside and what had been a door was no more than the entrance to a room open to the sky.

'Used by hunters, according to Lejeune,' said Chalmers.

'It's a ruin. We'll have to improvise.'

Together they put down a groundsheet and after half an hour's work with stones and the cycle capes succeeded in erecting a rough shelter that would keep out the worst of any rain. The silence of the wood was reassuring. The only sound was an occasional car on the road. There was not even any birdsong.

'Let's have something to eat,' said Chalmers. 'Then we'll look around.' They ate Célestine's bread and cheese before going back to the main road. It was as deserted as it had been before. The cloud had cleared and a thin moon lit up the countryside. 'Here's the hill,' said Chalmers. 'They'll come up in low gear.'

'Car coming,' said Johnson suddenly.

They scrambled into the trees. Johnson put a foot in a water-filled ditch and swore. Headlights shone upwards and levelled off as the car reached the top and speeded up. 'Jerry,' said Chalmers. 'Staff car – four men. Probably dining in Saulieu. The restaurants have a reputation. I read about it in a guide book at La Rippe. It was a posting stage for horses on the Paris-Lyon road for years – even Rabelais praised its cuisine. Before the war it was a stopping place for motorists on the N6 heading south.'

'Dining with collaborators?'

'You're becoming cynical. Let's see how long the hill is.'

They clambered back, and set off down the hill. Trees closed in and the gradient became steeper. Eventually the road levelled off and widened out. 'That's it,' said Chalmers. 'Perfect – assuming they're all together. We stop the first one at the top and the rest will be strung out down the hill. It's not wide enough for them to turn round. Lejeune says this is the best place. I trust him.'

'My foot's soaking,' said Johnson, stamping on the ground. They went back to the hut, laid out blankets under their shelter and made themselves as comfortable as they could. 'You a Boy Scout?' asked Johnson, arranging a pile of ferns on a stone he had put down as a pillow.

'No – were you?'

'Oh, yes. My father was an enthusiastic camper. Said any fool can be uncomfortable. Some of the men I joined up with had never spent a night out of doors – or away from their parents. My first barrack-room was full of Welsh miners. If they weren't crying for their mothers, they were singing. All night long. It was purgatory, I can tell you.'

They held a desultory conversation about their experiences in the forces, but were soon asleep. Both woke at different times, but they did not speak and dawn was breaking when they awoke together. There was birdsong now and the rising sun cast shadows through the trees. 'Too bright too early,' said Chalmers. He pointed east. 'Red sky in the morning . . . Your feet are going to get wet again.'

They ate more food – bread and ham this time – and were ready for a recce before seven o'clock. To start with they went further into the forest to look at escape routes and see where vehicles could be parked. Everywhere was deserted; they did not meet a single person and they soon knew the area intimately. Then it was back to the cycles and the road the convoy would use. Occasionally they deviated into side lanes and other possible ambush sites, but nothing was an improvement on Lejeune's suggestion.

They turned down the lane to the hut. 'Will they come separately?' asked Johnson.

'I think so. Lejeune hasn't taken a risk since I've been here.'

They put their bikes in the hut and sat down on convenient stones. 'We'll hear them turn off the road,' said Johnson. 'What time did you say?'

'Three o'clock. I want them to have two hours to see the ground and know it as well as we do. The convoy leaves Le Creusot at five. I can't see them getting here before six. We'll be ready from five in case they set off early. Belt and braces. We haven't come all this way to miss them.' Chalmers spoke almost automatically. He was thinking about something else. 'What's best to block the road. A car's simplest. Just drive it across in front of the leading lorry. Once they're on the hill they'll be stuck. But we can't afford to risk losing a car and if anything went wrong the Germans could trace it. A tree's safer.'

'Steal a car?'

'We could.' Chalmers considered the idea. 'It might lead the Germans to pick up the wrong people.'

'There's a branch the other side of the road – where we crossed and I stood in the ditch. Big enough stop a lorry, almost a tree trunk. It would do if we could move it.'

'Show me.'

They crossed the road and found the branch. 'It's been down some time,' Johnson said, giving it a kick. The branch was embedded in the ground at one end and covered in ivy.

'See if we can shift it. It's big enough.' They got hold of the branch at strategic points and made a joint effort. It moved marginally, but was heavy. 'We could do it with two more. We'll try again when they get here. It's the answer.' Chalmers was confident. 'Just wish they'd get a move on.' He glanced at his watch.

'Someone's coming.'

They waited in the wood and two cars passed. 'False alarm,' said Johnson. They returned to the hut and were about to sit down when another car approached from Saulieu. It slowed as it reached the junction and turned off towards them. 'René,' said Chalmers. 'He's got Lejeune, Chantal and Gambert.' He ran through the ferns to show where he wanted the car parked.

'Sorry we're late,' said René, turning off the engine. 'Boche traffic on the main road. They're holding everybody up in Avallon. How have you got on? Wet?'

Ten minutes later Georges and Henri arrived in the *camionette*. 'Thank the Lord for that,' said Johnson, watching it turn in. 'I meant it when I said I couldn't go back on the *vélo*. I'd rather walk.'

Chalmers gave a quick briefing before taking them to the tree he wanted to use. With four of them it moved easily. Then for the best part of two hours they walked the tracks in the forest and the road to Autun. They were discussing how to deal with the French drivers when Johnson said, 'Nearly five.'

'Back to the hill,' said Chalmers. 'We're not missing them now. Spread out and keep out of sight. Note everything – drivers, passengers, anyone in the back, any sign of an escort.' He turned to Johnson. 'Go down to the first bend, make sure no one can see you. Wave the moment you see the first lorry. It's only a trial run, but we'll need time to shift that log when we do it for real. I want to know how long we've got.'

They scattered on both sides of the road. Chalmers and Lejeune stayed together, unconsciously recognising the support they gave each other. From their position behind two oak trees they could see Johnson down the hill. Chalmers felt Chantal crawling in behind them. It gave him a warm feeling when she gave his ankle a squeeze.

Chalmers said, 'Only a handful of cars in the past twenty-four hours.'

'No petrol,' said Lejeune. 'This is *la France profonde*. You're more likely to see a horse and cart.'

As if to prove his point there came the sound of horses' hooves from Saulieu and a farm cart driven by a lad and girl of no more than seventeen went past. They noticed nothing of the watchers, being taken up with each other, kissing and giggling. The boy's hand was under the girl's skirt; the horses plodded as though taking a familiar route home. Chantal squeezed Chalmers' ankle again, her fingers sliding up his leg.

For more than forty minutes they lay concealed, lowering their heads as one or two vehicles passed. The only tricky moment came when a pair of cycling farm workers debated whether they should stop to relieve themselves in the bushes. As it was, the prospect of an effortless downhill ride proved more attractive and they freewheeled past. A shout from Johnson alerted everyone. Chalmers acknowledged with a wave. Within seconds there came the sound of straining engines. 'More than one,' muttered Chalmers.

'At least three,' said Lejeune.

'Close together,' said Chalmers, watching Johnson's arm. The arm dropped as the first lorry approached the final bend. Seconds later a grey, unmarked lorry, lights on, reached the top. Immediately behind came a second lorry, identical to the first. There was a short gap before the third, but within the space of two minutes six lorries had laboured up the hill. Bringing up the rear came a black Citroën like René's, the driver wearing civilian clothes. 'Is he with them?' asked Chalmers. 'Gestapo?'

Lejeune was laconic. 'Might be someone local held up by a convoy he couldn't overtake.'

Chantal crept up alongside. 'A driver in each,' she said. 'The third had a passenger – a woman – but that was the only one. Canvas at the back of each lorry tied up. You couldn't see in.'

'Heavy loads,' responded Chalmers. 'The hill was difficult.'

'Time short for the tree,' said Lejeune. 'We need longer.'

Chalmers got up, brushing leaves from his jacket and trousers. 'We'll put someone further down for an earlier signal. The important thing is that they're close together. When we stop the first, we stop the lot. And there was nothing to link them to the Germans at all. Unmarked French lorries, civilian drivers, no escort. Let's go home. We've got a week to get it right.'

That night Chantal came to Chalmers's room. 'I know you're tired,' she said, lying down beside him. 'Give me a kiss and we'll go to sleep. It's going to be all right, isn't it?' She had watched him all day, her emotions deepening the more he took charge.

Chalmers kissed her. 'I liked it when you put your hand on my leg this afternoon. I thought your father might see.'

'I was careful. Did you think of Mary?'

'Unfair question. You know I think of Mary. But I think of you, too. I shan't let you down.'

'What does that mean?'

Chalmers was silent. She had touched the nerve he wanted left alone. He had not forgotten Mary – the idea appalled him – and he knew he never would. But she was not there now; she was part of the past, increasingly insubstantial. His feelings for Chantal could not compete; but she was *there*; she was warm and tangible, soft and gentle. She was the woman who had made him a man. He felt for the hem of her nightdress.

'Not tonight. You're tired. I'll come tomorrow.'

'Promise?'

'Have you known me break promises?'

'I trust you completely. You know that.'

She held him close. 'I know that. Go to sleep now.'

***

The plan was developed the next morning and details were

honed later. From contacts in Auxerre Lejeune discovered his guess about the black Citroën following the convoy had been accurate: it belonged to a doctor in Saulieu, so there was no escort. They were clear about the destruction of the lorries and their contents. The doubt centred on the French drivers.

'We can't kill them,' said Chalmers when he and Lejeune were on their own after supper.

'Why not?' asked Lejeune, pouring two glasses of red wine. 'They're collaborating and if they make trouble they can't expect mercy. Our safety comes before theirs.'

'I can't kill anyone in cold blood. They just want to keep life going, even when they're driving for the Boches. I begin to understand the compromises.'

'I'll make them see sense,' said Lejeune. 'We've got guns. They'll see their lorries blown up. They can make their own explanations to the Boches. They weren't responsible, so they'll be convincing.'

Chalmers changed the subject. 'We've got to get Johnson away from the Poiriers. It's too much strain on the family.'

'I've been against it, but he could go in the barn. I can persuade Marie.'

'What does the old man know about me?'

'I told him about the RAF men. You're one more. He doesn't know you're different. I've spoken to Célestine. She keeps him happy.'

They fell into a companionable silence, a measure of their mutual respect. Chalmers looked at the flame of the oil lamp, appreciating the characteristic smell that reminded him of his grandmother's farm on Bodmin Moor in Cornwall, visited as a child. 'Difficult,' he said. 'Killing in cold blood.'

'Different from dropping bombs?'

'Very different.'

'No choice if it's them or us.'

'Killing someone would stir up a hornets' nest. They'd shoot hostages. Having said that, we'll obviously be armed next week.' Chalmers pointed at a photograph on the wall behind Lejeune showing Jacques with a group of friends with shotguns and a dead wild boar. 'You hunted a lot?'

'I used to. That was in the Ardennes.' Lejeune stubbed out a cigarette and lighted another. 'Chantal likes you,' he said. 'I've seen the way she looks at you – and the way you look at her.'

'Do you mind?'

'No.' The lines by Lejeune's eyes creased humorously. 'It wouldn't matter if I did. I had trouble with the old man over Marie. It only made me more determined. That's human nature.'

'Did he change his mind?'

'Time heals. Marie's kind to him and she understands about Célestine. So you like Chantal?'

'We've been thrown together.' Chalmers was determinedly vague. 'I've got a girl in England. She probably thinks I'm dead.'

Lejeune drained his glass and pushed his chair back. 'I'm going to bed. Market tomorrow and I'll have to take Maurice. Only one word. Don't ever let her down.'

The two men stood up, their eyes meeting across the smoky oil lamp.

'I shan't let her down,' said Chalmers. He wondered if Lejeune suspected how far their relationship had gone.

28

In the fortnight before the next convoy, summer gave way to autumn and the temperature dropped in the valley of the Yonne. One night there was an early frost and locals discussed the likelihood of a hard winter. Célestine started a fire for old Lejeune in his bedroom, a fire she kept going throughout the winter.

'We know the spring's come when she lets it out,' said Chantal. 'It's his winter treat.'

A week later Johnson moved into the barn, much to the relief of Madame Poirier. He rigged up his wireless in the loft and his eyrie was protected by hay as Chalmers had been. Célestine hinted at disapproval, seeing a cause of additional work. She was modestly mollified when Chalmers and Johnson helped carry logs upstairs for the old man, though Jacques stipulated that neither should be taken to see him.

Two days before the convoy, London reported all seemed normal for the next delivery. Le Creusot also confirmed that the drivers were unarmed Frenchmen unconnected with Vichy or the Germans. Chalmers had been waiting for this before putting the final touches to his plan. They would travel in René's car and the *camionette*, which Lejeune had insisted should be available. 'You'll have to cut your profits,' Lejeune said when Georges was doubtful. 'This comes first. And don't give a hint of where you're going. Most will assume it's a Morvan group and we want everyone to think that – French and German.'

They were in the kitchen late at night discussing the details. René had not been able to come and Marie, Marguerite and

Célestine had gone to bed, but Chantal remained with the men. Two candles stood on the table, each in a brass candlestick. Shadows flickered on the wall.

'You understand the explosive, Henri,' said Chalmers. 'We leave that to you. You wait in the forest with all your kit. We block the road and get the lorries into the trees. You deal with the first driver, Jacques. We'll make the others follow. We have guns and we show them, but we shouldn't be too aggressive. Just make it clear they've no choice. Peter, you'll be further down the hill, so you deal with the last lorries. Once they're into the forest, we clear away the tree.' He turned to Gambert. 'Jean, you've got the trickiest job. I want you on the road from Saulieu. If anything comes, wave it down and say there's been an accident. You're a professional and you'll be convincing. Say something medical about an injury if you have to. They'll believe you. They can't see anything down there and it shouldn't be necessary to produce a gun. Hold them as long as you can – five minutes will be enough. The lorries will be off the road.'

'How far into the forest?' asked Henri.

'At least a quarter of a mile – right into the trees. We don't want anything seen from the road. Our own vehicles will be further in, down that track to Saulieu. The French drivers mustn't see them. If they turn nasty they could give details to the Boches. A quarter of an hour, Henri?'

'Everything will be ready. I only have to attach it. You wait in the cars.'

'We get out down the Saulieu track. It's rough, but joins the main road further on. We'll be out of the forest before anyone can investigate. The weak point is the road. Something could come at the wrong time – at worst a German car. That would be difficult.'

'We have the advantage of surprise,' said Johnson. 'We could shoot without asking questions.'

'Only if we have to,' said Chalmers. 'We keep it simple. Just the lorries. If we start a private war there'll be trouble for everyone – the locals and ourselves. Besides, what experience have we got of firearms?' He looked at Lejeune. 'So what about the drivers, Jacques?'

Lejeune had remained quiet, letting Chalmers take control. 'We put them back on the road. They can do some walking – whichever way they want. We get out fast. We keep the vehicles separate and come back by different routes.'

Gambert had been quiet throughout. Now he pursed his lips. 'We've got these guns. I've never held a pistol, let alone fired one.'

'We don't use them unless we have to.' Chalmers turned to Lejeune. 'But we ought to know what we're doing. Where can we fire shots without being heard?'

'In the top wood. No one for miles.'

'Tomorrow?' Chalmers looked round the table.

Henri looked doubtful. 'What time?'

'Ten o'clock?'

'All right. I've got the shop – and Alphonsine. But I'll be there. You all right, Jean?' His hoarse voice lifted to a higher register.

Gambert nodded. 'I'll see the coughs and colds and then I can be called to an emergency.' He changed the subject. 'I shall only fire if my own life's in danger.'

'You've only got a holding operation,' said Chalmers. 'Hardly any cars the whole time we were there. I don't think you'll have to do anything. But we can't risk someone coming at the wrong moment – just when we've blocked the road.'

The next day they took the revolvers and fired shots at bottles. Johnson, who had done a handgun course, gave simple instruction. Gambert closed his eyes every time he fired. After an hour they returned to the farm.

'Better than nothing,' said Chalmers to Johnson, when the others had gone. 'We'll look dangerous, even if we're not. You did that well.'

'The doctor's more dangerous to us than them. But at least he realises it.'

That night Chantal came to Chalmers's room He was reading the guide to local châteaux and cathedrals by the light of a candle. She took off her blue woollen dressing-gown and slipped in beside him. 'I'll show you some of those,' she said, lying down at his back and putting an arm round him. 'You'll like the cathedral at Auxerre – and Sens.' She pointed at a picture over his shoulder.

'Thomas Becket was at Sens.'

'Thomas Becket?'

'English archbishop. Had a row with his king – Henry II – in the twelfth century. Went into exile to Sens. Henry had him killed later. He'd been the king's friend. It didn't pay to get too close to kings in those days.'

She held him closer, pressing her face into his back. 'It's cold. If you lie down, we can pull the blankets up.'

'You were good with the pistol,' he said. 'Better than Jean.'

'I don't want to fire it.'

'You would if you had to. I'm not sure about Jean.'

'He won't let us down,' said Chantal. 'I know him.' Her hands were under his pyjama jacket, her fingers moving gently over him. 'I'd like a kiss.'

'So would I.' He pulled her to him, almost roughly. She responded in the way he had come to expect. Then he pushed her away, holding her almost at arm's length. 'We've got to get it right tomorrow, Chantal.'

'We shan't let you down.' She nuzzled into his shoulder. 'Is that all we're going to talk about? I was more optimistic.'

'Come here, woman.' Chalmers felt the fullness of her breasts against him and the softness of her body. Only for the briefest of seconds did he think about Mary. Each time was becoming easier.

Chantal loved the physical firmness of the man she began to believe was hers and she knew the weight of responsibility he was taking on. Her respect grew with the other emotions she was recognising in herself. It made her hesitate to confide something she had been concealing for some time.

***

Chantal crept away at dawn, huddled in her dressing-gown. When Chalmers went downstairs later, Johnson was already there and had earned unspoken approval from Célestine by carrying her early morning water from the pump.

'Beautiful morning,' said Johnson. 'I've always liked autumn. Lovely sky.'

Chalmers looked at him anew. He had not thought of him as someone who appreciated nature. 'Nervous?'

'Are you?'

'I'd be daft not to admit it. But we've done our planning and I trust Lejeune. Any flaws?'

Johnson shook his head.

'Two things we can't be certain of. First, the French drivers. Second, other traffic. There's not much – but there's always sod's law. Suppose a German convoy appears out of the blue? Or just an inquisitive farmer? We really need another half dozen men.'

'Luck comes into it.'

'If Germans appear, we abort the whole thing – as long as we haven't started. Think we're lucky, Célestine?' asked Chalmers.

Célestine put a jug of coffee on the table. As a concession to autumn, she had a beige woollen shawl round her shoulders. The details of the attack had been discussed in front of her almost as though she did not exist. Chalmers was conscious of her exclusion and always tried to draw her in. Now she shrugged with apparent indifference. 'We must kill another pig,' she said.

One thing Chalmers had learned was that farms like La Rippe were a law unto themselves when it came to killing animals. Lejeune said farmers everywhere evaded the rules, partly to feed families, partly to make money. 'And everyone buys on the black market – Pétainists, communists, collaborators. No one's going to starve.'

'A pig-killing used to be a special occasion,' said Célestine. 'Now we keep quiet. And if we kill a cow we bury the hide. Once we sold it to the tanner in Courson for leather. Not now. He might inform.' She was back at the stove putting on wood. 'We need more logs.'

'We'll do that,' said Chalmers. He looked at Célestine who almost smiled.

The door to the yard opened and Lejeune came in, blowing on his hands. 'Everything in order,' he said. Georges and Henri have the van. They'll be here at ten. René will be here before that.' He poured some coffee. 'I'll have this while we've got it.'

'Maurice?' said Chalmers.

'Knows we're going out, but doesn't know why. He'll do the animals. Célestine will look after him.' He looked at her with a confidence born of years of understanding.

Célestine was at the sink washing dishes. Unexpectedly she looked up. 'You be careful,' she said. 'All of you.' Her tone was different, softer, and Chalmers sensed affection not detected before. Servant Célestine might be, and never allowed to forget it, but her role in bringing up the brothers had left a mark.

Shortly before ten René arrived to pick up Chalmers, Johnson and Chantal. Each had a pistol and ammunition, though no guns were loaded. Marguerite had taken a day off from the shop to help on the farm and she and her mother watched them get in. She had reluctantly accepted her father's decision that she could not take part. Célestine watched from the kitchen door.

'Drive carefully, René,' said Lejeune. 'Nothing to draw attention. We shan't be far behind. And remember, right into the wood – well down the track, further than the lorries.'

René nodded. The lines on his face, still youthful, hinted at a maturity Chalmers had not noticed before. For the first time he realised René might be good in a tight situation. As the car turned into the lane he let his hand run against Chantal beside him. She wore a tweed skirt and high-necked brown jumper under a thick grey coat. His hand was against her thigh, but the layers of clothing removed intimacy. Momentarily he recalled the *frisson* when feeling Mary's suspender through her dress on the London train.

When they had gone, Lejeune ran over a list of jobs with Marie and Marguerite. Shortly afterwards Georges and Henri arrived in the van. Lejeune embraced his wife and daughter, putting an arm round both at the same time.

'Don't forget,' said Marie.

'I promise,' said Lejeune. 'No heroics.' Marguerite hugged him and Lejeune gently pulled away. 'We'll be back.'

Georges was driving and Henri moved closer to him to make room for Lejeune. All three raised a hand to the waiting women as they pulled out of the yard.

'You're silent, Georges,' said Lejeune. 'Everything all right?'

'Petrol was difficult. I paid over the odds. If we use too much today there won't be enough for Tours on Sunday.' Georges's face was impassive, his tone less so.

Henri was smiling. He knew how much Georges resented anything costing money. And he knew the Sunday trip to Tours would be profitable.

'I've never had a gun in my pocket,' said Georges.

'None of us have,' responded Lejeune. 'And we don't want to use it. If the information's reliable, it should be easy.' He turned to Henri. 'Your big chance, Henri.'

Henri's bony face with its long chin for once looked confident. He nodded over his shoulder at the explosives in the back. 'All ready. No more than ten minutes.'

Georges, usually an erratic driver, took unexpected care with his sensitive load. When they reached the forest and pulled in behind the Citroën, the others had been waiting more than half an hour and were ready for lunch. Chantal had organised it and they sat under the trees. Chalmers briefly remembered a picnic with Mary then, more graphically, his failure when Chantal had first offered herself.

Lejeune looked at the wine his daughter had brought. 'No wine,' he said gruffly.

'No?' This from Georges.

'No risks. That means clear heads. No wine.'

Chalmers nodded agreement. He was standing with bread and cheese in his hand looking towards the main road. 'I'm going to check the tree. Peter, it's worth making sure the track's clear further in. We don't want to find a tree's fallen down since we were here. We depend on a quick exit.'

'Right.' Johnson swallowed a mouthful and set off into the forest clutching more bread and cheese.

Henri and René took the explosive to the glade where the lorries would be parked. René handled it gingerly, Henri with confidence. Henri laid it out methodically. 'If it's the usual six, we'll give one of them an extra dose.' He laughed, the characteristically high-pitched sound Chalmers had found irritating before he knew the man better.

Chalmers rejoined them. 'Nothing different,' he said. 'The tree's there. Now we've got to kill three hours. If anyone wants a sleep, have it now. The Germans stick to routine, but we'll be ready an hour before they're due.'

'Waiting's the worst,' said Chalmers, rubbing his hands together before pulling on gloves that had once been Robert's. 'The time between briefing and take-off seemed endless. It was easier once we were off the ground. The imagination has to be controlled.'

'I couldn't do it – not night after night,' said Lejeune.

'You do something more difficult. If you'd made mistakes, you wouldn't be here – and nor should I.' In a rare moment of male closeness, Chalmers stretched out a hand and touched the Frenchman on the arm.

Somewhere down the road to Autun a lorry changed gear in preparation for the hill. They looked at each other. For a full minute they listened, waiting to see what appeared. In the event it was a lorry full of bricks belching smoke. 'We're getting jumpy,' said Chalmers.

'Rely on Boche punctuality.'

'Henri reliable?' Chalmers asked the sort of question the growing relationship with Lejeune made possible.

'There's a man in Clamecy who was with him in Africa. He had a reputation.'

'Sorry. It must look as though I don't trust you. It's because I'm used to my crew. We knew each other inside out. I'm still learning here.'

They eyed each other again then looked away. Chalmers was with his crew, remembering the tense jokes on take-off, the relief on the way home. Lejeune thought of Robert, his trusting nature as a child, and the emotions when told of his death. Chalmers thought of Mary and the first kiss by the tail-plane of Z-Zebra; Lejeune remained with Robert, comparing Marie's tears with his own inarticulate silence. 'The mind's a funny place, Jacques,' said Chalmers, aware of their joint pre-occupation. 'Do you ever dream?'

'Sometimes.'

'What about?'

'The farm, the old man, Robert. And you?'

'Strange things – no logic really. The crash made a difference. I've been through that more then once. Looking for somewhere to get down, the burning engine, the mist, my own panic.'

'Your friends?'

'Still alive in my dreams. I don't think I've accepted the truth.'

'Like Robert. He's alive, working on the farm.'

Another companionable silence ensued. A car from Saulieu passed, battered and covered in mud, the driver looking like a local farmer. It was followed by a horse and cart carrying milk churns. Otherwise the road was deserted. For half an hour they made desultory conversation, the sort of conversation held by close friends. Suddenly, after a pause, Chalmers said: 'Getting dark. We ought to be ready.'

'I'll get them.' Lejeune vanished into the trees. Within minutes the others set off to prearranged positions, Gambert tense as he went down the hill towards Saulieu. Lejeune rejoined Chalmers. 'Half an hour,' he said.

Chalmers turned to René and Georges. 'Get the feel of the tree. Make sure it's loose.' The four of them took hold of it and it shifted easily. Across the road Henri and Chantal waited for Johnson's signal.

The last quarter of an hour seemed endless. Chalmers fingered his revolver; it was cold. He looked at his watch again: the hands had barely moved. Once more his mind wandered. He had never done anything criminal in his life, yet for a moment he imagined he was a crook waiting to carry out a robbery on a money delivery to a bank in London. In that second of aberration he wondered how he might spend the ill-gotten gains. A ring for Mary took priority.

His reverie was interrupted by a shout from Henri. '*Attention! Attention!*' From Autun came the rumble of engines. The four men got hold of the tree and had blocked the road before the first lorry was half way up the hill. Chalmers had an ear cocked for sounds from the opposite direction. Silence. He took out his pistol and waited at the edge of the road.

The first lorry, grey and drab, struggling in low gear, rounded the bend at the top of the hill. The driver saw the tree immediately and halted a few yards from it. Lejeune was up to the driver's door before he stopped. He showed his weapon, but did not point it threateningly. The driver was middle-aged, his face unshaven and covered with a network of grained lines; grizzled hair curled from beneath a dirty beret. His expression conveyed a mixture of questioning and ill temper. He did not look surprised and said nothing.

Lejeune indicated with his gun. '*A gauche*. Into the trees. Do as we say and you'll be safe. Stay in the cab until you're told to get out.'

The driver gave a shrug and remained silent. He turned the wheel and drove into the trees. Chalmers was at the door of the second lorry. He, too, flourished his pistol. The driver was older than the first. For a moment Chalmers thought he was going to argue, but he saw the gun and followed the leading vehicle. Further down the hill Georges, Johnson and René dealt with the others.

Only one questioned the order, the man in the last lorry, dark-haired and younger. '*Pourquoi?*' he asked. 'Who are you?' A coarse-featured girl in a raincoat sat beside him in the cab.

René was curt. 'Do as you're told and you won't get hurt. Cause a problem and you'll be dead. You're working for the Boche.' Before the man could reply, the woman said: 'Do as he says, Pierre. Don't argue.' The young man looked at her sharply but said no more. René climbed on the running-board by the driver as he followed the others into the trees.

As the last one turned off, Lejeune returned to help shift the tree off the road. In the forest matters went more smoothly than they could have hoped. Marshalled by Henri and Chantal, the lorries were drawn up together, drivers in their cabs. The smell of petrol had taken the place of damp bracken.

Lejeune took charge. 'Get out,' he shouted. 'Over here – *vite.*'

The drivers gathered in front of him in the twilight. Most were middle-aged or older, the man with the girl the only one under thirty. It was the girl who spoke. She was petulant. 'What do you want? They're working men earning a living.'

'You know what's in them?' Lejeune looked at one of the older men, indicating the lorries.

The man nodded. The girl said: 'Of course they do. It's a job.'

'A Boche job. You knew the risks. You're Frenchmen and you'll not be harmed. You'll have a long walk – Autun, or anywhere else. We're destroying the trucks.'

The driver of the first lorry spat. '*Canaille*. They'll say we set it up.'

The drivers turned to each other, grumbling. Chalmers's military training took over. 'Any questions?' he asked.

The woman took the lead again. 'We can go now?'

'No.' This was Lejeune. 'You stay till we've finished.' He turned to Johnson. 'Get them out of the way.'

Johnson pointed with his pistol to a track beyond the lorries. The drivers and the woman sullenly went the way he indicated. He took them some four hundred yards off to a depression where they would be safe. 'Get down,' he ordered, 'and you'll be all right.' He kept the pistol in his hand, but it remained by his side.

The others were already at work on the trucks: doors and bonnets were opened, the tarpaulin at the rear was untied. Henri busied himself with explosives and lengths of wire, climbing in and out of the vehicles with unsuspected agility. Within minutes he was satisfied. He nodded to Lejeune. 'All done,' he said.

All except Henri and Johnson ran to the cars where they were joined by Gambert. There was a moment of silence, then a crunching explosion. A flash of orange and crimson ripped through the first lorry and in a matter of seconds the six vehicles were ablaze, burning more fiercely as the flames reached petrol tanks. The lorries' metal skeletons stood out amidst the fire and the light etched the outlines of the surrounding trees. The flickering flames sent Chalmers's mind off on its own track. Shelley this time. '*Yellow, and black, and pale, and hectic red, pestilence-stricken multitudes . . .*' The colours lighting up the forest changed constantly; the smell of explosive and burning rubber drifted across. He turned to Lejeune. 'Henri's good. Get rid of the drivers.'

They got up, brushing off leaves. Henri appeared running, his gaunt face shining with pleasure. '*Mon Dieu* – the right stuff! We can do it again – and again.'

'Well done! Spectacular, Henri,' exclaimed Chalmers. 'Into the car. We're getting out.'

Chantal squeezed Chalmers's hand as he slid close to her. 'Perfect,' she said, 'perfect.' He ran his hand under her skirt and up her thigh in the darkness. He leaned towards her. 'Perfect,' he said.

Johnson ran through the trees and poked his head into the Citroën before getting into the van. 'They're going to Autun,' he said. 'The woman decided. She won't be looking for a lift with them again.'

'Time to move,' said Chalmers. He felt the others did not share his sense of urgency. 'Did you stop anyone?' This to Gambert, who had got in beside René.

'Nothing came.' His relief was apparent. 'I'm not doing that again.'

The vehicles stayed close together, the *camionette* leading, following the forest track. The headlights probed ahead, creating grotesque shapes and shadows, giving the trees a life of their own. For Chalmers they brought back tales of forests and witches read by a grandmother during a childhood illness long buried in his subconscious. René nursed the car's suspension, easing it over the uneven ground; eventually, after more than a mile at a snail's pace, they emerged onto the Saulieu road. Looking back through the rear window, Chalmers could see a smudge of smoke in the sky.

In Saulieu the vehicles separated. René took the Citroën back on the N6 to Avallon; Georges tacked the van back to Clamecy on side roads. Inevitably the Citroën arrived first at La Rippe where Marie and Célestine had a meal waiting. By the time the others arrived, a steaming *cassoulet* was on the table, together with red wine and fresh candles. Maurice sat in his usual place, yawning.

'*Ah, du vin,*' said Georges. 'I'm ready for that.' He got out a fresh cigarette, lit it from the stub of his last, and tossed the stub into the kitchen range. He was breathing heavily.

Marguerite filled glasses. 'Tell me what I missed,' she said, looking at Chalmers. Before he could answer, she added, 'I'm coming next time.'

'There may not be a next time,' said her father.

'Why not?'

'It went well because we planned every move and covered everything.'

'Surprise was the key,' said Johnson. He looked at Marguerite. He appreciated her appearance and was increasingly attracted. 'We can't do the same thing twice.' He picked up his glass and took a sip. 'Worth it if we get welcomed back like this.'

'Fatted calf,' said Chalmers, smiling at Chantal, who looked tired. 'Smells good.'

'Goose,' said Maurice, suddenly. 'I like goose.' He yawned again. He showed no interest in their doings.

'Goose,' said Marie, taking the lid off the *cassoulet*. 'Célestine's special for Maurice.' She was already filling a plate for the old man upstairs. 'We've started the cider,' she said to her husband.

They took it in turns to describe the ambush and as they drank revealed more of their characters. Chalmers and Johnson, the outsiders, drank little and watched quietly. Henri was flushed with success and his confidence grew. He gave an account of his wiring of the vehicles. Like most technical men he overdid the detail.

Lejeune cut him short with praise. 'I knew you could do it. *Magnifique, Henri, magnifique.* We thought you'd blown up the whole forest.'

Gambert drank more than anyone. He had agreed to stay for supper with reluctance, but now looked as if he was settling in for the night. 'Never again,' he said gloomily. 'Why did I agree? I'll come with you, but I shan't do that sort of job.' His sallow complexion was touched with red. He put his pistol on the table. 'I don't want it,' he said.

Georges, too, was drinking steadily; the wine seemed to confirm his surliness. 'It won't be available every time – the *camionette*,' he said.

Maurice chose that moment to open his eyes. He looked at Gambert's gun with puzzlement. 'I like goose,' he said.

Later that night Chantal slipped into Chalmers's bed. She put her arms round him and said, 'I was proud of you. And I loved it when you put your hand under my skirt on the way home.' Her fingers touched the smooth, hairless skin on his chest. '*Chéri*, I must tell you something.'

'Mmm?'

'I've been putting it off because I'm not certain – and I'm nervous of telling you.'

'Nervous?'

'*Je pense*' – her voice fell to a whisper – '*je pense que je suis enceinte.*'

Fluent in French though he was, the words shocked Chalmers into a moment of incomprehension and silence. Then realisation took over and he exclaimed in English: 'Pregnant? You're *enceinte*?' The clumsiness of the English word and the beauty of the French struck him even as he spoke.

'I'll see Gambert this week.'

Chalmers's arms remained round her, warm and tight. Not a nerve in his body gave away his surprise.

29

Chalmers and Chantal lay silently for half a minute. It was a shock, but he wanted to be sure his response was right. Whatever his own feelings – and they were not clear – he knew he must reassure her. Mary floated into hazy focus in the background, but she was peripheral. Chantal and a baby were here and now. Momentarily he thought of Célestine and her history. He must show understanding and warmth and that would be easy: it was in his nature. What did Chantal feel? Did she want a child or was it the embarrassing encumbrance he felt it must be? His own first rational response was that it was a disaster, proof of manhood but a problem for her, for him, above all for the situation they were in. How could he have been so foolish? But Chantal was a practical woman; she must have considered the possibility.

'A shock?' Chantal's voice was soft.

'You want honesty, don't you? How we've always been.'

'Of course. It's a shock, isn't it?'

'I'm wondering why we never considered it.'

'I did. I'm a woman.'

'We never talked about it.' Chalmers was anxious to share responsibility without sounding too stupid. 'I think I thought it was . . . safe. What will your father say?'

'He may blame you to start with, but he knows me. He'll know the initiative was mine.'

'Was it?'

She held him close, laughing into his hair. 'Of course.'

'What do you feel . . . really?'

'I know you love Mary. But I've come to love you. A woman

who loves a man wants his child. That's true of any woman. Mary would be the same.'

His initial reaction altered marginally. If she wanted the child, he was pleased he was the father. She was here in his arms, warm and dependent. 'When shall we tell them?' he asked.

'I'll see Gambert this week.'

'If you want a child, *chérie*, I want it as much as you. We'll support each other. I can cope with your father . . .' – he laughed – 'I *think* I can cope with your father.'

'I'll deal with Papa.' She spoke confidently, knowing how close she and her father had become since Robert's death. 'Shall we go to sleep? I think you're tired.'

'I'm never too tired for you. But sleep would be good.' Enough light came in from the window to show the pale face on the pillow beside him. 'If you're pleased, I'm pleased. Of course I am.' He pulled her to him and they adjusted themselves to the position they adopted for sleep, his chin on her shoulder.

***

Two days later Chantal went to see Gambert. She had already spoken to him privately and arranged to go when no one else was there. She stayed less than half an hour and when she came out she was smiling. Of course there would be problems, and she suspected her mother would be more difficult than her father, but Gambert's confirmation made her very happy. He predicted the end of April or early May.

Outside in the Place de l'Église where the first leaves were falling from the chestnut trees she remounted her bicycle with care. She pedalled past the flying buttresses and strange little turrets of the thirteenth-century St.Adrian's church towards the road down to the river. She reached the hill, gravity took over and she freewheeled down, skirt billowing behind her. At the bottom she raised a hand to Georges, standing at the door of *Les Pêcheurs*, waistcoat unbuttoned, hands in pockets. He responded with a nod but no more. From the inception of the group it had been agreed they should never draw attention to the fact that they knew each other well. Then, without thinking, instead of taking the lane directly back to La Rippe, she turned off and crossed the bridge over the Yonne with its little chapel. Conscious of the glowing health of her body, she was following a roundabout route home to have time on her own.

She pedalled for some time, enjoying the solitude, until the tower of the church on the hill at Châtel-Censoir became visible over the trees and the silence was broken by the sound of the Clamecy train clattering over one of the river bridges. She avoided a rough piece of road then turned into a lane running back to La Rippe. After a while the gradient changed as the lane went uphill to the ridge on which the farm stood. Normally she pushed hard on the pedals, but today, remembering the child, she got off and walked to the top. 'No need for special care,' Gambert had said, 'but get the men to do the heavy work. James will do anything for you. I've noticed, you know.' His eyes twinkled.

'He loves a girl in England,' she had replied. 'If he gets home he'll marry her. He wouldn't let her down. Meanwhile we only have one life – and I love him.'

Back in the saddle she coasted down the final slope to La Rippe. Everyone was in the fields except Célestine peeling potatoes in the kitchen. 'Where's James?' Chantal asked.

'Top field with Jacques.' She wiped her hands on her apron and said: 'Are you all right, Chantal?' Her tired eyes assessed the girl she had looked after for so long.

Chantal took a swift decision. 'I'm fine, Célestine. Absolutely fine.' She paused for the difficult bit. 'And I'm *enceinte*.'

Célestine went to the sink and rinsed her hands. 'Monsieur Chalmers?'

'You guessed?'

Célestine wiped her hands again on her apron in a movement that had become second nature. 'I've eyes in my head. I can understand, *ma petite*.'

'That's why I told you.'

'Things are different now.'

Chantal moved closer to the old servant and took her hand. 'It was hard for you.'

The wrinkled face, grey and worn, almost smiled. 'Hard for anyone then. You've got a better man.'

Chantal had never enquired about the father of Célestine's child, though she assumed he had let her down. 'I'm glad you came to us, Célestine. We couldn't have done without you – and Grandpa certainly couldn't. I'll be fine. I've got you to look after me. And war alters everything.' Her voice had an edge. 'It took Robert.'

'And brought Monsieur Chalmers.'

'I knew you'd understand – and be kind.' She stood back and looked at the old woman. Feeling ashamed for not asking before, she said, 'Did you love him?'

'I loved him. He didn't love me.' Her tone was philosophical, not bitter. 'It brought me here – and to your grandfather. He's been good to me. Life could have been worse.'

'You lost the child.'

'God's will.' Célestine crossed herself. Her thin lips pulled themselves inwards on her toothless gums.

The sound of a door shutting in the yard broke up the conversation. Marie and Marguerite came in from the dairy. Marie carried a basket of eggs which she took to the pantry. 'Laying well,' said Marie. 'Enough to get coffee from Brialou when I go to Bazarnes.'

'If he's got some,' said Marguerite. 'He only gets it because his daughter goes out with that German in the stores in Auxerre.'

'I don't care where he gets it. Cider again tomorrow, Célestine. James can help.'

At lunch conversation centred on farm matters as usual. Chantal had no chance to speak to Chalmers until afterwards when he went up to his room. She followed him, shutting the door. 'It's true,' she said. 'End of April.' She put her arms round him from behind.

Chalmers turned and held her to him. 'So when do we tell them?'

'Straight away. No point in putting it off. And Papa's in a good mood about the other night. I've told Célestine. I knew she'd understand. And I must tell Marguerite first. After supper's the time if I can get them on their own.'

'Are you sure? Shouldn't it be me?'

She gave him a kiss. 'No, they're my family. I know you'd do it, but you're the guest.'

He laughed. 'Some guest!'

That afternoon Chantal took Marguerite aside and told her. The sisters were close and Marguerite was as supportive as Chantal knew she would be. She joked that Chalmers was a handsome fellow and she would have been after him if Chantal hadn't got there first. She was nervous about their parents. 'Maman will be difficult.'

At supper they talked about the ambush. 'I want to know the locals weren't harmed,' said Lejeune. 'The last thing we want is reprisals against innocent people. Wine?' He nodded towards Chalmers and indicated the bottle.

'Thanks.' Chalmers poured more wine for Chantal and himself.

'I like wine,' said Maurice. Chalmers looked at Lejeune. He nodded approval, so Chalmers poured some into Maurice's glass. Maurice drank it in one draught and clearly wanted more. Lejeune shook his head.

Johnson looked at his watch. 'London tonight. All right to do it here?' He too looked at Lejeune.

'You haven't done it here for six weeks. We'll risk it. See if the Morvan news has reached them.'

After supper Johnson vanished to the barn to set up his kit and Célestine went up to the old man. Chantal made signs to Chalmers suggesting he should help Marguerite, so the two of them cleared the table and started the washing up while she manoeuvred her parents into the sitting room on her own.

It did not take long. She was quite blunt and explained that there was no question of marriage. Both were stunned, but to Chantal's relief neither condemned her. Lejeune, cautious at any time, was concerned about the child and the future; Marie, predictably, thought about neighbours and reputation. Chantal was relieved that neither blamed Chalmers. Both recognised that war changed things. 'Who are we going to say is the father?' Lejeune asked.

'That's my problem, Papa. You can plead ignorance and say I won't tell you. You're very good at telling people how wilful I am.' She spoke with affection.

'You really want the child?' asked her mother. 'What am I going to say to the curé? He'll say it's a punishment for not coming to Mass.'

'I love James and I want his child. While he's here I shall love him – and if he goes . . . Well, we none of us know what will happen, do we? We once had Robert and – now he's gone. Who knew James would come down in that field? And what do you think the bodies of his men in the *cimetière* at St.Pierre mean to him? I've decided to live my life while I have it – and James is the same. If the Cossacks come back and catch us, they'll shoot us all without giving it a thought. That's reality.'

Lejeune loved his elder daughter and was fighting his emotional reaction. But his respect grew as he saw she had summed up the situation more realistically than he had. 'And James?'

'Who knows? He wanted to tell you himself, or with me, but I said I wanted to do it on my own. He's a good man and in his way he loves me. He'll look after me while he's here . . . If the war comes to an end, who knows? He hasn't hidden his love for Mary. There's nothing I can do about that – and nothing he can either.'

Marie folded her arms, the posture making her look plumper. She was still taking the news in and the expression on her face made her seem older. 'There'll be gossip, my girl,' she said. 'I want to say the right thing. It's not easy. Who'll tell the old man?'

'I'll tell him,' said Lejeune. 'I can handle him. And if I'm wrong, Célestine can.'

For a moment they stood quietly looking at each other across the room. Then her mother took Chantal in her arms. 'We'll look after you, you know that,' she said. The tone of her voice, previously neutral, was warm and accepting, but there were tears in her eyes. Chantal saw her emotion and her own eyes watered. Lejeune put his arms round both of them.

***

Later Lejeune and Chalmers joined Johnson in the loft. 'It's all right,' said Lejeune, as they crossed the yard. 'It's not what we wanted. But it's what Chantal wants. Marie will be all right – eventually. I know you care for Chantal.'

'I'll do anything for her – within the possibilities.'

'I know that. You'd be a good son-in-law. Pity you're spoken for.' Lejeune was a serious man, but there was a note of humour in his tone.

They climbed into the loft where Johnson had more or less finished setting up. He put on headphones and the usual noises started. Initially he was merely waiting. Then he made contact and worked at his morse key. It was a lengthier communication than usual, so much so that Lejeune began to worry that it might give the Germans a fix. From time to time Johnson made jottings on a pad. Eventually he took off the headphones. 'They know,' he said. 'Congratulations on a job well done. Their man at Le Creusot reported.'

'Anything else?' This was Chalmers.

'The convoy will be escorted in future. Don't want us to do it again. The drivers lost their jobs. Another possible target next transmission.'

'What?' asked Lejeune.

'A train to the south. Don't worry, I said it was your decision.' He looked at Lejeune. 'Next transmission Friday.' Johnson's speech was as episodic as his communication with London.

'Where?'

'Not clear. I got the impression there's no hurry. They mentioned Migennes.'

'We're not messing about with the Reds.'

'We must wait,' interposed Chalmers. 'Get the details. Then we can assess it.' He looked at Johnson. 'No details at all?'

'They mentioned tanks. Going south.'

'We might do it,' said Lejeune, 'if we choose the place. We're not doing anything in a hurry. Transmission Friday? Not from here. Go to the barn in Vézelay. Brocard's agreed – if we tell him.'

Johnson dismantled his equipment. Chalmers watched, his mind elsewhere. He saw his first days in the loft and the memories that went with them: the sickness and headache; his naked fear during the German search; the slivers of sunshine lighting up the spider's web; and most clearly of all, Chantal's face at the end of the tunnel. He saw it all, but so much had happened it seemed in another age. Inevitably Mary appeared too. He realised he hadn't taken her photograph out of his wallet for a week. In the loft he looked at it every day.

'That's it,' said Johnson, breaking his concentration. Together they pushed the wireless into the darkest corner and covered it with hay.

Lejeune inspected it critically. 'We need more hay.' He looked at Chalmers. 'We'll do that tomorrow – and more for the horses. Plenty in the barn opposite.'

They climbed down the ladder. The older of the two horses, a grey, eyed them speculatively from its stall. The other, younger and worked more often, snorted as they passed. They went into the yard where Célestine was drawing water from the pump in light from the kitchen window. Her breath showed in the cold night air. 'I'll carry it,' Chalmers said. Briefly he was back in the loft with the peasant faces from Millet's *L'Angélus*.

Lejeune was at his shoulder again. 'I meant it,' he said quietly. 'We'll cope. Chantal's tough. Marie's upset, but we're a close family. She'd like you to marry Chantal. She's said so, even though you're English.' He glanced sideways at Chalmers. 'And I understand my daughter. She's a strong-willed girl and she knows what she wants. She likes you – she loves you. This wouldn't have happened otherwise. She's not that sort of girl.'

'I know.'

They went into the kitchen where the smell of candles and cooking onions permeated the room. Chalmers felt Marie looked at him reproachfully, but knew it could be his imagination. His feelings, initially disturbed, had somehow become frozen. He was not sure what he really felt at all. He just hoped he and Chantal would have some time together. It seemed more important than any attack on a train. And deep down there was Mary. The child would be proof of his betrayal.

Quite naturally Chalmers and Chantal held hands in front of them all when they said goodnight and went upstairs. Chantal followed him into his room. 'No need to hide now,' she said. 'I want to be loved.'

30

Johnson took his equipment to Vézelay for the Tuesday transmission. He had not been there for two months and it suited Georges to drive him. He had cigarette dealings with a fellow bar owner in Vézelay who had been dilatory in making payment. It gave the opportunity to turn up unexpectedly. 'Good business,' he explained. 'He's done it before. He knows it's illegal and hopes I'll let it go.'

They went in the afternoon, taking minor roads. It had been raining hard and La Madeleine on the brow of Vézelay's hill was barely visible through a curtain of mist. Brocard's farm, no more than a cottage and a few rough outbuildings, was a dismal place of mud and water. Georges left to chase his debt and Johnson had an evening meal with Brocard and his wife before setting up. Brocard had been wounded in the Great War and was now a peasant farmer doing his best to survive. His Pétainist sympathies had evaporated and his son had recently fled to the Morvan to avoid labour service in Germany. His wife had remained loyal to Vichy for longer, but the safety of their son had changed her mind and she was now more enthusiastic about resistance than her husband. They ate in the kitchen, a small dark room with a black cooking range and powerful smell of garlic.

'I didn't agree the first time,' said Brocard, pushing bread round his plate. He was a small man, nut-brown from life in the open. For once he had taken off the battered hat from which he was usually inseparable. 'There've been reprisals round here. Our girl's still at school. And Yvonne isn't well.' He gestured with his knife towards his wife, a pale woman in an

322

old-fashioned blue dress who looked frail. 'But Jean wasn't going to Germany. He persuaded me to let you use the barn. Lejeune said it would be safe if you didn't come often. I trust him. I've known him at the markets for years. Good beasts at La Rippe, I've always said so.' He cleaned up the sauce on his plate and again pointed his knife at his wife. 'Cooks well, doesn't she? Do the English cook well?'

'Not as well as the French,' Johnson said tactfully. He maintained a stream of non-committal pleasantries. He barely knew them and did not want to be thought rude.

'More logs,' said Brocard to his wife. 'Fire's going down.'

His wife said nothing, but pulled her shawl round her and went out into the yard. The moment spoke volumes.

'Lejeune – a *parachutage*?' asked Brocard.

'Do many people know?' Johnson felt he should find out what he could.

'There was talk of a plane and parachutes. Most thought it was for the Maquis who blew up the lorries.'

Johnson feigned ignorance. 'Lorries?'

'Lorries from Le Creusot. The Boches are furious. We wondered if our boy was there. We haven't seen him for weeks.'

Johnson looked at his watch. 'Time to get ready,' he said. 'That lamb was good – and the wine.' He stood up, looking at Madame Brocard who had barely spoken. 'Thank you again, Madame.'

Madame Brocard inclined her head, but did not speak. Johnson went out into the dark. It had stopped raining, but his feet were covered in mud by the time he reached the tumbledown barn. Georges joined him while he was setting up. He looked ill-tempered.

'Successful?' Johnson asked.

'Cognac?' Georges handed him a small bottle with the top off.

'He paid up?' Johnson took the bottle.

Johnson thought he wasn't going to reply; Georges was looking at the wireless with his usual dour expression, avoiding eye contact. Then he said, 'He paid up. Didn't expect me. But found the money he told me he hadn't got. And gave me the cognac.'

'Will you do more business?'

'*Mais oui*. I get what he wants. I know he eventually pays – and Vichy knows nothing. The way France works now.'

Johnson put on the headphones and sat down at the rough table on which the wireless stood. Johnson concentrated, listening before clicking the morse key. He was on the air for fully ten minutes, Georges standing by a broken, cobweb-covered window looking into the darkness. Eventually Johnson took off the headphones and relaxed. 'November the fifth,' he said. 'A good choice.'

'Good choice?'

'You're French. You wouldn't understand.'

'Why not?' Georges again looked like a pugilist, chin jutted.

'English history. Heard of Guy Fawkes?'

Georges shook his head. 'Guy Fawkes?'

'Catholic who tried to blow up Parliament and the King. Caught in the act – all a long time ago. We celebrate it every year. Bonfires and fireworks – and we burn a figure on the bonfire called a guy.'

'I'm a Catholic.'

'It's stopped since the war started. Blackout – no lights or bonfires allowed. It'll start again when this lot's over. National celebration – like Bastille Day. The train they want derailed is on November the fifth – military train.'

'Jacques will decide. You've finished? Time to go.'

Georges was monosyllabic driving back to La Rippe and did no more than raise an eyebrow in dismissal when he dropped Johnson outside the farm. Inside Johnson found a domestic scene. Lejeune was reading the latest copy of *Résistance*. Chalmers was studying a map and planning another recce of local lanes. Marie was knitting, Chantal was sewing, and they were discussing a young blacksmith from St.Pierre whose family had invited Marguerite for supper. Célestine was with the old man and Maurice, always a law to himself, had gone to bed.

Chalmers spoke first. 'Possible?' he asked.

'A train – Paris-Dijon. Military train – troops and tanks. I've got suggested grid references. They want it stopped before Dijon.'

'I'm coming,' said Chantal. 'Time for a baby later.' She had decided to stress her condition at every opportunity.

'Where do they suggest?' asked Lejeune, ignoring her.

Chalmers had opened the map. 'The first suggestion's between Ancy-le-Franc and Montbard. Forest on both sides. The other's near Alise-Ste.Reine.'

Lejeune looked over his shoulder. 'Some way from Migennes. We'll look at it. Not before Sunday – markets in Châtel-Censoir, St. Pierre and Clamecy. If I'm not there it'll be noticed, not always by friends.'

'Your decision, Jacques,' said Chalmers.

'The earlier, the better. If we do it, we plan properly. Sunday it is. Georges won't bring the *camionette*. No petrol. It'll have to be René – he's got the reserve. Chantal's not coming. She's stopping the messenger work.'

Chantal pulled a face. 'I'm still coming when you do it,' she said, 'baby or no baby.'

Lejeune pointed at the map. 'North of Montbard. Forest, few villages, and several roads out. The Burgundy Canal and the river alongside the railway. There may be a bridge. Easier for Henri. He's always wanted a bridge. We'll look at Alise-Ste-Reine as well.'

'I've heard about Alise-Ste-Reine,' said Chalmers. 'The original name was Alesia. Famous in history. Where Julius Caesar defeated Vercingetorix, the Celt who united the tribes against him. There's a statue of Vercingetorix on a hill – I've seen photographs. Put up by Napoleon III – part of his French aggrandisement campaign. A fine statue. He got Millet to do it.'

Lejeune was indifferent. Chalmers had yet to detect any hint of artistic appreciation in him. 'Statue?' he said. 'Never heard of it – or Alesia.' He prodded the map. 'Too many people. We want a place where locals won't get the blame. The forest's better.'

Chantal watched Chalmers with quiet admiration. 'Perhaps we could see the statue?'

Her father was blunt. 'There won't be room for you, Chantal. Only one car. And safer. No argument.'

***

René had no problem with the following Sunday. Chalmers found his attitude had thawed and they laughed at the way René had managed to get extra petrol. His sister had persuaded a German corporal to hand over half a dozen cans for what he hoped would be feminine entertainment over the week-end. She was an experienced flirt and this was not the first time she had acquired goods with the flick of a skirt and unfulfilled promises.

'He'll realise he's been fooled,' said Chalmers.

'Too late. He daren't tell his officers he's sold petrol. He'd be in trouble – probably the Russian Front. Only a bit of it needed for Montbard. Nine o'clock Sunday?'

'I'll ask Henri,' said Chalmers. 'I'm going back via Mailly.'

'It'll depend on Alphonsine,' said René. 'I'm not getting married. I'm the only one who doesn't have to ask a woman before we do something. Even Jacques has to prepare the ground with Marie.' Chalmers was relieved René could talk so naturally. The gulf of Mers-el-Kébir was being bridged.

It was raining again when Chalmers remounted his cycle and he pulled the woollen scarf Chantal had given him more tightly round his neck. The days of biking in the autumnal sun seemed a long way off and by the time he had pedalled up the hill to Mailly-le-Château he was soaked through. Henri was surprised to see him, but still basking in the glow of his success did not need much persuading. He would be there on Sunday.

'The stuff from London's good,' said Henri. 'Gambert coming?'

'No need. Nor Georges. They trust you and Jacques to get it right.'

Chalmers dropped in on Gambert before returning to La Rippe. As he had predicted, the doctor was happy to be omitted. On two things he was firm. 'I'm not stopping traffic and I'm not taking a gun. *Mon Dieu, non!* I'll do anything else.' He switched to the subject he thought Chalmers had come about. 'We've got to look after Chantal. It's going to be difficult for her.'

'I'll do my best.' He had got to know Gambert well enough to put out a hand and touch him on the arm. 'It was a surprise – but not to Chantal. She wants a child. That was a surprise, too. We'd never talked about it.' He felt himself blushing. 'I'm glad you'll be looking after her.'

'It's other people I'm worried about. Tell Jacques and Marie I'll do anything to help. No one need know yet.'

Back at La Rippe, Chalmers took off his soaking clothes. He had not been so uncomfortable since recovering from the crash. Chantal helped carry buckets of hot water from the kitchen and washed him in the huge old-fashioned bath in the scullery. He seemed to have been cycling for hours and his legs were aching.

'You'll get used to it,' she said. 'It can be wet in Burgundy.' She rubbed his back vigorously, reminding him of the tough matron who had scrubbed him at prep school.

'The summer was good – and the early autumn. I began to think the sun shone all the time.'

Chantal handed him a towel. 'I got really wet once cycling

from Vézelay. It's further than you think. I know I can't come to Montbard. Papa's right.'

'The operation comes first. Anyway, I want you safe.' He stood up, towelling himself, revelling in the closeness of the moment.

'You don't think I'm a fool, do you?'

Standing in the bath and only partly dry, he threw the towel over his shoulder and pulled her to him. His arms were round her, his hands under her sweater. 'Silly girl,' he said. 'You know what I think of you.'

They kissed and her fingers touched him intimately. For the first time Mary did not intervene.

31

After three days of rain Sunday dawned with a pale blue sky, crystal clear from Mailly-le-Château to the Morvan hills. René arrived in the Citroën as Chantal was driving the cows out after milking. Lejeune and Chalmers got in immediately. Johnson was staying to help on the farm; with a transmission due in the evening he could not risk a late return. They were picking up Henri in Mailly to save him the early morning cycle ride. He and his wife Alphonsine were waiting in their shop doorway facing the Place de l'Église as the car drew up. 'You'll be back for supper,' Alphonsine said firmly. Arms akimbo, she left no room for debate.

The narrow country roads to Montbard were more or less deserted. Recent wind and rain had stripped the woods of most leaves, but a few beech trees still showed the reds and yellows of autumn. Here and there a peasant was ploughing and they met occasional carts carrying hay or vegetables. There was no sign of Germans. Lejeune knew four men in a car would be suspicious, so they wore dark clothes and black ties. If challenged, they were attending a funeral at a village near Fontenay. Lejeune knew the name of the deceased and the officiating curé.

They stopped at Noyers, the medieval town in the bend of the River Serein with half-timbered houses overhanging cobbled streets. René had an uncle there who ran the smithy and garage and would have local information. He was a middle-aged man with a nicotine-stained moustache and a cast in one eye. He was working on a jacked-up Renault, its rear wheels off the ground.

'No Boches,' he said. 'I haven't seen one since the summer. July – it was hot. Wehrmacht corporal and an officer. Asked me to fix the steering on their Hooch. I fixed the steering,' he said. He touched the side of his nose in a knowing way.

'Ancy? Montbard?' René asked.

'Troops at Montbard a month ago – they didn't stay long. They were looking for men hiding from the labour order. None there now. Some in Dijon. And the *milice*.'

Lejeune said, 'Resistance? Where's the nearest?'

Up to now René's uncle had answered with confidence. Now the cast in his eye made it seem he was looking behind them. He drew his own conclusions about his visitors. He shook his head and ran the back of his hand over his moustache. 'Can't say. There's a rumour about a group near Beaune. Don't know if they've done anything.'

'Nothing at Montbard?'

The eye apparently shifted to the pepperpot towers in the medieval ramparts. 'No support for Resistance round here. The Marshal's strong – old soldiers don't forget. And we don't trusts the Reds – only railway and factory workers. The labour order may change that.' He appeared about to say more before thinking better of it.

René noticed the change of mind. 'Go on.'

Without looking at them, he said, 'Don't make trouble round here. We don't want trouble.' He turned away, wiping the spanner in his hand with an oily rag.

'It looks safe,' said Lejeune as they drove out of Noyers through one of the ancient gates. 'No reason for the Boches to protect the line if they haven't had problems.'

'A beautiful little town,' said Chalmers, catching sight of a statue of the Virgin in a niche in the arch of the gate. 'I haven't seen towers and ramparts like that before. I hope it doesn't get bombed.'

'No one's going to bomb Noyers,' said Henri. 'Nothing worth bombing.'

'Accidents happen,' said Chalmers. He remembered the night he had jettisoned a pair of bombs stuck in the bomb-bay. The relief of being able to shed them before landing had overcome any concern about where they landed in France.

They were in the countryside now, pale sunlight lighting up rolling fields and woods. Chalmers sat in the front, Michelin map on his knee. When they had gone about seven miles and passed a ruined chapel, he said: 'Next turning left – only a lane. About ten kilometres to the railway. I can't get used to kilometres – and France is a big country. No wonder it's difficult for the Jerries.'

René slowed down on the lane; the surface was rough, grass growing through in places. 'Forest most of the way,' said Chalmers.

At one point and for no apparent reason the lane deteriorated into a stony track. The gloom of the forest dominated. The only sign of human activity was an occasional pile of felled trees waiting to be logged for winter fires. 'Main road coming up,' said Chalmers. 'Ancy-le-Franc at one end, Montbard the other. Runs in the valley with the canal, the river, and the railway. No houses. Turn right, René, and take the first left to a village called Cry. The railway crosses a bridge. Might be a good spot.'

They met nothing on the main road before turning towards Cry. They were in a shallow valley with forest on either side. Shortly after they came to a brick bridge covered in ivy, the railway crossing the road. 'How about this?' said Chalmers, turning to Lejeune in the back seat.

'Stop where you can,' said Lejeune. 'We'll get onto the line.'

They drove under the bridge and René turned into the trees. When he switched off the engine, the forest was quiet. They got out, their feet crunching in dry leaves.

'Listen,' said Chalmers, holding up a finger. They stopped moving. 'Silence. I've appreciated it since I flew my first Lancaster.'

'That way,' said Lejeune. He pointed to a path leading up onto the railway some fifty yards from the bridge. Two lines ran more or less due south and north. Visibility was good in both directions. Towards Dijon a gentle curve took the lines into a cutting; to the north the bend was nearer, about a half a mile, and there were more trees. The other side of the line was a small railwayman's hut.

'They make good time here,' said René. 'Nothing to hold them up.'

Chalmers raised his hand again. 'Listen. Train coming south. Quick – under cover.'

The sound was distant, but Chalmers had got used to hearing trains during his days in the loft. They retreated into the trees as the train approached. It was an express with ten coaches, the engine steaming powerfully as it pressed down the gradient towards Dijon. The noise was overwhelming as it passed, as overwhelming as the silence that preceded it.

'Good place,' said Henri as they watched the rear of the train vanish towards Dijon. Blow the line when it comes into sight and it'll have no chance of stopping.'

'Not the bridge?' This was Lejeune.

'Easier,' said Henri, 'but the drivers will be French. They may survive if we blow the line. Less likely if we do the bridge. I'd give them a chance.' Henri was kneeling beside the line. 'Get things right here and we'll derail most of it. What about trains in the opposite direction? We could have a disaster on the up line to Paris if anything's passing at the same time. Innocents could be killed.'

'We'll find out,' said Lejeune. 'René, you know people on the railway. We'll know the exact time of the Boche train after the London transmission tonight. If there's a Paris train, we'll find a better place.'

'How long will you want, Henri?' This was Chalmers.

'Half an hour.'

'We'll give you an hour. Allow for the unexpected. We'd

look foolish if we turned up and found railwaymen doing something to the track – or anything unpredictable. And there'll be ordinary trains as well.'

Lejeune nodded in agreement. 'Anything else to look at here? We're away from the road, it's remote, and we can clear off when the job's done. Now we'll look at Alise-Ste-Reine.'

They were inspecting the line near Alise within an hour. Again they parked in forest, this time with a ten minute walk to the track. There were other differences. One side of the line was overlooked by a wooded hill; the line itself had a more pronounced curve and the view in both directions was more limited; there were two bridges, one for the line to go over the river, the other for a country lane over the line. The villages of Alise and Venarey were not far away. In the short time they were there two trains passed, a goods to Paris and an express to Dijon.

'Busy,' said Chalmers. As a boy he had collected engine names and numbers and in a modest way considered himself something of an expert. 'The down express was slower here than at Cry. The gradient's changed – not so favourable. Or it could have been the coal. Judging by the smoke, the first one had better coal. God knows what that's running on.' He pointed at the heavy grey-black smudge left in the sky.

'Coal's short,' said Lejeune. 'Two bad winters when the Boches arrived. All right in the country – plenty of wood. People stole coal in Paris. It had to be guarded.'

'Terrible in Paris in 1940,' volunteered Henri. 'My brother runs a bar on the Left Bank.' His long face creased with a smile. 'It was so cold the artists sacked their nude models and painted still life instead.'

Lejeune's expression did not change. 'All right here, Henri?'

'No different here,' said Henri. 'Either will do. *Facile comme tout*. I leave the choice to you.'

'We've seen enough,' said Lejeune. 'I go for the first. More time to see the train. Easier to get out. You agree, James?'

'Less chance of locals appearing unexpectedly.' Chalmers remembered standing on a bridge in High Wycombe collecting engine numbers. 'Do boys collect engine numbers in France?'

'Engine numbers?'

'Names and numbers – a hobby. Like collecting stamps. You get books to cross them off as you see them. I spent hours doing it before going to boarding school. I had all the GWR Kings and most of the Castles.'

The Frenchman was nonplussed. 'Kings? Castles?'

'Names of engines. The best engines had names.'

'Strange,' said Lejeune. 'Never heard of it. Perhaps in towns.'

Chalmers said: 'Vercingetorix? Statue?'

'You want to see it?'

'There's a photograph in the guide book in my room. It's not far.'

'Too much risk. Four men in black ties going to a funeral. Difficult to explain on Mont Auxois. You can cycle here in the spring – when you want to escape from cleaning out the pigs.'

'Have you seen it?'

'Farmers don't look at statues.'

Chalmers sensed the rebuke. 'It's famous,' he said weakly. 'I'll persuade Chantal.'

'She'll be busy.'

Again the rebuke. She would be busy because of the unexpected child on top of farm work. For the first time he felt they were on different wavelengths. It must be the child. They were quiet on the drive home. They ate the bread and ham Célestine had prepared and Chalmers fell asleep. They delivered Henri to his shop and were back at La Rippe in time for evening milking.

The transmission that night was short, to Johnson's relief; he saw Lejeune's distrust of anything lengthy and did not want to go to Vézelay again until he had to. London confirmed the date of the train and said it would be near Cry at approximately

7.30 in the morning. It was a regular slot the Germans used and they did their best not to upset Vichy by interfering with timetables. London knew nothing about trains on the other line.

***

That night Chalmers held Chantal closely as he told her about the day. 'Feeling all right?' he asked.

'I want to come,' she said.

'Only if Papa agrees. I sensed his disapproval today. He must be disappointed about the baby. You're his little girl.'

'Did he say so?'

'No, I felt it. There's a change. What does your mother really think?'

'We talked while you were out. She's worried about gossip – and the curé. She's very traditional, and you know how she treats Célestine. If anything goes wrong I'll get the blame. She knows it was me rather than you.'

They lay with arms entwined around each other, aware of each other's heartbeat. Then Chantal eased closer and her breathing become deeper. Chalmers felt protective and marvelled at the thought of the new life in her body.

***

In the days before the attack Lejeune and Chalmers polished the details. The first decision was that they did not need everybody. As long as they delivered Henri and his explosives to the right place the only essential was to protect him. René's enthusiasm meant he would always be available, so it was agreed that Henri and the explosives would go in the car with Lejeune and Chalmers. Georges and Gambert were happy not to take part. Georges had *marché noir* activities and after his previous experience Gambert's relief was obvious.

'There won't be room for you, Chantal,' said her father. 'Nor you, Peter. You'll have to make yourself useful here. Someone's got to take the milk to the station. Maurice can't do that.'

They sat in the parlour, listening to Marie and Célestine cooking and washing in the kitchen next door. Gloomy, black-framed, sepia photographs of generations of Lejeunes looked down.

'Your father's right,' said Chalmers, giving Chantal an intimate smile. 'We'll be there and back in no time.' He turned to Lejeune. 'Henri's worried about the other line and I agree with him.'

'René's telephoning *Les Pêcheurs* about the timetable. Go and see Georges this afternoon. Take the *vélo*.'

After lunch Chalmers cycled to *Les Pêcheurs*. He confirmed the German train at 7.30 and nothing was scheduled on the Paris line until 7.55. His informant was cautious. Timings were unreliable and it was always possible that a train coming up from Lyon might be late. A recent Allied raid on Le Creusot had come near to wrecking rail movements in Burgundy completely.

Lejeune and Chalmers agreed there was no point in checking further. They'd done their best. It remained to deal with their own timings. As before they planned to arrive early, allowing for the unexpected. René would come the evening before and sleep at La Rippe. They would be ready to plant the explosives an hour before the train was due and that meant leaving at about 5.30 am.

London had said it would confirm the German train with a message the night before. It would be an extract from Shelley's *Adonais*: 'Life like a dome of many-coloured glass stains the white radiance of Eternity . . .' Chalmers was surprised by the choice. Keats had been his favourite poet at school and he had always been moved by Shelley's tribute on his early death. He wondered if anyone in London had been researching his literary taste. Absurd. No one would have been told of his survival. He remained posted as 'Missing'.

The days went slowly. The weather remained clear, cold at night, weak sunshine by day. Farm routine dominated. More cider was made, Jacques and Maurice harvested late vegetables and continued autumn ploughing. A pig was killed and dismembered. The labourer from Coulanges was no longer a security problem; he had been working for Blanchard since the *vendange*, as he always did.

The night before, they went to Célestine's bedroom for the messages. Célestine was there as well. She had moved her chamber pot and got out the radio before they arrived. The broadcast followed the pattern, the announcer intoning *Ici Londres, ici Londres* before launching into his messages. They did not have to wait long. The third message, sandwiched between 'The vultures are flying tonight' and the instruction that 'Anatole should take his geese to the station at the first opportunity', could not have been clearer: 'Life, like a dome of many-coloured glass, stains the white radiance of Eternity . . .' As always the announcer repeated it. Célestine and Marie, neither of whom had any English, were puzzled.

'Bed,' said Lejeune. 'Up early tomorrow. René will be here any minute.' Even as he spoke, lights lit up the back of the farm and the Citroën pulled into the yard. Lejeune turned off the radio and Célestine restored it to its hiding place. Lejeune touched her on the shoulder as they left her room. 'We may not see you in the morning.'

'You will.' The old woman adjusted her shawl. 'I'll be up before you. I always have been since you were little.'

The next morning she had lit the kitchen lamps and was raking the fire in the range when Lejeune, René and Chalmers came downstairs. Chantal joined them in her dark blue dressing-gown, hair tousled, devoid of make-up. Célestine made coffee and there was bread and ham on the table. It had been agreed they would eat a meal at a café in Noyers on the way back. By chance it was René's birthday and a modest celebration would provide cover for the last part of their journey. It was too early for extended conversation and they ate in silence, punctuated only by the sound of Célestine putting on fresh logs and clattering pots and pans.

'Time to go,' said Lejeune, eyeing the clock over the door. He stood up, pulling on an old grey coat. The others followed, wrapping themselves up for the cold of the morning. Outside it was dark. Stars shone from a clear sky and the barn roofs were covered in a rime of frost. Woken by the car's arrival, the horses stirred in the stable.

'Be careful,' Chantal said, holding the lapels of Chalmers's coat and tucking the woollen scarf securely round his neck.

'You be careful, too. I'm only blowing up a train. You're looking after two people, both valuable and both mine. Come here.' They kissed before Chalmers joined René and Lejeune in the car. The others watched from the warmth of the open kitchen door. Within ten minutes they were outside Henri's shop in Mailly. Henri was waiting, holding a sack containing his explosives. Alphonsine stood beside him in a dressing-gown. He opened the boot and put the sack in carefully.

'Everything there?' asked Lejeune. Chalmers was glad it was Lejeune who had asked.

Henri paused by the open door, mentally checking off the items in the sack. 'I won't let you down, Jacques,' he said. He gave his wife a perfunctory kiss, got in and slammed the door. He shivered. '*Mon Dieu, il fait froid.*' Alphonsine had gone inside before they moved off.

The drive went without a hitch. There was nothing else on the road, not even carts. The only signs of life were the odd glimmer in a cottage window or chimney smoke from an early morning fire. Streaks of dawn came up as they followed the track through the forest and the first light made the crystals of frost glitter in the whiteness carpeting the countryside. They reached the lane to Cry and the railway bridge. As before, René drove well into the wood. 'All yours, Henri,' he said.

The silence was pervasive and they did not speak; they

338

closed the car doors with hardly a sound. Lejeune led the way onto the railway, followed by Henri with his sack. Again their feet crunched through the leaves. Chalmers studied the twin parallel lines and then remembering how his crew had needed reassurance before take-off, he said, 'Plenty of time.'

Henri was already on his knees by the line. Around him lay small boxes and lengths of wire. 'Glad it's not raining,' he said quietly. 'Easy to keep the detonators dry.' The others watched and it was apparent he was dealing with both rails. 'I'm not blowing them early because other trains may come.' Almost at once, as if to prove his point, there came the distant sound of a train running towards Dijon.

'Take cover,' said Chalmers. Minutes later a slow-moving goods train with closed wagons passed on its way south. As its rear red light vanished they came into the open again.

Henri's bits of equipment lay where he had left them. For the next quarter of an hour he placed charges and there was an obvious competence about him that contrasted with his normal diffidence. 'Hope there's nothing else,' he said. 'The vibration won't set it off, but it might shift it.'

Chalmers looked at his watch. 'Another goods is possible, or a local. An express is unlikely. It would catch the goods before Dijon. The next one should be ours.'

Henri stood up, running a wire into the bushes some way from the charges. 'I'll do it from there. They may hear it on the engine, but they'll never stop the train. I shan't need you. Once it appears, leave it to me. Get in the car, engine running. What's that?' He looked startled. 'Early?' Something was coming from the north.

They retreated to the trees and a lone engine and tender passed. With no load and a friendly gradient it was barely steaming as it idled past the watchers, its badly maintained conrods clanking. Driver and fireman in oily blue overalls looked at the passing forest with indifference.

'I wonder,' said Chalmers, thinking aloud. 'It could be

picking something up at Montbard or Dijon. But you know what it could be doing?'

The others looked blank. René said, 'Engine on its own?'

'Advance guard – pilot run. Check the line before the main body. German efficiency. They haven't had to cope with attacks here, but if they've got something important, they may play safety first. I'd put money on it.'

'They weren't looking very hard,' said Lejeune.

'Don't have to. Only want to see the line's intact. They were Frenchmen anyway.'

'Surprise to come,' said René, scratching his head and making his hair stand up more than it did already. 'How much longer?'

'A quarter of an hour,' said Lejeune. 'Get the car ready. We don't want to find it won't start.'

René went down the bank; Chalmers put his ear to the shiny metal of the line. For ten minutes no one spoke. Only the mewing cry of a buzzard broke the silence. Behind them René started the car. A bead of sweat had appeared on Henri's forehead. Confident he might be, but his reputation was again at stake. Lejeune held up a hand.

Chalmers shook his head: 'No – nothing,' he said. Then, a second or two later, 'Wait – wait. I think . . . .'

In the distance came the faint sound of a train. The engine was working hard on the favourable gradient and approaching faster than the goods. Henri stooped by the track, looking up to the northern curve. The sound increased and quite suddenly the engine appeared, grey-white smoke pouring from its squat black chimney.

'Double-header,' muttered Chalmers involuntarily, seeing smoke from a second engine behind the first. 'Heavy load, going well.'

Henri shouted, 'Take cover,' and dived into the bushes behind him. 'Get out!'

Chalmers and Lejeune ducked behind the bank, waiting for

the explosion. It came quicker than they had expected and both ran down into the trees. They had reached the bottom when another two charges went off, sounding more destructive than the first. René was waiting, engine running. Henri joined them within seconds. '*Allez!*' he shouted. '*Allez!*' René let in the clutch and they were in the lane before the train arrived on the straight stretch to the bridge.

They stopped further up the lane, windows open, looking behind them. None was prepared for the spectacle that followed. The engines, both steaming hard with no hint of braking, reached the destroyed line and heeled over in a haze of smoke and steam, tumbling onto their sides before the bridge, crushing bushes and trees, dragging tenders and two carriages with them. Behind were flat trucks carrying tanks and at least four followed the engines, tank gun barrels waving helplessly like dying elephants as they rolled off the line. Some trucks and their tanks fell across the parallel track; the last part of the train remained on the line, but tanks broke from their chained moorings and were thrown into the wagon in front or onto the trackside. The sounds shattered the morning's silence, a cacophony of screaming metal and splintering wood as bits of the train were flung into the trees.

Chalmers had seen enough. 'Go!' he exclaimed. 'Go now!'

René already had the car in gear. He accelerated away as the frenzy of destruction continued behind them.

32

The return journey was as uneventful as the drive out. They stopped in Noyers and had a meal at *La Petite Auberge*, where René knew Auguste, the son of the *patron*. They had been at school together and played in the St.Pierre football team. Like most cafés they kept food for regulars and friends and René knew they would not ask questions about anyone he brought. For Lejeune it provided cover for the last leg of the return to La Rippe.

Auguste, a bulky young man, had been hunting the week before and shot a wild boar. Like so many he had not handed in his gun. His father was a sound cook and washed down with a Pinot Noir from nearby Irancy the remains of the *sanglier* made a good lunch. 'We eat better than they do in the cities,' said Auguste, taking off his apron and sitting down with them. 'You won't get a lunch like this in Orléans or Nevers. They say people in Paris breed rabbits on the balconies of their houses. Have you heard that? Thousands of them, they say. Not as good as *sanglier*, eh?'

'Germans?' asked Lejeune.

Auguste shook his head. 'Wish they would come. More money than Frenchmen. Trade's bad.' He looked round at the tables where a handful of elderly men were drinking, smoking and playing cards.

Chalmers had been largely silent, soaking up the atmosphere of provincial France, relaxing after the tension. On the bar a voice jabbered from a bakelite wireless. He thought he caught items of news. 'News?' he asked. 'The wireless – Vichy?'

Auguste went to the bar and turned up the volume. The

sound quality was poor, but the voice could be heard. It was a young man's voice with a touch of a Languedoc accent. It described the enthusiastic reception given to Marshal Pétain during a visit to Clermont-Ferrand. There followed an extract from the Marshal's speech urging children to work hard and grow up good Frenchmen and women of whom France and their parents could be proud. He made no reference to the occupation or the war. The voice continued with various Vichy announcements about prices and rationing, followed by details of an exemplary prison sentence on a butcher from Lyon convicted of black market profiteering. Later, he added an item almost as an afterthought. There had been a train accident near Montbard on the main line to Dijon. Both lines were blocked, he said. Services to and from Paris were suspended. There was no mention of cause or casualties. It sounded a mundane affair of no consequence. The voice was replaced by popular dance music.

Auguste did not notice his guests' concentration. His parents, a well-upholstered pair in aprons, red-faced from the warmth of their kitchen, chose that moment to appear. His father carried a tray of glasses. 'Champagne,' he said, putting it on the table and flicking a napkin over his shoulder. 'The last in the house. Have to wait till after Christmas before we get any more. Thank the Lord for local vineyards or we wouldn't have anything to sell at all except this disgusting coffee.'

***

René returned Henri to his shop before delivering Lejeune and Chalmers to la Rippe and making his own way home. Though willing to take part in any operation, he was not foolish enough to believe his absence would go unnoticed in a place as small as St.Pierre and always returned as soon as possible. Apart from anything else, he did not want talk about his use of the car when his neighbours found it virtually impossible to get petrol. Rumours abounded of Resistants denounced to the authorities by locals whose envy got the better of their patriotism.

Back at La Rippe Chantal was in the orchard waiting for them. She had spent an uneasy day trying to keep herself occupied. Now she was hunting for the eggs of independent minded hens who laid in the hedges bordering the orchard. When the car appeared she put down her basket and flung her arms round Chalmers the moment he opened the door. 'Safe?' she said. 'All safe?'

'All safe,' said her father. 'Come inside.'

The others were waiting in the kitchen. Maurice had no idea what he was waiting for and Célestine took him up to the old man. 'Take logs, Maurice,' she said. 'The basket's empty.' He picked up logs from a pile in the corner, adjusted them in his arms and headed for the stairs without a word.

Lejeune and Chalmers gave their account of the morning. Lejeune had been taken aback by the scale of destruction and was more animated than usual. Chalmers was full of praise for Henri. 'He's done it twice. He knows what he's doing with a stick of dynamite. And such a mild man.' What he really meant was that Henri's high voice and lugubrious personality had not impressed him and he had to admit his initial assessment had been wrong. 'It was on the Vichy news. The line will be hard to clear with the tanks in the wreckage. They'll need heavy lifting gear. They won't leave it unguarded again.'

'I want to come next time,' said Johnson. 'Transmission's dull compared with your excitement.'

'No hurry,' said Chalmers. 'See how this stirs them up. If they shoot hostages, we shall need to think again. We're not here to kill Frenchmen.'

'A price may be needed,' said Lejeune. 'The Resistance knows that. Your friends in the cemetery paid the price. We can't let Englishmen die on our behalf without taking risks as Frenchmen. I'm ashamed so many have settled for a quiet life, and even more ashamed of the ones who've done a deal with the Boches. Some of the women can't help it. They're poor and Germans have got money. It's the people who compromise to keep their lives going as before. I was like that once.'

'How shall we know about reprisals?' asked Johnson.

'They'll publicise it,' replied Lejeune. 'No point in doing it if they don't spread the news. They'll make sure it's on the Vichy wireless, as well as putting up posters. We'll hear all right.'

'Henri was worried about the drivers and the firemen on the engines. I don't see how they could have survived,' said Chalmers. 'It would have been worse if we'd blown the bridge, but it was bad enough. The engines just keeled over. And two crews with a double-header.'

Chantal was sitting next to him and her hand crept out to him under the table. He linked their fingers. 'I'm coming next time,' she said. 'I'm not letting you out of my sight.'

'There may not be a next time,' said her father. 'We'll see.'

'I'm not going to sit back and do nothing – baby or no baby.'

'You may have to do as you're told,' said Chalmers, squeezing her fingers. 'Your father and your man are a powerful combination. You can stay and look after Maurice.' Their eyes met and Chalmers saw the love he had once seen in Mary's. He looked away.

Marie watched them. She liked the Englishman and was only sorry he could not be Chantal's husband. She recognised the love in Chantal's voice and remembered her own courtship. Lejeune had treated her well. She looked at his lined face now and knew she was happy. Then she remembered something else, something she had meant to tell Chantal earlier. 'When you were out at Mailly this afternoon, Jean-Claude called.'

'Jean-Claude? What did he want?'

'Nothing much. I told him you were in Mailly, but he wouldn't wait. He'd cycled to Prégilbert and wanted to get back to Vézelay before it was dark. He'd come out of his way to see you. Business isn't good, he says.'

'I've never encouraged him. Didn't you say anything?'

'Come on, Chantal. You wouldn't thank me if I ever said anything to anyone who wanted to see you. I've learned that lesson.' She smiled at Chalmers. 'Mothers can never do the right thing.'

Chalmers was struggling with the situation. On the one hand he was revelling in the success of the railway operation and the bond he was making with a group of Frenchmen of whose existence he had known nothing a short while ago; on the other, he was increasingly involved with Chantal and complications he could barely contemplate. His feelings were strong and getting stronger. And now he was aware of a pang of jealousy at the thought that Jean-Claude had been to see her. That was new. He responded to the pressure of her fingers under the table and slipped his hand onto her knee.

Chantal looked at her mother with affection. Her love for her had been strengthened by her unexpected acceptance of her child. 'Mothers can do the right thing sometimes,' she said. 'Jean-Claude's all right, but I'm spoken for and I shall have a baby soon. He'll run a mile when he finds out.'

Marguerite returned from Mailly and shortly afterwards Célestine came downstairs and started to get supper. Marie laid the table and lit lamps and candles. Once Marguerite had caught up on the excitements, Lejeune switched to the farm and plans for the next day. Autumn was giving way to winter and one of the quieter periods of the year, but the animals always needed attention and Lejeune was shrewd enough to take advantage of the extra labour Johnson and Chalmers provided.

By seven o'clock when they sat down for supper the action of the morning seemed an age away: the mundane farming world had taken over.

33

For several weeks life at La Rippe reverted to routine. Johnson had regular contact with London, using different sites under cover of darkness, but he and Chalmers spent most of their time helping on the farm, Johnson totally hidden and unable to go into the fields during daytime. Georges and Henri paid no visits and Gambert came only to see his bedridden patient. Lejeune followed his policy of caution and the group almost ceased to exist. Only Chalmers remained active, exploring the area, making himself known in local bars.

News of the derailment and its consequences filtered through. The drivers and firemen of the engines had not been killed, but all were in hospital and one had lost a leg. Several German soldiers had also been injured and half a dozen tanks were damaged beyond repair. The Paris-Dijon line had been blocked in both directions for a week. Initial German reaction had been to round up suspects in Montbard and Dijon, but a commander friendly with local dignitaries had stopped the shooting of hostages and German energies were directed towards looking for suspects outside the area. The *cheminots* at Migennes were the first port of call.

Slowly the family adjusted to the idea of Chantal's pregnancy, though no one told the old man. Hiding his true feelings from Chantal, Lejeune expressed his doubts to Marie. She, too, for the most part managed to suppress her natural reaction, though every now and then Chalmers saw her looking at him in a way that made him feel uncomfortable. He rightly surmised dismay, but was also honest enough to assess his own emotions of guilt. In the background was Mary, but she was increasingly peripheral. He could not betray her totally by marrying Chantal; he had been clear about that from the beginning. But Chantal was carrying his child, was facing her family and would soon be coping with the prejudices of neighbours. War changed things as everyone kept saying, but it was a complication he could have done without. He was baffled by his own naïvity.

Winter closed in. Frosts were frequent and there was a heavy fall of snow before Christmas. The rounded contours of Burgundy were bathed in whiteness; here and there lanes were blocked and cycling was difficult. By January of the new year Chalmers was a familiar figure in local bars. One crisp, sunlit day, snow still lying in places, he and Chantal walked to Mailly-le-Château to be on their own. Chantal was starting to expand and had stopped cycling. Her friends knew of her condition and had been supportive, as she knew they would be. Gossip among mere acquaintances was a different matter and her mother and Marguerite heard critical comments in local shops. Chalmers and Chantal walked slowly, holding hands, picking their way between patches of ice on the deserted lane. Though acutely conscious of the present, both were curious about the past.

'Tell me about Gaston,' said Chalmers. 'Did you love him?'

'I thought so. I thought he loved me. I thought we'd marry. That's what he said. Then I found out the truth – just before he went to the front. I didn't even have the chance to say what I thought of him.'

He was holding her hand and he pulled her closer. 'I'm sorry.'

'I'm not. I discovered the truth. And I might have found myself with his baby. He'd have let me down. Anyway I didn't know it then but I wanted your baby. I'm complete now. And I know you can't marry me – don't say it.'

'And the last you heard?'

'I didn't hear from him but a friend of Marguerite's says he was captured in the first few days. It sounds awful, but to begin with I wanted to hear he'd been killed. I can say that to you, but not to anyone else.'

'I can understand.'

'He was Robert's friend. They were at school together. Robert was killed and he survived. It's all wrong – I cried and cried. I loved him once.' She paused. 'I love you now.'

'We don't know the future. We live in the present.'

'That's what I've thought every day since you arrived.'

'Every day? Does the baby change anything?'

'He proves our love.'

'He?'

'Or she. Would you like a little girl?'

'If she was like her mother. But she'd be the future not the present.'

'She'd have a love story to tell. She'll know she means something special. Some children get no love. Have I told you about the Dutourds in St.Pierre? They hate each other and their children were taken away by their grandmother when the oldest girl was nearly killed by her father. Our child will get love, I know that.'

'For a practical girl you don't always look at the possibilities. She'll get love – if we're here. Suppose the Boches catch us? I'll be shot as a spy if my papers don't stand up the first time someone asks for them – and suppose Montbard had gone wrong?'

'Pessimist.'

'Realist. And the war? There are terrible losses over Germany, you know that. Can we go on taking that pain? The Russians are doing well, but can we depend on them? Suppose they have a row with the Yanks or Churchill and do a deal with Hitler? They've done it before. Can we even bank on the Yanks? They only came in when the Japs attacked them – they were hopeless at the start. Suppose the invasion of France is a disaster? I could see the Yanks backing out and leaving the rest of us to get on with it. And how easy is the invasion going to be? There'll be massive casualties – I told you what happened at Dieppe.'

A jay flew across the lane as they reached the river, perching on the parapet of the bridge, its bright colours sharply defined. On the bridge they met a horse and cart coming down from Mailly; the horse was thin, the cart empty. The old man driving held up a hand in greeting. He knew Chantal well and had met Chalmers in *Les Pêcheurs*. 'Cold,' he said. 'More snow in the Morvan. They've got wood to burn up there. We're short. I'm cutting more.'

'You're right, François.' Chantal turned to Chalmers. 'François knows the weather better than anyone. The locals do their harvesting when he tells them. Never wrong. Isn't that right, François?'

'*Bien sûr*. Bones don't lie,' the old man repeated. 'Not at my age.' The horse moved slowly and François saw Chalmers looking at it. 'The one the Boches left us. They stole the young one the first year. Took three at La Rippe, didn't they? You had more than most.' Chalmers detected the envy of a subsistence peasant. The horse slowed almost to a stop. The man flicked the rein and the cart jerked forward. '*Bonne chance, Chantal*,' he said, looking pointedly at her.

'He knows,' said Chalmers when he had gone.

'Everyone in the village knows.' She shrugged with indifference. 'I knew what it would be like. Maman and Papa are more worried than I am. They're nearer Célestine's generation. Times change.'

'It would be the same in England.'

They crossed the bridge and were about to go into *Les Pêcheurs* when a German dispatch rider roared down the hill from Mailly. He was followed by a slow-moving convoy of lorries carrying soldiers and towing guns. Chalmers and Chantal watched from the door of the bar. 'Avoiding obvious routes now,' said Chalmers. 'Keeping off the railway.'

It was cold. Chalmers pushed the door open and they went in. The usual characters were there, several drawn to the window by the commotion outside. Ernestine, plump and cheerful, was behind the bar. She was knitting.

'Georges?' asked Chantal.

'Business,' responded Ernestine, smiling. 'You know Georges. *Oui, Albert?*' She turned to an old man who had come to the bar. '*Du vin?*'

The man, stooped and unshaven, was a regular and nodded. 'Going south,' he said. '*Les Boches.*'

Ernestine handed him a glass and his usual *pichet*. 'Plenty going that way, they say.'

Albert took out a grey-looking handkerchief and blew his nose. 'Invasion,' he said. 'They won't be here for years. I'll be dead.' He looked at Chalmers and Chantal. 'You might see it. And what about the Reds? They'll take our land. They'll kill *le curé* like they did in Spain. The Resistance . . .' – he waved his arms despairingly – 'The Boches'll shoot hostages.'

Chantal spoke sympathetically: 'The Resistance isn't all communist, Albert. Be fair.'

'They want my land,' he said. He took his wine and joined two men of similar age thumbing greasy playing cards at a table near the window.

'Georges has got petrol,' said Ernestine. 'Gone to Irancy. Cigarettes from Paris. We don't ask questions. Nor do our customers.' She looked across the room as the door opened, creating a draught. The schoolmaster Ronson came in. He wore the same nondescript suit. He had not spoken to Chalmers and Chantal since their first meeting but once he held a cognac in his hand he made straight for them. He detected Chalmers's intellect and gossip had told him of Chantal's condition. He raised his glass in greeting: '*A la vôtre!*' His eyes were sharp and questioning behind the metal-rimmed glasses. 'All well at La Rippe?' he asked.

'Plenty of work. That doesn't change, war or no war,' responded Chantal. 'Madame Ronson?'

Ronson fielded the question as he always did. Everyone in Mailly knew his wife was a hypochondriac. 'As well as can be expected.' He looked over his shoulder and lowered his voice. 'You heard about Montbard? The Gestapo arrested five at Migennes. My friend – I told you about him, didn't I? – my friend says they had nothing to do with it. They're as puzzled as the Boches. Think it might be a group from Beaune. They're not pleased. Say planning should be better. If they had their way they'd have complete control of resistance in Burgundy.' Again he looked over his shoulder. 'I think they're right.'

Chantal countered: 'You're not communist, Monsieur. You were Pétainist in 1940 – I remember that.'

'Times change, Mademoiselle. And it may be sensible to change with them.'

'It doesn't matter who organises resistance,' said Chalmers. 'The Allies don't care.' Momentary irritation made him forget his role as the cousin from Provence. 'The pilots risking their lives for a *parachutage* don't care who they drop supplies to.' He moved into imaginative mode, aware of growing confidence in dealing with men like Ronson. 'I met an English pilot shot down near Bourges who couldn't understand us. Thought we were all on the same side. Had no idea we're so divided. He understood when he was nearly caught by the *milice*.'

'Escaped?'

'Passed down the line. I don't know where he ended up. The chain wasn't communist. Just Frenchmen – patriots.'

'Are you joining the Resistance, Monsieur?' Chantal spoke quietly.

Ronson looked away, then back at Chantal. 'I'm too well known. I can't commit myself. One day perhaps. Too difficult now.'

Ernestine had been watching. She disliked Ronson and only the fact he was a regular customer stopped her speaking out. She said: 'Most of us are waiting, Monsieur. I'm surprised Migennes doesn't know anything about Montbard.'

'They're trying to find out. Think the railway's their business. My friend says there could be trouble if they find out. Even talk of giving them away. They want control.'

Ernestine maintained her equilibrium. Used to dealing with awkward customers, she said: 'Politics and religion – not in *Les Pêcheurs*.' She laughed. 'Well, not too often.' She turned to Chalmers. 'We tried to stop talk before the war – Georges had to get tough. Frightened them away – and they stayed away. Go to the bar by the church,' – she pointed up the hill – '*Les Mousquetairs* – you can say anything up there. They've had fights.'

Ronson seemed not to be listening. He turned to Chantal. 'I saw young Coulet the other day. I used to teach him. Said he wanted to see you.' The eyes behind the spectacles, mischievous now, were no warmer. 'You've got an admirer there, Mademoiselle. Solid property in Vézelay. You could do worse than young Jean-Claude. He'll inherit the café one day. His father's ill – and his mother's older than his father. Says there are other girls in Vézelay showing an interest. He's more interested in you. None of my business, of course. I said I'd tell you if I saw you.'

Chantal was irritated and showed it. She had never had more than a passing conversation with Ronson, though he was a fount of local gossip. 'None of your business, as you say, Monsieur. And if Migennes betray anybody I'll remember what you said.' She turned to Chalmers. 'You didn't come up from Provence to hear this.'

Chalmers was trying to detach himself from his own anger. A phrase from a history lesson at school ricocheted round his mind – 'Perfidious Albion.' Who said it? Someone French. And look at them now. Defeated, divided – pusillanimous like Ronson. For an instant he forgot the risks the Lejeunes and others had taken on his behalf and the unity they had found together. The shame of his thought made him edge closer to Chantal. He touched her foot with his. She returned the pressure.

353

Ronson accepted Chantal's rebuff without visible response. 'Betrayal's a nasty word. The Reds know what they're doing. Whoever blew up the train at Montbard could have destroyed them. They're not going to be ruined by others. Particularly people with orders from London.'

There was bright winter sun outside, but it was dark in the bar. Shards of sunlight coming through the windows lit up individual tables and showed dirt on the glass. The card players beneath one window grunted from time to time. Sepia photographs on the walls added to the gloom. Chalmers hoped it was dark enough to hide the emotions he thought must show on his face. Again he felt the pressure of Chantal's foot. She said: 'Better than orders from Moscow, Monsieur.' She turned towards Ernestine. 'Blanchard told Papa he's had a good year.'

'Last year he sold the best to the Boches. Good prices. You can't blame him.'

Ronson looked as though he was about to speak, but thought better of it. Insensitive he might be, but he saw his enthusiasm for Migennes was not shared by everybody. He took his cognac to a table where a regular was reading a newspaper, the front page dominated by a picture of Pétain surrounded by crowds in Vichy.

'You're all right?' Ernestine spoke softly to Chantal. She had been one of the first to hear of the child and had given immediate support.

Chalmers leaned across her. 'Thank you, Ernestine. It means a lot to us.' It gave him pleasure to link himself with Chantal before one of her friends.

'You can count on Georges and me, you know that.'

'I know.' Raising her voice to a normal level, Chantal said: 'I'll play the Schubert again when we get home.' It was common knowledge that Chalmers was giving her piano lessons and when lost for a subject in public they reverted to it. 'You're patient with a poor pupil.'

Outside there came the sound of another military convoy.

Lorries came down the hill in low gear and braked almost to a standstill for the bend at the bottom. Engines revved as they picked up speed towards St.Pierre. The card players paid no attention. Ronson joined a younger man watching from the other window. 'Good place for an ambush,' he said.

The man was unimpressed. 'We don't want trouble here. I've a friend in Bordeaux whose brother was a hostage. The Boches shot him and ten others when a Red from Paris killed a Boche officer. They won't forget. The assassin won't dare to go back to Bordeaux.'

'The Allies are winning,' said Ronson. 'Stalingrad hit the Boches hard. A mistake to be on the wrong side when the invasion comes.'

Chalmers and Chantal had their backs to Ronson, but his voice carried. 'Time to go,' said Chalmers. 'He's making me angry.'

Outside they pulled their scarves and coats tightly about them. An icy wind blew in their faces as they turned towards La Rippe. The road was empty; the Germans had gone. Leafless trees outlined against the sky formed a moving filigree in the wind. Chantal held Chalmers's arm.

'Are there many like Ronson?' asked Chalmers.

'Too many,' she said. 'Plenty of Pétainists see they backed the wrong horse. But the old man did the only thing he could. He picked up someone else's mess. His mistake was getting too close to the Boches. Most supported him when France collapsed.'

'Ronson's just a slimy toad. Would Migennes betray Frenchmen?'

Chantal held his arm more tightly. 'I used to believe no Frenchman would betray another. We know better now. The *milice* will do anything for Vichy. And the Reds want power. Papa's met Spaniards in the Morvan maquis who are all communists. Ruthless. Can't get over losing to Franco's fascists.'

'I met one.'

'Papa's cautious. Ronson knows nothing about us. He likes to give the impression he knows everything. Typical small schoolmaster. And he knows nothing at all about things going on under his nose. I think that's funny.'

'Reassuring,' said Chalmers. 'I expect you see the next problem? We're established in the eyes of London. They've sent arms – and they'll send more. But they'll want action – another target.'

'Papa will have ideas.'

'So will London. They won't wait for ever. I'm as cautious as your father. Something simple, something that can't go wrong. More difficult each time.'

The wind was against them and their eyes watered. Chalmers pulled Chantal's scarf up over her mouth before doing the same for himself. Chantal loved his concern and clutched his arm tighter. She said, 'You know de Gaulle was seen as a traitor when he went to England? Vichy claimed *they* were the patriots. Confirmed by Mers-el-Kébir. Plenty think the English more dangerous than the Boches. Traditional enemy – instincts are strong.'

'Like Ronson's nonsense about Joan of Arc last time we saw him. *Idiot.*'

'We haven't attacked a convoy like that,' said Chantal, looking backwards.

'Too risky. We'd need more men. And the consequences could be awful. Best to keep it at a distance. London chose the targets well.'

They were out of Mailly now, the lane rising towards La Rippe's ridge. The pale sun lit up a stark countryside of bare trees, leafless hedges and occasional patches of snow. They came to frozen snow in the lane and their feet crunched through it. It was the only sound before the faint hum of an aircraft emerged behind them. Automatically they looked back towards Mailly. 'Something small,' said Chalmers. 'Small and slow.'

At first nothing was visible in the blue of a cloudless sky.

Then a small single-engined, high-wing monoplane appeared flying south at about a thousand feet. Chalmers checked off the aircraft in the recognition manuals remembered from training days. 'Storch,' he said. 'Fieseler Storch – army support plane. Probably watching the convoy. Short take-off and landing – like our Lysander.' The aircraft flew more or less straight over them, black Maltese crosses clear on its wings, before disappearing beyond La Rippe. I wish we'd met that over Augsburg. No guns – simple reconnaissance. A pity there isn't an airfield for us to attack. Where's the nearest?'

'There's something outside Dijon. I don't know what it's used for.'

'No fighter bases? That's what I'd like to have a go at. Anything to help the night bombers.'

'Risky.' Chantal tightened her grip on him, wriggling her fingers in her woollen gloves. 'I'm concentrating on our baby. My aims are domestic. I can admit that to you.'

'I could stay with you in France for ever. Let's forget targets. Let's think about us.' Chalmers was ashamed of what he was saying, but he meant it. The beauty of the day, Chantal's affection, and his involvement in the day to day running of the farm made him feel increasingly detached from England. He guided her to the side of the lane under a tree and put his arms round her, feeling the swell of her body. 'I mean it,' he said. 'It must have been a miracle that brought me here. We could have come down anywhere.'

'I'll have you on any terms,' she said, noticing he still said 'we'. He never forgot his men in the *cimetière*. Night after night she comforted him.

He kissed her long and hard, almost bruising her lips. His physical force reflected a multitude of male emotions she was beginning to understand. Thinking back to Gaston she realised how she had been deceived by facile charm. For a full five minutes they remained locked in a silent embrace. Then without a word they continued back to La Rippe.

***

That evening after supper Chalmers took Lejeune aside and told him about Ronson. 'He believes Migennes would betray anybody in their own interests. And he's sitting on the fence himself.'

'Plenty like him. Human nature. And the Resistance is made up of a thousand pieces – not all fitting together.'

'You were wise not to link up with anyone.'

'I'd have had a *parachutage* earlier if I had. London dropped to the Maquis Bernard and Maquis Camille. You made the difference – and Johnson.'

Chalmers enjoyed the moments when Lejeune praised his contribution. His sense of failure over his crew lay so deep that the slightest compliment gave reassurance. Only slowly was he recovering his confidence. Lejeune, plainspoken, shrewd, but fundamentally a farmer with limited psychological understanding, saw nothing of this. For him Chalmers was a military man bringing skills he needed and, above all, recognition in London. The relationship with his daughter was a different problem and one he could have done without.

Johnson came in shortly afterwards. He had cycled back from a transmission in Coulanges. He was flushed from the ride and his fair hair was windblown, but his eyes showed excitement he wanted to share. 'More praise for Montbard,' he said. 'And a new target.'

'If we want it,' said Lejeune.

'I made that clear.'

'The railway again. The same line – further north. The other side of Joigny.'

'How far the other side?' asked Lejeune.

'Why?'

'Joigny's near Migennes.'

'We don't have to do it. I made that clear,' said Johnson.

'What is it?' asked Chalmers.

'Not a train – just put the Dijon line out of action for as long as possible. Simple sabotage. And they want the telephone lines cut.'

'One of the busiest lines in the country,' said Lejeune. 'It'll upset the French as well as the Germans. And it's closer to Migennes.'

'Can't we speak to Migennes? After all you distribute the papers.' Johnson's view of French politics was still simple.

'That's all they know. The Reds know nothing else about us. They couldn't betray us even if they wanted to. The Boches might shoot hostages – probably *cheminots*. Second time the line's been attacked.'

'Risk worth taking?' hazarded Chalmers.

Johnson stood up. 'I want my supper. I'll see Célestine.'

Lejeune and Chalmers sat in silence for a while. At length Lejeune said, 'We'll look at it. You're right. Preparation and planning – that's what matters. Migennes knows nothing. You, me and Johnson. No commitment.'

'And Chantal, if she wants to come. She's as committed as any of us. You know that.'

'I know that.' The worn face formed a warm smile. 'Thank God she's got you and not Gaston. I always had my doubts, a father's doubts. Marie thought they'd marry, even encouraged it. Now we've got honesty, honesty all round. I trust you. Marie's upset and has to face the gossip. Women are different.'

Chalmers felt the reassurance. 'I love Chantal,' he said. 'I shan't let her down.'

Lejeune stood up. 'We'll look at the railway – the day after tomorrow.'

34

The day Lejeune wanted to look at the target Chantal was not feeling well. Her mother said it was the child, but Chantal had a sore throat and although Célestine kept a good fire going in the kitchen she shivered and huddled herself in a coat. She guessed she had a cold brewing. 'I'm not coming, Papa,' she said when Lejeune and Chalmers came in from the yard. 'James says I mustn't take risks. I expect he's right.'

Her mother agreed. 'You can help with the cream and butter – and we'll do it in here. The barn's cold. With three of us we can finish in half the time and I can get into St.Pierre. I promised Dépargneux pork and eggs. He pays good money.'

'Dépargneux?' said Chalmers.

'Wealthy,' said Marie. 'Lived in Paris and came out to St.Pierre during the *Exode* – the Exodus when thousands fled from the Boches. Refugees on the roads for miles – a terrible time. He's had the house here for years, but hardly ever used it. Two old servants look after it. He's a bachelor – and he's got money. The war hasn't affected him much. He gets wine from Blanchard and food from us. He probably forgets there's a war on. And why not? He was wounded in the trenches during the last one. Thinks he's owed something – that's what he says. It pays us to keep him supplied.'

'Something odd about him,' said Chantal. 'All that money and never married. He's a lonely man.'

Chalmers was silent. He was back at Wynton Thorpe, inching Z-Zebra forward behind the Lancaster in front of him on the perimeter track. He bent forward, his eyes watching the plane ahead. Around him his crew, the men he called his friends, chattered and joked with the tensions of take-off. Had they realised the realities in France? Wealthy men with servants living in comfort. Collaborators hunting with German officers. Farmers exploiting the strength of their position on the land. He said: 'Sorry, I was back in England. It was simpler there. We knew what we had to do – everything was black or white, no shades of grey. Would Dépargneux help if we were in trouble?'

'He might,' responded Chantal. He's short tempered when the old wounds hurt. No one knows where his money comes from.'

'He hates the Boches,' said Marie. 'He might help. Why?'

'He sounds independent,' said Chalmers. 'We should know where friends might be.'

'He knows nothing about us,' said Lejeune. 'No need to tell people if we don't have to.'

'Big house, you say. Suppose we got another RAF man?'

'Reliable servants – been there years,' said Chantal.

'Don't worry, Jacques. I'm cautious, too.' Chalmers poured himself coffee. 'I'll be ready once I've drunk this.'

René arrived shortly after. As they set of for Joigny, Chalmers, in the back with Johnson, leaned forward. 'Know anything about Dépargneux, René? Not far from your place.'

'He's got a car – a Renault. Mended a puncture once. But he can't get petrol. No visitors or family. Michel and Janou have been there for years – looking after an empty house.'

'He might help,' said Lejeune. 'We know the collaborators – not so much about people who might help.'

They drove through an empty countryside and eventually turned onto the main road to Auxerre. This too was relatively deserted until they caught up with a grey van. 'Don't overtake,' said Lejeune. 'Nothing to draw attention.'

'Boches,' said René suddenly. They were passing a roadside café with a German staff car outside. 'It was near here that girl was run over by a German lorry,' said René. 'Killed immediately.'

'Her fault I was told,' said Lejeune. 'The driver was very upset.'

'Probably,' said René. 'But a Boche. Locals would kill a few.'

They fell into a companionable silence as they reached the outskirts of Auxerre. It was cold and the few people in the streets were well wrapped up. Near the centre of the town a woman in a fur coat, high heels and smart cloche hat fiddled with a key at the door of a nineteenth-century mansion.

'*Bordel*,' said René. 'The early shift. Girls from Paris. Germans only.'

'How do you know?'

'I know one of the girls.' René spoke without embarrassment. 'Too expensive now.'

Chalmers recalled his sad excursion to Paris and his search for sexual manhood. Now he was faced by the emotional upheaval of his betrayal of Mary and fulfilment with Chantal. Sex seemed simpler for René and he was envious. They continued north through the ragged outskirts of the town. René slowed for the villages of Appoigny and Charmoy before accelerating on the straight stretch to Joigny.

'Not too fast,' said Lejeune. He handed the map to Chalmers. 'We're parallel to the Yonne. Migennes to the right.'

René slowed obediently. Chalmers was again impressed by the respect Lejeune commanded. As before Lejeune had covered the possibility of an unexpected roadblock. Today the story was that René was visiting a fellow garage proprietor in Villeneuve to pick up spare parts; his passengers were taking advantage of his journey to see an eighty-year old uncle of Lejeune's who had said he would do anything to help.

A curve in the road brought Joigny into view, a tumble of houses on the far bank of the Yonne; the older houses with ancient woodwork and mansard roofs climbed the hill behind. They crossed the railway and grey smoke drifted across the road showing a train had passed beneath the bridge.

'Busy before the war,' said René. 'Main road south to the

Riviera – the N6 had a reputation. That's why my father started the garage. Sold gallons of petrol in the summer and cars were always breaking down.'

Chalmers looked out of the window. 'We could do real damage if we destroyed these bridges,' he said. 'Odd London didn't suggest it.'

'They've got Frenchmen who know the area,' said Johnson. 'They'll know the best place. Destroy these bridges and we cut the town in half and make life difficult for everyone. The Resistance can't afford that.'

Over the river they turned left towards Villeneuve-sur-Yonne. Chalmers followed every twist in the road on the map. Apart from the occasional hamlet the area was deserted and heavily wooded. 'Railway parallel the other side of the river,' he said.

'We get back to it at Villeneuve,' said René. 'Two more bridges, like Joigny. Minor road – little chance of Germans. More dangerous here on the N6. I was stopped twice when I went to Avallon. I was on garage business – genuine.'

Even as he spoke a German staff car materialised coming towards them followed by a motor-bike and side-car. 'Someone important,' said Johnson. 'Not interested in us.'

Chalmers watched the forest passing. In a flash of private thought Chantal vanished and he imagined bringing Mary to France. She loved peaceful countryside and he was beginning to feel a mastery of Burgundy with its forests and vast open vistas. They would come by car and stay in a country auberge where no one spoke English. They would drink wine and mix with locals like he did at *Les Pêcheurs*. He had a vision of the old woman tipping cognac into her coffee, just the sort of moment Mary would enjoy.

René brought his musings to a halt. '*Merde*,' he said. 'Boches.'

They had reached the medieval entrance to Villeneuve, an arched gateway in the walls with pepperpot towers in the

Burgundian style. To one side, partly on the pavement, stood a German lorry and under the arch three soldiers, two with slung rifles, were checking everyone entering or leaving. René wound down the window. Chalmers was glad his normal scowl had been tailored to something approaching geniality.

'Papers,' ordered the young NCO. 'Business?' He had been on duty since early morning and regarded his job as a boring chore. His French was limited but adequate. His colleagues were talking together and not looking at the car. René explained that he was getting spares and his passengers were taking advantage of his petrol to visit a relative. They wound down the windows and proffered their papers. The German was perfunctory. Posted to Villeneuve after a winter on the Eastern Front, he welcomed the peace of Burgundy. He handed the papers back, glancing at the car's occupants to see they fitted their photographs. '*Bien*,' he said, gesturing in a way he thought was French. '*Ça suffit. Allez.*' He waved them through.

'Thank God for that,' said Chalmers. 'The first test.'

'Not a serious one,' said Lejeune. 'They looked more closely when I was in Chablis buying pigs.'

'They don't expect trouble. Where's the garage, René?'

'By the church. It's only a small town.' Within moments they drew up at a garage. It was an untidy affair with battered cars outside. Near the solitary petrol pump a rusty Peugeot, tyreless, windscreen broken, lay like a beached whale. In the garage a mechanic tinkered with an engine. René went to speak to him. 'I won't be long.'

'The old man's near here,' said Lejeune. 'We shan't have to see him. Once we've got the spares we'll go straight to the railway.'

Chalmers looked at the town. A faded advertisement for Martini dominated an end wall; a group of women, mostly elderly, huddled together outside a *boucherie*; a small bar, its sign as faded as the Martini advertisement, stood next door; a clergyman in a soutane and biretta crossed the road towards the church. It was the sort of place Mary would love. It renewed his guilt.

René put boxes in the boot. The mechanic, hands covered in oil, brought several more. There was a minimum of conversation. 'Brake linings,' said René laconically, getting into the car. 'The old man?'

'No, straight to the railway. No risk.'

René waved to the mechanic, and they were soon out of the town. 'Pretty place,' said Johnson as they left the last houses. 'No sign of war except the three Jerries.'

In the woodland of the river valley Chalmers followed the map. 'Railway beside us,' he said. 'Nothing closer than St.Julien du Sault down there. We can get out in any direction. Pull off and have a look.' He glanced at Lejeune for confirmation.

Lejeune nodded and René turned into the trees. 'As good as Montbard,' he said.

They got out, easing muscles, closing the doors quietly. 'Can't be more than a couple of hundred yards,' said Chalmers. They made their way through the trees and soon met the fence edging the railway. Forest covered both sides and the lines ran more or less north-south as they had at Montbard. To the north the line curved westwards, to the south it was straight as far as the eye could see.

'Good place,' said Lejeune. 'Do it at the right time and warn them. No train need be damaged. No threat to Frenchmen.'

'Timetables again,' said Chalmers. 'We wreck the line and phone a warning. But we must have time. A lot could be killed if we get it wrong – ordinary people. They'll go fast here. Something coming now.'

It was almost a replay of their first visit to Montbard. To the south there was a faint sound and a mushroom of smoke. 'It's shifting,' said Johnson. They crouched in the bushes and a passenger train stormed past. Carriage signboards proclaimed a Lyon-Paris express.

'Broken rails here and the wreckage would be awful,' said

Chalmers. 'You're department, René. We want a slot where there's nothing either way for half an hour.'

'There can be goods at any time.'

'A goods only risks the driver and fireman, and the speed factor's gone.' He turned to Lejeune. 'We wreck the line then telephone the railway people. They'll stop the trains themselves.'

'Calls can be traced,' said Lejeune.

'Night job?' said René.

Johnson interposed: 'We've got till next week-end. And don't forget the wires.' He pointed at the telephone poles. 'Easy?'

'Henri said so. He's looking forward to playing with his toys again,' said Chalmers. At the same time, looking at the lines running through the forest, he felt a strong sense of *déjà vu*. The site was more or less identical with Montbard. He saw again the clouds of smoke and steam as the engines rolled off the track.

Lejeune was impatient. 'We've seen enough. Tell London tonight.' He pulled his overcoat round him, tightened his scarf and led the way back to the car. 'Different way home, René.'

***

With the men away, the women at La Rippe had a busy day. Marie and Marguerite concentrated on the farm chores with Maurice. Chantal stayed indoors to nurse her cold and help Célestine with butter and cream for the market. When they finished the cream, they sat down with a glass of milk.

'James will look after you,' said Célestine. Her worn face fell into unusually warm lines.

'I love him, Célestine. But I can't control the war. The war brought him, the war may take him away.' She stretched out a hand and touched the old woman affectionately. 'You've been loyal a long time. Grandpa and Maurice can't do without you. You've had a hard life.'

'It's been hard. It would have been harder without a home. My family never forgave me – I've told you. The curé stopped me going to Mass. Some will feel the same about you, but times are different.' Her rheumy eyes seemed to fade. She drew in her cheeks and made a sucking sound. 'War . . . I told you about the old lady, my mother's mother? Dead these fifty years. I did tell you?' Her eyes moved vaguely, searching the wreckage of a decaying mind. 'Her mother – taken by two Boches when the Boches came the first time. Years ago – the first time. You know when I mean? When the Emperor was beaten. Nearly killed herself with shame. The village knew – blamed her. *Mon Dieu* – nothing she could do. Big men, men with guns. They killed a girl in the village who wouldn't pull her skirts up. War again – *Mon Dieu, les Boches.*'

Chantal, who had heard the story many time before was about to reply when there was the sound of a bicycle in the yard and someone knocked. She went to the door and found herself face to face with Jean-Claude Coulet. He was a dark-haired man in his late twenties with a pale, thin face and intense brown eyes. He wore a thick coat over rough working clothes and looked cold. His expression softened when he saw Chantal. 'I came before,' he said. 'You were out.'

'I've been busy. Papa keeps us at it.' She smiled a welcome. 'Don't come too close. I've got a cold. Come in. It's warm inside.' With the others out it was safe to invite him in and it would have been odd not to. 'Business good?' she asked, taking his coat and hanging it behind the door.

Coulet shook his head. '*Non, difficile.* The *Café Momus* – remember it, higher up the hill? – that's closed. We get more Germans because we're near the bottom. Why haven't you been to see us? Maman thinks I've done something wrong.'

Célestine liked Jean-Claude more than the others who had shown an interest in Chantal. His property made him doubly attractive in her peasant eyes. She fetched wine from the pantry, poured it and wiped her hands on her apron. 'I'm cleaning,' she said. She clutched her skirt and slowly climbed the stairs in the corner of the room.

Coulet watched her go. 'Célestine doesn't change. Papa and Maman well?' His eyes flicked round the room, looking at the onions hanging from a beam.

Chantal nodded. She liked Coulet and did not want to be rude, but Chalmers had changed everything. The trouble was that she could not tell him. She was wearing an apron and hoped her swelling body was not apparent. 'We're all well – but busy. You know what that means.' She had told him of black market sales before and he understood. He knew nothing of the Resistance. 'Killed a pig,' she said, laughing. 'I can trust you. Can you smell it?' She pointed at the range where a pot was cooking.

Coulet leaned forward, eyes more intense. 'Of course you can trust me. We've known each other a long time.' He drank some wine. 'Better than our stuff at Vézelay. Blanchard again? Sells to the Boches, doesn't he?'

'Keeps some of the best. Worth his while. He'll have something off the pig. Do you want anything?'

Jean-Claude had had food before and Chantal was consciously scheming to avoid difficult questions. He shook his head. 'We hoped you'd come to see us. Maman's missed you – and so has Amélie. They thought you'd come and stay the night. I'd like that, too.' Jean-Claude's sister Amélie had been at the convent school with Chantal and they were good friends.

'I might do,' she prevaricated. 'I'd like to,' she lied. 'It's my turn to come, I know. But we're very busy. The old man's in bed all the time now and' – her voice dropped – 'we miss Robert.'

'Of course. I liked Robert.' He paused. 'I heard about a cousin from Provence. Still with you?'

'Yes. He helps out.' She was not surprised the news had reached him. 'Less use now. Broke his leg falling in the barn. That's his crutch.' She pointed at the crutch in the corner of the kitchen which she had noticed seconds before.

'When will you come?'

'When it's warmer. You looked frozen. What are you doing over here?'

'Coffee. A man in St.Pierre knows someone in Nevers. He got some last time. We pay a lot, but we have to keep the café going. No cognac or Pernod for months and only this other muck for coffee. The Germans will stop coming.' Coulet scanned the room as he sipped his wine. 'You had the Boches here. Ronson told me at *Les Pêcheurs*. What did they want?'

'Boches and Cossacks. Looking for Englishmen from the plane. I thought the Cossacks'd kill the old man. He lost his temper and didn't know they were Cossacks. They searched all the farms. They're camped near Chablis – the Cossacks. Too near.' Chantal looked softly at him. She had always liked him in spite of his concern for accounts. She looked round the kitchen, hoping there were no more signs of Chalmers's presence. Then she saw his boots by the door, the fleece-lined flying boots he had recently resurrected in the cold weather.

'Bad crash,' Coulet was saying. 'Brings the war nearer. There'll be trouble if the Allies invade. There's a man in Vézelay who listens to messages from London. Says de Gaulle is important. I listen to what they say in the cafe and they haven't turned against Pétain – he can't do anything on his own. Laval's different. We ignore the regulations, like you. No one's going to starve if they can help it.'

'*Résistants* in Vézelay?'

Coulet shook his head. '*Non* – nothing. Talk about the Morvan. I've heard names. Something called the *Maquis Camille*. The Boches don't like the Morvan. Hills, forest, places to hide. We don't want trouble in Vézelay. The shopkeepers all feel the same – they're as frightened of the *résistants* as the Boches. In the south *résistants* have attacked shops and taken what they wanted. Attacking Frenchmen.' His thin face smiled unexpectedly. 'You'll come? I can tell Amélie and Maman?'

'The first sign of spring. You still look cold. Don't you feel warmer?' She saw the boots again and wondered how she could stop Coulet noticing them.

'Don't worry about me. I wanted to see you. It's been a long time.'

Chantal watched him, hoping she looked sympathetic, but hoping also she was maintaining a careful distance. 'So it's coffee? Successful?'

'Perhaps. Chevreau didn't promise. It might be February. I'll be third on the list – but we'll have to pay. More than last time.'

'Amélie enjoying school?' Amélie had recently started teaching in the village school at Vézelay and Chantal had not seen her since. She looked at the boots again. She felt hypnotised by them.

'She's very happy. You thought of teaching once.'

'The farm needs me now. Papa needs us all. War's changed everything.'

Coulet eyed her over the rim of his glass. 'It hasn't changed what I feel for you. I told you once.'

'Accolay?' Chantal played for time, her eyes still on the boots. Coulet's words took her back to a summer's day by the canal two years before when he had unexpectedly held her hand and told her she was beautiful.

'Yes – Accolay. I'm glad you haven't forgotten.'

'A lot's happened since.' She searched for words. 'We were younger. You meet lots of people at the café. I'm very dull – we can always be friends.'

'Friends?'

'That's how I think of you. An old friend.' She stood up, crossed to the door and picked up the boots, together with a pair of her own shoes beside them. 'I must clean up.' She was doing everything possible to avoid eye contact and feared he would stretch across the table and take her hand. 'I'll come to Vézelay when it's convenient for both of us – and Amélie. I won't come if she's in school.'

'Soon?'

She put the boots and shoes in a corner at the bottom of the stairs, hoping he was paying no attention. He did not appear to be. He seemed so anxious to pin her down that he noticed nothing else. She was wondering whether to ask him to stay to eat when Marie, Marguerite and Maurice came in from the yard.

Her mother took the decision for her. She liked Coulet and was disappointed by the way things had turned out. 'Pork, Jean-Claude? I expect Chantal's told you about the pig.' She looked at Chantal, wondering what she had said about her husband's absence.

Chantal picked up the unasked question. 'Papa's with René from the garage. They've gone to Villeneuve. Taking advantage of his petrol. Do you get any?'

'Might as well put the car in the garage and leave it there. I'll forget how to drive. I'd like some pork. I can stay until we've eaten, then I must get back. I told Maman I'd be back early. She'll understand.' He looked at Chantal, somehow indicating that his mother understood other things as well.

Chantal, anxious to get Coulet away before the men came back, went to the stairs and shouted: 'Célestine – Jean-Claude's staying. We're eating straight away. Come down.'

For Chantal the meal was tense and she longed for it to be over. Her mother and Marguerite seemed not to share her concern. Neither of them responded to glances she threw in their direction. Eventually Jean-Claude said he had to go and she tried not to show her relief. At the door, saying goodbye, she was more relaxed than at any time since his arrival. 'I won't kiss you because of my cold,' she said, but gave his hand a squeeze. 'I'll come, Jean-Claude. Tell Amélie.'

Coulet wrapped his heavy coat round him and picked up his bicycle. 'Soon?' he said. 'I'll be waiting.'

'Thank goodness he's gone,' Chantal said as the door closed. 'He saw James's crutch. I hope he didn't see his boots – his flying boots.' She pointed. 'I moved them over there.'

'Jean-Claude won't let us down,' said her mother. 'He's a nice boy. I hoped you might like him too.' Her head tilted sideways with a look both humorous and knowing. 'Not now though. I understand.' She cleared the table with Célestine while Chantal picked up a pile of clean washing to do some ironing. She had already put two flat-irons to heat by the fire.

'When will Papa be back?' asked Marguerite. She was close to her father and always thought of him first.

'It depends what they find,' said Chantal. 'Papa won't take risks. He won't do what London wants if it's not safe – and James won't press him.'

'You love him,' laughed Marguerite.

Chantal was blushing. 'Of course I love him. I wouldn't be having his baby if I didn't. I realise how much I love him when I see Jean-Claude. Jean-Claude's a nice boy, but James is different James is – .' She paused. 'He didn't notice I'm pregnant.'

Chantal was about to go up the stairs when she realised Célestine was half-way down. She waited while the old woman negotiated the last stone steps, carefully holding the broom and her full skirt. Only six months ago she had fallen badly and was nervous. She saw the boots. 'He didn't see them,' she said. 'He was looking at you.' Her tone managed to imply a criticism.

'I know,' said Chantal. To Marie she said: 'Maman, what would you have said if they'd all come back?'

'I'd have thought of something – or you would have done. Papa would have dealt with it.' Her confidence in her husband was total. 'Here they are.'

Outside came the sound of the car drawing up in the yard.

35

J ohnson reported to London the next evening and René got timetable details the day after. The last scheduled train was at 12.30 a.m., an overnight sleeper from Paris to Marseille. As usual freight trains might come at any time, particularly when the lines were free of passenger traffic. Likewise German demands were unknown and they could insist on specials to suit themselves. When René had gone, Lejeune, Chalmers and Johnson sat down to discuss his information.

'Straight forward?' said Chalmers, looking at Lejeune.

The older man was cautious. 'We shan't need everybody.'

'Henri's the only essential. Two others, I suggest. One to drive and another as look-out. The fewer, the better. We can keep the Doctor and Georges out of it. I could drive, if René will trust me with the car. He doesn't like leaving St.Pierre too often – causes questions. Peter, you could come with me. You missed the last one, and,' – he looked at Lejeune –'you could have the night off.'

The lines on Lejeune's face were deeper in the candlelight. He trusted Chalmers implicitly and deferred to his military experience, but he had controlled everything so far and no mistakes had been made. He was on home ground. If there was an emergency, he would know what was possible and what was not. 'I'll come,' he said.

Chalmers didn't argue. 'I thought Marie might like you to stay here.'

'Marie understands. I'll come. You, me, Peter and Henri.'

'High time you had some fun,' said Chalmers, looking at

Johnson. 'Anything to get you away from that frightful wireless. Every time you open up it must be audible to the Gestapo in Avallon. But we've got to keep you safe, Peter. None of us could cope with it.'

'Don't worry. I'll look after myself. I sometimes think I've landed up with a load of lunatics anyway. I look forward to Henri's pyrotechnics. Difficult to believe he's an explosives maestro.' He looked at Lejeune. 'You were lucky to find him.'

'Known him for years.' Lejeune shied away from Johnson's lighter tone. 'We all know each other. We trust each other. I've learned to trust you, too – and London.'

Chalmers looked at the two men – Lejeune, the weathered countryman who had saved his life, and Johnson, the fresh-faced young Englishman dragooned into the Special Operations Executive with all that implied. Thinking of his own experiences, he decided Johnson's cold-bloodied parachuting into enemy territory was braver and more nerve-racking than anything he had done. He had simply coped with crises as they occurred, and in the end luck was all that mattered. He felt unworthy of the respect he detected in Johnson. He wondered how far Johnson had been aware of the dangers he might face. Thinking of the time since his crash, he realised he had expected something to reveal his presence more or less every day. In the first weeks he imagined everybody was looking at him when he went out. Only slowly had confidence grown as he merged into the scenery. Johnson must have faced the same thoughts months before he was dropped.

A candle faltered in a draught and shadows flickered round the kitchen. Chantal had told him about his flying boots and he cursed his carelessness for leaving them in the most public room in the house. What else might there be? Lejeune had destroyed the rest of his kit and English clothes when he moved out of the barn. The only thing he had preserved – apart from the boots – was a woollen scarf and that was safely in his room. There was still his wallet. But that was emptied of anything incriminating before every operation. That left the photograph of Mary. That, too, was upstairs in his room. There could be nothing else to incriminate him or the Lejeunes. As he checked off the possibilities, he realised he had not looked at Mary's photo for several weeks and felt more guilty for leaving the boots which might have betrayed Chantal.

'Villeneuve? When?' asked Johnson, looking at Lejeune. 'London wants it before next week-end.'

'Tuesday. Alphonsine's sister comes to Mailly for lunch on Tuesday and stays the night. Henri can't stand her and she can help Alphonsine in the shop. And there are no markets, so it suits us. All right?'

Chalmers could see Lejeune had considered it before Johnson asked his question. He said: 'First principle of leadership, "Keep the troops happy." Henri should be pleased.' Chalmers, too, had done some planning. 'If we leave here at about 10 p.m. we can be there well before the Marseille sleeper at 12.30 a.m. Once that's gone we can deal with the line, and we'll have time for anything unexpected. How do we warn the SNCF?'

Lejeune had already decided this. 'We telephone René's garage from a public telephone in Joigny. He'll phone his cousin in Avallon – he runs a garage too. He's prepared to telephone the SNCF from a public phone in Avallon. Keeps everything at arm's length from us and takes it closer to the Morvan maquis if the Germans find out where the call came from. Anyone could phone from there. Nothing to connect it with his cousin – or us.'

'Maurice can shift hay tomorrow,' said Lejeune. We need more in the barn by the river. We may have to buy more before the winter's out. A poor year in the Yonne. Prices are high.'

Later that night in bed Chalmers told Chantal of the plans for Tuesday. Her cold was already fading, but she agreed to stay on the sidelines. She understood her father's insistence on taking part. 'He's controlled everything so far. The others trust him completely. He doesn't want to let them down.'

Chalmers held her close. 'It's all right. I shan't interfere – you know that. He's done too much for me. It's straightforward anyway. Like Montbard.'

***

Tuesday was a dull, blustery day. Work on the farm was limited to the animals. Chalmers cycled to St.Pierre and picked up the Citroën. René had filled it with petrol and was relieved he did not have to leave the village. 'Bring it back safe,' he said. The warmth of his tone cheered Chalmers. It was a measure of his success in winning him over. Later, after supper, he and Lejeune picked up Henri and set off to Villeneuve. There was no hurry and Chalmers drove slowly. It was the first time he had driven in France and the right-hand side of the road was a novelty. If stopped, the cover story was again a visit to the Lejeune uncle. 'His memory's gone,' Lejeune said. 'He's confused and won't remember anything if the Germans question him.'

The drive was uneventful. They saw no Germans and Joigny and Villeneuve were more or less deserted. There was no moon and it was dark. When they stopped in the forest beyond Villeneuve they needed torches to find their way to the gap in the fence they had used on their first visit. They climbed through and hid behind bushes to await the final trains.

The line was busy until midnight with late expresses and several goods trains. While waiting for the Marseille sleeper Henri set explosive charges against three of the nearest telegraph poles. Then he went further up the line and dealt with three more. '*C'est bien*,' he said when he got back. 'The wires will break in both places. Enough for London?'

Johnson looked at his watch. 'It's running late.'

For another ten minutes they stood behind the bushes without speaking. Occasionally there was the sound of an animal moving in the forest; on the other side of the line an owl hooted. 'Do we go ahead if it doesn't come?' muttered Chalmers. It would be Lejeune's decision.

'Yes,' he responded without hesitation. 'No risk to us. Ten more minutes, Henri.'

'Not so long,' said Johnson. 'Something coming – from Paris.'

'Sharp ears,' said Chalmers, as he too heard it. 'Coming fast. Making up time.'

From distant hints of approach to a crescendo of noise the Marseille express roared past on the down line, the sound magnified by the silence of the forest. Henri was out on the line clutching explosives and detonators before its red tail light was more than fifty yards away. The others, holding torches, joined him, lighting up the track as he had instructed. Henri had prepared as much as he could and it took him no more than ten minutes to lay the charges.

Henri, who had been crouching by the line, stood up and stretched. 'Get in before I blow it.'

Within moments the others were back in the car. Henri waited till he heard the engine start, then unleashed the explosives. Once again the forest was riven by noise and light, the initial impact ending with the sound pieces of metal and stone falling far and wide among the trees. After a pause there was another double explosion as the telegraph poles came down.

Henri rejoined them, clutching the bag from which he had not been separated the whole evening. 'Finished,' he said. Chalmers let in the clutch and eased the car onto the road. It was deserted. Hardly anything had passed the whole time they'd been there.

'They'll have heard it in Villeneuve,' said Lejeune. 'This is the difficult part.' But Villeneuve showed no sign of having been disturbed when they drove through. No lights showed and the streets were empty. They met nothing on the way to Joigny, equally deserted, where they parked in a side road for

Lejeune to telephone René. He was laconic. 'Finished,' he said. René put the phone down without acknowledging and immediately contacted the cousin in Avallon. Within fifteen minutes of the first explosion the SNCF knew their main line south had been broken.

When they reached Mailly-le-Château they dropped Henri by the church. 'Quiet with the door,' said Lejeune, conscious of the sleeping village.

Henri crossed the road to his house and the others set off for La Rippe on sidelights. None of them noticed the light come on in one of the cottage bedrooms near the Mairie. The clock on the tower of the Mairie struck two as they turned out of the square.

***

Back at La Rippe they went to bed immediately and next morning the farm took over as usual. Chalmers escaped after lunch to return the car to St.Pierre. René was busy working on another Citroën and the exchange between them was brief.

'Simple?' asked René, wiping his hands on an oily rag.

'Simple enough. The tank's half full.'

Chalmers picked up his bicycle and was back at La Rippe within twenty minutes. Chantal was waiting. She was anxious to know what might be in line for the future.

'Up to your father,' said Chalmers. 'London thinks we're good. Peter's transmitting tomorrow. Anything on the news about last night?'

'Nothing. They take a day or two to decide how to handle it.'

It did not take a day or two this time. A Vichy news broadcast at 4 pm reported the suspension of services between Paris and the South, but gave no indication of the cause. The newsreader suggested a temporary hold-up and predicted normal services by the end of the week. Again the news item was followed by a reminder that any hostile action towards the Germans would be followed by severe penalties.

The next evening Peter transmitted from Vézelay. London expressed gratitude for a job well done, promised more supplies and new targets. The same day Lejeune followed Chalmers's advice and paid a call on Dépargneux. He manufactured an excuse to get into the house by suggesting he might provide more food if they could agree a price.

Armand Dépargneux was a lugubrious man with flowing white hair. Looking at him, Lejeune remembered the rumour that he had been an artist in his youth before inheriting wealth and the family business. He looked unemotionally at Lejeune as they sat down in his dark, heavily curtained drawing-room. Unusually for Mailly it had electric light.

'Vichy wouldn't approve,' he said. His voice had a hollow quality somehow in keeping with his deep-set eyes and he gave the impression of being older than his nearly sixty years. He sucked at an unlit pipe.

'You've paid before.' Lejeune was the blunt farmer. 'I don't offer to everyone.'

'You offer because I've got money. I'm nobody's fool, Lejeune. And I buy without questions. It's devil take the hindmost these days. The Boches dictate the terms and we dance to their tune – like Vichy. I pay for extra because if I don't somebody else will. I'll buy anything you'll sell me – and I'll give some to the Michelets. Only servants, but here for years. The house has to be looked after.'

'You've stayed in St.Pierre?' It was a statement phrased as a question. Lejeune wanted to shift the ground.

'Safer here.'

'Why?'

'You never know what will happen in Paris. My factory's in Lille. The English don't care who or what they bomb. As I say, safer here.' Dépargneux was uncommunicative.

'You make things for them?'

'Who?'

'The Boches.'

'Of course. We all do.'

'Willingly? After your experiences. The trenches, the last war?'

'Why do you want to know?' His eyes were sharp. He was being led into areas normally kept to himself. He counter-attacked: 'Resistance? Any round here?'

Lejeune shook his head. 'Rumours. There was talk of an escape line for airmen – broken by the Boches. Have you heard that?'

Dépargneux's face revealed little. 'I heard something. A disaster,' he said. 'I keep out of politics. Too much to lose.'

'But you're sympathetic. You must be. We'll have to make a choice one day.'

Dépargneux was suspicious now. 'What do you want, Lejeune? Are you looking for something?'

Lejeune shied away. 'Nothing. I'll keep you supplied, pork, eggs, beef – pork next week. Send the Michelets to La Rippe. There'll be plenty for them, too.'

Cycling home, Lejeune considered the exchanges. Dépargneux had been as evasive and non-committal as he had expected. His intelligent eyes had suggested sympathy, but his voice had been hard. There was no point in risking further contact. There was no hint of willingness to become involved in spite of his obvious hostility to the invader. His instincts had been right. He had only spoken to him to satisfy Chalmers.

***

The same evening there was a telephone call to a railway trade unionist, one Marcel Pourrat, at Migennes. It came in response to enquiries Pourrat had been making since the sabotage at Villeneuve. He and fellow resistants at Migennes were irritated by what they saw as another invasion of their territory. The caller was a communist living at Lormes in the Morvan. 'Nothing from here,' he said. 'Montbard wasn't from here either. I'd know. Someone would talk. Auxerre?'

'No contact with Auxerre or Clamecy – not since the line was broken.'

'A new group?'

'Perhaps. They've got explosives – and someone who knows how to use them. The Gestapo are all over us. Three were taken for questioning yesterday. They're furious. Not Camille?'

'Definitely not Camille.'

'We're going to find out. Tell me if you hear anything.'

The conversation was brief as all such calls were. Pourrat trusted the caller, a long-standing Party member called Lebon whose knowledge of Resistance in the Yonne was second to none. He was about to hang up when Lebon added, 'There's talk.'

'Go on.'

'There was a wireless operator – sent from England. Escaped when the line was broken. Had only just arrived. Went to Bernard, but isn't with him any more. He's gone somewhere.'

'Bernard will know. Find out.'

'I haven't seen Bernard or any of them for two months. They don't trust me. They're not Party members.'

Pourrat did not hide his irritation. He rang another number, this time Ronson, the schoolmaster at Mailly-le-Château. They had spoken before and Ronson had passed on odd bits of information about the defunct escape line. Ronson suspected La Rippe had known more about it than Lejeune admitted and had kept his eye open in that direction. He had no intention of becoming involved with the Resistance, but enjoyed picking up knowledge useful to others and indulging in what most people would call gossip. Pourrat had assessed his character long ago. 'Anything to interest me?' he asked cryptically.

Ronson had finished supper and was sitting on one side of

a log fire with his wife on the other. 'Not much. Troops moving. South and West.'

'Avoiding the railways. We know that. Nothing coming through here. Someone wrecked the line at Villeneuve.'

'When?'

'Yesterday.'

Ronson and Pourrat communicated disjointedly. Both knew the dangers of telephone interception and the conversation remained bland and non-committal. 'I'll be in Migennes tomorrow,' said Ronson. 'To see my brother. You heard about his wife?'

'Worse?'

'Much worse. I'll come to see you when I've seen them.' He spoke carefully, his tone implying something of importance to be imparted. He looked at his wife who was knitting. 'We'll go earlier tomorrow,' he said. 'We'll catch the 9.10. Pourrat wants to talk.'

His wife was counting stitches. She waited until she had finished, then shifted to a more comfortable position and said: 'Don't get too close to *les cheminots*. You said you didn't want to have anything to do with them. Not changing your mind, I hope.'

Ronson did not reply. He was not changing his mind, but he saw that times were changing. It was time for reassessment.

36

Winter in northern Burgundy was harder than usual. A cold north-easterly wind swept in more snow and it lay for several weeks on the higher ground. Animals were kept inside and Lejeune spent as much time fretting about a shortage of fodder as he did about the next target. Some days after the success at Villeneuve he took Chalmers aside when they were feeding the pigs. He said, 'Nothing now – nothing at all.'

'Nothing?'

'*Rien,*' Lejeune was firm and curt. 'Enough here. The farm comes first – and Chantal.'

'We should tell London.'

'The next transmission?'

'Day after tomorrow. I'll tell Peter.'

'He can do it from here if he's brief – very brief. The Boche tracking van was in Auxerre for two days last week – down from Sens. The first time it's been around since it was in St.Bris.'

Johnson was shifting hay in the other barn. He was still concealed from the outside world and Lejeune kept him busy. Johnson did not mind the shadowy existence. His relief at not being picked up at the monastery was so great he would put up with anything. Chalmers was pleased Lejeune was taking a firm line. He was increasingly concerned about Chantal and their child. Gossip in Mailly had grown as Chantal's condition became more obvious and most knew he was the father. Visits to *Les Pêcheurs* had led to ribald comments when there were no women present. Elsewhere he detected a certain *froideur*, even from Georges.

Johnson's transmission two days later was brisk and to the point. Together they concealed the equipment afterwards. 'At the rate we're using this hay there won't be enough to keep it covered much longer,' said Chalmers, as the last items vanished. 'Lejeune's worried about the animals.'

'It's me I'm worried about,' joked Johnson. 'It's got to cover my trap-door whatever it does.'

Later that day Chalmers went to *Les Pêcheurs*. Johnson didn't go. He only accompanied Chalmers when they went further afield and his point of departure could be concealed. Chalmers enjoyed the riverside inn because it marked his first acceptance as a genuine Frenchman and he knew several regulars. At the same time the atmosphere of the bar, *la France profonde*, appealed to his romantic streak. More practically he realised he was better than Lejeune at picking up items of local knowledge. Lejeune was the most substantial farmer in the area and his success was resented by some. On this occasion there were more customers than usual as two canal barges had tied up and the bargees were drinking the real coffee Georges had recently obtained. Chalmers murmured a greeting before picking up a *pichet* of red wine and joining an old fellow he knew as a regular.

'Good trade,' said the man, an ex-railwayman called Cordier, knocking out the contents of his clay pipe and nodding towards the bargees. 'Money in barges.'

'How far do they go?' Chalmers feigned ignorance, though he had discussed the barge trade with Lejeune several times.

'Depends on the cargo. A lot off the roads with no petrol. Horses are cheaper. They take wine to Paris – or Montereau. The Yonne joins the Seine there.'

'Always French cargoes? Nothing for the Boches?'

Cordier dropped his voice, looking sideways at the bargees. '*Quelquefois*. German money's good. They make what they can – families have to be fed. Some take things to the caves where the Boches build the aircraft.' He scraped the bowl of his pipe with a knife. 'Last of the tobacco. Georges promised more next week.' He wanted to change the subject.

'Do you know them?' Chalmers indicated the four bargees.

'Might have seen the old one – not the others. Ronson knows them.' He pointed at Ronson, who had just joined the group.

'He seems to know everybody.'

'Like a woman – everybody knows that. He's been talking about the railway at Villeneuve – you heard about that?'

'What's he been saying?'

'Says he knows more than the Boches. Talks to Migennes – the Reds.' Cordier looked round again. 'He wants to help them.'

'Why? He's not a Red.'

'Sees how it's going. Wants to be on the winning side. Not a Vichy man now. People remember him in 1940 – Pétainist like most of us. Doesn't like the English or Americans – turns to the communists. A lot of schoolmasters do.'

Chalmers's shrugged in what he hoped was a Gallic way. 'On our side,' he said. 'I'll support anyone who gets the Boches out.' He brought his imagination into play in a way he had not done before. 'We had land in Alsace. They killed two women in my family in 1870 – my great-grandmother's generation. We don't forget les Allemands.' He pulled a face.

He was watching Ronson and listening to snippets of conversation drifting across the room. The bargees had come down from the Loire and were catching up on news. Ronson was a source of information and they kept him primed with drink. At one point he said, 'I know more than Migennes. You'd be surprised. Resistance is growing.'

'Here in the Yonne?' The oldest bargee, a thin man wearing a Breton cap, moved nearer to him.

'Spreading from the Morvan. The Boches caught some at the monastery. You heard about that?'

The bargee nodded. Ronson went on talking. Chalmers

tried to listen, but his voice had dropped and Cordier was speaking again. 'There'll be plenty say they helped the Resistance if the Boches go – too frightened to do anything now. I don't know anyone in the Resistance. Do you know anyone?' His watery eyes looked at Chalmers.

'No.' It was Chalmers's turn to be uncommunicative. 'Difficult to say if I did,' he added, drinking his wine. '*Du vin?*' He offered his *pichet*.

Cordier nodded thanks as Chalmers refilled his glass. He finished cleaning his pipe and laid it on the table. 'Young Pageot from Coulanges went to the forest to avoid the Labour order. The Morvan – others there. His mother hasn't heard anything since he went.'

Chalmers nodded sympathetically. 'They take food where they can. Doesn't please farmers. Worse than Boches requisition. The Resistance isn't popular everywhere. You know that and so do I. Some say they're bandits. They take what they want because they've got guns.'

'They stole ration books and tobacco in the Vaucluse. There'll be a reckoning one day – I'll be dead.'

At the bar conversation had become more general. Ronson's metallic spectacle frames nodded up and down. The bargees were complaining about problems with locks and food prices. Chalmers had almost stopped listening when Ronson took centre stage again. 'There's Resistance here,' he was saying. 'They can't hide everything. They've no idea what I know.'

The youngest bargee, fair-haired, wearing blue overalls and a red scarf said: 'In Mailly? But no Boches?'

'No Boches.' Ronson plainly thought he had said too much. He turned his head sideways, his glasses briefly opaque at the new angle. He repeated, 'They don't know.'

'*Juifs?*'

'No Jews. Went a year ago. God knows where. Only two families. Both taken.' He looked round. 'Most weren't sorry.

Not popular here. The Church is strong – and support for the Marshal. And you?'

The young bargee drained his coffee and cognac. 'Frenchmen, Boches, Jews – all the same to us. As long as they keep the canal clear. It's overgrown near Baye – the narrow cut after the tunnel. If it's blocked, we shan't get through from the Loire. The lock at Villiers is rough as well. It'll be closed soon. Tell the Resistance to do something. More important than blowing up trains.'

Chalmers looked at his elderly companion, who was also listening. Cordier drained his glass and stood up. 'Monique's cooking – I'm going.' He nodded towards Ronson. 'He talks too much. The bargees are different – work and survival. All that matters. *Demain, Monsieur?*'

'*Peut-être. Bonsoir, Monsieur.*'

Chalmers waved a farewell to Ernestine behind the bar and made his way back to La Rippe. The wind had dropped, but he kept the collar of his overcoat turned up and his hands deep in his pockets. One thing exercised him. What did Ronson know?

***

For Chalmers the next weeks passed swiftly. Chantal remained well as her pregnancy developed and winter gave way to spring. Chalmers had to be firm to get her to take the regular rest Gambert advised. Lejeune and his wife were equally concerned, but Chalmers knew the real powers of persuasion lay with him and he made sure she spent time sitting or lying down every day after lunch. She went on doing the dairy work as though nothing had changed.

Chalmers and Johnson continued with chores about the farm and Chalmers felt he had been looking after animals the whole of his life. By April he had helped with everything and even done some ploughing with Maurice. Maurice might be in a world of his own for much of the time, but he was a skilled ploughman and could not understand why Chalmers found it so difficult. Lejeune would not yet countenance a new operation, but the group met from time to time at la Rippe and discussed the war. The BBC kept them informed of the Allies' progress in Italy and they speculated about the prospect of an invasion of France.

From time to time they saw aircraft at a great height leaving con-trails in a blue sky. 'Fortresses,' said Chalmers one day as he and Chantal watched them from the orchard. 'Flying Fortresses – American. I wouldn't swap a Lancaster for one of those. They do the day shift. I prefer the night. They lose as many as we do, often more. You can't hide during the daytime.' He changed the subject. 'I still wonder what Ronson knows. I don't trust him.'

'He wouldn't betray anyone, whatever he knows.'

'But he talks – he never stops. The Boches have eyes and ears. What about the bargees? Probably reliable Frenchmen – but what is a reliable Frenchman? Remember what you said when I arrived? Everyone faces two ways. Vichy, local officials, gendarmes – everyone has his own interests.'

Chantal, who was not wearing a coat, shivered. 'Cold,' she said. 'I'm going back inside.' She turned at the kitchen door and looked over her shoulder. 'One of us may have let something slip out. Georges? Henri? None of us is perfect.'

Chalmers followed her, putting a comforting hand on her waist. 'Possible – quite true. Do you know, I don't even know Georges' and Henri's family names. Never liked to ask. Your father's never mentioned them.'

'Bourget and Lacoste. Georges Bourget and Henri Lacoste – there've been Bourgets and Lacostes in Mailly for generations. They've half filled the *cimetière*. Didn't I show you when,' she paused, embarrassed at her tactlessness, 'when we went there?' No one was in the kitchen and she put an arm round his shoulder. She knew he was not thinking about Georges or Henri.

'It's all right, *chérie*. More important things now.' He ran his hand over her swollen body. 'New life. Ours.'

'Four weeks if Gambert's right. He's got a reputation. People trust him.'

'He did a good job on my leg – but you were helping. Come on, sit down. You're still doing too much. Any chance of Marguerite giving up the shop and doing more here?'

'She might – when she sees what I can't do. She won't let us down, or Papa. She'll help with the baby – and so will Célestine.'

'And Maman?' He looked at her quizzically, one eyebrow raised.

'And Maman. She's getting used to you. She likes you.'

'She wants us to get married. Do you think she understands?'

Chantal held his hands to the baby. 'She understands – and so do I. I told you that a long time ago. It doesn't stop me loving you.'

He said nothing, but held her close as he did every night. He wondered if he understood himself.

37

The final weeks passed more slowly. As the time of Chantal's confinement drew closer, she and Chalmers shared work around the farm whenever possible. Chalmers joined her in the dairy, helping with the butter, cream and cheese; together they collected eggs and sold them in the Châtel-Censoir market; Chalmers even helped with the making of bread. Emotionally they drew closer too. Chalmers became more protective, hovering in the background in case someone asked her to do something he considered unwise. He showed little signs of affection: a touch on the arm, a hand on her waist as she went through a door, a kiss on the neck when they were on their own. For her part, Chantal revelled in his care. She had never experienced such warmth and it confirmed the strength of her own emotions. The family watched with mixed feelings: Lejeune, the realist, recognised the situation; Marie, the optimist, hoped the child might alter it; and Marguerite, envious of the love she saw, wondered whether she would ever experience anything similar.

Spring was late and April was wetter than usual. Gambert became solicitous, visiting almost daily, rain or shine. He had already prepared the Mailly midwife, Madame Mothe. She, too, cycled to La Rippe and Johnson made himself scarce when she appeared. She knew Chalmers was the father and accepted him as the distant relative from the south without making moral judgements. One day after an afternoon visit she stopped at Gambert's house and told him the birth was imminent. 'This week,' she said. 'Tomorrow or the next day. I'll be there.'

Lucille Mothe, a widow with grown-up children, had the

tired look of many of the inhabitants of Mailly-le-Château. She wore black at all times and her hair, grey and speckled with the remnants of its original auburn, made her look older than she was. She had known Chantal for years and had it not been for her father's prohibition Chantal might have told her the truth about her Englishman. As it was, Lejeune was adamant; no one, not even Lucille Mothe, could be trusted. A tactless word and everything could be exposed. The likelihood of her making such a mistake was in fact remote. Twenty-five years as a midwife had given Lucille Mothe extensive knowledge of her village flock and she would have been the last person to reveal a confidence however startling. For her, motherhood was both practical and, in a sense, holy. Wise in a simple, peasant way, she kept many secrets confided over the years.

Her prediction was accurate. Two days after speaking to Gambert she was summoned to La Rippe and shortly before sunset she and Gambert delivered a healthy boy. Chalmers spent the time tensely, part with Johnson making a brief transmission from the loft, and part on his own in the fields in gathering darkness. He was back with Lejeune, Marguerite and Célestine in the kitchen when Gambert eventually appeared and announced a son. The birth had been relatively easy and Chantal had recovered well when they went up to see her.

Gambert was smiling, putting things into his bag. Madame Mothe was tired. It was her second delivery that day and the disarray of her hair suggested she had made as much effort as Chantal. Marie had tidied up her daughter, who held the scrap of a child in her arms. Chalmers hugged Chantal and looked with wonder at the baby for whom they were responsible. Trite words spilled out: 'Clever girl – I knew you were a clever girl. He's beautiful, as beautiful as you.' He wished they were alone.

Marie was smiling at her daughter. 'You did well,' she said.
'I tried.'

Lejeune's lined features softened when he saw the baby and momentarily the hard-nosed farmer showed a sensitivity

Chalmers had not suspected. His arm lingered round Chantal's shoulder. He did not speak. Marguerite did not speak either, but kissed Chantal gently, confirming Chalmers's observations of their closeness. Célestine approached the bed last. 'A boy,' she said. 'A beautiful boy.' Then with a sigh she added, 'You're a lucky girl. I'll look after you.' To the midwife she said, 'What needs washing? I'll get warm milk.'

The birth of the baby altered the focus of life at La Rippe. Chantal recovered quickly, but she now concentrated on the baby and paid little attention to the farm or the Resistance. She was more concerned about a name, which she and Chalmers had not yet decided. Likewise, Marie saw the arrival as an opportunity to swing her husband's interest back to the family. She was not cool towards Chalmers and Johnson, but both saw what she was doing. One evening, after a day of clear blue sky hinting at the first Burgundian warmth, they discussed it up in the loft before a transmission.

'Are we still in business?' asked Johnson. 'It's up to you.'

'Of course we are.' Chalmers's response was immediate. 'I've got to think of Chantal and the baby, you can see that. But Lejeune's as dedicated as ever. He just wants to keep Chantal safe and Marie happy. We talked about it yesterday taking the churns to St.Pierre. Give him another couple of days.'

'Is that what we tell London? They're getting impatient. They reminded me they'd sent explosives.'

'Ask if there's a target. Don't commit us. They've been understanding – and complimentary. Just remember Lejeune won't have anything to do with other groups.

Johnson contacted London at the expected time. Lejeune had agreed to another transmission in the loft as long as it was brief. Chalmers sat in the hay, watching Johnson concentrate on tapping out the Morse responses. Once their eyes met and he detected concern. Eventually Johnson took off the headphones and packed the equipment. He had promised Lejeune that would always be the first priority.

'Lejeune won't like it,' said Johnson. 'A moving convoy. Troops going west – to Rommel on the Channel coast. About a fortnight's time if intelligence is right. They want it held up.'

'Where?'

'In the Puisaye. It's expected to go through St.Fargeau from Auxerre. Anywhere we choose. Before they get to the Loire. They don't expect us to do more than delay them. Other groups are waiting the other side of the Loire. We'll be part of a bigger picture. They know it's difficult. Said they'd understand if Lejeune turns it down.'

'He won't like it. We're only a handful. Not our sort of thing. We could only hold them up a short time. How many troops?'

'Could be a few hundred. They're not certain. Ammunition in the convoy and the possibility of armour – tanks.' Johnson paused. 'I got the impression it's important. Flattery, too. We've been faultless so far. One of the best groups they've got.'

They climbed down the ladder and covered the trapdoor. Chalmers knew an attack on a convoy was too difficult. But there were other possibilities – destroy a bridge, block a road. 'A bridge would be best,' he said as Johnson hid the ladder. 'Destroy it before they get there – so they have to go back and find a different route. If we anticipate where they go next, we could destroy another one at the last moment. The delay could be considerable. I'll tell Lejeune we've ruled out a straightforward attack. Easier for him if we do it.'

Back in the warmth of the kitchen domestic matters dominated. Chantal was feeding the baby; Célestine was ironing, heating and reheating the black flat-irons on the fire. 'I agree with you,' said Chantal, as Chalmers and Johnson came in. 'Paul. The same in English and French. Nice name. I haven't known a Paul I've disliked.' They had spent hours discussing names and were both anxious to agree. One of Chalmers's best friends at school had been called Paul, a leg-spin bowler in the School XI of which he had been captain. He'd become a pilot, too, killed earlier in a raid on Stuttgart. 'Maman's pleased. Her favourite uncle was called Paul.' She hugged the baby, laughing. 'Paul, you're called Paul.'

Lejeune had been working with Maurice in the fields by the river and they came in for supper at about seven. Afterwards, still wearing farm boots, he joined Chalmers and Johnson in the dining room. It was light, but he pulled the velvet curtains and lit the oil lamp. The room felt damp from the winter. 'Tell me,' he said. He held a glass of wine against the light. 'Poor stuff,' he said.

'Difficult,' said Chalmers before Johnson could speak. 'Not our sort of thing, Jacques. Too risky in every way. Gambert would have a fit.' Johnson reported on the contact with London before agreeing with Chalmers. 'We could delay them. London trusts us. Look at the map. I've marked a couple of possibilities.'

Lejeune's finger, dirt of field work deeply ingrained, hovered over the map. 'Daylight or night?'

'They don't know. They may nearer the time. It wouldn't matter if we blew a bridge. There are rivers and lakes all over the place in the Puisaye. Plenty of bridges on the D965. Look at my red crosses. If we destroyed the bridge on that straight stretch before St.Fargeau, they'd almost certainly turn back to Mezilles and take the D7 to St.Sauveur and St.Amand. Once they're committed we'd have several choices to blow another one. You know those roads?'

'Poor farming in the Puisaye. Too wet, too much forest. Everyone knows that. Only been there once.' He looked at Chalmers, his eyes reflecting the suspicion Chalmers recalled from his first days at La Rippe. 'I want ground I know – ways in, ways out, friendly people. We can't attack a convoy carrying soldiers.'

'Agreed. We destroy a bridge and get out. They turn back and go another way – we blow another bridge. We'd do the usual reconnaissance and can always cancel at the last moment.

Don't worry, Jacques, I shan't influence you against your better judgement.'

Lejeune looked at the map again. Chalmers and Johnson watched the grimy finger moving over it. He looked up unexpectedly. 'Do you know what I heard today?' He did not wait for an answer. 'There are Frenchmen building Heinkels – and engines for U-Boats. Making profits, wining and dining in Paris with Boche industrialists. And others making binoculars and uniforms. It's in *Combat*. These are Frenchmen.'

'Survival?' hazarded Chalmers. 'Their factories would be taken over anyway. And the Allies can bomb them now. Any different from girls in brothels? Or Dépargneux?'

Lejeune's finger prodded the map. 'There,' he said. 'Henri could destroy that bridge. If there aren't any houses.'

Chalmers and Johnson watched. Lejeune was coming to terms with the idea. 'No decisions now, Jacques,' said Chalmers. 'Let's have a look. Henri must see the bridges.' He laughed. 'He's always wanted a bridge. Timing's important. It's only worth it if we get the bridge when the convoy's almost there. No point doing it the day before. They'd go round anyway. We want more information. Use your contacts in Auxerre. When they get there, when they leave, numbers and so on. Information on the day itself will be vital. Someone we can speak to by phone.'

It was Lejeune's turn to laugh, something he did rarely. 'Who's in charge here? I used to be.'

Chalmers blushed, as he was prone to when embarrassed. '*Pardon, Jacques. Excusez-moi.*'

Lejeune straightened up, his voice gruff. 'I can't do without you. London takes us seriously. You, too, Peter.' He nodded towards Johnson. 'We can't do without either of you. I'll speak to Henri.'

Later that night Chalmers lay in bed with Chantal's head on his shoulder. She was deep in sleep in the crook of his arm. Beside the bed Paul lay in the wooden cradle used by the

Lejeune family for three generations making the sounds of a satisfied, sleeping baby.

Chalmers was half awake. The wonder of Paul's birth stirred painful emotions. He could share Chantal's delight in the mystery of new life, but there was darkness, too. Immersed in the deep featherbed, his wandering mind took him to the St. Pierre cemetery. Again he saw the mounds of newly dug earth and rough wooden crosses. Night after night they had seen death all round and known it could be their turn next. As friends they had drunk in The White Horse, as friends they had faced the final test together. And he had failed. Their faces floated before him. Somehow representative of them all, appearing again and again like Banquo's ghost, was poor Les Ricketts, so anxious to please, the inexperienced boy whose life had barely begun. 'He'll be all right, Mrs Ricketts. I'll look after him.' Thoughts tumbled together in the waking dream. He had failed Mary, too. She was still waiting, longing for him to return – he had no doubt of that. Was she listening to the Schubert? How could he tell her he had another woman, and a child to prove his infidelity? How could she possibly understand after all they had said, all they had believed? He remembered their first kiss in the Bedford, their ecstatic but unfulfilled night at The Royal Charles, the promises made about the future. And poor Les Ricketts had had no woman at all.

The child whimpered in its sleep, shifted sufficiently to make the cradle creak, and settled down again. It was enough to alert Chalmers and end his waking dreams. He put both arms round Chantal, pulling her closer. The problem of the convoy took over. Should they tell London it couldn't be done?

The next morning he was prepared to tell Lejeune to scrap the whole thing. But Lejeune had been thinking, too, and come to a decision. 'We look at the bridges,' he said at breakfast. 'It might be easy if we know enough about the convoy. Will London tell us more?' He looked at Johnson cutting a chunk of bread.

'They'll give us everything they can. No date yet, remember. Your Auxerre contacts should help.'

'They may,' said Lejeune. He was looking at his wife as though they had shared a private conversation. 'We'll find out something for ourselves. We won't decide until the last moment.' He looked at Johnson. 'Say we're considering. I'll talk to Henri and the others.'

That evening he arranged for Gambert, Georges, Henri and René to pay a late-night visit. René brought them by car and Lejeune and Chalmers outlined the possible plan round the kitchen table when the women had gone to bed. As usual they sat in the light of flickering lamps drinking red wine.

The doubter was Gambert, his confidence dented by his role in the Morvan. 'Troops and tanks,' he said, looking at the map. 'We haven't talked about that. Not wise?'

'We shan't see any of them,' said Chalmers. 'We blow the bridge and we get out. And if they take the alternative route, Henri will have blown the second bridge before they get there too. No-one need see us and we won't see them. We'll look at the bridges beforehand, of course.' He looked at Lejeune. 'When?'

'The day after tomorrow. We need the car and you can manage a Tuesday can't you, René? Next week might be too late. We can't take everybody. Only one car. Henri, you must come. Georges and Jean stay at home.'

'There's talk,' said Georges in his blunt way.

'Talk?'

'In *Les Pêcheurs*. Ronson. He doesn't know much, but keeps suggesting he does. Hints at something here in Mailly.'

'Talk,' said Lejeune. 'That's Ronson, just talk.'

Chalmers was looking at the map again. Remembering the solitary engine running ahead of the train at Montbard, he thought of another possibility. If the convoy was as substantial as London predicted, there could be motor-cycle outriders and possibly guards on bridges. If so, any approach to bridges would involve risks. Lejeune had thought of it as well. 'Only two go to the bridge – whichever we choose – Henri and one other. We go on foot. Any sign of a sentry and we call it off.'

The Tuesday reconnaissance went as smoothly as before. They looked at five possible bridges, starting with the one over the river before St. Fargeau. As usual Chalmers deferred to Lejeune when it came to assessing targets and Lejeune approved the first. It was surrounded by woodland and there were no houses. A bridge on the D955 beyond St. Sauveur, the likely second target, also earned approval. Henri chuckled as he looked at it. 'Better than the first. The arch is higher. Gaps in the stones everywhere and a bigger drop for the Boches.' They looked at three more bridges and only one, overlooked by cottages on the edge of St.Amand, was rejected. Chalmers took notes and jotted comments on the map. Back at La Rippe he spent a silent half hour on his own putting his thoughts together.

He was considering the best route to the Puisaye when a thought that had been lurking in his subconscious surfaced. They had come back through Mailly-le-Château and as they passed through the square by the church he had seen Ronson outside the Mairie. He was with two men Chalmers did not know and as usual seemed to be doing most of the talking. His arms were gesticulating, but he stopped in full flow when he saw them. Now Chalmers wondered what Ronson would have thought when he saw the five of them crammed into the Citroën. He wasn't aware he had seen them together as a group before, but he would know René's car. Remembering Ronson's unhealthy curiosity and the conversation overheard in *Les Pêcheurs*, Chalmers hoped he was not jumping to conclusions about La Rippe. He would also have seen Johnson and wondered who he was.

After supper, when they had shut up the animals, Chalmers spoke to Lejeune. 'Do you think he might have guessed?'

Lejeune was laconic. 'Possible,' he said.

'And dangerous?'

'He wouldn't betray anyone. But he talks to Frenchmen and that's just as dangerous. He lives in the square near Henri. He might have seen Henri coming and going. And he talks to Alphonsine. She could have complained about Henri. She talks as much as he does.'

'Should we check?'

'Leave it to me.' Lejeune was brusque. Chalmers was articulating a concern lying dormant in his own mind. Ronson was the man whose gossip was dangerous. And he had done nothing about him. 'Leave it to me,' he repeated.

***

Three days later Ronson cycled to Vézelay. His aged mother, a widow in her nineties, lived there and when he had paid her a duty visit he dropped in at Jean-Claude Coulet's café at the bottom of the hill. Coulet had a soft spot for his old schoolmaster and usually gave him a free cognac and coffee if he had it. Neither realised this casual meeting was to have tragic consequences.

38

The crucial transmission from London was set for the Saturday evening and Johnson agreed to do it in a barn near Châtel-Censoir used before. As usual they took precautions. René drove the wireless to the barn in the morning and Chalmers and Johnson cycled there in time for the nine o'clock contact.

Information was brief and to the point. The convoy was scheduled for the following Wednesday. There were fewer troops than previously thought, no more than a hundred, but Tiger tanks were anticipated and the route through St.Fargeau was confirmed. Timings were uncertain. The vehicles were refuelling in Auxerre in the afternoon, but it was not known when they would leave. London hoped Lejeune might find out more from his own sources. The night before the convoy was due its passage would be confirmed by the BBC with the message 'The Campbells are coming,' a sly reference to Chalmers's onetime Scottish background.

'Still got a sense of humour,' said Johnson, taking off his earphones.

'I'd have a sense of humour if I had a pub round the corner and a safe London bed. That damned wireless van's been around again – Vincelottes last week. They'll get a fix if we're not careful.'

'Best not use La Rippe again.'

'You know more about the wretched thing than I do. The further away from La Rippe the better. Now let's skedaddle.'

They tidied the equipment away, hiding it under stones and old beams in a corner. René would pick it up later. The barn was ruinous and only part of the roof was intact. Its owner had given permission as long as he was not involved.

***

Chalmers and Johnson were right to be worried. The Germans were aware of their messages, but because of their constant movement and brevity had not yet tracked them down. The circle was narrowing however, and the Wehrmacht officer in charge was moving inexorably towards Mailly-le-Château and Châtel-Censoir. He was not to know how pure chance would solve his problem.

Ronson was the unwitting catalyst. His visit to Vézelay and Coulet's café had consequences he could not have foreseen. Jean-Claude had been pleased to see his old mentor and had given him the anticipated cognac and coffee. There were few customers and Coulet took advantage of a calm moment after lunch to join Ronson at one of the tables outside in the fitful sunshine. Coulet knew Ronson's capacity for gossip and with his interest in Chantal hoped for unguarded comments about La Rippe.

He opened with a blunt question. 'Could there be someone else, Monsieur?'

Ronson realised he knew nothing of the baby. 'You haven't seen Chantal for a long time?' he asked obliquely.

'I've visited once or twice, but she hasn't been here since last year. She came with her mother and Célestine for the special service in La Madeleine. They always come for that. Do you think they'll come this year?'

Ronson looked at the young man with his serious face, long apron and rolled up sleeves. He came to a decision. 'Jean-Claude.'

'Yes?'

'Have you had anything to do with the Resistance?'

Coulet looked over his shoulder nervously. '*Prenez garde,*

Monsieur. Prenez garde,' he said. *'Non,* nothing at all. I don't know anyone. There are rumours – always rumours. Customers talk, I listen. But nothing here.' His discomfiture was obvious. 'Why?' he asked.

Ronson leaned backwards in his chair. The sun shone on his spectacles, his sallow skin seemed older in the sharper light. 'La Rippe?' he said. 'Have you thought about La Rippe?'

'La Rippe?' Coulet looked puzzled. He had known the Lejeunes a long time. The idea had never occurred to him. He was shocked. 'Do you mean . . . ?' He paused and again looked over his shoulder. 'Monsieur and Madame Lejeune? Chantal?'

Ronson sipped his cognac. 'I don't know anything,' he said. 'But I keep my eyes open. I see things. And I know the *cheminots* at Migennes. Resistance there – everyone knows that, including the Boches. They don't want competition. Communists. Plenty like them all over France. There'll be changes.'

'La Rippe?'

Ronson touched his nose in a knowing way. 'Forget what I said. You've noticed nothing, you've seen nothing. But there are people in the Resistance you'd never suspect. We all know that.' This time it was Ronson who looked round. No one was paying attention. A woman two tables away with her back to them was reading a newspaper, apparently waiting for someone. 'Have you thought about me?'

'You, Monsieur Ronson? You're Pétainist. Everyone knows that.' Coulet's puzzlement increased. 'And La Rippe?'

Ronson shook his head. 'Jacques Lejeune isn't communist,' he said. 'And you know more about La Rippe than I do. Your sister stays there. You know Chantal.' He backed away from the idea he had suggested. For once – a rare occurrence – he wondered if he had said too much.

The sun shone on the tables outside the café. Ronson finished his coffee and toyed with the remains of his cognac. Coulet went over to serve an old man and his wife who had just sat down. The woman reading the newspaper, middle-aged, attractive, well dressed in a provincial way and wearing a smart blue hat, greeted a tall man, prematurely grey, who had parked a black Citroën on the other side of the road. He wore a summer suit and had wire-rimmed spectacles not unlike Ronson's. He apologised for being late.

The woman smiled, suggesting she was pleased to have the advantage of him. 'You usually are.' Quietly, she said: 'You should have been on time. You've missed something.'

The man raised an eyebrow. 'Yes?'

'Where are we going for lunch?'

'I told you. Pontaubert – *Les Fleurs*. Good food, no problems with German money. You won't feel guilty eating with the enemy.'

'Who's good to me.'

'I missed something?'

Ronson got up and went into the café to make his farewells. He knew Jean-Claude's parents and his sister. He heard nothing of the exchange behind him.

The woman, her face mature yet attractive and dominated by dark mobile eyes, moved nearer her escort and again spoke softly. She nodded towards the table where Ronson had been sitting. 'Talk about the Resistance. Anything round here?'

'Not here – nothing in Vézelay. We'd know. The Morvan – over there' – he waved an arm vaguely towards the Morvan hills – 'yes, plenty of problems. We know more than they think. But they don't come out. They can stay there. We won't waste troops. More difficult here in the Yonne. What did I miss?'

'Railwaymen – *les cheminots*, you know about them?'

'We know about Migennes – Reds. Always causing trouble. We've got hostages. They'll be shot if they do anything. What did they say?'

'La Rippe?' she said. 'Mean anything?'

'No.'

'Nor me. Village? Farm? Could be anything.'

'Who was talking?'

'Middle-aged man and the young waiter. They know each other. He had a free cognac. The man was Pétainist – the waiter said so. Changing his mind now. Wants to be on the right side.'

'Plenty like that. I'll find out who he is. He'll regret it.'

'He knows something. Talked about Migennes and La Rippe.'

Ronson came out of the café shortly afterwards, mounted his bicycle and rode off down the hill. The grey-haired man leaned forward to the woman. 'I won't let you down. Don't worry.'

Coulet came to their table. He had already decided the man was German. It made no difference to him. '*Oui, Monsieur?* Coffee, cognac? Wine perhaps? Real coffee this morning.' He automatically wiped a tray picked up from another table and flicked the cloth over his shoulder.

'Coffee,' said the German. 'Two coffees – and I'll have some Armagnac.' He turned to the woman. 'You won't, will you?'

'No. Just coffee. Real, you say? The first I've had for two months.'

The man eyed Coulet, conspiratorial yet friendly. '*Marché noir?*' he said. 'Don't worry. I won't tell anyone. Pleased to get the real thing.'

Coulet looked embarrassed. He had regular German customers to whom he could admit such things, but he did not know this man. He hedged: 'Our turn. It's taken long enough. Things are getting worse.' He looked at the woman, whom he had not seen before either. Her clothes were expensive, the sort of clothes possible for women linked with the occupiers.

When Coulet returned, the German had moved his chair closer to the woman and was smoking a cigarette. He looked relaxed, leaning back in the sunshine. '*Merci,*' he said as Coulet put the coffee and Armagnac on the table. He knew he got better service if he spoke French. And he wanted information. 'Your friend,' he said, pointing down the hill where Ronson had vanished. 'Local dignitary? These are difficult times. He looked the sort of solid Frenchman who holds things together.'

'My old schoolmaster – St.Pierre.'

'Ah.' The man exhaled smoke and looked at the woman. 'I told you he was a pillar of the community. He had that look.'

'Keeps up with old pupils.'

'I see one of my old schoolmasters,' said the German. 'Told me not to join the army,' he confided. 'A mistake. I shouldn't have seen France. You have a beautiful country, Monsieur. He lives in St.Pierre?'

'Mailly-le-Château. Village not far away.'

The woman motioned to her escort and he produced a cigarette for her from a silver case. She fitted it into a tortoiseshell holder before leaning forward for a light. She blew a slim line of smoke and nodded in a curt way that dismissed the waiter. Coulet had already assessed the relationship and was glad not to have to answer more questions. But Ronson's mention of La Rippe concerned him. He had long hoped he might be a prospect for Chantal and liked to think he knew everything. The idea he might have been excluded from family secrets was more disturbing than the possibility that they might be linked to the Resistance. And he wondered how much the woman might have overheard. He had only seen her back and she had seemed preoccupied with the paper before her escort had arrived. He had barely noticed her.

He was right to worry. The woman was in love and had been the German's mistress for three years. Their relationship was close. They had already agreed to go back to Germany together if the war was lost. 'I'll follow it up,' the German said. 'We pick up hints here and there. People can be indiscreet, fortunately for us. I won't let you down, Louise. No one will know where I got the information. I love you – you know that. You've known that for a long time. No secrets, darling, no secrets.' He stretched a hand and put it on her nylon-clad knee under her skirt.

She leaned back in the sunlight, holding her cigarette-holder at an elegant angle. 'La Rippe,' she said. 'Only an idea. If I heard the name correctly. I wasn't really listening. Probably nothing. The schoolmaster only mentioned it.'

The man was smiling as he let his hand slip higher under her skirt. He was technically on leave and anticipating an amorous afternoon at *Les Fleurs*. He knew the proprietor and had already booked a room. But he would telephone his office before that. La Rippe would be investigated.

***

That same evening one of his officers reported back. La Rippe had been identified, a substantial farm near Mailly-le-Château. Records showed it had been searched and nothing suspicious had been found. Vichy, too, had been contacted and they knew nothing. Ronson had been investigated and his pro-Pétainist stance confirmed. In view of his contacts with Migennes he would be watched. At the same time a junior intelligence officer was deputed to look into La Rippe.

This young man, a fluent French speaker who had managed to ingratiate himself with a French farming family on the edge of Auxerre, was efficient. By devious means he discovered details of the Lejeune household, including the presence of a relative from Provence and the recent birth of a child to one of the daughters. There were also rumours that someone else might be living there, but there was no evidence of Resistance. Locals were sceptical when the idea was mooted, even peasant farmers who might have been expected to be envious. Only one thing attracted his attention. A talkative shopkeeper in Mailly-le-Château said he had twice seen Lejeune and Dr. Gambert in a car driven by a garage man who serviced his own car in St.Pierre. He had been resentful because on the last occasion the doctor had cut short his surgery just when it would have been his turn to be seen about his crippling lumbago. The officer saw nothing suspicious here, but he had the sort of mind that chased up everything. He started enquiries into Gambert and the St. Pierre garage through known collaborators.

His enquiries bore fruit. A man in St.Pierre with a grievance over a garage bill reported unexpected closures of the garage and the inconvenience of the unavailability of petrol. Gossip suggested René was having an affair with a girl in Châtel-Censoir, but the collaborator was unconvinced. He knew René's brothers had been killed in 1940 and would not be surprised to learn he was involved in the Resistance. German Intelligence immediately produced money and the man, who happened to live opposite the garage, promised to report the next time René left the village. At the same time he arranged for an informant in Magny to watch vehicle movements at La Rippe.

***

Two days before the Wednesday convoy Lejeune and Chalmers confirmed their plan. First they would destroy the bridge on the D965 before St.Fargeau. They would then deal with the other bridge Henri had found such an attractive target, working on the assumption that the convoy would double back and take the D955 through St.Sauveur. Johnson wanted to go too, but Chalmers saw no point in risking him as he was the essential link with London. Reluctantly he agreed to stay out of it. The problem came when they went into the kitchen where Chantal was sitting at the table giving Paul a late feed.

'I'm coming,' she said. She looked not at Chalmers but at her father. 'I won't stay at home. Not now Paul's born. He's safe.'

'That's why you should stay here,' said Lejeune.

'Célestine will look after Paul. I'm coming. Remember what we said at the beginning. You can't stop me.'

Her father looked at Chalmers. Chalmers was about to

support him when Chantal spoke first. 'I'm coming, darling, you know that. Papa and I agreed we would do everything together when we started. You've changed my life, but nothing alters what I said before you came. We share all risks. Doubly so now you're here. I'm coming.'

'We don't want two cars,' said Lejeune.

'There'll be room in one. I'm coming.'

Chalmers said nothing. Close as he and Chantal were, he knew there were times when her determination would pay no attention to him. When they were alone upstairs he said, 'I didn't want to interfere between you and your father, but he's right. Paul needs you. We shan't be long.'

'You can persuade me about most things. But not this. Paul will be fine with Célestine. She'll enjoy looking after him. I met you because of our group. We take the risks together.' She put her hands on his shoulders. 'No argument.'

39

On the Tuesday evening the BBC broadcast its messages. One of the last, so late they thought it was not coming, was the one they were waiting for: 'The Campbells are coming.' Lejeune had already checked with his source in Auxerre who confirmed the convoy was on the way. Everything was set.

Wednesday was grey and overcast with rain in the air. René picked them up promptly, unsurprised to find Chantal joining them, and after an uneventful drive they reached the woods between Mezilles and St.Fargeau in the Puisaye by eleven in the morning. As usual they took the car well off the road and set off on foot towards the first bridge. Lejeune, Henri and René led the way, taking a track through the trees marked on the map but so unfrequented as to be barely passable. Chalmers and Chantal, anxious to be together, followed slightly behind. It had been agreed they would stop just short of the target and that Chalmers would go ahead to check for sentries. If all was well, he would call Henri forward with his explosives. Lejeune's information suggested the convoy would arrive between three and five in the afternoon. They would be ready from one o'clock, destroying the bridge the moment the first vehicles were heard.

Chantal walked a pace or two behind James as he pushed through the undergrowth. Occasionally she spoke, but Chalmers was uncharacteristically silent. He concentrated on the path and the seemingly endless brambles, worrying about the return journey and the need for speed when the job was done. Eventually they caught up with the others at the agreed spot, deep in the wood.

'Close enough,' said Lejeune. 'All safe so far.'

'So far,' said Chalmers. 'Ready, Henri?'

'*Mais oui.*'

The two of them pushed forward, Chalmers leading, Henri clutching his sack. Chantal reluctantly stayed with the others. They moved cautiously, crouching down as they reached the glade just before the bridge. 'All quiet,' Chalmers whispered, looking up at the curve of grey, lichen-covered stones ahead. The only sound was the river to their left. The bridge had three arches, the river cascading over boulders through the central one, before broadening out on the nearside. 'Wait' – Chalmers held up a hand – 'Stay here. We must be sure.' He inched forward under such cover as there was and eventually climbed onto the road through the bushes edging the bridge. There were no sentries. He looked back and waved Henri forward. Henri joined him behind the parapet and they peered in both directions. The road was deserted.

Within a quarter of an hour Henri had placed his explosives under the central arch, Chalmers keeping watch. Nothing came. Chalmers, who had had presentiments of trouble for some time, began to relax. Henri laid his wires to the cover of the nearest trees and signalled that all was well. With three o'clock approaching, Chalmers moved to a spot with a clearer view towards Auxerre. He could see for more than half a mile as the road, originally Roman, ran straight as an arrow through the woods. As usual he felt excitement rising. They would blow the bridge the moment there was a hint of German activity, even if he could not confirm it was the convoy. With the bridge gone the convoy, whenever it came, would have to make a substantial detour.

As in the Morvan only a handful of vehicles passed: a farmer's overloaded *camionette*, exhaust throwing out thick blue smoke; two or three horse-drawn carts, one full of pigs; several locals on bicycles. At one point a motor-cyclist and a builder's lorry approached together and nearly convinced

Chalmers the convoy was imminent, but he held back at the last moment and silence returned. Fifty yards away a fox, looking neither left nor right, crossed the road. As usual in a moment of calm before action, Chalmers's mind wandered. Thinking of the fox and the wild flowers in the grass verges, he pondered the way Nature went about its business indifferent to man. A poem contrasting the activities of men with the peace of nature by the mad John Clare flickered into view:

'I long for scenes where man has never trod, A place where woman never smiled or wept; There to abide with my creator, God . . .'

What conjured such ideas? He never knew. Then he saw them. Far in the distance, at the extreme end of his vision, several vehicles appeared and a quiet but insistent rumble broke the silence. He held up a hand. 'Wait,' he called. 'Wait.' For a fraction of a second he hesitated, then jumped off the road and ran back to the trees. 'Now,' he ordered. *'Oui, Henri* – yes, now.'

Henri needed no second bidding. Almost before Chalmers could throw himself to the ground, two explosions smashed the silence. Stones were hurled into the air and the central arch of the bridge disintegrated. Debris was still falling into the trees around them as they ran back to the others. Lejeune clapped Henri on the back. Chantal took Chalmers's hand, and René led the sprint to the overgrown path. Excitement gripped them all, but it did not stop Chalmers saying as he plucked Chantal's skirt off a bramble, 'I told you to stay at home.'

She was breathless. 'I don't always do as I'm told.'

The path seemed shorter than on the way out. 'Not far,' said Chalmers. 'I recognise that tree.' By now he, too, was short of breath. Running, crouching, checking Chantal was immediately behind him, he felt responsible for the whole operation. After the shattering noise of the explosion the forest had fallen silent. René got to the car first and had the engine running before the others were in. Henri, holding his sack, closed the rear door. René edged the car forward through the closely spaced trees. Reaching the apparently deserted road he turned towards St.Fargeau, accelerating the moment they were on tarmac.

Then they saw it: three hundred yards away a grey German lorry stood in the trees. It was not hidden and was the sort that carried troops. 'Trouble,' said Chalmers. 'Speed up, René.'

'Get down,' said Lejeune.

'Too late,' said René.

Ahead, each side of the road beyond the lorry, German soldiers with raised rifles emerged from the trees. Another had a pair of Alsatians on a leash. An officer held up his hand. René stopped and wound down his window. The officer, with highly polished boots and a harsh voice, was imperious. *'Raus!'* he shouted. 'Out!' he pointed at the side of the road.

René did his best. *'Pourquoi, Monsieur?'* He suggested puzzlement.

'Do as he says.' Lejeune was back in charge.

'No heroics,' Chalmers said quietly. 'No excuse for them to shoot.' He fingered the pistol in his pocket and got out, pulling Chantal behind him. Within him every emotion fought for supremacy: intense fear, a fear never experienced before; love and protectiveness, as he held Chantal's hand, seeing in her the reflection of his own fear; shock at the German presence; and, numb and paralysed, recognition that this was the end. The five of them stood at the side of the road, Henri clutching his sack, the car behind them, doors open, engine running.

'Merde', Henri said quietly.

The officer drew a Luger and waved them towards the trees. Behind him his men moved threateningly, rifles to their shoulders. 'Over there!' he shouted. 'Against the wall. *Schnell! Vite!* All French? Papers *immédiatement.'*

They did as they were told, Chalmers pulling Chantal with him. Chantal was comforted by his presence, but every nerve vibrated with a shared fear: fear for him, for herself, for Paul.

Her life was crumbling. Like Chalmers she saw the hopelessness of the situation. She clutched his hand and realised one of her shoes had lost its heel in the woods. She was sweating, her dress sticking to her. Without thinking she pulled the skirt down modestly.

They stood together by the wall fumbling for papers they knew were irrelevant. Behind the soldiers a radio operator in the lorry could be heard, a muffled rumbling in the background. The officer pushed the Luger back into its holster and looked at the papers held out before him. He seemed indifferent. 'Maquis,' he said, eyeing his captives. 'Mailly-le-Château? La Rippe?' He pointed up the road. 'The bridge? Search them.'

The man with the dogs approached, together with two others who had put down their rifles. Lejeune took a step forward. 'Bridge?' he asked. 'What bridge? We're visiting an old man. He hasn't seen us since the beginning of the war. Going together to save petrol.' He played his last card. 'I got the petrol from the Wehrmacht in Auxerre. The officer will vouch for us.'

A soldier had seized Henri's sack and was inspecting its contents. 'Explosives,' he shouted. He struck Henri with the butt of his rifle when he tried to pull the sack back.

'Show me,' said the officer.

The soldier held out one or two items. 'No doubt. Explosive, detonators, wire.'

Chalmers had his left arm round Chantal. He felt as helpless as when caught in searchlights over Germany. He whispered: 'Do as I say. Last chance. They're going to shoot.' His fingers closed round the pistol in his pocket. He whispered again: 'I love you. Run when I say. Just do it. Go left. Behind the wall.'

Chantal looked at him despairingly and let go of his hand. What followed, every detail etched in sharp relief, seemed to Chalmers to unfold in slow motion. He felt for the trigger of his pistol.

He watched the officer, seeing triumph and ruthlessness. 'Against the wall,' the man shouted. He had drawn his Luger again. He stood with his legs apart, a line of sweat appearing above his upper lip. 'Maquis,' he shouted. 'Traitors to France, enemies of the Reich. Against the wall. You die now.'

Chalmers pulled the trigger, at the same time shouting at Chantal, 'Go.' The shot rang out, the officer exclaimed in pain and seized his left arm. Chalmers fired again, this time missing. Chantal ran for the end of the wall.

The soldiers did not wait for further orders. Rifles already at the aim they fired a volley at more or less point blank range. They reloaded and fired again. At such range, each man with his own target, the result was inevitable. The figures before them crumpled.

Chalmers fired one more shot. Simultaneously the first bullet struck him in the shoulder. There was time for pain and more fear of death. He turned his head to watch Chantal going for the wall as he was hit again in the neck. She did not make it. Behind the others she sprawled full length, skirt riding up her thighs, blood spurting from her chest, the shoe without a heel thrown off. Lejeune, René and Henri had already fallen, their blood mingling and staining the dusty ground. As misery and darkness enveloped him, Chalmers's last thought was that he and Chantal were dying together. There was a poem, a medieval poem . . . A bullet from the third volley hit him in the head. He knew nothing of it.

The officer swore with pain as one of his men tightened a bandage round his shattered arm, blood dribbling down his fingers. His men stood back, lowering rifles and watching for signs of life in the bodies. They were not veterans. This was the first time they had killed and they eyed each other nervously as the officer's wound was dressed.

Eventually the Oberleutnant took charge. He pointed at the bodies. 'In the truck,' he ordered. 'Manfred, you're responsible. Take them to St. Pierre. Report to Colonel Hagen at the Mairie.

Tell him the suspicions were confirmed. He'll have a report by eight this evening. We're going to St.Fargeau. We'll commandeer transport there. Move!'

Under Manfred's instructions the soldiers loaded the bodies. They were as tentative about this as they had been about the shooting. They were young, with limited experience of death. One by one they picked up the warm corpses, treating them with respect and trying to avoid the dripping blood. They picked up Chantal last. The death of the woman had affected them most. Manfred had seen Chalmers holding her in the final seconds.

'Put them together,' he said. 'They were together.'

Three men held Chantal and laid her next to Chalmers. One pulled down her skirt, another picked up the shoe without a heel and put it on her foot. Her head lay on Chalmers's shoulder. Her blood ran freely over the man who had fathered her child.

EPILOGUE

The tables outside Madame Breton's bar were now in the shade of the plane trees. Beyond them the sun beat down on St.Pierre's deserted village square. A pair of old men, entirely silent, sat drinking marc. The only other customers were the man in the linen suit and the elderly woman in the flowered dress who had visited the cemetery. The man had put his panama hat on the table. The other holidaymakers from the hotel barge had gone back to the boat.

'We're missing lunch,' said the man.

'More important you should know the truth, Paul.'

'It's a shock.'

'I knew it would be.'

The man stretched an arm across the table and closed his hand over hers. 'It doesn't alter anything. You're still my mother.'

She squeezed his hand in return. 'I knew you'd say that. You're still my son.'

'I'm glad I didn't know till now. It seems like ancient history – almost nothing to do with me. Someone else's story.'

'It is ancient history – all a long time ago. But I can't forget.' Their eyes met. 'I can't forget because I loved him.'

'Can you bear to tell me the details? When did you know he wouldn't be coming back?'

'I really knew the night he went missing. But I managed to keep a glimmer of hope alive. I discovered the truth on a Tuesday in September,1944 – about eleven in the morning. I'll never forget the time or the day. It was raining and I'd just brought the washing in from the line I'd fixed up outside our hut at Wynton Thorpe. I was still driving crews out to their aircraft. My C.O. sent a message to say she wanted to see me about something personal. I went round to her office. She was a tough woman – she wouldn't have been C.O. otherwise – but she could be kind and thoughtful. She stood up when I went in and asked me to sit down. I could tell it was something serious and my first thought was that it might be one of my parents. Then she took my hand and said the War Office had confirmed that the whole crew of Jamie's Z-Zebra had been killed. Up to that time they had been posted 'Missing' and, as I say, I suppose I'd avoided the truth. She waited a little while, still holding my hand, then said the liberation of France had given the chance to find out the whole story. They discovered Jamie had been killed with the Resistance, not with his crew. London had known he'd survived the crash but maintained secrecy to protect the Resistance.'

'And the rest – La Rippe, the Lejeunes – Chantal?'

'That came about a month later. The war went on – the Lancasters flew from Wynton. No one had time for personal problems. But I had an advantage. My father had an old friend in the War Office – he'd been his fag at Sherborne – and he did a bit of research into the group at La Rippe. He got hold of the wireless man, Peter Johnson, the man S.O.E. sent to the Morvan. He escaped from La Rippe when the others were killed, went back to the Maquis Bernard in the hills, and eventually helped with the liberation of Burgundy. He was back in England when Dad's friend was trying to find things out and he came to see me. Told me everything. He's a nice man – he knew how upset I'd be. He did his best to let me down lightly."

'He told you about me?'

The woman's face tightened and cracks in her careful make-up emphasized the lines of age. 'Yes, he told me about you – and Chantal. And what happened to you after they were killed.'

'What did happen?'

'The Germans arrested Lejeune's wife and Chantal's sister. They were taken to Auxerre first and later deported to Buchenwald. No records, but they didn't come back and it's assumed they died there. La Rippe – the farm – was burned down and the land sold to a Vichy collaborator.'

'And me?'

'Célestine looked after you. She and the old man and Maurice were turned out of the house before they burned it. She took you with her.'

'Where did we go?'

'A good Samaritan stepped in. A man called Dépargneux from Mailly-le-Château with a big house and servants. He took you all in. Old Lejeune died soon after the Germans had destroyed the farm. Dépargneux looked after you, Célestine and Maurice. He was a wealthy man, unmarried. He had a factory near Lille. Maurice disappeared.'

'Disappeared?'

'He left Dépargneux's house one day and never came back. Dépargneux did his best to find him – and so did the gendarmerie. No sign anywhere. Anything could have happened.'

'You met Dépargneux?'

'Oh, yes. I went to France as soon as we were allowed to after the war. I loved your father and I know he loved me. Whatever happened was caused by the war. None of us controlled our destinies then. He was a man. He needed a woman. Chantal was there. From all I heard I believe he loved her too. She certainly loved him. And you were born. You were born of love. And I've loved you from the moment I saw you. Célestine was nearly eighty. She loved you, too, but she knew she couldn't bring you up. When I appeared, I think she was relieved – though she didn't say so. I offered to bring you to England and she eventually agreed. You were the second child she'd lost. Dépargneux persuaded her it was best for everybody. He was a good man. He had a conscience for not joining the Resistance.'

'Was?'

'He died some years ago. But he kept in touch with me. He looked after Célestine until she died. About eighty-five. I wrote to her regularly to let her know you were all right. I think she had some peace at the end.'

'So you adopted me?'

'No.' She looked at him with the look of a mother to a son. 'No, I wanted you to be mine, genuinely mine. No recognition of anyone else. I smuggled you back to England – that's a story in itself – and I had documents created, birth certificate and so on, to prove you're mine. There was a lot of confusion after the war. With money in the right places it wasn't too difficult.'

'Money?'

'That's another story. It wasn't my money.'

'But you sent me to public school. I assumed you inherited something from you father.'

'A country vicar? Time to go, Paul. They'll sail without us.'

The clock on the Mairie on the far side of the square struck two. The old men at the other table who had looked at empty glasses and barely moved for the past hour stood up. The man in the linen suit picked up his hat. He helped the woman to her feet. 'Money,' he said. 'Who paid?'

The woman clutched his arm a trifle unsteadily. 'Dépargneux,' she said. 'Stranger than fiction, isn't it? The war cast a long shadow. He felt guilty. He saw what had happened to the Lejeunes – and, above all, he saw what had happened to Chantal and your father.'

'And you?'

'And me. Célestine told him the whole story. He didn't know any of us, but he felt he'd let us all down. Lejeune apparently sounded him out once to see if he might help the La Rippe group. He brushed him off. He wanted to make amends.'

'He did that as far as we were concerned.'

'He did, indeed. A good man. Let's get back.'

They crossed the sun-scorched square, the woman holding his arm. At the edge of the village they followed the same grassy track through the trees lining the canal. Léonore was still there. Lunch was over and several guests were on deck drinking coffee and liqueurs under coloured umbrellas. Others had gone to their cabins for a post-prandial sleep. The young crew were getting the barge ready to leave. The girl in shorts had already detached the stern rope and was waiting for orders to cast off.

'Well timed,' shouted the skipper from the bridge. 'We were about to send out a search party. Moving shortly. The locks are open.'

The man helped the woman up the gangplank onto the barge. As they reached the deck the man put an affectionate arm round her and took off his hat.

'Time for a sleep,' he said gently, 'a long sleep.'